CHOOSE ME

The Lindstroms #4

Katy Paige

Please visit my website at **www.katyregnery.com**
Cover Designer: Marianne Nowicki
Formatting: CookieLynn Publishing Services
First Edition: May 2020
Choose Me: a novel / by Katy Paige—2nd Ed.
ISBN: 978-1-944810-68-9

*For Henry, who listened patiently the very
first night Mommy started writing
this book. This one is yours.
I love you.*

xoxo

CHAPTER 1

Lars Lindstrom had drawn the short straw.

It was a feather in the cap of Lindstrom & Sons to be contracted by *Trend* magazine for such a high-end job, but the fact that Lars was saddled with picking up some lowly assistant at the Bozeman airport and chauffeuring her around all weekend while she did errands and whatnot was infuriating. He was a capable tour guide with sought-after park expertise, not a glorified taxi driver.

At thirty years old, Lars had been working with his father and older brother for over a decade, and both would agree that Lars knew Yellowstone better than anyone. Almost as if Lars and Yellowstone had a personal, symbiotic understanding, the park cooperated with him in ways that it didn't for other tour guides, who often surrendered their business to the Lindstroms without a fight:

You'd like to see grizzlies? Lars Lindstrom will know where they are.

Wolves? Yup. Lars Lindstrom again.

Looking for hidden waterfalls? Look up Lars Lindstrom when you get to Gardiner; he'll hook you up.

Part of this expert knowledge was due to the sheer number of hours Lars spent in the park, familiarizing himself with every nook and cranny in the northern parts, particularly around the Grand Loop. But it was more than that: his connection to the park felt visceral, palatable. Like the tree in the children's story *The Giving Tree*, the park almost seemed to want to please Lars as much as possible, in exchange for Lars's sheer love for it.

With the park as his partner, Lars grew adept at leading tours throughout his adolescence into adulthood, careful to ensure a sense of adventure without compromising safety. He was requested specifically for corporate fishing tours— ice *and* fly—which he handled with equal savvy. He was also the tour guide of choice for the all-female groups...especially since his little brother Erik had gotten hitched and moved away to Kalispell.

Still, despite everything Lars offered to Lindstrom & Sons, he was continually relegated to what he considered the drudgework, and he blamed this on two factors, one static, and one long past due for review. He was the youngest employee, which he couldn't do a thing about, but more irritating to Lars was that his father and older brother, Nils, each owned forty-five percent of the business. That left Lars, who was a teenager when the original papers were drawn up, a paltry ten percent.

It smarted to be treated as the youngest when in fact he wasn't the youngest of his siblings. And while his salary was good, his stake wasn't, and it bothered him. He was treated like the lowest man on the totem pole because, well, that's exactly what he was.

Lars glanced out the window of the van, following the signs for Bozeman Yellowstone International Airport. He knew the way by heart. Not more than a week of his life in the past ten years had been spent without at least one trip to or from Boze to pick up or drop off tourists. There was no public transportation from Bozeman to Gardiner, which worked to the Lindstroms' benefit. If you wanted to get to Yellowstone from the airport, hiring the Lindstroms for a transfer was a good way to go.

"Heya, John."

Lars waved to the gate attendant at the short-term parking lot, stopping the van to exchange hellos.

"Heya, Lars. Who'ya got coming in today? More pretty girls?"

"Nah, not today. But, one *very* pretty girl coming in soon. You ever heard of Samara Amaya?"

"Who hasn't? Dated the Viking's QB last season, right?"

Lars nodded, grinning. "That's the one. She's coming to do a magazine photo shoot in the park, and guess who's in charge of getting Miss Amaya everywhere she needs to go?"

"Lucky Lars, I'd wager."

"You got it!"

"What I wouldn't give to have your job, brother. She's smokin' hot."

"Tell me about it." He winked at John, who chuckled. "But, I'm a professional."

"So, who's comin' in today?"

"Location assistant. Gotta babysit her until Miss Amaya gets here. She comes early to get everything set up, I guess. You wouldn't believe the kind of things these famous people ask for. Water cooled to such and such a temperature. Organic, no-salt peanut butter and Hendrick's Gin. Like it would kill her if she had Jif and Beefeater. Goose-down pillows with no feathers."

"Down without feathers? How do ya do that?"

"Beats me. Couldn't stay in any of the local hotels either because they weren't fancy enough. We had to rent a cottage for her and get it all fixed up. But with the kind of money she's paying? I don't ask questions."

"You got that right. When you coming back for the supermodel? I'll be sure I'm in the terminal getting a cup of coffee that day!"

"She'll be here on Tuesday, after the long weekend."

"Alrighty, then. Park it wherever you want, Lars. And have a good Labor Day weekend!"

"You too, John. Hope you see some fireworks!"

"I don't know about *me* but it sounds like *your* fireworks are on the way!"

Lars saluted the parking attendant and pulled into the lot, but something about John's parting words stuck around in Lars's head.

Fireworks? With Samara Amaya? Talk about reaching for the stars. *Lucky me, I'm just stuck with the location assistant.*

Lars pulled into a parking space and cut the engine on the tourist van, resting his hands on the steering wheel in thought.

As much as he griped about the job of babysitting Miss Amaya's assistant because it hurt his pride, this job intrigued him. Last night, he'd had a very vivid dream—one of those dreams that feels so real, you're shocked when you wake up to find out it wasn't. It faded quickly. He didn't remember much—just a blurry-faced girl with dark hair, wearing a poodle skirt. She'd made him laugh—made him feel something more than attraction, something greater than lust. And he had woken up breathless, hard as a rock, confused by the realness and intimacy of the images, and melancholy to realize they weren't real.

As he made his way through the parking lot to the terminal, he couldn't shake the feelings brought on by the dream—like this was more than just a job, like it was something more important.

Rationally, he knew his intuition had nothing to do with Samara Amaya or her location assistant, but the timing of the job and the dream had gotten all mashed up together in his head today. He couldn't help it. There was something that felt...*possible* about the dream. Almost as if—if Lars had believed in such nonsense—it was more of a *premonition* than a dream. His heart pounded a little faster as he walked through the sliding glass doors.

He checked his watch. *11:42.* Her flight would arrive from New York in thirteen minutes, and then she would have to deplane and make her way down to baggage claim. He stopped in the men's room to check himself out in the mirror, running his fingers through his short, thick blond hair and giving his reflection a wink and a winning smile before heading back out to the terminal. Assistant or not, she'd get the full Lindstrom & Sons treatment that *Trend* had booked and paid for, and that included Charming Lars, her flirty, friendly tour guide.

As he sauntered over to the escalator adjacent to the baggage carousel, he took the cardboard sign out of his back pocket and unfolded it. He looked down at the neatly penned sign in his hand, thinking *"Jane Mays"* was about as plain as a name could get, and shuttling her around for the next few days wasn't exactly the stuff of fireworks.

Dream or no dream, the only fireworks Lars expected this weekend were the ones set to go off in the Gardiner Community Park on Monday evening. There was no reason for Lars to feel extra excited or expectant.

No reason at all.

***

Jane Mays looked out the window of the taxiing Boeing 757, still groggy from the nap she'd taken from Chicago to Bozeman. Leaving LaGuardia Airport in New York at seven a.m. meant arriving at the airport at five-thirty a.m. That meant waking up at four a.m.

And since Jane was the furthest possible thing from a morning person, now it meant she was feeling crabby and sluggish, even after her catnap.

It didn't help that Jane had left her favorite camera at her cousin's downtown loft last night while she was there packing her cousin's things for the trip, which meant going back to get it at one o'clock in the morning. But there was no way Jane was going to spend a week on location without her camera. Returning from Sara's apartment, she had packed until about two-thirty and then fell asleep for ninety minutes draped across her kitchen table before the alarm on her phone buzzed her awake.

Turning toward the small airplane window, Jane rubbed her eyes, noting snow-capped mountains in the distance. The window didn't afford a great view, but she admired it as best she could through the scratched, cloudy plexiglass. She hoped to get some good shots in before Sara came to town on Tuesday, but there was so much to do between now and then, she probably wouldn't have the chance.

In the five years since Jane had graduated college and been pressured into taking on the job as her cousin's assistant and location coordinator, Sara—er, um, the model professionally-known as *Samara*—had progressively become more demanding, more needy, never fully satisfied with anything.

And Jane, who had developed the skill of tuning out Sara's over-the-top drama, abusive language and absurd demands, was once again reaching her breaking point. It happened cyclically. Jane would have just about enough of Sara's attitude and share with her uncle her intent to quit. But then between Uncle Mays cajoling Jane to give it another month and Sara choosing to behave herself, Jane wouldn't walk away.

There was something about her uncle, the identical twin of her deceased father, beseeching her with her father's face that made Jane's gumption fold and crumble every time. The words "Something is better than nothing" circled in her head, and quite simply, her uncle, Sara's father, was all she had.

Jane turned on her phone and waited for it to boot up

as they reached the gate. She couldn't remember the name of the tour operator she should be looking for. *Trend*'s travel department had made all of the ground arrangements and Jane had been assured that all of her instructions pertaining to Sara's needs had been passed along.

Her phone buzzed noisily, downloading messages, as she put on a beat-up Red Sox cap and tossed her chic Coach backpack over her shoulder. Five messages from Sara: two calls and three texts—even though her cousin knew good and well that Jane was flying—and it was all nonsense: *Make sure there's Burt's Bees lip gloss on my bedside table; Did you pack my fave slippers?* and *What did I get my daddy for his birthday?*

Jane had packed a dozen Burt's Bees lip glosses for Sara, had purchased an extra pair of her favorite slippers for Yellowstone so that she wouldn't have to be without them in New York for even one day, and had sent her uncle Patriots season tickets, signing the card from both girls.

Jane had taken a small measure of satisfaction in signing her own name first—she had, in fact, *purchased* the tickets and card with her own money—sure that Sara wouldn't remember his birthday anyway. If Sara hadn't read the email Jane sent advising Sara of the gift, that was *her* problem.

There was a voicemail from Sara's agent, Sebastian, who would be traveling with her on Tuesday morning, as well as two calls from Sara's trainer, and a text from her makeup artist, Ray, which simply read: *Wow! 3 days to u-self, girl. U deserve it. Enjoy. xo*

Jane smiled at that text, shoving her phone back in her pocket as she made her way down the jetway and into the airport. *I do deserve it.* And damn it, if she had to spend a week in the same house with Sara once her cousin arrived for the shoot, the least Jane could do was to enjoy a little time to herself before Sara arrived.

Once upon a time the cousins, who were only a year apart in age, had been best friends. Both only children, the girls spent every holiday and school vacation together—at Jane's house in San Francisco or Sara's house in Boston, at Disney World over spring break and in Cape Cod for two weeks every summer. But when Jane's parents had been killed in a car crash a few weeks after her tenth birthday, she'd been sent to live with her aunt and uncle Mays permanently. Her sudden presence in the Mays family had upset the careful balance that had pre-existed her. Spectacularly beautiful nine-year-old Sara, who was unaccustomed to sharing her parents—her father, especially—had quickly come to regard her older cousin Jane as an interloper, and whatever friendship that had once flourished between the cousins met a hasty demise.

Jane sighed, shaking herself out of her reverie. Distracted by the barrage of texts, she had forgotten to look for the name of the tour operator who would be meeting her flight. As the escalator gently lowered her to the ground floor, Jane dug into her back pocket to find her phone. She tapped on her email and scrolled through the messages filed under *Yellowstone Trend Shoot*, looking for ground details. Ah-ha. *Lindstrom & Sons. Lars Lindstrom will be waiting to collect you from baggage claim…*

She looked up as she stepped off the escalator and

realized she needn't have bothered looking him up since she couldn't have possibly missed him. Aside from the fact that Bozeman Yellowstone International Airport was one of the *least* bustling places she had ever touched down, making him a standalone figure at the bottom of the escalator holding a sign reading *Jane Mays*, he was, hands down—and Jane had seen the best-looking men in the world up close and personal—the most jaw-droppingly handsome man she had ever seen.

Not that it could possibly matter for Plain Jane Mays.

***

There weren't a whole lot of people arriving from Chicago, and without the benefit of a photo, Lars just assumed that the assistant of Samara Amaya would be a fashionable woman. She would also sit in first class, thus be one of the first to deplane, but as he watched the passengers step onto the escalator, no one fit the bill. There was an older couple, two businessmen, a middle-aged lady struggling with a rambunctious toddler, and a teenage kid in jeans and a sweatshirt with a baseball cap pulled low over her eyes, and a few brown curls escaping over her ears.

The couple, the men and the lady made their way to baggage claim without giving Lars a second glance. The kid in the baseball cap got off the escalator and walked purposely toward Lars. Huh. Maybe she needed directions.

But as she walked closer, Lars realized that she wasn't a teenager, as he'd originally assumed, but a young woman in baggy clothes. His glance flicked to the strap of her backpack. He could tell it was real leather, and it looked expensive. Flipping his gaze back to her face, he saw diamond studs glistening in her ears. Suddenly she was in front of him, and putting two and two together, Lars realized just in time that *this* must be Jane Mays, the woman for whom he was waiting.

"Miss Mays?" he asked, hoping she didn't notice the surprise in his voice or on his face.

She looked up at him from under the brim of her beat-up cap and grinned. "Mr. Lindstrom?"

"Lars, yeah."

"Well, *Lars-Yeah*, thanks for picking me up."

Her voice. Oh man, her voice. It was distinctly low and gravelly, like Demi Moore or Kathleen Turner, and he wondered if she was recovering from a cold or if she always sounded that way. The way she said *picking me up* made him do a double take, though her body language read friendly, not flirtatious.

"Just Lars," he clarified.

"Okay. Over this way, *Just-Lars*?" She gestured to the baggage claim area where the battered carousel had just started to make its first lazy rotation.

"Lars."

"Yeah, I know. I'm just—" She half-smiled, about to say something, then turned and walked over to the conveyor belt, speaking over her shoulder. "Did you bring a big car, Lars? This could be ugly."

Lars stared after her, trying to figure her out. She dressed like a hobo-teenager, but she was low-talking, playful and dry. She was throwing him, and women *never* threw Lars.

"U-ugly?" he asked.

"Ms. Amaya doesn't travel light."

"Ms. Amaya didn't travel."

"Touché, *Just-Lars*. Nicely done." Her green eyes twinkled as she shoved her hands in her back pockets. "What I mean to say is that Ms. Amaya's luggage generally precedes her. It all came with me so that I could unpack for her. I think it was eight bags. Maybe nine. Maybe eighty-six thousand and twenty-four. I can't remember."

Remember. The low rumble of her voice made the word sound unaccountably sexy, which was momentarily distracting. For a second, *just a second*, he stared at her, trying to reconcile the voice with the woman. A millisecond later he shook his head, focusing on her words instead of the way she was saying them, and rolled his eyes inwardly at this news. Another spoiled famous person who couldn't make do with a duffel and a backpack like a normal person. Great.

Though he couldn't fault Jane for the habits of her boss. Jane didn't look like trouble at all, in fact. She looked boyish and spare. Physically, she wasn't Lars's type at all.

She was several inches shorter than he was, maybe five-foot-five, and not much to look at. A fan of big breasts and a small waist on full display, Lars couldn't make out Jane's figure from under her oversized Boston College sweatshirt. The worn-out, loose, faded jeans that pooled around her expensive loafers didn't do much for her either. Her face was partially hidden under her cap, and she wore tortoiseshell-framed glasses that concealed her eyes. Her hair escaped from under the cap in little waves over her ears that looked soft and inviting, but her face was unremarkable…well, wait, *mostly* unremarkable.

There was something about her eyes when she grinned at him—the way they crinkled a little around the edges when she asked if he brought a big car—and the way her lips had tilted up tentatively, like she was giggling on the inside, but not letting him in on the joke. He sensed a bit of mischief in that smile, and it appealed to him.

"Ready to go to work, *Just-Lars?*"

Just-Lars.

And that voice.

It was—by far—the most distracting thing about her.

Silky and low, it belonged to a woman much taller, more voluptuous, with heavy-lidded eyes, and oozing sex appeal. He didn't believe she was a smoker; he didn't smell a whiff of tobacco while standing beside her. But, her voice was low and raspy *like* a smoker's, like Jessica Rabbit's, like the voice of a lounge singer or the *femme fatale* from a black-and-white movie. Like Lauren Bacall telling Humphrey Bogart to put his lips together and blow. And she had that smart-ass sort of confidence going for her too. He sensed that she wasn't purposely suggestive, but he couldn't help wondering about the subtext he'd add to a voice like that. Something like: *Yeah, I'm wearing a baggy sweatshirt, but I'll bet you're wondering what's under it, aren't you, you bad, bad boy?* And he didn't really *want* to wonder, so it confused him that that's where his mind headed every time she uttered a word. Man, her voice was something. Honestly, it made the hairs on his arm stand up; it was so sexy and so damn unexpected.

"*Voila. Numero uno,*" she said, gesturing to a large Gucci suitcase, black with a distinctive red and green decorative stripe.

Lars stepped forward and grabbed the bag off the belt with ease just as Jane reached out to grab the one after.

"Hey, let me do that."

"I don't mind helping," she said.

"It's my job." Plus, he just wasn't comfortable watching a smallish woman heft heavy luggage. "You stay with the bags and I'll bring them over. Do they all look like this?"

Jane nodded, sitting down gingerly on *numero uno*, and watching as Lars went back to the belt again and again until she was surrounded by eleven almost-identical Gucci suitcases and four black garment bags.

"Is this it?" he asked Jane, who was counting the bags, and comparing the claim numbers against the collection she had stapled to her boarding pass.

"Uh—," she replied, "One more…"

She jumped up and hurried to the belt, picking up a simple leather duffel bag. The most unassuming bag circling the belt, it had clearly done its fair share of traveling and had the scars to prove it. She hefted it onto her shoulder and smiled at Lars.

"Mine."

The way she purred *mine* while she grinned at him made his throat go dry.

He swallowed and tried to smile back at her but couldn't help staring at her lips. Flustered, he dropped his eyes quickly, where they rested, inadvertently, on the words

14

Boston College. Suddenly recognizing that he was essentially staring at her breasts, he snapped his eyes back up to her face.

She raised an eyebrow at him, conveying surprise and amusement with the clean, elegant gesture.

He cleared his throat nervously and made himself useful, reaching out to loosen the beat-up leather bag from her shoulder and toss it on the mountain of Samara's luggage.

He wasn't the sort to get flustered around women in general, let alone someone as average looking as Jane.

That damn voice of hers was making him crazy.

He rubbed his forehead, staring at the pile of luggage, suddenly noting the contrast of Jane's simple duffel on top of her boss's fifteen pieces of luggage.

She's just a normal person with a duffel and a backpack. Then…*That pile of black Gucci bags must have cost a small fortune.*

As if reading his mind, Jane piped up beside him. "Each one costs thirty-eight hundred. Don't add it up. It'll hurt your heart. All those starving people in India…" He looked at her and she shrugged. "What can I say? Ms. Amaya likes her comforts."

Comforts.

The way she said it reminded him of warm honey.

He needed some air. Stat.

Putting up his palms as if to say: *Hey, none of my business*, Lars backed away from Miss Sexy Pipes.

"You wait here," he said. "I'll get the car."

***

Jane didn't know what to make of Lars.

Or rather, Jane didn't know what to make of what Lars was making of Jane.

She couldn't remember the last time someone tried so hard to conceal a quick glance at her chest. Come to think of it, she couldn't actually remember the last time someone had glanced at her chest at all.

She looked over at him as he drove them out of the airport complex and onto a major highway. He had explained to her that generally a client would sit in the back, relaxing during the trip to Gardiner. But because of the volume of Ms. Amaya's luggage, he had needed to collapse the back seats, leaving Jan no other option but to sit up front with him.

"I'm sorry about it, Miss. I didn't realize there'd be so much…"

"What? You didn't realize you were picking up the luggage of the diva to end all divas? Don't sweat it. I like the front seat. And by the way…I'm not "Miss" anything. Jane's good."

"Well, *Jane's-Good*, I'm glad to hear it. There's water and trail mix in the glove compartment. Help yourself."

His eyes had sparkled as he turned her little trick around on her, and she rewarded him with a little tip of her cap.

It wasn't unusual for Jane to get along with people. By and large, she enjoyed meeting new people and had a knack for quickly establishing a comfortable, playful rapport.

Working with Sara meant she had to deal with a lot of

different personalities, from fun and easygoing to quite difficult and demanding, but Jane didn't really alter herself for anyone, and that seemed to work for her. Maybe people were so anxious to work with Samara Amaya that they didn't mess with the gatekeeper, but Jane worked hard to treat people with kindness and respect, which wasn't altogether common in her business. Anyway, it didn't surprise her that she was getting along easily with Lars Lindstrom.

What did surprise Jane was how *affected* she was by him. Oh, she was doing a bang-up job covering it up—you couldn't be in the same room as movie stars and models without learning how to control your fawning—but Jane was really flustered by him in a way that wasn't common for her.

It was baffling. And annoying.

(Because it couldn't possibly go anywhere.)

But, whew…he was stunning.

A good bit over six feet tall, Lars was broad-chested like an athlete, like someone who regularly worked out. "Regularly" meaning hours a day to maintain that sort of form. He was tan and his face was rugged and maybe a little prematurely aged in a sexy, outdoorsy sort of way. She guessed he was in his thirties, strong-jawed and hard-bodied. Jane didn't need for him to take off his shirt to be certain she'd find a tight washboard under there.

Damn.

You own your body like a Greek god, she thought—like he didn't have to work for it.

Despite his near-perfect physique, however, it was his eyes that had really startled her. A clear, ice blue, they were almost supernatural. You didn't expect someone to have eyes *quite* that blue, *quite* that icy; it was shocking, and if she wasn't more practiced at staying composed, she would have stared an extra minute every time he made eye contact with her. It helped—him, not her—and was probably no coincidence that his polo shirt with his company's logo matched his eyes perfectly. They were unsettling to her— captivating and a little too intense for Jane's general comfort.

Bottom line? Lars was youngish, buff and unusually good-looking. And he'd already proven himself quicker than most with a couple of witty rejoinders. But all of that interesting personality would be lost on Sara, of course, whom—Jane predicted from a lifetime of experience with her cousin's wily ways—would have Lars in her bed within a day of her arrival.

When Jane glanced at him again, Lars offered a friendly grin in return, but she didn't smile back.

Best not to get too attached, she thought, looking away from him, out the window.

Already been down that ugly road once before.

***

A little over a year ago, on one of their very first international photo shoots, Jane was sent ahead to make sure everything was ready for Sara's arrival. Met by her local contact in Cairo, Ben Abaz, she spent a blissful weekend enjoying exotic Egypt, being wined, dined and romanced to the hilt by the handsome modeling agent.

After an instant connection at the airport, Ben had impetuously kissed her and they had ended up on the floor of Sara's hotel suite, quickly consummating their hot little flirtation. Afterward, Ben had taken Jane to the ancient marketplace, held her hand as he pointed out the shoot locations, made a toast to her sparkling eyes and joined her in bed for two nights of bliss preceding Sara's arrival.

But, when Sara arrived, Jane saw an instant change in Ben's behavior toward her. He turned from hot and playful to politely professional in the course of an afternoon. Jane watched as he followed Sara around like a puppy, eager to do her bidding, to make himself useful, to make himself indispensable. Unable to bear the sudden change in his behavior, Jane had pulled him aside during one of Sara's costume changes and demanded he explain the sudden shift.

Ben had touched Jane's face, running one long, tan, tapered finger from her forehead down her nose, over her lips to her chin before pulling away. "Oh, Jane. The sun has come out from behind the clouds. I am blinded to anything but the sun."

As if on cue, Sara had exited her tent covered in sparkling gold body paint, with snake-like, gold, cuff bracelets circling her arms, and delicate, gold, anklets tinkling as she approached.

She had smirked at Jane, and then she touched her own lips with one manicured, gold-painted fingertip. As she walked by Ben, she brushed his lips with that fingertip lightly and murmured, "Later."

And stupid, pathetic Jane understood.

Or rather, she was cruelly reminded:

Samara was the sun.

Jane was nothing but a shadow.

***

"So, we have the house all set up per your instructions, and—"

"Later," Jane interrupted Lars, looking out the window, adjusting her cap. She wasn't ready to start working just yet. She softened her tone, offering him a small smile. "We can talk about all of it later, if that's okay with you. When we get there."

"Sure. Whatever you say." Her driver ran his hands over the wheel, and she sensed he was wondering if he should make conversation. A second later, he added: "This is the, uh, Bozeman Pass we're heading through right now."

Jane glanced over at Lars, then back out the window, noting the mountains up ahead, capped with white. The sky was big and bright blue with picture-perfect puffs of clouds at pretty intervals. She considered taking out her camera, but you never got great shots riding along in a car...plus, she was too relaxed with the afternoon sunlight streaming in through her window, making her tired body feel mellow and warm.

"Bozeman Pass, huh?"

"Yes, ma'am. To the left over there is the Bridger mountain range and out your window is the Gallatin range. We're about to pass between the two ranges."

"Ergo, Bozeman *Pass*."

"Ergo, Bozeman *Pass*," he repeated, seeming to warm to his subject. "You've heard of Sacajawea, right?"

Honestly, it had been a long time since Jane had studied up on American exploration, but she had always admired the story of the intrepid young Indian guide who carried her infant son on her back from North Dakota to the Pacific and back again. She had admired her strength and bravery. So, yes, in fact. She *did* remember Sacajawea.

"I have."

"Well, she guided Lewis and Clark through this pass."

Jane looked around admiringly at the landscape, which wasn't very developed, aside from the four-lane highway on which they were traveling. It wasn't hard to imagine what it looked like two hundred years ago.

"Would have been a tough journey, shackled to a man she'd been sold to with his baby on her back," she commented.

"Whoa!" He whipped his head to glance at her before turning back to the road. "You actually know her story!"

"Hard one to forget."

"Huh. You surprised me. Nobody ever knows the story or remembers the details."

"Well, *Just-Lars*, I guess I'm not 'nobody'."

"Means you're somebody, I guess."

She knew his words didn't have any special meaning, but they made Jane smile as she looked out the window at the Gallatin range, thinking again: *You'll be wasted on my cousin.*

"Hey, would you like some music?" he asked. "We've got a little bit of a drive ahead. An hour or so."

Jane shifted toward him, recrossing her legs in his direction. "Why not? What'cha got?"

"Mostly they play country out here."

She gestured to the CD player. "No CDs?"

He didn't answer her right away and seemed to be considering her question. "I mean, I have CDs. But, they're—"

"Are they dirty?"

"Wh-what?"

"Dirty. Like, dirty lyrics or something?" asked Jane.

"No!"

"Racist?"

"What? No!"

"Hmmm. Celtic? You into Enya?"

"Absolutely not."

"Japanese flute?"

"I don't even know what that is."

"Sitar? You like Bollywood tunes?"

"You are very strange."

"I've been called worse," said Jane. She readjusted her cap, tucking some stray curls back under, and trying not to smile.

"Sorry," Lars said. "That wasn't professional. Your questions are *unusual*."

"Actually, I preferred strange, *Just-Lars*. I can live with that."

He sighed. "I like…I mean, I like music from the 60s. When I'm driving alone, that's what I listen to. That's what I have on CD."

And the thing was? Jane *loved* 60s music.

"Cool. I don't mind 60s music."

"Really?"

"Nope. It's your van. We can listen to it if you want.

22

Where are the CDs?"

Lars flicked his overhead visor down and twelve CDs, neatly arranged in a flat holder, appeared underneath.

"May I?" she asked. Jane reached over, careful not to block his vision with her arm, and collected the twelve CDs one by one, depositing them carefully on her lap.

"Let's see…"

The soundtrack to *American Graffiti*, the soundtrack to *Peggy Sue Got Married*, Top Hits of the 60s, Beach Boys' *Endless Summer*, Peter and Gordon—

"This one. Track three."

She slipped the disk into the slot, only waiting a moment before the familiar guitar riff from "I Go to Pieces" made unexpected tears spring into her eyes. She was instantly jolted back in time to 1995. She was a six-year-old in the back of her father's car on the way to school, and he was playing this song, telling her it was his mother's favorite, telling her that it was one of his favorites too.

Do you hear the longing, Janie? Can you hear it? This must be the saddest song in the whole world.

She stared out the window at unfamiliar Montana.

…and I go to pieces and I want to hide, go to pieces and I almost die, every time my baby passes by…

"Hey," said Lars, "you have a decent singing voice, Jane Mays."

Jane didn't realize she'd been singing along.

"I bet you say that to all the girls who end up in the front seat of your van listening to random 60s music in the Bozeman Pass."

"You found me out."

"It was one of my dad's favorites."

She took a bottle of water from the glove compartment, unscrewed the cap and took a long sip.

"Huh. Mine too. I grew up listening to these songs. My dad loved the 60s stuff, and my mom tolerated it, so…"

"Lots of car rides singing along to 60s music, right? Sounds familiar."

"I wouldn't trade those memories," he said softly.

"Me neither," she whispered. "Do you mind if I open the window?"

"No, go for it."

With a good, deep breath of fresh air, Jane allowed her memories to linger. She leaned into them, even, which was unusual for her. It had become difficult, over the years, to differentiate real memories of her father from memories that were actually of her uncle. But, with the old chords drawing her back in time, she thought of her *father's* profile, driving her to school, his dirty-blond hair cut short and neat, and his light-blue dress shirt open at the neck. He was very handsome, and he had loved her with no strings attached.

Do you hear the longing, Janie?

She suddenly recalled, with a heart-pounding feeling of elation, that her father's voice had been slightly grittier than her uncle's, with a stronger Bostonian accent; almost as if he'd worked harder to hold onto it after moving to California. Hearing *his* voice in her head after so long was like uncovering a long-forgotten treasure.

"Penny for your thoughts?" asked Lars.

Um, no way. This belongs to me, not to you.

"Oh. Um. I don't know. I was just thinking that they don't write songs like these anymore."

"I agree." He glanced at her, then back to the road, smiling. "They're sweet, right? Heartfelt."

"Heartbreaking," she murmured.

"Little of that too, I guess."

"They're emotion," she said, looking over at him. "The music now is all so cool and slick. These songs were *all* heart."

Lars chuckled. "Sure were. And the way their voices blended, right?"

"Yes! The harmonies. Like butter." Jane sighed, shuffling through the CDs on her lap. "Hey…do you have the Kingston Trio here?"

"I do at home. But, um, I think I have The Fleetwoods if you're looking for a three-part sound."

"Yes! Here it is!"

"Give it to me," he said.

Suddenly the voices of the late-50s trio filled the car.

"I love this one," Lars sighed, gently beating his fingers along to "Come Softly."

Jane leaned back in her seat, letting the soft harmonies and sweet tune envelop her. *Come softly, darling. Come to me, stay. You're my obsession forever and a day…*

Her afternoon was not turning out as planned.

She should be doing work on her phone, not listening to obscure music with a hot tour guide. But she was so tired, and the music was so nice. It was such a relief to be far away from New York, and it had been weeks, maybe months, since her father felt so *real* to her.

She glanced at Lars and felt her stomach flutter. His lips were moving as he sang softly, but she couldn't actually hear any sound. She watched his lips, almost mesmerized, wondering what it would be like to—

"Take a picture, it lasts longer," he said, staring straight ahead.

"A throwback to our shared youth. How very sophisticated of you to quote Pee Wee Herman," she muttered, looking down quickly, feeling her face flush hot.

"I mean it," he said in a decent imitation of the Paul Reubens' character. "Do you need a camera? I could loan you one. Do you want me to smile? Pose?"

She squirmed in her seat, peeking at him with an embarrassed grimace. "Fine. I admit it. I was staring. You were mouthing the words, but no sound was coming out."

It was mostly the truth.

He flicked a glance to her. "Smooth."

"Conceited."

"Quick."

"Forgiven."

"Intriguing."

She grinned. Since when was Jane Mays intriguing to anyone? Especially anyone as hot as Lars Lindstrom? She felt a little chuffed, a little saucy, maybe even a little sexy.

Or maybe she was feeling sexy because of the ass massage her phone was giving her. She'd been so distracted by Lars, she hadn't realized it was buzzing. She shifted in her seat to pull it out of her back pocket.

Samara. Jane stared at her name and beautiful face on the iPhone screen, the familiar heaviness of servitude compressing her chest. She clenched her jaw, knowing that if she answered, she was going to have to listen to some long tirade that required *immediate attention.*

But Jane was tired. She was tired of being at the beck and call of a fully grown woman who had no appreciation, respect or understanding of what Jane did for her every day.

Maybe it was time Sara found out.

For one day, after five years in manacles, she wanted to be free. She just wanted to be Jane, with her own thoughts, her own experiences, a conversation with a handsome blond and a little 60s music. Was that too much to ask? She was sick and tired of being an extension of Samara Amaya, a nobody, a shadow.

Oh, she wouldn't get involved with Lars. This wasn't *about* Lars, and the memory of Ben was still fresh enough to sting. No, this was about *Jane.* This was about Jane having a few hours to herself.

In a second the phone would start playing Sara's favorite song, Christina Aguilera's "Beautiful," whose meaning had been totally lost on Sara, but which she had programmed into Jane's phone as her ringtone anyway.

Jane's finger hovered over the green Talk button for a moment, but she impulsively hit the red End button instead, exhaling loudly, then almost giggling with the outlandish reality that she just hung up on Samara Amaya. Throwing all caution and sanity to the wind, she pressed hard on the power button until the phone powered down completely. She stared at the screen for three seconds, realizing she'd never seen it so black and still.

"Anything important?" asked Lars, turning down the volume.

"No," answered Smooth, Quick, Intriguing Jane. She turned the music back up and tossed the phone into the outer pocket of her backpack.

Right now I'm just going to be Jane Mays. Nobody's assistant. Nobody's cousin. Nobody's niece. Sadly, nobody's daughter. Today is for me. Just for me.

She turned to Lars and smiled, feeling a thousand-pound weight slip off her shoulders. Oh, she'd pay for her rash decision later. But, for now, as Ray had kindly pointed out, she had three days to herself.

And damn if Jane wasn't going to make the most of them.

***

Lars pulled up in front of Sara's on-location housing in Gardiner, Montana, and all Jane could think was: *Sara is going to have a fit.*

A month ago, after looking at the four or five hotel options in Gardiner, and as politely as possible, Jane had insisted that *Trend* rent a house for the entirety of Sara's stay. She reminded *Trend* that Samara Amaya was accustomed to a two-bedroom suite at the finest hotels in the world when on location, and she would not be comfortable in a hotel room. The magazine had graciously arranged for a house to be leased while Sara was in Gardiner, and while they didn't have a photo for Jane, they had assured her it would be the local equivalent of a two-bedroom suite.

Jane lowered her Chanel sunglasses, looking up at the shiny, new fluorescent sign over her head that read "Kozy Kabins" with a jaunty red arrow that blinked cheerfully toward the four brand-new housekeeping cottages.

On one hand, she could see why they had been chosen. The construction was new, that was obvious. Obvious by the fact that there was not one blade of grass, bush or tree to be seen around the full perimeter of the solitary four cottages, whose medium-toned, orange-hued logs were almost a perfect match to the dust at her feet. There was no driveway, no patch of grass, no other sign of life. Just four log cottages with green metal roofs plopped down in the middle of nowhere with a view to an expansive meadow that extended to a faraway mountain range.

"This is…for *Samara?*"

"Yep." Lars nodded, standing next to her on the red soil. "Got it all fixed up just in time too."

Oh, my God, he doesn't even realize how unacceptable this is.

"Are those," she gestured to the other three cottages, "for her staff?"

Lars shook his head. "Nope. We were only asked to secure a cottage for Miss Amaya. Those three aren't even finished yet. I'm not sure they even have the electric wired in yet."

Jane turned to face him, her eyes wide. "This is a …a vacation cabin."

"Uh-huh."

"This is…not what she's used to."

Lars furrowed his brow, and then shrugged. "We don't exactly have six-bedroom, million-dollar houses lying around Gardiner waiting for someone to come rent for a week. The travel department at *Trend* said that the minimum requirement was a two-bedroom suite. None of the local hotels *have* suites, let alone a two-bedroom suite. We figured if we fixed this up, it'd be the closest to what Ms. Amaya requires."

"Yes, but—" Jane rooted around in her bag until she found a Tootsie Pop, unwrapped it, jamming it into her mouth and letting herself out of the van. She cringed at the dust and dirt that surrounded the small cottage and swirled around her feet, and the *Eau d'Construction Site* odor.

This is a disaster.

As she made her way toward the front door of the cottage, she turned back and waggled her lollipop at Lars. "You want one?"

"Umm, a *sucker*?"

"Yeah. They're delicious. And there's a secret in the center…" she cajoled, in a sing-song voice.

"I don't remember the last time I had one."

She fished another out of her bag. "Then it's time."

While he unwrapped his treat, he looked to her left.

"So those cabins are…empty?"

"Yep. This one here's the only one that's furnished. It's brand new. Wasn't supposed to even be open until next spring. They rushed this one and got it all set up nice for Ms. Amaya."

Jane looked up and noted two satellite dishes on the roof. Shiny and garish in the mid-afternoon sun, they looked ridiculously large on the small roof. She gestured to them with her lollipop. "What's with those?"

"TV and Internet. Said you needed them."

She glanced at him and realized he was staring at her, so she nodded.

Sara would have plenty to say about that, starting with the fact that they weren't *aesthetically* pleasing, perched on the green tin roof over the front door. That was *after* she got finished screaming about the Kozy Kabins, in general, of course.

Jane shuddered. "Do you have the keys?"

While Lars unlocked the door, Jane watched him from where she stood in front of the cottage, arms crossed, sucking on her lollipop, glad her sunglasses shielded her eyes.

For all he knew, she was evaluating the cottage. But she wasn't. She already knew everything she needed to know about this disaster of a housing debacle. And she had a feeling it wasn't going to get any better when he unlocked the door and showed her around the inside. No, Jane was checking out his long legs in worn jeans and the way the muscles in his back flexed when he reached forward to unlock the door. She sighed, finally removing her sunglasses, and headed up two concrete steps into the living room of the small cottage.

She couldn't help it: she had this sudden mental picture of Sara's face in her head and she burst out laughing.

The room had a cream, low-pile, wall-to-wall carpet, a

living room set from Sears, a modest dining room table with four chairs, and a kitchen area with a white linoleum floor. The two cheaply paneled walls in the living room had several stock photographs of elk, deer and wolves blown up and framed without mats in serviceable medium-wood frames.

Lars crossed his arms, staring at her, his eyes wide and surprised, and a sour expression puckering his lips.

Jane stopped laughing.

She gestured to the four picture windows that spanned the length of the room, offering sweeping views of the vast meadow and mountains beyond.

"The view is very nice," she said quietly, putting the lollipop back in her mouth.

"It's brand new," he explained again, his voice cool, though his cheeks were red. "It was just an empty cottage before. We had it…fixed up."

"Yes. So you said." She swallowed, noting his embarrassment, and suddenly she felt ashamed of herself for laughing, for making him feel bad. "It's just…um…different from what she will expect."

"I can't do anything about that," he said. "Unless you want to go back to Bozeman." When she didn't say anything, he shrugged. "Maybe I should start bringing her stuff in."

"Lars," she started gently, stopping him on the way to the door, though he didn't turn around. She took the lollipop out of her mouth and crossed the room, touching the bare skin of his upper arm with her free hand. He turned around slowly, looking down at her hand first, then into her eyes. "Just so you know…if it were *me* staying here, I'd be thrilled.

The views are beautiful, and"—she spread her arms, gesturing to the furnishings and decoration—"I have pretty simple tastes. *I'd* be happy here. Very happy. Very pleased. It's clean and snug and new and—"

"*She* won't like it?"

Jane shook her head slowly, adjusting her cap and putting the lollipop back in her mouth. "No. I'm afraid she won't."

"Anything we can do about it?"

Jane sighed and walked to the back of the cottage, peeking into the small bathroom, master bedroom and smaller guest bedroom. Lars leaned against the front door, probably *trying* to look nonchalant, though his arms were still crossed protectively over his chest.

There was no way, in a million, trillion years, that Samara Amaya was going to *happily* stay in this six hundred-square-foot, third-rate vacation cottage. Didn't matter that the carpet smelled new, and the linoleum was spic and span. Didn't matter that no one had probably dared sit on the toilet yet, and the views were gorgeous. Didn't matter that good people had gone out of their way to make it as comfortable for her as possible. She was going to pitch a proper fit.

Lars tilted his head to the side, raising his eyebrows in question, and she couldn't bear to disappoint him. Jane smiled at him with unforced warmth.

"We'll just have to make it work."

***

In the end, Lars upended the bed in the guest bedroom and

put all of Samara's luggage in there. It would serve as her dressing room, and Jane told him that she would get a room at the hotel with the rest of the crew, coming back to the cottage early in the morning to be on-hand for Samara before she woke up each day. Lars said he'd have an extra key made so that Jane could come and go freely.

To save his life, Lars couldn't understand the fuss. For heaven's sake, it was a perfectly nice little place, not to mention Miss Amaya would only be staying there for three nights before relocating to a resort in Jackson Hole next weekend.

He sensed that Jane was still uneasy about the arrangements, but he had been honest about the lack of options. There was simply nowhere else for Miss Amaya to stay that would meet her demands.

Since Jane had a good hour or two of unpacking to do, Lars said he'd be back to pick her up at five o'clock to take her to dinner and then to the Best Western to check into a room of her own.

Frankly, he was glad to get back in the empty van and drive away from the cottage. Aside from the fact that he was uncomfortable and embarrassed by Jane's reaction to the tidy little cabin, two burning questions had been driving him crazy for almost an hour:

What grown woman walked around sucking on a pink lollipop?

And what red-blooded man was supposed to be able to concentrate on anything she was saying when she kept taking that pink lollipop in and out of her mouth?

It's not like she was trying to be sexy with it. He would

34

have known if that was her game. It wasn't. Most of the time she had it wedged in the back of her cheek. But she couldn't keep it in there indefinitely. It had to come out every time she said something.

In and out, in and out, and *incredibly* distracting.

As he made his way back to the small office of Lindstrom & Sons, feeling more than a little annoyed, he had to admit that he was sort of fascinated by her.

Her. Jane.

She was incredibly quirky, liking the same obscure music genre he did and softly singing along all the way to Gardiner. She wore that Red Sox cap low over her eyes like she was shielding herself from the world, but then she made all of these smart-ass comments that surprised him and kept him on his toes. And just when he thought that was all there was to her, she put her hand on his arm and assured him that she wasn't the snob that her boss was, showing him a womanly, softer side of herself before popping that pink lollipop back in her mouth.

His breath came out in a *whoosh*, remembering.

He definitely didn't have her figured out.

That, in itself, was new to Lars, because it had never been tough for him to figure out women. He was good at picking up on female body language, reading between the lines of what they said and what they meant. He knew when a no meant maybe and a maybe meant yes. Unlike many members of his sex who were constantly stumped by women, Lars had always felt comfortable and confident; he had cracked the secret code so long ago, he took it for granted.

And it didn't matter if the women were pretty or plain, they all seemed to want to be with him, disarmed by his easy manners and enticed by his hard body. So, Lucky Lars had the pick of the litter and naturally he chose women that turned his head: exceptionally pretty, above-average beauties who—after a mild or overt flirtation—ended up in his bed.

Which is why it was out of character for him to be spending so much time thinking about Jane Mays. Aside from a mischievous smile and those twinkling, minxy eyes, she was…well, sort of plain next to the women he generally pursued. Unless she was really hiding something spectacular under those baggy clothes, she wasn't pretty enough to tempt him. So *why* was she getting under his skin?

Most women didn't joke with him; they lowered their lashes and flirted.

Most women would have taken off the cap and the sweatshirt, run a hand through their hair and at least *tried* to show off their assets, but she didn't seem to care how she looked.

Most women wouldn't have gushed over 60s music— hell, they wouldn't have known any of the words, either.

Most women wouldn't have admitted to eating a piece of sugary, fattening candy, and if they did? They would have been suggestive with that stupid lollipop, rather than just sucking on it like a good ol' piece of hard candy from a penny store.

Lars turned into a parking space in front of the storefront that read "Lindstrom & Sons: Yellowstone

Tours," and cut the engine, resting his hands on the steering wheel as an unlikely conclusion took root in his mind.

She didn't flirt. She wasn't trying to impress him. She wasn't putting on airs. And she wasn't trying to seduce him.

Huh. Why not?

It hit Lars like a ton of bricks as he put the pieces together, and he sat back in his seat, a little stunned, a little bemused, and maybe even a little impressed.

She doesn't want me.

As he identified this reality, *impressed* shifted quickly to *bothered.*

Wait. She *doesn't want* me?

And *bothered* was swiftly followed by the compulsory reaction of any confident man in the face of such an ego-bruising realization:

Challenge accepted.

You don't want me? Well, we'll just see about that, Jane Mays. We'll just see.

CHAPTER 2

"Lars!" His father looked up from the desk where he was sorting client files and grinned. "How's the New Yorker?"

"Fine," Lars grumbled, plopping down in the loveseat across from his father's desk and feeling ornery. "Kind of a smart-ass."

The store-front offices of Lindstrom & Sons were simple and serviceable: in the front of the office was a small table with six chairs for client meetings, and beside that, a simple khaki loveseat and glass coffee table on which a handsome leather album sat with the words *Lindstrom & Sons: Adventures* embossed on the cover.

The rear half of the office had two prominent desks and several file cabinets lining the walls over which hung photos of Pop, Nils, Lars, and Erik leading various tours of Yellowstone. Two doors in the back led to a washroom and a small kitchen that had a table for two and a Keurig that made the worst coffee in Gardiner.

"Smart-ass, huh?" His brother Nils came from the back room stirring a cup of coffee and took a seat at the desk behind their father. "Code for: She's immune to Lars's famous charm. Ha ha! Wonders never cease!"

Nils plunked down at his desk and picked up a Nerf football, throwing it over their father's head in Lars's direction. Lars caught it easily and tossed it back. He didn't have his own desk, which grated on him most days. If he needed to handle paperwork, he was left sitting at the conference table in the front window which, more or less, broadcasted to the world: *There's Lars Lindstrom, not important enough to have his own damn desk.*

"She's here for work, Nils, not pleasure," Pop said, without looking up. "I'm sure she has more important things to do than make eyes at Lars here."

He winked at Lars over his glasses then went back to sorting the files. "Mess of work getting all these magazine people sorted out."

"Can I help?" Lars asked, leaning forward.

"Nah, *Midten*. Me and Nils'll handle the business. You're our face man. You handle the talent and the locations."

Face man. Don't you see I can be more than that?

But Lars wasn't in the mood to face off with someone else today.

"I'll drive out with her tomorrow to check out the locations. They chose Sheepeaters, Old Faithful and Yellowstone Lake. Had to convince 'em of that one. They considered Hayden, but I told 'em I couldn't guarantee sightings." Hayden Valley was home to a good number of Yellowstone wildlife, but Lars didn't like it for a photo shoot. Without animals grazing it was unimpressive, and the animals were too unpredictable.

"Sounds good," his father mumbled, distracted by work.

"Have to go pick up Jane at five," Lars said, wondering if she'd wear her baseball cap at dinner. "Said I'd take her to a restaurant for supper and then to the BW. She had fifteen bags to unpack for the model. Can you imagine?"

"Fifteen bags? For a week?" His father looked at him over his glasses. "I will never understand these city people. All you need is a backpack and a duffel. Don't even need the duffel for less than a week."

Lars smiled to himself, thinking of Jane's leather backpack and beat-up leather bag. His father would probably like Jane.

"Call her "the talent," son. They like it better."

Lars rolled his eyes. He knew to call Samara Amaya the *talent*. He didn't need a reminder. *Just an excuse to treat me like a baby.* Grr.

"When're Erik and Kat getting to town?" he asked, changing the subject.

"Week from today. Erik said they'd leave at dawn, so probably here by Saturday lunchtime. Same with Jenny-girl and hers. Magazine people leave for the airport on Friday night and the talent's headed down to the resort in Jackson Hole for Saturday and Sunday."

Lars's little brother Erik and his wife Katrin were having their twin daughters, Dagmar and Heidi, baptized at Grace Church in Gardiner next Sunday, which meant that next weekend would be packed to the gills with family time while Samara Amaya and Jane Mays enjoyed the delights of the five-star Amangani Yellowstone Resort.

And thank God. Lars could use some time with his

family. His very, very Swedish-Norwegian family.

Only once in a while, although he would never admit it aloud, it felt slightly embarrassing to be so overtly ethnic. It made him feel protective and defensive at once. If Miss Smart-Mouth thought that the cottage all trussed up like the suite at a grand hotel was provincial, just wait 'til she heard his father's outdated style of speech. Then again, she didn't seem snotty like that, and Lars liked it that she was with famous people all the time but somehow managed to seem so normal.

"*Midten*, all okay?"

His father regarded Lars with his own ice-blue eyes. Lars realized he'd been frowning in thought.

"*Ja, Pappa.*" Lars looked at his father's aging face with love and nodded, "*Allt är okej.*"

His father smiled, returning to his work.

Lars caught Nils staring at him and raised his eyebrows, but Nils shrugged, throwing the football back to his younger brother.

Lars caught it, then got up, grabbing a Lindstrom & Sons embroidered fleece jacket from the coat tree by the front door. "Guess I'll go make sure the BW has a room ready for Miss—for Jane."

"Don't let the door hit you on the way out," Nils cautioned merrily, and Lars turned and threw the football back, hitting Nils squarely in the forehead before pulling the door closed behind him.

***

Jane was unpacking bag number six when she remembered

her phone was still off.

"Craaaaap!"

She ran into the little living room area and fished it out of her backpack, turning it on.

"Crap, crap, crap," she muttered, shifting her weight back and forth. It was one thing to take a break from her phone for a two-hour car ride from the airport, but believing that she could remain unavailable all day was not realistic or smart.

"Damage control," she whispered as soon as the main screen came up.

Oh my God. Eighteen voice messages, twenty-one emails and thirty texts. *Good Lord!*

First, she accessed her email and typed an out-of-office automatic reply:

Jane Mays is on location and may be difficult to reach. Please be patient and she will return your email as soon as possible.

Second, she accessed her voicemail and left the identical out-of-office message there.

Third, she turned off the "Read Receipts" function on her texting. People wouldn't know if she got their text or not, so they'd have to call or email to be sure, and then they'd hear the out-of-office messages.

She scrolled through the texts, and immediately figured out the cause for so much clamor. Laney was sick and wasn't able to join Sara for the shoot.

Jane put one hand on her hip, rolling her eyes as she read back through the message chain between SS (*SuperStar*, Laney's nickname for Sara) and LL (*LovelyLaney,* Sara's nickname for Laney).

> *It's strep AND an ear infection. MD says I can't go to
> Montana.*
>
> *-LL*
>
> *LL, I can't do the shoot w/o u! Will b all alone!*
>
> *-SS*
>
> *SS, u know I'd do anything for u! But, ears could burst on
> plane and am contajus.*
>
> *-LL*
>
> *Thx for leaving me all alone with GR, PJ and Bassy. Sux.
> Mad @ u, LL. Still*
>
> *love you forever.*
>
> *-SS*

Jane rolled her eyes. GR was "Gay Ray", PJ was "Plain Jane" and "Bassy" was Sebastian Together, they were her makeup and hair artist, assistant and manager. *How nice.*

Jane read the remaining texts quickly, wherein LL encouraged SS to still have a good time, be beautiful, be fierce, and get laid. *Classy.*

For as much as Jane questioned Laney's influence over her cousin, Jane had to admit that Sara was always easier to manage with Laney in play.

After Sara met Laney in a nightclub about a year ago, she'd become a regular part of Samara Amaya's entourage, which had been a considerable relief to Jane.

Whereas some personal assistants might act as a coordinator, manager and *friend* to a supermodel or actress, Jane and Sara didn't have that sort of connection anymore, so Jane handled the business while—more and more—Laney handled Sara.

Laney went to premieres, hung out with Sara at parties, held back her hair at the end of the night as she threw up into the closest toilet, worked out with her, and was for all intents and purposes Sara's best friend. Well, a best friend who got paid to be a best friend and agree with everything Sara said and did.

Only once had Jane taken a shot at Laney by taunting Sara—after a particularly brutal bitch-out session—by exclaiming, "It's no wonder you have to *buy* your friends!"

But Jane had had the poor taste to make the remark within earshot of Laney, and regretted it when she saw the wince of embarrassment and hurt on Laney's face.

It made Jane realize that while Laney was firmly on Sara's side of things, she had feelings like everyone else, and Jane took pains to treat Laney with kindness after that.

Laney was actually very useful. Sara was calmer and happier with Laney around, and Laney was quite good at getting Sara to do things that Jane couldn't get her to do, like charity photo ops or goodwill appearances. Not to mention, Laney's presence in Sara's life took a lot of pressure off of Jane. Without Laney, Jane wouldn't be able to arrive two or three days early for location shoots; she'd be forced to attend dreaded industry parties and be around Sara a lot more.

"This shoot just got a whole lot tougher," she sighed aloud.

Jane shook her head, deleting the messages. She wrote back to tell Laney she hoped she felt better soon and reassured Sara that all would be ready for her upon arrival.

Her phone dinged angrily in response:

Where were u, Jane?! U know I hate it when LL is sick. Don't piss me off.

Ding again, and the next text showcased all of her cousin's charm:

Don't forget I can fire ur ass, Janie.

Jane raised the phone over her head as if to smash it on the floor, then took a deep breath and lowered it back down slowly. Her thumbs flew as she typed a quick response.

Sara, cell service here is terrible. Have contacted local government to ask for

improvements since you're coming to town. Getting things ready for you. Hope

Laney feels better soon. -J

A minute later she received a two-line message back:

My name is SAMARA. Don't fuck with me, Jane.

She wrote back:

My bad. Sorry, Samara. Have to go finish unpacking your bags now. —J

Jane turned the phone over, swallowing painfully against the indignant lump in her throat. With Laney down, Sara was on the warpath. Great. Just great.

She shoved the phone into her back pocket and braced her hands on the windowsill staring down at them, at their freckles and whiteness against the medium-toned wood.

I miss my parents.

Tears welled up in her eyes, and she blinked, wishing them away. After almost fifteen years, she'd learned that tears didn't help anything. Tears didn't resurrect your dead parents or change your uncle into your father, no matter how much they looked alike. Tears didn't change the fact that Jane had had to grow up in the shadow of her profoundly beautiful cousin, always outshined, always second best.

She took her phone back out, and clicked on music, then on her 60s Playlist, then on Peter and Gordon, then on "I Go to Pieces" and let the music swell around her as she lifted her gaze to the mountains beyond the meadow.

Do you hear the longing, Janie?

Jane took a ragged breath, wrapping her arms around her body and sighing heavily.

She didn't like where her life had ended up.

She didn't like that her cousin owned her, her parents' untimely death forcing Jane into indentured servitude to the closest branch of her father's family in payment for them taking her in.

She didn't like it that she'd given up her own dreams in order to please her beloved uncle.

She didn't like it that she'd put aside her longing to be a professional photographer in exchange for the monetary comfort of a well-paying position with her shrew of a cousin. Here she was, in one of the most beautiful places on earth stuck making sure that Sara's underwear was neatly unpacked into a bureau, and her favorite lip gloss was ready on her bedside table. If Sara had her way, Jane would wipe her backside too.

What kind of life is this?

Jane sniffled lightly, wiping her eyes with the backs of

her hands.

I'm just tired, and I know Sara—Samara will be a handful without Laney.

Buck up, Jane. Turn off the waterworks. You'll be okay. You have two days to get your head around it.

The song ended and she glanced down at her phone, realizing it was four-forty.

Lars would be here in twenty minutes, so she would just have to do the rest of the unpacking tomorrow, and then maybe he could show her the shoot locations. Sara liked to see pictures of her locations prior to her arrival so Jane would have to get some good pictures and send them before Sara arrived on Tuesday morning.

Jane closed the door to the second bedroom, which looked like the aftermath of an explosion of clothes, jewelry, shoes and makeup. She'd been able to remake the bed in the master bedroom with Sara's sheets, and she had gotten most of her cousin's lingerie and pajamas sorted out. Everything that required a hanger was neatly hung in the closets. Tomorrow Jane would unpack everything else, down to Sara's last toiletry, arranged just so in the bathroom so her cousin wouldn't have trouble finding anything.

Jane paused in the bedroom, looking at herself in the mirror over the bureau. She took off her glasses and folded them gently, leaving them on the counter next to the sink.

She looked tired and drawn.

Two hours of sleep will do that to you.

Glancing down, she noticed that all of Sara's travel makeup was in a large fabric pouch, open in front of her.

There were darker-than-usual circles under her eyes, so she opened one of Sara's concealers and ran a thin strip of beige cream under her eyes. *Better.*

She took out the mascara and swiped her lashes. *Hm.*

She rummaged around until she found some bronzer and brushed lightly over her cheekbones and the tip of her nose as she'd seen Ray do for her cousin a million times. *There.*

She picked up a tube of Burt's Bees tinted and glided it over her lips. *Not bad.*

Okay. Okay. She was no Samara Amaya, but it's not like she was working on a top-drawer canvas either. Anyway, she felt better.

Taking off her omnipresent cap, she looked at the mop of brown waves that framed her face in soft, unfashionable curls. She opened a can of Samara's mousse and squirted a plump puff of white onto her hand, rubbed her hands together, then drew them through the curls, making them look more styled and manageable, then pushing them off her face and into elegant waves.

Under her sweatshirt, the plain white cotton tank top wasn't crisp but it was clean, hidden under her sweatshirt all day. She fished around in her leather bag until she found an olive green, cropped, cabled wool cardigan sweater and threw it on over her tank. She liked the way the bottom of the cardigan skimmed the top of her jeans, making her waist look smaller. She took off her socks and loafers and found her favorite brown, leather flip-flops in the bottom of her bag, slipping them onto her pedicured feet. Folding her cap in thirds, she shoved it in her left back pocket, and pushed her phone in the other.

Walking into the living room, she took out her sunglasses and put them on, tossed her backpack on one shoulder, her bag on the other, then went outside to wait for Lars.

***

Before Lars had time to get out of the pickup and help her with her bags, Jane had tossed the duffel into the flatbed of his truck and opened her own door. He looked over to see her pull herself up into the front seat beside him.

She wasn't wearing that old Red Sox cap, and her hair looked slick and styled, the waves swept off her face and far more sophisticated than earlier. She wasn't wearing her sweatshirt anymore either, and he could see that the pale skin of her chest was dotted with cheerful freckles as he caught the appealing swell of her small, rounded breasts under a simple white tank top.

Perfect handfuls. Well, well, Jane Mays.

"Heya," he said, offering her his sexiest smile.

"*Heya?*" She buckled her seat belt without sparing a glance for him.

"Yeah," he said. "It's what we say."

"Okay. Heya, *Just-Lars*. Where we headed?" The belt clicked closed and she ran her fingers through her hair from forehead to nape, looking straight ahead, out the windshield.

Huh. Not even a look? Damn it.

"I'm at your service, Miss Mays. Dinner? Sightseeing? Hotel?" He drawled the last word suggestively.

"Sightseeing?" she asked, pulling her purse onto her lap.

He cleared his throat, furrowing his brows. He wasn't accustomed to his efforts at being sexy and charming going unnoticed. "Beautiful downtown Gardiner is at your disposal."

She fiddled around in her bag, looking for something, all but ignoring him. "Umm…okay. Whatever."

He watched as she fished a Nikon D3X out of her bag. Interesting. It was possibly the best handheld professional camera that Lars knew of, and he saw an awful lot of cameras in his line of work. She must be pretty serious about photography to have spent several thousand dollars for a camera like that.

"Some camera," he said.

"My baby," she crooned.

My baby.

He hadn't expected her to say something like that. It made his breath catch. It made him think of kissing her, touching her, feeling her fingers running through his hair as she murmured *baby* low in his ear. Did she have any idea how sexy her voice was?

When he glanced over, she was caressing the black plastic casing of the expensive camera. *Lucky goddamn camera.*

"Hey, um…I found this for you," he said, slipping a CD into the player and choosing his favorite.

"The Kingston Trio!"

She finally turned her face to him, then, beaming at him as she pushed her sunglasses up onto her head.

His eyes slammed into hers and he realized that the sweater she was wearing was the same color as her eyes. He hadn't noticed the color before—probably because of her glasses and cap—but they were sort of an earthy, olive-y green with gold flecks. He'd seen that color a million times before in the park—in the forest and woods, in the mosses and meadows. Just never in another person.

"Your eyes are green," he observed softly.

"Yes, they are," she said. The smile she offered him was guileless. "I love these guys."

"I guessed. You, um, you asked for them earlier."

Her eyes twinkled as she nodded at him, bright and pleased, and it made his quick stop at home, to rummage through his CD collection, totally worthwhile.

"'Chilly Winds'," she murmured. "Good song."

"Yeah," he whispered, anxious not to break the moment.

"Wow, this is dreamy," she sighed, sitting back against her seat and staring straight ahead at the meadow and mountains beyond the cabins, listening to the soft guitar riffs and gentle harmonies filling the truck.

He leaned back against his seat too, and tried not to turn his head to stare at her, but couldn't help stealing glances as she mouthed the words, her head tilted away from him at a gentle angle.

She was right; it *was* a dreamy song, and it *felt* incredibly dreamlike to be sitting beside her, sharing the mellow love song while the late afternoon sun caught strands of her loose curls and turned them from brown to gold. She looked over at him and his stomach fluttered. He wished he could figure out the deal with her—with how she made him feel.

"Out where them chilly winds don't blow..." she sang softly, taking a deep breath. "Thanks for this, *Just-Lars*."

"I aim to please."

"You succeed," she murmured, holding his eyes for an extra moment as her cheeks flushed pink. Her lips twitched into a slight smile and she blinked at him, as though seeing him for the first time.

He stared back at her, unable to look away, lost in those mossy-green eyes, wondering what she was thinking.

"Where's the case?" she asked softly. "The CD case?"

His breath came out in a rush, like he'd been holding it. "Home."

He took a shaky breath and grinned back at her, grateful that her question had broken the intimacy of the moment. He turned the key in the ignition and pulled out of the dusty area in front of the cottage, headed back toward town.

"Does this one have 'Take Her Out of Pity' on it?"

"Yeah, umm...track six, I think." He glanced over as she leaned forward and pressed the fast-forward button on the CD player.

The banjo and guitar started, and Jane sang along, softly but faithfully, as she looked down, playing with the buttons and switches on her camera:

I had a sister Sally; she was younger than I am. Had so many sweethearts, she had to deny them. But as for sister Sara, you know she hasn't many. And if you knew her heart, she'd be grateful for any...

don't let her die an old maid but take her out of pity....Sara's almost twenty-nine, never had an offer...

He looked over at her. At the end of the verse, she shrugged her shoulders in delight and resumed the chorus with gusto, still staring down at her camera. It was as if there was a hidden message in the song that only Jane Mays could hear and enjoy. He was glad she was looking down; he was glad he could keep stealing glances of her unobserved.

"What's up with this song, Minx?"

She turned to him, surprised at first, then smiling mischievously. "Minx?"

Man, that voice. "The way you're smiling. Like the cat that got the cream."

She shifted her body toward him. "This song is about an old maid who can't get a man."

"Yeah."

"And her name is Sara."

He nodded, not entirely sure where she was going with this train of thought. "Yeah."

"Sara is my cousin's name."

"Huh. Okay. You're not a fan of your cousin, eh?" He stopped at a stop sign and looked over at her, amused.

"Wait 'til you meet her."

"Does she work for Miss Amaya too?"

Jane's eyes widened in surprise and that sweet twinkle died as surely as a fire doused with a bucket of water.

"I'm sorry. Did I say something wrong?" he asked.

"She *is* Miss Amaya." she muttered.

"Samara Amaya is your *cousin*? No. Wait. You said your

cousin's name is Sara."

She nodded, reaching over to turn off the CD player.

Lars pulled into a parking space on Main Street and faced her. "I'm sorry, I'm trying to understand. You're Samara Amaya's *assistant*."

"And her *cousin*," she said. "Samara's cousin. Actually, Sara Mays's cousin. Sara Mays. That's her real name. Our fathers are brothers. *Were* brothers."

"Whoa," he murmured, putting pieces of this family puzzle together.

She turned to look at him, facing him squarely. Her shoulders were rigid, and her eyes were guarded…almost worried, like she was waiting for—for what? What had she said? Were. *Were.*

"Who lost her father?" he asked gently.

"Wh-what?"

"You said *were* brothers. You can't undo brothers. I assume one brother, um, one *father* passed away?"

"M-mine. I was raised by my uncle. My father's twin."

He couldn't get a read on what was going on in her head, but her face was softening as she gazed at him. Her olive-green eyes searched his face intently and she looked like someone had just shocked the hell out of her…maybe even like she wanted to cry.

Talking about losing someone you loved can do that, Lars thought. He knew from experience.

"I'm really sorry," he said.

Those vulnerable green eyes searched his, her face softening all the way to tenderness as she stared at him.

For me? whispered his heart.

No, Stupid, his mind answered swiftly. *She's thinking about her father, not you.*

"I'm sorry, Jane," he offered again.

"It was a long time ago."

Her shoulders relaxed as she said this, and her lips tilted up in a small smile. He reached out and bumped his knuckles tentatively against the side of her thigh on the seat beside him.

"Doesn't matter how long...it fades a little, but it doesn't ever stop hurting."

"Who did you lose?" she asked softly. She glanced down at his hand, but didn't say anything, so he kept it where it was, lightly grazing her jeans.

"My mom. Cancer."

She nodded.

"What about your dad?" he asked.

"Both my parents," she murmured. "Car crash. When I was ten."

He winced. "Oh, no. *Both* of your parents? Aw, Jane, that's...I'm so sorry."

She placed her hand beside his on the seat and he gently hooked his thumb under hers. He watched as her fingers curled softly around his.

"Thank you," she whispered, her husky voice even deeper with the emotion.

When he looked back up at her, her green eyes were slightly glassy. He leaned closer to her, mesmerized, vaguely aware that if he kept staring into them, he might do something stupid.

Suddenly, she looked away, squeezing then releasing his hand and smiling up at him—that wonderful minxy smile he was starting to like so much—as she lowered her sunglasses. It sure wouldn't be hard to get used to that smile.

"Hey! You said *sightseeing*, right?"

"I did, indeed."

He smiled back at her before opening his door and rounding the truck to open hers.

His heart beat faster than usual between the long strides of his steps.

Something unspoken had passed between them—something bigger and more important than he'd ever expected. He felt it keenly, and sensed she felt it too.

***

Jane was surprised by how appealingly quaint she found Gardiner's Main Street, probably owing to its connection with and proximity to Yellowstone. She tried to stay focused on the various stores and businesses Lars was pointing out as they strolled along, but she was having trouble composing her thoughts. She was all turned around. What had just happened to her in Lars's truck had never, ever happened to her.

When she'd realized he wasn't aware of the close familial connection between her and Samara Amaya, she'd braced herself for what always came next. She always found it awkward, and sometimes downright painful, to settle into a friendly relationship with someone, only to have them realize she was Sara's first cousin. They'd look her up and down, wondering why Samara got daintily brushed with pixie dust and Jane got whacked with the average stick.

Sometimes they registered total and complete shock before narrowing their eyes and inspecting her face and body for similarities. Finding none, their reactions would vary.

Once or twice, people in the modeling business had actually cringed looking at her, mentally comparing her looks to those of her stunning cousin, but in fairness, most people were decent enough to just look a little uncomfortable—sorry for her, maybe, shrugging good-naturedly as if to say *You can't win 'em all.*

The *most* tactful people—who were few and far between in the beautiful world of modeling—just smiled and nodded, probably assuming Jane had been adopted, because there was no way the two women could possibly share such similar DNA and look as different as they did.

He clearly hadn't known she was Sara's cousin – his face had registered total surprise. So, she'd taken off her glasses and faced him, making it easy for him to stare at her, make his mental comparison, find her lacking, cringe—or whatever else he needed to do—and get the whole mortifying ritual over with.

She wanted to weep when it didn't happen.

He didn't inspect her like a third-rate cow at a state fair. Instead, he asked about her father, told her how sorry he was, shared how much he missed his own mother. It made her lonesome heart contract with longing at the unexpected goodness of it, the sweetness of the reprieve, his sheer kindness. And something substantial shifted inside of Jane—

something instinctually inconvenient and risky to her heart—
as she searched his handsome face for censure and found
none.

In that moment Lars Lindstrom felt…*possible.*

She took a deep breath of air into her lungs, trying to
get out of her head, but familiar doubts already started
creeping in.

*Don't fool yourself. He is out of your league, Jane. This will end
badly if you don't let go of it now.*

She shushed the voice in her head, but it was persistent
in its concern.

*What's gotten into you today, Jane? Turning off your phone?
Calling "Samara" Sara? Walking beside Lars Lindstrom right now
like it could actually go somewhere? Like he could ever actually be
interested in a Plain Jane like you? Make no mistake; if you get
involved with him, he will dump you the moment Sara gets to town.
Stop throwing caution to the wind. Remember Ben. Protect yourself
before you get hurt.*

She looked up at him. He was pointing out a bridge up
ahead and saying something about the Yellowstone River,
talking animatedly, smiling at her, then gesturing behind
them, talking about the source of the river. She nodded at
him with a vague grin, but she hadn't paid attention to a
word he was saying. They paused at the bridge, leaning over
the railing to look at the rushing water below.

Finally he turned to her. She could feel his eyes.

"Hey, you know who you kind of remind me of a little
bit?"

She looked up. He leaned on the railing, staring at her

and she felt her heart leap in her chest beholding those light-blue eyes, so searing, so fixed.

She swallowed. "Who?"

"Did you ever see that show *Felicity*? When the main character cut her hair? It sort of looked like yours does." He smiled at her, and reached out, pulling on a curl gently, then watching it spring back.

"You're talking about Keri Russell," she said, cheeks flushing from the unexpected compliment.

"Yeah! Her. You look like Keri Russell!"

It was on the tip of her tongue to point out that Keri Russell was a famous—and very beautiful—actress, while Jane was just her cousin's plain assistant, but opted to joke with him instead: "So, are you big into the chick shows, or…"

"Nah. My mom liked that one. I pretended I hated it. But, I—"

His mood changed on a dime and he shrugged, dropping his hand and turning away from her.

"You watched it with her. While she was sick."

He nodded, still looking out at the river, the silence strangely comfortable between them for several long minutes as the water rushed white beneath their feet.

The sun lowered to the horizon as they stood side by side, so Jane took off her sunglasses, tucking them into the front of her tank top. He looked over at her and she watched his eyes flick to her breasts, linger for a moment, and then return to her face.

His cheeks pinkened, and she couldn't resist teasing him.

"I've heard…if you *take a picture it lasts longer*. Do you want to borrow my camera or anything? You might need the zoom lens, but you can use it if you want…" She wiggled her shoulder, letting the camera strap slip down her arm.

His face was an appealing shade of salmon as he rolled his eyes at her. "You stole my line."

"You stole it first."

"You're trouble, Minx."

"Aw, I'm harmless." She shoved her hands in her back pockets, which pulled her shoulders back and flaunted her measly—but apparently, compelling—assets.

"Mmm," he hummed, narrowing his eyes. "Harmless my ass."

"Now, your ass is another story."

"Minx, again!"

She giggled. "Had enough of your ass and my chest?"

"I honestly don't know how to answer that. Damned if I do…"

"Then don't. Take me to dinner?"

"Now, *that* I can do."

***

After dinner Lars drove her to the Best Western where he had already reserved a room under her name. He got out of his truck and pulled her duffel from the back, holding it out to her.

"Unless you want the door-to-door service?" he asked.

"Not necessary, *Just-Lars*. I'm the low-maintenance cousin."

"We're a full-service operation, Minx."

She had been smiling at him, but her smile faded. "Better not call me that when Sara—I mean, *Samara*, gets here."

"Why not?"

"She wouldn't like it."

"Maybe I'll take my chances."

"You'll make my life harder if you do."

"What's *with* your cousin anyway? She can't be *all* bad."

Jane looked away, her face blank, guarded. Finally she sighed. "How about we talk more tomorrow? While we look at the shoot locations?"

He was curious about Samara Amaya, but honestly, he was more curious about Jane, and how exactly Samara, of whom she didn't seem overly fond, fit into her life. He predicted it was complicated. Lars hated complicated. Lars avoided complicated like the plague.

"Sure. Tomorrow. What time do you want me here?"

"I still have to unpack a few more of her bags too."

He nodded. "I can take you to the cabin at nine? I don't mind helping, if you need me."

Jane smiled. "Yes, I'm sure you'll be very effective lining up her Jimmy Choos. I tell you what. Maybe I could give you a grocery list while I finish the unpacking? You could grab her some supplies?"

"Who's Jimmy Chews?"

Jane giggled. "You're definitely on grocery duty, my fine friend."

"Okay. It's a date. I'll be here at nine, drive you to the cottage, head to Arnold's, pick up whatever you need, and

I'll get some lunch for us too. We'll drive out to the shoot locations around eleven? We can have lunch somewhere in the park."

"Sounds perfect. Thank you, Lars."

"Well, I'll—" He sort of saluted her awkwardly but as he was walking back to his truck door he heard her call his name. He turned around.

Jane approached him, a leather bag on each small shoulder, slight smile, sweet brown curls, her shiny eyes the color of spring moss in a summer shower. For a moment it seemed like she didn't know why she had called him back, and for a brief instant he considered leaning forward and kissing her.

He didn't, but damn, he *wanted* to.

She tilted her head to the side, must have remembered what she wanted to say.

"If it's sunny tomorrow...do you have the Beach Boys? We could listen to *Endless Summer* to mark the end of summer?"

He swallowed and nodded at her as his heart kicked into high speed—*Please let it be sunny for her tomorrow*— before she grinned, turned, and walked into the office.

***

Jane lay in bed staring at the ceiling, unable to fall asleep. She had finished all of her emails, sent several texts and made the few phone calls that required immediate attention.

Sara had evening plans tonight and tomorrow—a vodka launch tonight and a gala at the MoMA tomorrow—which usually made her happy, but less so with Laney unavailable to join her. Though she loved to be on display, Jane knew Sara preferred to attend these events with a wingman. Jane talked to Sara's agent, Sebastian, who was traveling with her on Tuesday morning, and he said he'd offer to join her for the launch tonight. Sara wasn't a fan of Sebastian, but Jane knew she'd probably say yes to his company and end up ordering him around all night. Jane had two thoughts. First, *Poor Sebastian*, quickly followed by, *But, better him than me!*

She tried to sleep, but she was exhausted. *Beyond* exhausted. She checked her phone: eight o'clock here was ten at home. If she were at home, she would pad out to the kitchen and put a cup of milk in the microwave as her mother used to do when she was little and had trouble sleeping, but there was no milk and no microwave in her hotel room.

She got out of bed and flicked on a light, putting her cap back on and grabbing her bag. She glanced in the mirror at her black fleece yoga pants and Boston College t-shirt, and shrugged—she wasn't about to change for a quick walk to find warm milk, and anyway, besides Lars, she didn't know a soul in town.

She hadn't seen a Starbucks during her sightseeing tour of Gardiner, but she was fairly certain she had noticed another coffee shop, and if she wasn't mistaken, it was just down the road from her hotel. She slipped her feet into flip-flops and locked the hotel room door behind her.

At the front desk, she was told that yes, the Prairie Dawn Café & Book Shop was a five to seven-minute walk from the hotel. *Perfect*, she thought. *A short walk and a cup of hot milk should put me to rights.*

The streets of Gardiner weren't buzzing with activity, but they weren't dead either. Jane saw a few tourists out and about, having dinner or getting the supplies they needed for their outdoor adventures in the morning. She saw a little boy and his father walking along with new fishing rods resting on their shoulders, and a group of four women in bikini tops, short shorts and hiking boots, headed for a local bar.

It didn't take long to get to the Prairie Dawn, and when Jane opened the door, she gasped lightly in pleasure, her lips turning up as she stood in the doorway with delight, taking in the quirky little bookstore/café.

It was one large open space, with wooden columns scattered throughout the room at intervals and brightly colored throw rugs covering parts of the wooden floor. Bookcases and windows lined the walls from floor to ceiling to her right, and there were jauntily upholstered couches and chairs, mismatched, waiting for a reader to find a book and get comfortable. Small, ceramic tiled bistro tables, each with two or three chairs, were scattered in cheerful bunches, and a shiny copper coffee bar with six stools took up most of the wall to her left.

Several of the tables and couches were occupied, as people of all ages sipped tea or coffee and flipped through newspapers, magazines and books. Soft music was piped in too, and Jane recognized the mellow voice of James Taylor singing about sweet baby James, which Jane's mother had always changed to *sweet baby Jane.*

Walking into the Prairie Dawn felt like an embrace, like

walking into a dream, like connecting with the past…and Jane breathed in deeply, smelling the books and the coffee beans, profoundly content with her decision to get out of bed and go on a quest for warm milk.

A petite, redheaded barista stood behind the bar with her elbows on the counter, deep in conversation with a blond man sitting on a stool at the end of the counter. They were practically head to head, and Jane didn't wish to disturb their conversation, so she pulled out a stool two down from where he sat.

The redhead looked over at Jane and smiled.

"We have a visitor, Paul."

The blond man looked over at Jane and smiled too.

"From Boston, no less."

Jane raised her eyebrows.

The woman pointed to her t-shirt and the man pointed to her cap at the same time.

"Originally San Francisco. Then Boston," Jane admitted. "Now New York."

The woman moved to stand in front of Jane and offered her hand. "Maggie Campbell."

"Jane Mays." She shook Maggie's hand and turned to Paul, who gestured to the stool beside Jane. She nodded, and he moved over to sit beside her.

"Paul Johansson."

"Heya," Jane offered, smiling at each of them in turn.

"Heya!" Paul looked at Maggie and smiled. "Only one family in Gardiner greets everyone with 'Heya'. Which of the Lindstroms were you hanging out with today?"

"Lars."

"Magazine shoot," said Paul.

"What am I thinking right now?" Jane asked in a rush, eyes twinkling.

Paul looked confused.

"Well, you must be clairvoyant!"

Paul chuckled. "Nothing so glamorous. Best friend to Lars."

"Ahhhh. *Just-Lars*'s best friend."

"So you work for Samara Amaya," said Maggie, and Jane picked up on a soft burr. Irish maybe...or Scottish? "D'you want coffee?"

"Um, yes, I do. And no I don't. This is a little strange, but I was wondering if I could have some warmed milk?"

"Havin' trouble sleepin'?"

"A little."

"Comin' right up, then. Want a wee bit o' sugar too?"

"Sure, Maggie, thanks."

"Samara Amaya dated the Vikings QB, didn't she? Last year? Year before?"

Jane shrugged. "The media makes a lot out of these things."

"Huh. Vikings fans around here were pretty steamed when she dumped him. Blamed her for the next two losses."

Jane wasn't comfortable talking about Sara, and her cousin would blow a gasket if she suspected Jane was gossiping about her with the locals. "I can't actually..."

Maggie interrupted smoothly, giving Paul a look. "She can't talk about her boss, now, Paul. You want yer milk

66

boiled or steamed, Jane? I'm thinkin' steamed, right?"

Jane nodded at Maggie gratefully, then turned to Paul, feeling bad that she'd been so cagey.

"Think about if you went on a date with somebody, and it was nice, so you went on another, and it was nice again. But then he went home. And home was a six-hour plane ride away. And you realized you were in New York and he was in Minneapolis, and you were both on the road all the time, so as much as you enjoyed each other, well, it just probably wasn't going to work out. So, you broke it off. And since it didn't hurt either of you very much, you knew it probably wasn't meant to be." She tilted her head to the side and glanced at Maggie, who set a steaming mug on the counter in front of Jane. "But suddenly there are all of these pictures of you together, magazines are photoshopping wedding dresses on you, and Cartier calls to offer you whatever diamond engagement ring you want. I mean, you were just a girl who went on a couple of dates with a guy. The world isn't supposed to explode over that."

Maggie rested her elbows on the counter, hanging on Jane's every word. "Is that what happened?"

Jane grinned. "Not exactly. But, isn't that a nice story?"

Maggie smiled and Paul chuckled.

"What d'you do for her, then?" asked Maggie.

Jane picked up her mug and blew over the top. *Just get it over with.* "I'm her personal assistant. And, um, her cousin."

She looked down at the mug, smiling at the tiny brown grains of nutmeg and cinnamon Maggie had sprinkled over the top and fashioned into a heart. Finally she took a sip and let the hot sweet, creamy goodness fall scalding down her throat. "Mmmm."

When she looked up again, Maggie was leaning closer, her eyes fixed on Jane's.

"What was it like growin' up together?"

Jane said the words by heart. "Like any other cousins. We loved each other. We hated each other. We watched *90210* and went for ice cream and opened our presents together on Christmas morning." She blew on the hot milk again, deciding to add her own addendum this time. "I know she's a supermodel. But, to me she's still just Sara."

"Is her name really Sara?"

Jane nodded at Maggie. "Sara Mays."

"Ahhhh. Sara Mays. Samara Amaya. I see."

Paul huffed softly, gesturing to Maggie for a refill. "No offense, Jane, but Maggie was giving me some advice before you got here. Do you two mind if we get back to web dating 101?"

"Oh," said Jane. "I didn't mean to interr—"

"You're not," said Paul. "Chime in if you've got any advice."

Maggie poured herself a cup of coffee too. "Paul's met someone online!"

Huh. That's it? They didn't want to talk about Sara and ask me questions all night? Well, wow! This is awesome. Regular people talking about regular things.

Jane turned to Paul with a delighted smile. "Do tell!"

Before he could answer Maggie whispered again, "And, how's this for a coincidence, Jane? She's from *Connecticut!*"

Jane had never actually seen someone so excited about *Connecticut*. Jane looked back and forth between them. "What am I not getting here?"

"Connecticut!" said Maggie. "It's between New York and Boston, isn't it? Where you're from? It's in the middle, isn't it? You been there?"

"Oh. Um…sure, a little. Samara has friends in Westport, and I know a few people in Connecticut too. Friends from college, mostly. It's pretty. What town is she in?"

Maggie beamed. "Mystic! D'you know it?"

"I do," answered Jane. "Not well, but I've been there. It's on the coast. Very picturesque. They have, um, an old-fashioned village there. And great seafood. And an aquarium, I think. Sailboats. Old houses. Sort of quintessential New England. Yeah, I remember it."

Maggie beamed at Paul, and he gave her a look.

"Can I ask you a question?" Jane asked, looking back and forth between them.

Paul nodded.

"Why'd you decide to get to know someone from Connecticut and not closer?"

"Maggie meddled," Paul blurted out. "She set up the profile and she wasn't totally clear about where I lived."

Maggie cringed. "I thought the question asked where he was *from*."

"And you're from…?"

"Maine. Originally." Paul rolled his eyes at his friend.

"Ah. I get it. So it fed you girls from New England.

Huh. You must have liked her a lot out of the gate," said Jane, "to get to know her from so far away. Once you realized the distance."

Paul smiled at Jane and she saw the sudden warmth infuse his blue eyes. "You could say that."

"*I* could say that? Look at you. You're a goner."

"I like her," he said softly. "I look forward to her emails and we're reading a book together. We talk about our lives, work, whatever, you know? I tell her everything lately. She's a teacher and I'm a principal so we talk about our students, our families, what we like to do on the weekends. Yeah, I like her."

"You like her a lot. Sounds like you're ready for the next step," said Jane. "When're you going to meet her? *In person?*"

"Heck, I'd love to meet her. But I can't just pick up and go to Connecticut. The school year's just starting. I have commitments here."

Jane took another sip of the now-cooling milk, feeling the warmth travel all the way down to her tummy. It was working. She was feeling warmer and mellower, but she liked Maggie and Paul and loved talking about regular people and their regular lives. She wasn't ready to say goodnight yet.

"You *really* like her?"

Paul nodded.

"Time to visit Connecticut," said Jane gently.

"You think?"

Jane shrugged. "Don't you have a break coming up? A few days off when you could make a quick trip?"

"Columbus Day's a four-day weekend."

"There you go." She thought of Ben dumping her so cruelly when Sara arrived in Cairo. If she'd have known how fickle he was, she might have expected things to go south, and his rejection wouldn't have hurt her so much. "Probably best not to invest any more of yourself until you meet her, you know? Anyway, that's what *I* think."

"Aye, the lass has some good advice, I think." Maggie winked at Jane.

"May as well put your cards on the table, Paul."

Paul bit his lower lip, nodding. "Guess so."

She downed the rest of her warm milk, and slid off the stool. "What do I owe you?"

Paul took out his wallet and put five dollars on the counter. "Let me get it. In thanks for the advice."

"Cool. Thank you, Paul. And good luck. I'm off to bed, folks."

"Give Lars hell tomorrow, Jane." Paul winked at her.

"Yeah?"

"Sure. Lars thinks he's the cat's meow."

"Does he?"

"Aw, you know. The girls from the park…the ones who pass through."

She didn't know. Her heart clutched painfully at this news, though she worked hard not to show it.

Of course. He was so good-looking. Too good-looking. He probably had his pick of the tourists that came into town.

It shouldn't matter to her. She hated that it did.

"Oh, shut up, Paul. Lars is a *good* man, Jane. An eye for

the ladies, aye, but what single man doesn't? *More* than an eye? Neither Paul nor I can say."

Paul scoffed. "We're good friends, Mags. He's certainly shared—"

"Gossip. A little chin wag. That's all. Our Lars just needs to meet the right woman. The right woman changes everythin'." She tilted her head to the side, smiling at Jane. "D'you play euchre, Jane?"

"Euchre? I don't know how—"

"Aye. It's grand. We'll teach you. As long as you're in town, come play with us. With Lars workin' so hard on your group, we need a fourth."

"Who's the third?"

"Lars's brother." Was it Jane's imagination or did Maggie's cheeks just turn a little pink? "Nils."

"His brother?"

"Aye. 'Twill be fun. Tomorrow night. Seven-thirty, and all the warm milk you like."

Jane smiled. Regular people doing regular things. She was never invited to do regular things with regular people.

"Thanks. I'd love it. I'll be here."

"See you then, Jane."

Jane walked back to the hotel slowly, warm and drowsy from the cool, fresh air and warm milk filling her belly, but she couldn't shake Paul's words: *the cat's meow…the ones who pass through.*

She couldn't shake the disappointment she felt in learning that Lars was a player.

If that's what Lars was all about, Jane had best steer

clear of him or she'd be in for some heartbreak when Sara hit town, because Samara Amaya specialized in flings. And she always got what she wanted. Always. Regardless of the collateral damage. And Jane wasn't interested in another Ben Abaz situation.

It was probably just that she was overtired, but she felt so sad, hot tears gathered in her eyes as she pulled the covers over her body and settled her head on the pillow. He hadn't treated her like Samara Amaya's ugly-duckling cousin, and it felt unusual and special. She'd had such a good time with him and he had seemed so…different.

But, he's not Jane. He's not different.

She flipped to her side, staring at the seam of light under the bathroom door, willing herself not to think about him anymore. But, try as she might, her last thought as her eyes drifted closed was of Lars holding her hand in the car, and she moved that hand to rest on her chest, curled up longingly against her heart.

CHAPTER 3

Lars stood in the doorway of the second bedroom of the cabin, watching Jane sort and organize shoes, jewelry and clothing, baffled that any one person could possibly require so much *stuff* for a four-day stay. It was ridiculously self-indulgent and he wasn't impressed.

Jane said she needed about twenty more minutes and then she'd be done. He checked his watch as he headed into the living room to wait for her, plopping down on the couch.

She seemed a little different this morning, but he couldn't put his finger on how. More professional, more businesslike, yesterday's repartee missing from their exchanges. She was perfectly friendly, but a good bit more reserved; he couldn't account for the change, but the longer it went on, the more he missed the warm, minxy Jane from yesterday.

When he'd picked her up this morning, he noticed right away how much a good night's rest brightened her eyes. Her hair was still drying from a morning shower which made her curls look tighter and springier, but he suspected they'd soften as the day went on. The dark circles under her eyes were gone, and her lips had tilted up in a polite smile as she pulled herself into his truck.

"Morning, Jane!"

"Good morning," she'd replied, buckling in.

"You ordered sun and we delivered!"

"Yes. It's a lovely day."

A lovely day? The Jane from yesterday would have made a snappy comment about how he must have a direct line to God, and could he order up a hot cup of coffee while he was at it.

She didn't smile at him, or offer any further conversation, but busied herself with her phone, checking texts and typing back, two thumbs moving like lightning.

"Did you sleep okay?"

"I did. Thanks."

"Well, I thought we'd start with breakfast—"

"I've already eaten, thanks. Have to get those bags unpacked, so probably best to get started," she said, still glued to her phone.

Lars had glanced over at her in confusion. She hadn't asked about the Beach Boys, but he had them all queued up and ready to go. He thought about pressing play, but the potential embarrassment of her not acknowledging them, or worse— not wanting to listen to them—made him think twice. What was going on with her?

She finally put her phone down and rummaged through her bag. Finding the object of her search, she ran a tube of lip balm back and forth across her lips then pursed them together. He could smell the tropical sweetness of it…mango or pineapple—sweet and incredibly distracting.

"So, I guess I'll drop you at the cottage and then…"

"Fine. And I have the list of groceries for you. Samara

75

likes really high-quality produce, so please take care when selecting, okay? And if the brand I specify isn't available, don't buy a substitute. Please just mark it on the list and I'll deal with it."

"Fine." He clenched his jaw. Nothing she was doing was wrong. She was polite and respectful. She was also in charge; he worked for her while she was visiting Gardiner. But, all of her warmth and teasing fun was gone, and he wanted it back. "Jane…"

She turned to him. "Hmm?"

"Is everything…okay?"

"Sure."

"Are you…*upset* about anything?"

"Upset?" She shook her head, but didn't look at him. "No. Not at all."

"You seem…different today."

"Just a lot to do today and tomorrow. Before she gets here."

Well, he had tried. *Business it is.*

"Fine. I'll drop you off, get the groceries, and then I guess we can go look at the locations?"

"Fine." She crossed her legs toward the window, leaning her elbow on the windowsill. "Mind some fresh air?"

"You're in charge," he observed.

She rolled down the window and turned her head away from him, effectively ending their conversation.

Since he had returned with the groceries, she'd barely said a word, except to ask politely if he would put the perishables in the refrigerator and freezer.

He stood up from the couch and walked to the window. Beyond the dirt and dust that surrounded the cottages, there was a large patch of green meadow that extended out toward the park. A small herd of bison made their way into the meadow as if on cue. Three, four, five, eight, ten, twelve, fourteen, with a calf among them. He watched them lumber into position, until they were all munching on the sweet grass in the mid-morning sun.

If *he* wasn't enough to bring out the sunny, teasing side of Jane, maybe *they* were…he walked back to the bedroom and stuck his head into the room.

"Jane!" he whispered.

She looked up at him and grinned, then seemed to catch herself and hurriedly looked down. When she looked up again, her face was cool and professional, eyebrows raised in question. "Yes?"

"I want to show you something."

"I really have to finish this."

"Bring your camera."

He saw the incremental widening of her mossy eyes, the twinkling she was trying to keep hidden. Curiosity won out as she opened the backpack hanging on the door handle of the room and took out her camera.

He put his index finger up to his lips, indicating that she should be quiet, and she nodded, her eyes bright and engaged.

There's my girl.

He led the way through the living room, pointing to the picture window.

He was rewarded with her gasp of surprise as she gazed at the herd, reaching for her lens cap with shaking fingers. Lars put his hand over hers.

"We'll go outside," he whispered. "You'll get better shots."

She nodded, curling her fingers around his hand. He was careful not to meet her eyes, pulling her along to the front door. He hadn't expected her to take hold of his hand, but he'd be lying if he said it wasn't affecting him, because it was. A lot.

He felt pathetically grateful that she was finally letting her guard down again after such a cool, composed morning. Suddenly he had a slight glimmer of hope that the rest of the day might showcase the funny, surprising Jane from yesterday instead of the cool, reserved one from this morning.

Lars opened the front door quietly, stepping down the two steps. He had no reason to keep holding Jane's hand, but he didn't want to let go. She stepped down beside him and they stood side by side.

"They're *marvelous*," she breathed.

He glanced down at her and felt his heart speed up as he stared at her face. Her mouth was slightly open, soft and surprised, and her eyes were wide and fascinated. He could still smell that mango or passion fruit, or whatever it was, from her lips, and wished he could lean down and kiss them. Instead, he adjusted his hand again, lacing his fingers through hers, hoping she wouldn't notice and pull away.

She turned to him and smiled. "Aren't they *wonderful?*"

He nodded at her, smiling back. But, he wasn't smiling at the herd—honestly, a herd of bison wasn't very compelling for him anymore—he was smiling at her.

From experience he knew that tourists were generally blown away by their first glimpse of a herd. He'd seen the *look* many, many times. But not on *Jane's* face, and it just about took his breath away to see her so unreserved, no trace of the smart-ass from yesterday or the businesswoman from this morning. Just a guileless young woman, enthralled by the sight of something pure and new in Lars's world. Watching her made Lars's heart swell and thump, drawing him to her in some otherworldly way he never saw coming. He squeezed her hand instinctively and she glanced up at him, pink lips still tilted up in delight, before she turned her gaze back to the grazing herd.

Finally she loosened her hand from his, and took the lens cap off, clicking the camera on. Moving stealthily, she approached them, then turned back to him, whispering, "How close can I get?"

He stepped up beside her. "We can move in a little. Just be really calm. No sudden movements. They're used to people, and they're pretty gentle, but you don't want to startle them. The bulls can gore you if they get riled, though they're more likely to run than charge. These are females, but with a baby out there, don't get too close. Stay low, okay?"

They moved calmly, quietly, until they were about sixty yards away, and Lars put his hand on her arm, motioning her to stop.

She raised her camera and started to shoot as he

squatted down next to her, whispering in harmony to the low whirring of her camera. "There used to be millions and millions of buffalo out here. But they were hunted, almost to the point of extinction. By the late 1880s, there was only a handful left. A couple hundred."

"Go humans." She stopped clicking and turned to him. "Way to almost wipe out a species. Then what?"

"Well, they took a small herd of forty-one captive and wild buffalo and moved them here to Yellowstone. Today there are over four thousand wild buffalo here."

"Well, at least they tried to fix things."

"I love to see the little ones," Lars whispered, smiling as he watched the calf trail along, bleating after its mother.

When he glanced at Jane, she was smiling at him, but it was a small, tenuous, uncertain smile. Her face was soft, as it had been in the truck yesterday while they were talking about her father, and her green eyes were serious, searching. Without thinking, Lars leaned forward, moving his lips closer and closer to hers.

She looked down suddenly, breaking their eye contact, breaking the moment. "Thanks for showing me this. I got some good shots. Time to finish unpacking."

He considered reaching for her as they stood up, to connect with her, to assuage the growing tension between them by kissing her senseless. But she stood up, still not looking at him, so instead he watched her walk purposefully back to the cottage without turning around even once.

***

Two hours later, Jane glanced over at Lars, who was driving

them to the first of three shoot locations so she could photograph them and send pictures to Sara. She checked her phone, even though Lars had warned her there wouldn't be reliable cellular service for as long as they were in the park.

No signal. No bars. More's the better.

She rolled down her window, which added white noise to the otherwise quiet of the car. Lars had seemingly given up all attempts to charm her out of her grumpy funk and drove in silence, which Jane hated as much as she suspected he hated grumpy Jane.

Not liking Lars was proving to be just about impossible, and the effort it was taking to be aloof and professional was draining, especially when he seemed so thoughtful; bringing that CD for the ride to dinner last night and showing her the bison this morning. But, whenever she felt her resolve slipping, she would think about Paul's words from last night—*the girls from the park*—and the coolness would return quickly. She felt sure that if she had let him kiss her earlier, that's all she'd be: a temporary distraction left in the dust once the "main attraction" arrived. *Just another girl from the park.* Jane didn't want that.

Well, she didn't *think* she wanted that.

Or *did* she?

Their chemistry was not just in her head anymore, not that she had ever *really* believed it was totally in her head. She felt Lars watching her yesterday, taking her hand, touching her curls. She could see how pleased he was to see her this morning.

She thought of him asking her if anything was wrong,

and how he had laced his fingers through hers as he led her out to the meadow earlier; she knew there was something between them, something crackling and interested, simmering just beneath the surface.

Jane peeked over at him.

Smokin' hot. Like, doing a double-take on the street, tongue rolling out of your mouth, rugged, western-model-perched-on-a-horse-with-a-cowboy-hat-and-a-lazy-smile hot. And Jane was pretty sure that if she wanted a fling with Lars, it was hers for the taking…at least until Sara arrived.

That was the rub. No way Sara *wasn't* going to hit that. Jane would be surprised if Lars *wasn't* her first order of business. And Jane knew her place. Every day, every moment of her life so far had impressed upon her that she couldn't possibly compete with Sara.

From a young age, Jane had believed what she had been told in a myriad of unspoken ways; Sara was vapid, but pretty and Jane was smart, but plain. Unfortunately for Jane, her smarts had never been a match for her cousin's beauty in the eyes of her guardians.

By high school, Jane's whole existence had been overshadowed by the breathtaking, luminous Sara. Graduating from high school, Sara was almost six feet tall, willowy and confident with a perfectly formed body, long, silky onyx hair and lavender eyes fringed with long, black lashes.

It was as though she had skipped puberty entirely, neatly developing within the time span of a mild New England summer before her freshman year with nary a blemish on her porcelain skin, and no need for the awkward machinery of braces. Her breasts followed a perfect trajectory from an A cup freshman year to a full B cup by the end of high school, ever accentuated by her increasingly tiny waist and adorable backside.

The beginning of the high school senior superlatives list was a veritable homage to Sara: Prettiest, Best Eyes, Best Smile, Best Hair, Best Figure, Most Likely to be in a Movie, and—especially baffling to teenage Jane, who shared a room with spiteful Sara—Best Personality. Indeed, Sara's true nature asserted itself privately. Her early insecurities at Jane's unexpected intrusion in her life imposed an unfortunate edge to Sara's demeanor that foreshadowed the demanding, difficult woman she'd become. Had, in fact, foreshadowed the international supermodel, Samara Amaya.

Jane, who barely bothered looking in the mirror by high school, wasn't exactly *jealous* of Sara, although she had many wistful moments wishing she was prettier. Alas, she was assured by her uncle's sympathetic glances that her own looks would always fall short beside Sara. It was the way of things. It was Jane's world.

And she knew without a shred of doubt that her cousin would choose Lars to be her "local flavor" of the week, just as she had with Ben Abaz on the Egypt shoot. So, here was the million-dollar question: Could Jane just enjoy today and tomorrow with Lars, and be okay if he turned his back on her once Samara Amaya arrived? Could she risk the hurt to her heart? Could she bear watching Sara take what had been hers for a few short, sweet days?

Wait now, Jane, she counseled herself. There was a big difference between Ben and Lars. She hadn't seen it coming with Ben. It had shocked her to see him switch gears to be with Sara; it had hurt her to watch him lose interest so quickly.

She'd felt ashamed of herself—foolish—for sleeping with him so impetuously, without a commitment, without the safety of true regard. She had, more or less, recklessly *given* herself to Ben physically and emotionally. She certainly would never be that stupid again.

But, benefitting from experience, the situation with Lars *could* be different, couldn't it? She could engineer it differently in her head. Jane could take a more modern, less emotional, approach with Lars. She didn't have to *fall* for him, did she? She certainly didn't have to sleep with him. She could just enjoy his company and a light flirtation before Sara arrived, with the full knowledge that he would turn his back and walk away the moment her cousin blew into town. As long as she knew that would happen, it wouldn't hurt, right? If she could anticipate it, she could brace for it. Be ready.

You might be modern, Jane, but you're not that modern. If you let him get close, you'll take a fall when he chooses Samara. That's all there is to it. Better just stick to business and not risk that long, hard fall. Business.

She looked over at him again, at the way his tan, muscular hands gripped the steering wheel. Her fingers tingled with the memory of holding that hand, the rough, calloused skin under her soft fingers as he pulled her closer to the bison. Her face softened.

It's not his fault that you like and can't have him. You could be a little warmer, Jane. Player or not, he's been nothing but nice to you.

"Been a stressful morning," she sighed, taking her phone from her lap and putting it back in her backpack. "Sort of nice not to have a cell signal."

"I told you."

"You did. I'll have to believe you when you school me on these things, Professor."

He grinned at her: easy, amenable, uncomplicated. It was part of why she liked him so much. "When it comes to Yeller, I am pretty knowledgeable, missy."

"Hmmm. That sounds almost like a dare."

"Ask me anything."

"Okay…how many acres in the park?"

"Two million, two hundred and twenty thousand."

"How many…um…waterfalls?"

"Five percent of the park is covered in water but that includes an unknown number of waterfalls. Probably hundreds."

He knows his stuff. She rewarded him with a surprised smile. "How many different animals live in the park?"

"Sixty-seven species of mammals…did you want bird and fish life too?"

"You're a *cocky* so-and-so! Um, visitors!"

"That's not a question, Jane. Are you asking how many people visit annually?"

Jane rolled her eyes at him and he chuckled.

"Three million, give or take."

"Give or take what, Professor?"

"One cute, wise-ass chick from New York."

"When's *she* getting here? She sounds like a blast."

"She *can* be." He said this slowly, without taking his eyes off the road.

Interesting. Okay. Maybe I deserve that after this morning's cold front.

"Those wise-ass New York chicks are often under untold pressure, you know."

"You forgot cute. I said *cute*, wise—"

"I didn't forget anything."

"You *know* you're cute, right, Jane?"

"You don't have to say that."

"I wouldn't if it wasn't true."

"All part of the service, *Just-Lars*?"

"Nope, that's my personal opinion."

Jane had had just about enough.

"You don't have to do that," she said, an edge creeping into her once-playful tone.

He pulled over to the side of the road, put the car in park and cut the engine, looking at her. "I don't have to do what?"

"You don't need to butter me up. You don't need to flatter me. I'm the assistant. Let me school *you* here, Professor… I'm the girl that's the *friend*, Lars. I'm the girl you *talk to* about the girl you're going out with on Friday night. I'm the girl who tells you which restaurant to take her to and what kind of wine she hopes you'll order. I'll even come over beforehand and help you pick out what shirt to wear, and if you forget your wallet while you're out with her, I'll jimmy your bedroom window open, find it in the pants you wore yesterday and drive it over to the restaurant. And when I hand it to you, she'll look at me like I'm nothing…and you'll—"

"Jane."

"What?"

"Stop talking."

He unsnapped his seatbelt, unsnapped hers, slipped one arm around her waist and pulled her across the seat next to him. Placing his hands on either side of her face—and before she could completely get her head around what was about to happen—he brushed his lips softly against hers.

Her eyes closed, tearing up from the unexpected sweetness of his reassurance, and as her lips opened in surprise, she kissed him back. His fingers played with her curls, tilting her face exactly how he wanted it, moving his lips with more urgency over hers as she arched her back to get closer.

She lowered her hands to rest her knuckles on his thighs, and he skimmed his fingers down her arms to her hips where his thumbs curled into the waistband of her jeans as the kiss deepened, as he slipped his tongue into her mouth. Satiny and stroking against hers, she felt dizzy from the contact, her breathing fast and fierce as her palms flattened, pushing down on the iron-hard muscles of his thighs.

Her heart pounded, her head was spinning, her insides a swirling mess of longing and warning, feuding in the overwhelmed territory between her head and her heart. She felt his fingers graze the skin of her waist under her shirt, which made goose bumps rise all over her body, somehow prompting her back to reality.

"Wait!"

She drew back, panting. Not daring to look into his eyes, she stared at her hands splayed on his thighs instead, listening to the sound of her breathing, which was amplified in her ears, heavy and ragged.

Lifting her fingers, she reached up to touch the tender, hot skin of her lips with a tentative caress, finally looking up at Lars. He was watching her, searching her face with an unapologetic, unwavering gaze.

"I wasn't...expecting that," she murmured.

He released her hips and smiled, reaching up to push an errant curl back from her forehead before leaning back against his seat. "You've got it all wrong, Jane Mays."

No. You've got it all wrong, Lars Lindstrom. You haven't met Sara yet. You don't know what I know. She stared at him, unsmiling, conflicted between her growing feelings for him and the pain of loss she'd feel later.

"Do I?"

"You're *not* just the friend," he said.

Yes, I am, her brain insisted, though her breath still shuddered from their kiss.

"We've got chemistry, Minx. Any way you slice it."

"But what does it mean?"

He leaned over her to pull her seatbelt back over her chest and she felt his breath hot against her cheek. She closed her eyes, longing pooling again in her belly and making her heart race.

"It means...you're different," he growled lightly in her ear. "Come to the Labor Day fireworks in the park with me tomorrow night."

"M-more sightseeing?" she murmured.

"Nuh-uh." He rubbed his stubbled cheek lightly against her flushed one and she felt his breath hot on her earlobe. "A date."

She swallowed, distracted by a thick haze of desire, her insides melting to liquid. Her pulse pounded in her ears. "A date?"

"Mm-hm."

Her seat belt clicked into place, her eyes popped open to find him smiling at her from his seat, amused, delighted.

"You want to go out on a date?" She straightened up, running both hands through her hair. "I don't know. I..."

"Such enthusiasm, Jane! You'll make me think you don't like me one bit."

"Maybe I don't."

"Aw, Minx. All evidence to the contrary."

"*So* conceited."

"So adorable."

Adorable! She grinned at him in spite of herself.

"So...how about it?" he asked.

She shook her head, even though her resistance was fading, and her decision to be "only friends" was disappearing with the rest of her self-control.

Because he felt inevitable, at least for now, she

surrendered.

"Yes. I will go see fireworks with you tomorrow night."

And we will have one sweet evening together before Samara turns your head on Tuesday. She thought of Ray's text, trying to hush her misgivings. *I deserve it. I do.*

"Fireworks. Excellent." He winked at her and buckled his own seat belt. When he turned the key, the truck didn't start. He tried again, but it grated and crunched.

Lars looked at her, trying again, and smiling with relief when the engine finally turned over. "She's temperamental sometimes. Like a cute wise-ass I know from New York."

And that time, because he said it so sweetly, she didn't argue.

***

Darn it, she thought, walking over to the Prairie Dawn that evening. She had meant to ask Lars how the heck you play euchre. But with the entire day fraught with sexual tension or packed with actual work, she never got around to it.

After he had kissed her and coaxed her out on a date tomorrow night, they had turned on The Beach Boys *Endless Summer* and spent the remainder of the day singing along, bonding over favorites and feuding over the worst.

The locations Lars had scouted for the photo shoot were inspired. They were all within about an hour of Gardiner on the Grand Loop to keep travel time to a minimum, but they were evocative, dramatic and beautiful, and would create a masterful editorial, possibly Samara's best yet.

The plan was to set out for one location each day—a

full crew from *Trend*, in addition to the photographer, Samara's team, Jane and Lars—on Wednesday, Thursday and Friday of this week. They prayed that the weather would hold each day, or the shoot would carry over into the second week. The *Trend* people had already been out two weeks before, scouting with Lars until they were satisfied with the locations, so Jane was really only taking pictures for Samara, per her request, so that she could anticipate her surroundings each day.

Jane used her Nikon to take shots of each of the three locations from different angles. The stark architectural beauty of Sheepeater Cliff, made of basalt columns. Old Faithful geyser, which proved *un*faithful in the short time Jane visited, but for which she knew they would wait a full day to get the right shot with Samara. Lastly, Lars had chosen a spot at Yellowstone Lake that he told Jane was his favorite.

As she took photos from a boardwalk that separated Black Pool from Yellowstone Lake, Lars leaned against the railing, looking out over the lake. Jane had lowered her camera to watch him for a moment, to take in his worn, faded jeans slung low on his hips, long legs and cowboy boots peeking out from underneath. He had on a white golf shirt, stark against his tan skin, which made his ice-blue eyes seem even more piercing. She raised her camera and took a picture of him in partial profile, his blond hair like burnished silver in the light of the afternoon sun. He heard the camera shutter and turned to her with an expectant look, a lazy smile tugging at her heart.

"What are we taking pictures of, Minx?"

"Can't help it if you're in my shot."

He had tilted his head to the side then, and she took one more: Lars smiling at Jane.

Later, in her hotel room, Jane was careful to rename and copy those two photos, and put them in their own separate folder, called simply *Lars*. One day, weeks from now, when she was home in chilly New York, she could open that file and remember the warm sunshine of today, the way his lips had felt when he kissed her, the fleeting sweetness of knowing he wanted her, even though by then he would surely be long lost to her. She could still have her memories, and the photos to prove that once upon a time Lars Lindstrom really happened to Jane Mays and for once in her life, Jane knew what it was like to be the pretty one.

She opened the door to the Prairie Dawn and, glancing at the teenage girl working at the coffee bar, searched the room for her new friends. Upon finding them she did a double take, because she was sure she was looking at Maggie, Paul and *Lars*, but a deeper look confirmed that while the family resemblance was striking, she was actually looking at Maggie, Paul and *Nils*, Lars's older brother.

Maggie saw Jane and stood up, waving her over.

"Jane! You made it! Grand!"

She made her way around the eclectic furniture of the coffee shop to join them.

"Heya, Paul." She grinned. "How're things with Miss Mystic?"

He smiled easily, winking at Jane. "I'll tell you all about

it, Janie."

She turned her eyes to Nils. "I'm Jane. I'd know you for a Lindstrom anywhere."

"The New Yorker. Good to know you." They shook hands and Maggie went to get Jane a cup of coffee. Jane took the empty seat between Paul and Maggie, facing Nils, who shuffled a deck of cards distractedly.

"Lars doing a good job?" he asked her.

"Very good," she answered. "Saw all of the scouted locations today."

"You like 'em?"

Wow, what a forward question. "Umm. Well, we've only just met, but you know, he seems really—"

"The *locations*. Not my brother."

"Oh!" She felt her face flush with heat as Maggie returned with her coffee.

"You teasin' her, Nils?"

"Just asked what she thought of the locations."

"They're—um, they're great. Great choices." Why was she so flustered? She could feel the blood rush to her cheeks. *Damn, Jane, get yourself together!*

Nils nodded, but she saw the merry twinkle in his eyes and suspected Lars would be hearing about this later. Her face coloring bright red was as good as showing her cards. Paul had noticed too.

"Hey, Jane…that stuff I said yesterday? About Lars and the park girls? He and Erik used to carouse a lot when they were younger, but he's really not like that anymore. He's my best friend." He glanced at Nils sheepishly. "Like a brother, really. Some as good, but none better, Jane. Really."

"Well, he's very good at what he does, which is what matters the most to me. He seems to know the park inside out."

"He's always been like that. In there all the time: winter, summer, rain, snow, didn't matter, still doesn't. Lars and Yeller are like two halves of the same thing. Sometimes you don't know where the park ends, and Lars begins."

Jane heard the wistful, affectionate undertones in Nils's voice. "He seems very knowledgeable."

Nils nodded. "He is, but it's more than that. Loves that dang park better than anywhere or anything in the world. I guess some folks would say that limits him. There's so much of Yeller, though, you could live a lifetime and never see it all." He made a bridge with the cards then slid them to Maggie who cut them. "But, our *Midten*'ll die trying."

"*Midten?*"

"Means *middle*," said Maggie, smiling askance at Nils who looked up at her and nodded in approval before looking back down at his cards.

Jane watched Maggie's eyes as they lingered on Nils and she was moved by what she saw there: a frank, deep affection that went well beyond friends who played cards together. There was a humming current that existed between Nils and Maggie. Were they a couple? They must be, though Jane saw no outward signs that they were anything more than friends. Maybe they were just very conservative in their PDA, because there was definitely something between them.

"Our *mamma* was Norwegian," said Nils softly.

"Called her three boys *Største*, *Midten* and *Minste*. Biggest, middle, and littlest," said Maggie.

"Not that Erik much appreciated being called *Minste*," said Nils, grinning up at Maggie again like she was the only girl in the whole room, the whole universe.

"Seems to be just fine with it now," Paul observed.

Maggie turned from Nils and smiled at Jane. "His bonnie wife Kat calls him *Minste*, and no complaints. And now, enough talk. More euchre."

"And Miss Mystic," teased Jane.

Paul grinned at Jane as Nils finished dealing, but it was a half-smile, wary.

"Are you going for a visit?" she asked, referring to their conversation last night.

"I bought a ticket," Paul confessed.

"Does she know yet?"

"She knows." A shadow passed over his face and he lowered his gaze. "I'm just not sure she loves the idea."

"Oh…well, I'm sure she will. Give her time to get used to the idea. Sometimes we have to protect our hearts, you know. Move forward with caution." Jane smiled at him, wondering if her words were intended for Paul or herself, hoping no one at the table had caught the transparency of her own feelings as she doled out advice to someone else.

"You know?" said Paul, brightening. "I think you're a good luck charm, Jane…or maybe you're just very, very wise."

Jane tried to pay attention as they explained to her how to play, but her mind was circling around Paul's words.

Very wise? *Not so much.*

A wise woman wouldn't have let Lars kiss her today.

A wise woman wouldn't be going out on a date with him tomorrow night.

Because, let's face it, a wise woman wouldn't set herself up for such a big fall.

CHAPTER 4

With Samara's cottage ready for her and the shoot locations confirmed, Jane didn't feel any pressure to jump out of bed the next morning. As the sun poured in through the curtained window of her hotel room, she lay in bed, checking her phone, which had been quiet throughout the night, except for some "boob" pictures Samara had texted to her.

One of Samara's favorite things was to occasionally send Jane pictures of her cleavage—and sometimes bare breasts—taken when she was drunk in an attempt to shock her cousin. Jane rolled her eyes, hitting erase, erase, erase. *Must have been quite a party last night.*

Jane sent herself a reminder to call Sebastian in a few hours and make sure Samara didn't send the photos to anyone else…and was in shape for traveling tomorrow.

Then she pulled the comforter over her head and went back to sleep.

The insistent buzzing of her phone rattling on the bedside table woke her up two hours later. She fumbled for the phone, pressing the green answer button and put the phone to her ear.

"Hello?"

"JANE!"

"Sara?"

"Who is that *delicious* piece of ass in the pics you sent me yesterday?"

Jane's eyes popped open, and her heart started racing. *No. No! I copied those photos and put them in a separate file!* She sat up, swinging her legs over the bed.

"I don't…" She raced to the table, opened her laptop and clicked on her email program. She scrolled through the pictures, and her heart dropped when she saw the two re-titled pictures of Lars included at the end of the location shots. Her shoulders caved in, and she sat down in the closest chair. Even though she put copies in the separate folder, she'd forgotten to delete the originals from the master file she'd sent to her cousin.

"Who is he, Janie?" Sara was using the singsong coquette voice that she used to get what she wanted.

"Local tour operator."

"He's hot."

"Hmm."

"Scalding."

"Well…"

"Well…nothing. Might be a spot for him in my shoot…if he's nice to me."

Jane shut her eyes tightly, holding her breath.

"Definitely a spot for him in my bed, if you know what I mean. Samara wants."

Jane lowered the phone, holding it in her lap, clenching her jaw until it actually ached. She could hear Sara still making her insane demands, even with the phone two feet from her ear. "…Jane? Jane! Did you hear me? I want him. Make it happen!"

You make it happen. I'm not your pimp.

Jane ignored her cousin, putting the phone back up to her ear and changing the subject. "Sara, you sent me boob pics last night."

"Yeah, so? I can do what I want."

"Just making sure…you didn't send them to anyone else, did you?"

"I'm not *stupid*, Jane. I know I'm a public figure. When I want to send boob pics, I only send them to you, so they're going to nobody."

Nobody. She bit her lip remembering Lars's words on the drive to Gardiner from the airport when they first met. *Means you're somebody, I guess.* Her heart twisted, thinking of him.

"Sebastian's picking you up in the morning, Sara. You're—"

"*SAMARA*, Jane."

"Of course, *Samara*. You're going to be ready at eight, right? Do you want me to call you to wake you—?"

"I hate traveling with Sebastian," she pouted. "He's so annoying."

"Well, Ray will be with you too."

"Whatever. Ray hates me. He's *your* friend."

Ray Cartier was *only* Sara's makeup artist because he was the best, which was the *only* reason Sara put up with his subtle digs. Jane adored Ray.

"I want my Laney," she whined. "The rest of you are

no fun. This sucks."

"Your whole team wants the best for you. I'm sure Laney will be better by the time you get home."

"Don't try to change the subject, Jane. I want the cowboy."

"Do what you want, Samara." *You always do.*

"Jaaaanie…I *know* you didn't mean to send me those pictures. They were re-titled. 'Lars' and 'Lars Smiles'. I *know* you, Jane. I know your type and he's it. I'm sure you've been making an ass out of yourself following him around." She paused, chuckling lightly. "But we both know…Sun's coming out tomorrow, Plain Jane. You know what they say about the sun."

Ben's words returned to Jane, and she winced. *I'm blinded to anything but the sun…*

"Travel safe, Samara. See you tomorrow." She managed to whisper the words before pressing the red end button on her phone. She threw it across the room and watched it bounce twice on the bed before clunking onto the carpeted floor. Then, she curled up in the chair where she was sitting next to her laptop, feeling the heaviness, the oppressive dread, return.

Tomorrow he will belong to her.

Her stomach was empty, but the thought of Lars with Sara made her stomach muscles contract and she retched bile into her mouth.

I'll quit, she thought frantically, wincing as she swallowed back the acid. *I'll call her back and quit and tell her to shove this crap job up her million-dollar ass. I'll catch the next flight out of here. I'll go back to San Francisco and take pictures. I'll – I'll –*

And where will you go for Christmas, Jane? For Thanksgiving? Who will walk you down the aisle one day? The old, familiar voice whispered the old, familiar questions, stopping her thoughts cold. *You don't know a soul in San Francisco. You haven't kept up with your college friends in Boston. Who will you have in your life? Ray? Sebastian? They're all in Sara's pocket. They'll turn their backs on you the moment you walk. Face it. You have no one. You'll be alone, Jane. Utterly and completely alone.*

You're. Not. Going. Anywhere.

Her eyes filled with tears at the unfairness of it, and she brushed them away. She had seen Lars first. He had liked her first. He had kissed her first.

She took a shaky breath, running her fingers through her springy curls, picturing his face in her mind, his hand laced through hers, his lips slanting across hers. After tonight, she would lose him.

After tonight. *After.*

"Not yet, Sara," she whispered raggedly. "You can't have him until tomorrow."

***

Lars had recently heard chatter about a mama grizzly and her two cubs getting a little close to the road near the north part of Lower Hayden where the Lindstroms often took their groups on day hikes, and he wanted to be sure he steered clear of her territory with hikers. But he also considered that knowing her routes would give him an opportunity to find viewing points for watching her. People would pay insane amounts of money to see a grizzly in her natural habitat, so he headed out on Monday morning to take a look around.

Unlike most days, when he was keenly aware of the park around him, he was distracted today. He couldn't remember the last time he felt so much anticipation looking forward to a date. Actually, he couldn't remember the last time he *went* on a conventional date.

When Erik still lived in Gardiner, they would go out on impromptu double dates with women just in town visiting the park—generally set up by Erik—and every other night felt like a party with the "Park Girls." That's what Lars and his brothers called the women who came to Yellowstone on vacation looking for a little something extra to spice up their adventure vacation. Women on tours, groups of friends coming to hike and sightsee, even women like Jane who came for work. They'd have the Park Girls back to their apartment or hang out at their hotel. The summer months were a seemingly endless parade of available women. He and Erik had pursued these short-lived flings like playboys, and enjoyed every minute drinking beers and bed-hopping with pretty girls.

But Erik had headed up to Great Falls for college about three years ago and married Katrin last fall. Nils was in love with Maggie but wouldn't do anything about it, he was so busy working and sucking up to their father. Paul had been crazy about Lars's sister Jenny for years so he never did much carousing anyway, but lately he was on his laptop all the time talking to some chick in Connecticut; besides, he was the principal at the high school—bars and girls weren't his thing. Surrounded by friends and family who had all at once decided to grow up, Lars was starting to feel his age too, and when he thought of his three small nieces, he had to admit the idea of settling down and having a family of his own had appeal.

The problem with settling down, though, was two-fold.

First, he couldn't think of any girls who lived in Gardiner who were potential marriage material. The permanent population of the entire town was only 720 people, and Lars knew every one of them.

The single, eligible, legal-aged women could practically be counted on one hand, with Maggie leading the pack. But Maggie and Nils were just a matter of time, and Lars didn't see Maggie like that anyway. There was Ms. Phillips, the church secretary at Grace Church, but she had to be in her mid-forties, and she was always talking about her shingles, which, frankly, grossed Lars out. There used to be Missy at the Blue Moon, but even she had found someone and moved away to Billings. And sure, there were a few other girls in Gardiner who he knew and a few divorcees, who were always on the lookout for their next "Mr.," but none of them exactly got his heart beating faster; none of them was the next Mrs. Lindstrom.

That left the Park Girls. But the Park Girls were transient, weekenders even, and he didn't imagine Gardiner out of season was enough to induce many of them to stay. To stay in Gardiner, you'd have to be looking for a small town—a small town on the outskirts of a very large park— and who was looking for that? A botanist? A naturalist? Maybe an artsy type like an author or a painter, but Lars imagined they'd be transient too, because the artistic types always went back to the big cities for the galleries and museums.

The bottom line? Women were scarce.

Second, Lars wanted to see some changes in his work life before he settled down. It was time for a change, a promotion of some kind. It was time for Lars to be treated like the man he was: like thirty-three percent of Lindstrom & Sons, not less.

Heck, he knew Yellowstone better than most seasoned vets of the tourism trade, definitely better than Nils, and possibly better than his pop. He had studied his facts, explored on his own and spent thousands of hours learning about the park firsthand. He didn't want to be relegated to the odd jobs and annoying errands, although he had to admit that once in a while they had their perks.

Jane.

She was something.

Aw, she wasn't the prettiest girl Lars had ever seen, but she was cute. She was the cute girl who might live next door, whose bedroom window you'd want to slip into if she'd let you. She surprised the heck out of him, saying unexpected things, making him laugh and shake his head with her unpredictable comments. He loved watching her taking pictures and by the looks of that camera, he suspected photography was more than just a hobby for her, which intrigued him. And yesterday, when she finally thawed out, it was like the sun had come out after a day of gray gloom, and Lars realized again how much he liked spending time with her.

There was something else he was starting to understand about Jane: her relationship with her cousin was complicated. She'd tried to give him that speech yesterday about how she was only friend material, implying that Samara was the girlfriend material. Lars wasn't buying that. Sure, Samara was pretty. He'd seen the same pictures everyone else had. But, how pretty could she be in real life? Weren't all of those pictures airbrushed and edited before they hit the magazines, anyway?

He understood the issue at the crux of Jane's situation: she was a normal-looking person who was first cousins with a supermodel, and that had to be difficult for her. But it didn't matter to Lars. He liked Jane and that's all there was to it.

And to Lars's thinking, it wasn't all that different from any other complicated family relationship, like being a thirty-year-old man who was still treated like some untried teenage kid by his older brother and father.

Huh. Jane and I have more in common than she knows. We're both working for family members who think they're more important than we are.

Lars checked his watch. In the past hour he'd finally made some headway on the mystery of the mama bear and her cubs, and he was pretty sure he'd figured out the reason for her gradual migration. Lars would warn Nils and Pop not to hike out too far anymore in this particular area.

He hitched his pack farther up on his back and headed to his truck. He'd need a shower and shave before tonight, and he was planning to pack a blanket and some wine too. He smiled, thinking of Jane's reaction to the small herd of bison from yesterday morning. Man, he'd love to see her face when a mama grizzly and her cubs lumbered across the valley.

He threw his pack in the truck and almost started to worry when it took three times until the engine finally turned over. He made a mental note to get the truck looked at soon and hoped he'd have a chance to show Jane the grizzlies.

***

Jane didn't bring any "fancy" clothes on location shoots because she preferred to be comfortable while she was working. Even though she had access to Sara's enormous wardrobe, Jane was a five-foot-six size ten, and Sara was an almost-six-foot size zero. Her cousin's fabulous clothes would be of little use to Jane.

Jane looked through her options: two pairs of jeans (one that needed washing), a pair of beat-up khaki cargos for shoot days, and a tired denim skirt from college. She picked up the skirt and slipped it on. It was old-school L.L. Bean— nothing mini or micro or sequined or trendy about it—two front pockets, two back pockets, front middle zipper, and it fell to right above her knees. The edges were frayed from copious wear, and it was as soft as flannel too.

Next, she surveyed her tops: two black camis, one white cami that needed washing, a cream V-neck t-shirt, her green cardigan and a Boston College sweatshirt. *Sexy choices, Jane. Wow.*

She took a deep breath and sighed, picking up one of

the black camis and slipping it over her head. Well, it wasn't glamorous, but the lines were okay. The black was slimming, and with her black sandals, it was the best she could do.

Next, she rummaged through her bag for makeup, but predictably she had none. Just some mango lip balm and some tinted moisturizer that she must have gotten as a sample. It was better than nothing. Jane swiped some on. She put her diamond studs in her ears, which had been her gift to herself when she'd lasted for one year as Sara's assistant.

She squirted some mousse into her hands and smoothed her curls back from her face, deciding to leave her dad's Red Sox cap in her room. *Felicity? Fat chance.* Maybe the hair, but that's where the similarities ended.

She shrugged into her green cardigan, slipped her feet into the black leather sandals then looked in the mirror.

If Lars had asked her out on a date in New York, she'd have put on a black dress, had her hair styled professionally, pulled out some of the makeup samples collecting dust in her bathroom and brightened her face. She'd have had tons of sample shoes to choose from and cute sweaters in her size sent to her from exclusive designers. She'd have had a fighting chance to make an impression before Sara got to him.

No, Jane. You wouldn't have a chance, fighting or otherwise. That's wishful thinking.

Her reflection wasn't a revelation, but she definitely didn't look as dumpy as she usually did. In fact, she looked sort of fresh and young. Thinking in terms of editorials—

which she never did for herself, but often did for her cousin—she had a certain girl-next-door appeal. *Modest* appeal, but appeal, nonetheless. She smiled at herself, timidly, unsure, and saw how the color of her sweater caught the green in her eyes. She'd never noticed that before. Her skin had tanned a little yesterday in the park, which gave her a little glow. She tilted her head to the side, feeling just the slightest bit of unfamiliar pleasure in the girl looking back at her.

Is this how it would be if I could get away from Sara? Would I stop judging myself so harshly if I weren't always standing next to her?

She sighed. Better not to tease herself with what could never be. It would be a cold, lonely world without Samara, thin comfort though she was. At least with Sara she had something, and something was better than nothing, wasn't it?

A light rap at her door meant Lars was here.

Most of the time, she amended, *something was better than nothing.*

***

I want to kiss her.

It was the first thought in Lars's mind when she opened the door, looking cute as hell in a short skirt and that green sweater that made her eyes greener than green. Her hair was pushed back off her face, but her curls were unruly behind her sunglasses, which perched like a hairband on top of her head. She looked cool but casual. Lars was smitten and his body tightened on its own.

"Heya," he said.

"Heya," she said, offering him a shy smile.

"You look really pretty."

Her eyes were wide and green, and a little pink crept into her cheeks.

"Thanks," she murmured, meeting his eyes. It was hard for her to accept his compliment, he could tell.

"When're you going to get used to it?" he asked.

"To what?" She stepped out of her room to join him, pulling the door closed behind her.

"To me saying you're pretty…or cute…or whatever you look like to me."

"I'm not going to be here long enough to get used to it."

"How about you try to get used to it tonight?"

"What's the point?" She gestured to his backpack which had a plaid blanket rolled up on the side. "Is that a picnic backpack? I've only seen those in catalogs."

"It is." He reached for her hand, and laced his fingers through hers. "I thought we'd walk."

"All the way to the park?"

"It's not far. And the company's good."

"Not far?" she grumbled. "Down the street, over the bridge, then some…"

"I've been walking all day," he said, as they walked out of the hotel parking lot, onto the Main Street sidewalk. "And I learned some interesting things."

"Like what?"

"I found a new route that a mama grizzly and her cubs are taking."

"New route?"

"Bears stake out their own territories. I've been noticing this one female, who used to hang out in a meadow between Dunraven Pass and Mount Washburn, but she's been gradually moving south to Hayden Valley, closer to the road. Well, I couldn't figure out why until today."

"Why?"

"There's a wolf pack settling in not far from the road. And the wolves, well, they are *great* hunters. So they take down an elk or a moose working as a team, and then the bears come along and finish off the kill. Big rivalry between the bears and wolves in the park. Typically, bears overpower better hunters, like wolves, and take their kill, because they've got size and strength over a wolf. Even a pack won't mess with a full-grown grizzly. Only time she'd retreat is if they threatened her cub, but she might even get them to back off in spite of the cub if he was a yearling. Anyhow, it's just easier for her if she hangs out near a wolf pack. She'll eventually benefit from their kill."

"I love it when you talk about the park."

"Yeah?" He licked his lips. Her words were practically *foreplay* as far as Lars's body was concerned.

"Yeah. You know so much. And it's a little dangerous. It's—I don't know—sort of a…" She shrugged, smiling up at him.

"Turn-on?" he asked.

She took a deep breath and sort of half exhaled, half chuckled as she nodded. "I guess."

He squeezed her hand as a tingly shiver went down his

back. Damn, he liked this woman.

"So, by tracking the bear, you actually found a wolf pack?"

"Um, yeah, I guess. I wanted to figure out why she was moving south, closer to the road, and it's because of a pack. Makes sense. Now I'll know where to spot her."

"Will you take me?"

I'll take you anywhere you want to go, Jane.

He looked down at her, smiling. "Sure. If you're here long enough," he said, teasing her with her own words.

"I'll be here long enough for that. I'd love to get some pictures of her."

"That was some camera you were using yesterday, Minx. Nikon 3DX is just about the best one out there for wildlife captures."

"Is that right?"

"Yeah." He smiled. "More than a hobby, I'm guessing."

She shrugged. "Sadly, no. Should have been, but…"

"But what?"

"Got sidetracked. Put that dream on hold."

"To work for your cousin."

"Mm-hm. Still don't know if I made the right decision."

"Working for family's not for everyone."

"Certainly seems like it's working out for you," she said.

"Things aren't always what they seem."

He adjusted and readjusted his fingers through hers, loving the feeling of holding her hand as they walked along together. "Sort of sick of being the low man on the totem pole."

"Are you the low man? I've only seen *you*. You almost seem like a one-man operation to me!"

"Ha. My father and my brother handle the business end of things. My father signed over a big chunk of the business to Nils on his twenty-second birthday, but I was three years younger and my share was smaller. Then Erik's share reverted back to my pop and Nils when he moved away. Oh, I don't know. I think things need to change. Sort of feels like I'm not going anywhere some days."

"I can relate to that."

"Can you? Because it seems like you're *always* going somewhere."

"There's a lot of travel involved with my job, sure. But I don't choose the places. I don't choose where we stay or for how long. I certainly don't have much leisure time. I travel, yes, but I haven't had a proper vacation in…geez, four or five years, I guess."

"Whew!"

"No rest for the weary, but complaining won't change it." She sort of chuckled low, ruefully. "I'm lucky, really. I make good money, and the people are, for the most part, really great.

"Anyway…my day was nowhere near as interesting as yours. I got an early morning call from Sara." She dropped his hand, lowering her sunglasses as they changed direction, walking into the low, setting sun. "Then handled a bunch of emails, confirmed the team's travel, made sure Sara was all set to go tomorrow morning. She liked the locations you chose, Lars."

Whether it was a coincidence or not, he noticed that Jane let go of his hand as soon as she said her cousin's name, crossing her arms over her chest in a move that looked defensive as she walked beside him.

"Who's on the team?"

"Oh, um…Ray. Ray Cartier." She chuckled again, but it was a warm, affectionate sound this time. "He's fabulous. Does makeup. Sebastian. He's Sara's agent. He's a pretty good guy. Sort of a worrywart, but I guess that's what she pays him for. Shanelle does hair. Margot handles wardrobe. And on this trip? I think Franco is coming too. He's her trainer-slash-nutritionist."

"Five people to tend to one person?"

"Six. Don't forget Jane."

"Aw, Minx…I could never forget Jane."

Lars reached for her hand again and felt his heart lift when she didn't pull away.

***

They made their way into the town park, where a small bandstand was roped with red, white and blue bunting and a band played jazzy Americana tunes as families and older couples sat on blankets and in lawn chairs waiting for the sun to disappear so that the fireworks could begin. Children ran around with glow necklaces and little American flags, visiting the ice cream truck or the hot dog stand. Jane loved it that small towns in America still had old-timey celebrations on national holidays; she just didn't have much of a chance to take part in them anymore.

The sun was already starting to set as Lars spread out a

blanket toward the back of the crowd and invited her to sit down. He took two wine glasses out of the backpack and poured some wine, handing Jane a glass.

"What're we drinking to?" she asked, sitting down with her legs straight out in front of her, crossed at the ankles.

He shrugged, sitting across from her, his long legs brushing up against hers. "I don't know, um—"

"Oh, wait, wait—wait!" she said, grinning. "I know a toast. It's good; I've never been able to use it, but—wait. Let me think of how it goes. Okay. Okay. Here we go…"

Jane cleared her throat, but knew from experience it wouldn't help her always-raspy voice, so she leaned into the rasp, and lowered it just a touch more.

Minx, right? Try this out, Lars Lindstrom.

She caught his eyes and let her lashes lower a little, murmuring slowly:

"When I want it,

I want it *awful* bad.

When I don't get it,

It makes me *awful* mad.

When I do get it,

Then life's *sublime*.

I'm talking about…"

She leaned forward toward him, but at the last minute, she started to giggle.

"…a glass of wine."

Oh, well. She blew it. She couldn't pull off the last line. She shrugged, looking up at Lars.

He was staring at her, eyes wide, slight smile on his

face, glass raised. Just staring.

"Lars?"

"I'll drink to that," he said quickly, shaking his head. "*Damn*, Jane."

"Damn…what?"

"That voice," he admitted, hefting the backpack meaningfully onto his lap.

She looked at his lap and her eyes widened. "Aw. It was just a toast."

"A toast is 'Cheers' or 'Bottoms up'. That was…Marilyn Monroe singing 'Happy Birthday, Mr. President'."

She smiled at him, feeling delighted.

"I can see you're very pleased with yourself."

Jane shrugged, taking a big sip of wine, and decided not to tease him about it. "Hey, I like this. What is it?"

"I'm not sure. Some film crew gave me the bottle a few months ago in thanks for giving them a hand."

"That's cool. What movie?"

"A TV show, I think. I don't remember. I don't watch much TV."

"Well, whatever it is, it's good." She offered her glass to him for a refill.

"Slow down, missy…"

"You *sure* you want me to slow down? You know what Dorothy Parker said?"

"I have no idea who Dorothy Parker is, but I have a feeling I'm about to be a big fan."

"She said…Wait. Are you ready for this?" She grinned

at him suggestively. "Can you handle this, Lars?"

He was lying on his side now, his head propped on one hand staring up at her. He set down his wine glass on the blanket and reached out to run a finger from her ankle to just above her knee, stopping at the hem of her skirt. It sent shivers all the way up the rest of her leg, and she felt her heartbeat kick in, fast and loud. He licked his lips and smiled at her, lazy, confident.

"Yeah, Minx. I think I can handle it."

Jane put her glass down too and maneuvered so she was lying on her side next to him, mirroring him, right down to the hand propping up her head. She cleared her voice again to amplify the rasp then met his eyes, trying not to smile or giggle and ruin the punch line again.

"Okay…here goes…Dorothy Parker on the subject of the second drink…

I like to have a drink,

Two at the very most.

After three I'm under the table," Jane licked her lips, smiling, then finished,

"After four I'm under the host."

Lars stared at her lips then flicked his glance back to her eyes.

"I *love* Dorothy Parker."

Jane started giggling and pushed herself back up into a sitting position, taking another sip of her wine.

"You're fun," she said.

He sat up too.

"So are you." He swallowed. "I want to kiss you, Jane."

"So kiss me, Lars."

So he did.

***

"You know, public lewdness isn't allowed in Gardiner parks, per section five of the Parks and Recreation manual. As a local tour purveyor, you should know that, Lars."

He'd know that voice anywhere. Lars leaned back from Jane, annoyed by the interruption. "Great timing, Paul."

"You've been busy, *Midten*. I haven't seen you in days." He winked at Jane. "Hey, Janie."

"Hey, Paul." She sat back with flushed cheeks, picking up her wine glass.

Hey, Janie? Hey, Paul? Say what?

Lars looked back and forth between his friend and Jane. "Do you two know each other?"

Paul sat down on the blanket beside Jane, a touch too close for Lars's comfort.

"Please. Join us." Lars couldn't possibly make his voice sound more unwelcoming.

"I would love to." Paul smiled askance at Jane. "Having fun? He bothering you?"

"Yes and…we'll see."

"What's going on here? You two are acting like long-lost best friends. How do you even know each—"

"Jane's our fourth for euchre while you're tied up with the tour."

"And getting pretty good," she added, winking at Paul.

Lars clenched his jaw and threw back the rest of his wine, pouring himself another glass. Lots of smiles and winks and teasing here. A little too much. He didn't like it. Not one bit.

He turned to Jane. "So, you've been in town for a day and you're the fourth at Prairie Dawn euchre? Wait…you've been hanging out with my brother?"

Jane smiled at him and nodded. "Mm-hm. Big fan of Nils."

Big fan of— "How come I didn't know this?"

Jane shrugged. "It never came up."

"Betting you didn't ask, Lars." Paul reached into his own backpack and took out a beer, cracking it open. "Probably going on and on about the park. Am I right, Janie?"

Lars gave his friend a look, wishing Paul would get lost.

"Yes," said Jane. "But, I like hearing about the park. Lars found wolves today."

"Wolves, huh? Imagine that." Paul smirked back at him, leaning back comfortably on his hands. "Well, Lars, I think Jane's the best thing that's happened to Gardiner in a long time."

Lars gave him another look that said: *I know we're friends, but I'm about to put my foot up your ass.*

Paul beamed. "She is simply a delight."

Jane tilted her head to the side, smiling at Paul. "That is so nice! You are too."

Lars moved a little closer to Jane, his knee grazing hers. "We're sort of on a date, Paul."

Paul gasped. "Oh, really? My bad!"

"It's no big deal. You can join us," Jane said, turning to

Lars. "Right?"

Lars smiled at her, nodding, while Paul's shoulder's shook beside her, obviously enjoying every second of Lars's consternation.

Paul stood up, finally throwing Lars a bone. "Nah, I gotta go. A few of my students were caught drinking beer back in the grove beyond the bandstand last year. Thought I'd go take a look and make sure no one's getting pregnant."

Paul downed the rest of his beer, swinging his backpack up on his shoulder. "Don't let him get fresh, Janie. I'll see you on Thursday, right?" He winked at Lars as he sauntered away. "See ya, Lars. Be good, now."

They sat cross-legged across from each other, knees to knees, as Lars stared at Jane. So Paul, who was young and good-looking, was acquainted with Jane.

Huh. He didn't like it. Man, he didn't like it one bit.

"So...*Janie*."

"Are you *jealous*?"

"Don't be ridiculous."

Her smile grew wider. "Pea green."

"And you're enjoying every second, Minx."

"It's never happened to me before!"

"Seriously. What's up with you two?"

"Me and Paul?"

"No. You and the man in the moon. *Yeah*, you and Paul...*Janie*."

She laughed at him. "We play euchre."

"What's Thursday?"

"Euchre."

"Just euchre."

"Just euchre." She nodded. "I'm getting good."

"Oh, are you?"

He didn't feel reassured. She didn't exactly clarify their status by saying "we're just friends" or something like that, which would have been reassuring. Euchre. He didn't like her playing euchre with Paul. He didn't want her playing anything with any man except him.

"Aye, that I am, as Maggie would say." She grinned at him so openly, his shoulders relaxed. *Maybe there was nothing between them, after all.*

"Janie."

"Mmm?"

"Come sit with me." He moved his knees up and put his arm around her waist as she backed into him. He pulled her up against his chest, between his legs, then wrapped his arms around her in the twilight, leaning down to nuzzle her curls. The fireworks would be starting any minute.

"You cold?"

Jane shook her head no, leaning back against him, and he tightened his arms around her.

His heart was pounding.

As far as he was concerned, the fireworks had already started.

***

The walk back to Jane's hotel room was too quick.

She listened to the faraway howl of wolves, thinking of them as Lars's Wolves now, and looked at the millions of stars in the clear night sky. The air smelled of burning wood from bonfires, campfires and barbeques marking the final night of summer. The end of summer. How Jane hated endings.

I much prefer beginnings, she mused, as she looked askance at Lars's handsome face. She couldn't remember the last time she felt like this. Frankly, she questioned if she had *ever* felt like this.

During the finale of the fireworks she had twisted her neck to look at him, catching his face illuminated in blues and greens. His eyes seized hers, one palm moving from her waist to cup her jaw, gently nudging her face toward him. His lips claimed hers, strong and soft, warm and purposeful. His tongue touched hers tentatively at first, but as she stroked his in welcome, he turned her in his arms until she was kneeling, facing him, her breasts pressed up against his chest, his hands splayed across her lower back. She laced her hands around his neck and lightly grazed the shell of his ear with her thumbs, sliding her tongue against his, her skin electric under his touch. When the explosive booming stopped, she ended the kiss by turning her head and resting her cheek on his shoulder as the crowd around them clapped with appreciation. The noise gradually subsided to the low hum of people packing up and heading home while he ran his hands distractedly up and down her back, holding her close.

Through the low din of activity, she'd heard him whisper, *I'm falling for you, Jane.* But she pretended she didn't, and he didn't say it again.

And now it was almost time to say good night.

Face it, Jane. To say goodbye. *Tomorrow at this time, there's a good chance he'll be in Sara's bed. Don't fool yourself. Remember Ben Abaz…*

As they neared her hotel, Jane sensed he was as sorry to see their evening end as she was. But she shouldn't have made those suggestive toasts and let him kiss her again, not when her intention was to say "goodnight" at her door and put an end to their flirtation. Spending any more time with him now was just going to end up hurting her later. She dropped his hand as they approached the hotel.

"Thanks for tonight," she said politely.

"My pleasure."

"All part of the service, huh?"

He shook his head. "Nope."

"Well, it was really great getting to know you—"

"Getting to *know* me?" He chuckled as if she was making a joke, then stopped, realizing she wasn't. "Wait. That sounds like goodbye."

"Sara's coming tomorrow. She'll…she'll need you."

"Of course. And I'll do whatever I can for her. *Trend* made it clear to keep her happy."

Jane nodded.

"What does that have to do with us?"

Us. She felt her heart break a little.

"You don't understand. Sara's going to *need* you. *Want* you."

"Want me for what?"

Jane stared at his eyes, then winced and looked away.

"She'll *want* me? Like…*want* me, want me?"

Jane looked down, jerking her head up and down once. "She doesn't even know me. And besides, *I'm* into *you*."

Her heart fluttered, despite the guaranteed ending to the short, lovely connection she had made with him. She sighed. "You won't be."

"Of course I will. I like you, Jane."

She couldn't look up. She knew he was telling the truth. She could hear it in his voice. She couldn't bear to see that truth in his eyes now, only to see them grow cold in a day or two, embarrassed that he had said these things to her, wishing he could take them back.

"Jane, I'm not some guy who walks away from the girl he likes just because another pretty girl walks into the room. I'm not that guy."

She looked up at him, locking her eyes with his, knowing what she knew from every photo shoot over the course of five years. It was the rule. There were no exceptions.

"Lars. She's *Samara Amaya. Every* guy is that guy."

He stared at her, rubbing his jaw, then put his hands on his hips. "Well, *I'm* not. I'm not going anywhere. We've still got a week together. I want to see what happens with *you*. I'm not that guy, Jane." He put his hands on her cheeks, and leaned down to touch her lips with his, whispering, "I'm not."

She nodded at him. There was no point in arguing about it anymore. He was so earnest, so sincere, tears pricked the backs of her eyes as he pressed his lips against her forehead, resting his hands lightly on her hips.

Turn away from him and walk into your room, Jane. Alone. At least you had this. At least you had tonight. Tonight was something, and something is better than nothing. Now, say goodnight. Don't let this go any further.

Her head and her heart were locked in a bitter battle.

Why not? Why can't I just spend a few more minutes with him?

You can't. You can't have him. Tell him to go now. Protect yourself!

No! Sara's not here yet. Don't push him away yet.

She will be here. Tomorrow you will lose him!

Her heart roared back, *It's NOT tomorrow YET!* brooking no further argument.

Jane tilted her head back up and whispered, "Do you want to come in?"

He leaned back, looking at her tenderly, his fingers still kneading the skin at her waist.

"Oh, I'm not offering *that!*" she said, eyes widening. "We could just…"

"I…I didn't think you were." Lars grinned, stifling a chuckle. "Sure, I'll—"

"Just…" She backed away from his hands, standing against the door, cheeks hot. "Come in if you want."

She unlocked the door and he followed her inside.

CHAPTER 5

When he told Jane he liked her, he'd only been telling most of the truth. He didn't remember *ever* feeling quite like this about a girl, and while he knew his feelings had intensified quickly, he couldn't help them. She was the most interesting person he had ever met, and he didn't care that her cousin was really pretty. Nothing was going to happen with her cousin and Jane would just have to trust him on that.

He pulled the door shut behind him then turned to face her, and try as he might to remember the words *I'm not offering that*, the idea of throwing Jane down on the bed and proving to her just how much he liked her felt like a pretty solid plan.

Ambient light streamed in from the parking lot through the venetian blinds, and he was glad she didn't flick on one of the overhead lights. He preferred the romantic half-light.

She put her sunglasses on the bureau and slipped out of her sandals. He hadn't noticed before, but her toes were perfectly painted with some color of dark polish and they looked slick and shiny. Sexy. An unexpected concession to beauty in such an unfussy girl—he felt the flush of heat across his skin just looking at them.

She sat down on the edge of the bed, crossing her legs, leaning back on her palms. She looked up at him, but her face was unreadable and for the first time in a long time, he was in a girl's hotel room, but he wasn't sure of himself.

Jane didn't give an inch.

She didn't pat the bed beside her in invitation, or tilt her head to the side with a teasing smile; just raised those serious green eyes to look at him. He wasn't sure if he liked it, feeling unsure of himself; he wasn't sure if such unpredictability was unsettling or exciting.

Without breaking their gaze, he let the backpack on his shoulder slip down his arm and carefully rested it on the floor. He leaned against the back of the hotel room door, staring at her with his arms crossed. She had invited him in with conditions. Frankly, he wasn't even sure *why* she had invited him in, and he sure as heck wasn't making the first move no matter how much he wanted to.

Her tongue darted out to lick her lips and she bit lightly on her lower lip, looking at him, but she still didn't say a word and Lars couldn't get a bead on whether she was flirting with him or nervous, but he watched her, fascinated, wondering what would happen next, trying not to think of better uses for that tongue than licking her *own* lips.

"This is awkward," she finally rasped, softly. "It's just a big bedroom, isn't it? If we were in New York and I invited you back to my place after a date, we wouldn't just go sit in my bedroom."

"Not that I'd mind if we ended up there, Minx." He didn't want her to feel uncomfortable or awkward. He had an idea. "So…what would we do? If you invited me back to your place in New York?"

Jane leaned forward, moving her crossed foot in lazy circles. "Well…we'd hang out in my living room…and I'd offer you a drink, for starters. Coffee or tea or another glass of wine."

"I can make that happen." Lars lightly nudged his backpack. "I have another bottle in here if we want another glass."

He squatted down, unzipping the backpack and took out the bottle. The glasses clinked together as he stood up, placing all three items on the bureau in front of her.

Jane smiled at him, standing up, and he was painfully aware of her so close to him in the dim light—and how close they both were to the bed behind them. His body tightened and he swallowed, looking down at her curly head.

"How about a glass of wine?" she asked with a tentative grin.

"Why yes, New-York-Jane, I would love one." He exhaled. *Stay cool, Lars. Let her relax a little.*

She unscrewed the top of the wine bottle and poured two glasses, offering him one. When he took it, his fingers grazed hers, a feather touch, but it chipped away at his self-control. His breathing got more deliberate as his eyes shot up to meet hers. She swallowed, watching him, then sat back down on the bed.

He took a sip from beside the bureau, his eyes holding hers.

"Then what?" he asked, unable to keep the huskiness out of his voice.

"I'd light a fire in my little fireplace. It's gas, not wood, but I like the glow. Makes my living room feel warm."

Through a fog of want, Lars remembered something. He put up his finger, telling her to hold on for a second. "Didn't use this tonight."

Lars squatted down in front of his backpack again, and when he stood up, he was holding a small, green plastic lantern. "It's an LED lantern. Came with the backpack."

Jane beamed at him. She stood up to take the lantern, then turned it on and placed it next to the open bottle of wine. When she turned, he had moved to stand between her and the bed. She was so close he could feel the heat of her body. It took every ounce of self-control in his tense, aroused body not to touch her.

"So…" he murmured. "We have our firelight and our wine. We're in New York. What comes next?"

"Music," she whispered. She swallowed. "You'd love my vinyl collection."

"I bet."

As she reached for the phone in her back pocket, her breasts grazed his chest. He cleared his throat to stifle the soft growl that he couldn't help as he gazed down at her.

"Ah-hem. Uh, cue up some music, New-York-Jane."

She reached around him, lightly brushing his waist as she placed her wine glass on the bureau. Tapping on the phone screen, she looked up at him. "What're you in the mood for?"

I'm in the mood to make out with you.

He looked down, feeling the uncomfortable pressure of his heavy breathing as he smelled the scent of her shampoo.

"May I?"

"Sure."

Looking down at the phone, he was distracted by the slight movement of her breasts in the shadowy light cast from the bright screen. She was breathing just as heavily as he was. He could hear her quick intake of breath as he grazed her hand with the back of his.

Yeah, Minx. Me too.

"What do you have?" he whispered.

One of her fingers pushed the song list up slowly, and he tried like hell to concentrate on the names, not on her fingers, or the warmth of her smaller body, or on her breasts moving up and down with every breath she took and released. He tried to focus on finding a song that would fit the mood, that would tell her what he wanted, what he was feeling.

"This one." He tapped lightly on The Beatles "Woman."

"Good choice," she murmured.

He nodded and tossed the phone on the bed as the guitar chords started playing.

"Would we dance?" he asked, needing to feel her in his arms, needing to touch her and be touched by her.

"We might," she whispered, staring up into his eyes.

"Then dance with me, Minx."

He watched as her smaller, whiter hand settled into his larger, tanner one and he carefully curled his fingers around it, pulling her up against his body until her breasts were finally, blessedly, pressed against his chest. Careful not to step on her little lacquered toes, he dropped her hand and slid his arms around her, resting his hands on her lower back, his breath catching as she reached her arms up and laced her fingers behind his neck.

She laid her head on his chest and they swayed lightly to the mellow music, to the words of a man beseeching a woman to trust him.

**

After tonight she would have to delete "Woman" from her playlist. She would never be able to bear hearing it again— even if she heard it fifty years from now, she knew she would wince, remembering tonight, remembering her terrible, fierce longing for the man holding her.

He had surprised her by choosing this song. It wasn't one of the innocent, lighthearted 60s tunes they had enjoyed listening to in his truck yesterday. There was something more mature, deeper and more complex, more…inevitable about this song.

Inevitable.

Like Lars turning his back on her tomorrow.

Her heart twisted painfully, and she closed her eyes against her thoughts, leaning her cheek against his chest, swaying back and forth with him.

Generally, Jane was satisfied with herself—who she was deep inside where true character lived. She had longings, of course: to belong to someone, to feel connected to family as she had before she lost her parents, to feel secure in her relationships. But mostly, Jane approved of the woman she had become. She had modest ambitions that she didn't realize through unkindness or manipulation. She had integrity. She was a good person. She rarely wished she were prettier. She had come to terms with her average looks a long time ago. She told herself it wasn't so bad being plain if you were kind and funny, interesting and well-liked—if you could look at yourself in the mirror and not feel shame or regret.

But, leaning against Lars Lindstrom's solid chest, with his tender words fresh in her head, she felt an uncharacteristic rebellion against the unfairness of being so plain, so average, so forgettable.

If I were beautiful, she thought, *he wouldn't be able to walk away from me. If I were beautiful…*

Her eyes watered, and she tried to shift her thoughts away, back to the moment.

Stop thinking about tomorrow, Jane.

Lars leaned back and Jane looked up at him. His eyes were large and black, surrounded by a thin band of icy blue, and they captured hers with intensity, flicking briefly to her lips then back to her eyes. She read his question and answered with her body, tilting her head to the side and running her tongue over her lips.

His lips twitched up for just a moment before he lowered them to hers.

Jane closed her eyes, her insides spinning and swirling with pleasure. He ran his hands over her sweater, up and down her back, slipping under her cami and touching the warm, smooth skin of her back.

She shivered, leaning into him, frustrated she couldn't

get closer. Every nerve ending demanded to be touched by him and her breasts ached to be flush against his skin. She felt him trying to push her sweater up, and she wiggled, breaking away from him for a moment to slip her cami and sweater over her head, leaving only her bra still intact. He found her lips again and his hands returned impatiently to her lower back. She felt his rough, muscular fingers kneading, adjusting and readjusting over her skin like pumice, making her tremble.

She moved her hands to his waist, pulling on the bottom of his polo shirt. He tore his mouth away from hers to pull it over his head in a quick movement, then put his arms back around her. He pulled her roughly up against him, crushing her lips with his as a growly sound rose up from his throat. Through the flimsy material of her black, sheer bra, she could feel the tickle of his hair, the heat of his chest pressed up against her breasts with only a thin barrier between them. She sighed into his mouth, loving the liquid fire of his tongue stroking hers.

Lars backed up against the bed, sitting down on the edge, and lifting Jane's so she straddled his lap. As he held her close, kissing her deeply, a soft, strangled sound rose from Jane's throat, a flurry of feelings and sensations poured into a single, low, erotic sound. Lars groaned in response, his fingers sliding into the waistband of her skirt.

"Wait," Jane breathed, breaking off the kiss. She leaned her forehead against his, lowering her hands to gently push his away. "Wait."

He took a deep breath and exhaled raggedly, putting his

arms around her and holding her in place. She rested her palms against the flat, hard planes of his chest, panting, trying to catch her breath, acutely aware, by virtue of her position, that he was more than ready to keep going and she was in the process of disappointing him.

"I'm sorry," she murmured, closing her eyes.

Her body protested her heart's decision, wanting him as badly as he obviously wanted her. But, her heart held firm: *You can't sleep with him, Jane. It will hurt too much later. You have to slow down.*

"It's okay. Don't be sorry."

Likely trying to calm himself, he rubbed his jaw with one hand while holding her with the other, a movement that made his chest muscles flex under her hand. She felt the contours of sinew under his warm skin and it made her clench her jaw, as she fought for self-control. *Oh. My. God.* She couldn't see very much in the dim light of the hotel room, but she could certainly feel the rock-hard muscles moving under her palms.

"Your chest is…um…firm."

His teeth were white as he broke into a smile. He reached one hand up and pushed her curls away from her face, cupping her cheek. "I work out a little."

"A *little*?"

He put his hands under her arms, lifting her away from him. She stood up by the foot of the bed and he stood up for a second only to turn and kneel on the bed, crawling to the headboard. He fluffed up a couple of pillows and moved her phone to the bedside table before settling in comfortably.

He had bared his feet at some point and all he was wearing now were low-slung jeans, ridiculously cut abs and a grin. "Come lie down with me?"

Jane stood at the foot of the bed, arms crossed, suddenly aware that she was standing before him in a black sheer bra and a jean skirt. She gave him a look.

"Come on, Minx. Come get comfy. We can just…talk. I won't touch you." He winked at her. "Unless you ask me to."

She took a deep breath and smiled at him. "Is that right?"

"I swear."

"On what?"

"On my good name, Jane Mays. That'll have to be enough."

"Now who's the minx?" she asked.

"You are. Come lie down with me." His voice was low and serious, and he didn't ask this time.

She crawled between his legs up the bed from the foot to the head, watching his eyes widen. She grinned at him then maneuvered to the left at the last minute, settling herself beside him innocently. He put his arm around her and she curled into him, her ear comfortably resting on the solid warmth of his chest. He ran his fingers up and down her arm, and then he laced his fingers through hers, taking a deep breath, and trying to relax.

"How many times has that song played now? Five? I must have set it to repeat."

Lars reached for her phone on the bedside table and switched the play mode from repeat one to repeat all, and "Julia" started playing.

HALF OF WHAT I SAY IS MEANINGLESS. *But I say it just to reach you…*

"Mmm. This is a good one too."

"Yeah," she murmured low. "I think this whole playlist is 'Mellow Beatles'."

They listened in the dark quiet of her hotel room until the song ended and he broke the silence.

"Jane," he whispered. "I need to be sure you know…I'm *really* into you."

She leaned back, looking up at him. She wished it didn't hurt her so much to hear him say things like that. She wished she could just believe him—smile and kiss him, feeling exuberant, hopeful about meeting someone so amazing with whom she had this searing chemistry, these growing feelings. She searched his eyes then leaned back down, feeling her eyes water with tears.

He put his fingers under her chin and tipped it back, catching her shiny, troubled eyes in the darkness.

"What, Minx? What is it? Why can't you trust me?"

She leaned back down, resting her cheek against his chest as his hand trailed lightly, comfortingly, up and down her back.

"There are no exceptions, Lars."

"Is this about your cousin again?"

"Listen…" she started, then hesitated.

He wouldn't understand unless she told him about Ben.

The thing is, she hadn't really told anyone, ever, about what had happened in Egypt. Aside from it being a painful story, it was hugely humiliating. He lived in her mind alone now, where he owned a huge share of real estate devoted to her crushed hopes and lonely reality.

Jane took a deep breath. She wanted Lars to understand why she didn't trust him. She wanted Lars to know that she would try to understand when he walked away from her tomorrow. It wouldn't be the first time.

"I didn't want to work for my cousin, but my uncle asked me to give her a hand and I couldn't say no. He'd been so good to me, like a second father after I lost my own. Right about the time I graduated from college Sara's career was starting to flounder. She was getting a bad reputation for tantrums and demands. Anyway, he asked me to step in and help her out. Essentially, I would be her front man, and she wouldn't have to deal with booking agents and photographers anymore. I'd book her jobs and handle her business and she would just show up for work. It's not what I wanted to do, but he took me in when I was little...he was—*is* important to me. Looking at his face is like still having my father alive in some ways. I mean, I just couldn't say no to him. I could *never* say no to him. Anyway, I didn't expect to work for her for more than a year or so, until she was back on track and could hire someone else. I knew my role. My cousin was the beautiful supermodel, and I was her plain assistant."

"Jane—"

"No, wait—please, just let me finish. It didn't matter

that those were our roles, because I had no time for anything else anyway. There was so much work and I was so young and so new to the business. I just worked, kept my nose to the grindstone, keeping her calendar, making bookings, arranging her travel. The only friends I had were the other people on Sara's team. I didn't…date. But, a year turned into two, then three, and I got comfortable. I knew what I was doing, and I could do everything faster and cleaner. I was more confident. It was less all-consuming, and I had more space…you know, in my life. Not to mention, right around that time Sara met Laney, her personal assistant, and that freed up some of my time too."

"Okay."

Jane gulped softly. "We did a shoot in Cairo last summer and I went early just like…just like here. Ben Abaz was my contact there, just like you are here. And we—well, I guess we fell into each other, we just—well, just like…."

"You and me," he said softly.

Jane looked down so she didn't have to look in his face, but she was comforted by his hand on her back, lightly stroking, making her feel connected to him as he listened.

"I had all of these wild hopes. It felt like falling in love, only it wasn't love. I know that now. In fact, when Sara got there, it was like—suddenly—I didn't exist. I mean it. It was like…well, the way he said it was, 'The sun has come out from behind the clouds. I am blinded to anything but the sun'."

Lars drew breath sharply, gathering her closer to him while Jane swallowed painfully, closing her eyes against the rush of hurt and embarrassment as she related the story. It would never get easier to remember how he had walked away from her so quickly, so finally, without looking back.

"Since then, I've never allowed myself to get involved with anyone again on a shoot. I swore I wouldn't. Never again. London, Oslo, Moscow, Rio…never. There were opportunities, I guess, but I wasn't even tempted." Jane raised her face then and locked her eyes with his. "Until I came to Montana. And met you."

He stared at her intensely, his face inscrutable in the soft light.

"And tomorrow you'll meet *her*," she finished softly. "Ben was right. You'll see. She *is* the sun, and I'm just—"

"Jane. You're just Jane. And I'm *Just-Lars*."

"I'm serious—"

"So am I." He cut her off. "I'm not him. Not Ben. *Lars*. I'm sorry he hurt you, but I'm not that guy, Jane."

She tilted her head to the side and took a deep breath against the assault of her feelings, against the dangerous, painful hope that exploded in her heart, unraveling like a ribbon of heat to touch the tips of her fingers, the tips of her toes, the shells of her ears, the place deep inside that clenched with longing, begging for his intrusion, until she was liquid, electric, until she almost couldn't bear the sweetness. He didn't know what she knew with such absolute certainty, but she adored him for trying to reassure her.

She swung her leg over his chest and sat on his abdomen, straddling him as she leaned down to press her lips against his. He jerked into a full sitting position, hands cupping her backside, edging her farther down his thighs until her skirt hiked up and she was flush on his lap, the hardness behind his jeans pressed up against the cotton of her panties.

Her feet were flat on the bed, bent knees holding his torso in a vise, and she wound her arms around his neck, running her fingers through his hair, shivering with longing for him. His hands kept her face captive, fingers threaded through her hair, not allowing her to move her face away.

Suddenly, he leaned back from her, panting, his face serious and hungry. He glanced down at her barely-covered breasts, then back to her face.

"Stop or go, Jane?" He breathed urgently. "Stop or…?"

Her mind was exploding with contradictions. She had never felt this turned on, this on fire. Her whole body was aching for him. She wanted to tear off the rest of her clothes. She wanted him to thrust inside of her over and over again until they both cried out in release. She wanted the weight of his body on top of hers, hot and hard, as he made love to her all night long until dawn.

The only thing stronger than her desire was her fear. She didn't want to have any regrets. Although her body screamed for his, she knew that surrendering so quickly was too risky for her heart.

"Stop," she whispered, hating the word with all her heart.

She leaned back, resting her hands gingerly on his shoulders and his face fell forward, his forehead on her chest, resting just above her breasts. His chest moved up and down, heavy and fast. She eased off his lap and he took a deep breath then released it in a slow hiss before leaning back against the headboard, his arm covering his eyes, still trying to catch his breath. She knelt beside him, not at all sure she had made the right decision, worried that he would get up and leave her, all the while knowing it would be best for both of them if he did.

He groaned and swallowed, then lowered his arm. He looked at her with searching eyes and shook his head—frustrated and disappointed—before reaching out his arm and pulling her gently against him. She placed her head back on his chest as before, listening to his racing heart under her ear. When she placed her palm on his chest, he flinched. *Sensitive.* He covered her hand so that it was flush against him, but still.

"You sure you don't want the 'or'?" he asked, gruffly.

"I do. But, I can't." *I can't because I can't trust what will happen tomorrow. Because you make me doubt myself. You put me in danger without meaning to.* Her voice was small when she asked him, "Do you want to go?"

"Do you *want* me to go?" he asked, his fingers trailing lazily up and down her arm.

She adjusted her head until she was comfortable against him, desperate for the solid warmth of his body. She sighed, closing her eyes, wishing she could escape from her thoughts.

"Jane?" he prompted in a whisper.

"Will you stay with me for a little?"

140

"I'll stay as long as you want."

***

The morning sun streaming through the windows of the small room woke her up. When Jane opened her eyes, the first thing she saw was Lars's chest under her cheek, tan and blond and perfect. He had pulled the comforter around them at some point, and she sighed from the warmth of her cocoon.

Pulling the covers down a little, Jane leaned up on one elbow to look at him. He had slept with one arm under her head and the other thrown over his eyes, which drew *her* eyes, like a magnet, to his exposed lips. Her stomach leapt as she remembered the sweetness of him kissing her last night as they danced to "Woman." She took a shaky breath and sighed.

His lips turned up. "Take a picture, Minx. It lasts longer."

"How did you—"

He lowered his arm. "I've got good instincts. That, and I peeked."

She grinned, lying back down and pillowing her head on his arm. He leaned up on his side, over her, and ran the back of his hand against her cheek.

"Morning, Minx" he said.

"Morning, Professor," she answered.

He leaned down and pecked her lips with his, then drew back, smiling into her eyes.

"I liked waking up next to you."

"Is that right, *Just-Lars*?"

"That's right, Minx."

"Can't call me that anymore. Starting today, I'm on the clock."

"You work for your cousin."

"I work for Samara Amaya. I don't forget it. You shouldn't either."

"Well, she's not here yet."

He kissed her again.

She will be. Too soon.

Jane rolled away from him and sat up, swinging her legs over the side of the bed, putting her back to him.

"Will you hand me my phone?" she asked, and a moment later he nudged her back with it.

More boobie shots, several texts from United Airlines reconfirming everyone's travel plans for today, a text from Ray, several from Sebastian and—of course—a few from Sara too, the most recent of which read: *On plane. Sebastian sux. Want the cowboy in my bed 2nite. —S*

Jane's shoulders rolled forward, and she bowed her head, her stomach turning.

"Everything okay?" he asked from behind her.

"Business as usual," she muttered without looking at him.

"Mind if I use your bathroom?"

"Nope. Go ahead." She still didn't look at him.

Jane scrolled through the other messages. They could wait.

The first thing she needed to do was tell Lars that this was over. She needed to say goodbye. If, by some miracle, they got to the end of the week and he had been able to resist Sara? Jane would jump into his arms and never let him out of her sight again for as long as she lived. But, it was a less than one percent chance that he could meet Sara and choose Jane. When he did, she didn't want any ties to him. She didn't want to feel the pain of losing something that she thought belonged to her.

She plugged in the phone to charge it and ran her hands through her hair, picking up her Boston College sweatshirt and shrugging into it. Her skirt had twisted around in her sleep, and she righted it. She pulled her curls up into a tiny, messy ponytail, and put her Red Sox hat on over it. Then she sat down in the chair at the desk and waited for him. Her heart started thumping like crazy when she heard him turn off the faucet and her breath caught when he opened the door, taking up the entire space of the doorway with his beautiful body. He had washed his face and hands, and must have run his hands through his hair, because it glistened. Sitting on the edge of the bed, he pulled his shirt on over his head then reached down for his shoes.

"Lars," she started, and he looked up, tilting his head to the side, blue eyes twinkling.

I am totally crazy about you, but I can't be with you. Whatever's between us has to end here and now so you're free to do whatever you want.

She stared at him, her heart racing, her brain willing her lips to say the words.

"What's up, Min—er, Jane? I might slip, but I'll try." He chuckled, finishing his laces and standing up.

And just like that…she couldn't do it.

She watched from her seat at the table as he reached down, grabbing the picnic backpack up and easily swinging it onto his shoulder. She could feel the moment slipping through her fingers and her mind raced through the past three days with him: meeting him at the airport, listening to music together, the moment he learned she was Samara Amaya's cousin, the first time he touched her hand in his truck, showing her the bison, kissing her in the truck near Yellowstone Lake, the fireworks, dancing in her hotel room, waking up in his arms…it had all been a little piece of heaven. Her heart twisted in her chest and she ground her teeth together, her nostrils flaring to keep from crying.

"I had a great time with you, Jane." He leaned forward and kissed her on the cheek. "It's going to be okay. I promise. Don't worry, huh?"

She nodded, swallowing against the enormous lump in her throat.

"I'll pick you up in an hour or so? We'll head to the airport?"

She smiled at him and it took every ounce of strength she had to pull it off. "Sounds great."

He winked at her, pulling the door shut behind him as he left her room.

Jane closed her eyes, exhaling until her lungs were empty and burning, and her shoulders fell forward under the sheer weight of her fear and sorrow. The first sob, as she drew a painful breath and exhaled again, was louder than she anticipated, so she covered her mouth with her hands to muffle the rest as her body shook with the force of her silent weeping.

She had promised herself she wouldn't let this happen again. She would never leave herself unprotected like this. She would never set herself up for this high a fall. She had promised herself she would never, ever let this happen again.

But, it had.

Only it was much worse this time:

She'd given Ben her body, but over a mere three days, she'd given Lars her heart.

***

Jane was all business when he returned to pick her up. That, and she was back in her banged-up jeans, baggie sweatshirt, glasses and cap, which made him miss the fresh-faced girl from last night and the warm, wide-eyed, tousled girl waking up next to him this morning, looking so sweet and young, her hair soft and loose.

She sat next to him in the van on the way to the airport, barely saying a word, alternately texting and making phone calls to confirm the flight arrival time, or to coordinate someone from *Trend* with Samara's personal team. Lars could see that she was efficient and professional, courteous in her dealings with people, saying "please" and "thank you" nearly constantly, chuckling politely and making small talk when people realized whom she worked for.

He looked out the window, wishing that they'd had one more day together before today, wishing they'd had one more night like last night. He sensed that she was putting some distance between them as she'd done before on

Sunday morning; too bad he didn't have any bison around this time to bring down that wall again.

He thought about the story she told him last night about the man in Cairo who had wined and dined her, then promptly dumped her when her cousin got to town. It was clear how hurt she had been by that episode and how much it made her distrust her cousin and the men she encountered for her work. He had a week to prove to her that he was different, and he intended to make the most of it. As long as she would give him a chance, he'd be sure she didn't regret it.

"Jane."

"Hmm?" She had a break between phone calls, but her thumbs kept moving like lightning, texting someone else.

"About last night…"

"Hmm?"

The phone was still commanding one hundred percent of her attention. He just wanted a little of it before Samara and her entourage arrived and they weren't alone anymore.

"Remember that last kiss before we fell asleep?"

"Mm-hm."

"Wasn't any good, huh?"

Her thumbs stopped abruptly, and she looked up, finding his eyes over the rims of her glasses. "You didn't think so?"

"Not good…" He grinned at her. "More like fantastic."

She looked like she was about to say something back, then she must have thought better of it, and looked back down at her phone. "Quit distracting me."

"Just wondered what it would take to get your nose out of your phone."

"I am very important today, Professor. No time for games."

"Okay. Then how about the direct approach…when do I get to see you again?"

"I think we're both going to be very busy."

Yeah, I'd like to be very busy. With you.

"Too busy for—?"

Jane took a deep breath, putting her phone down and crossing her legs toward him. "You don't get it. Tornado's coming, son. Keep your head down and take cover. Maybe I'll—maybe I'll catch you on the flip side."

"*Maybe* you'll catch me on the flip side? Why not take cover with me instead? I have *nice* covers."

When he glanced over, she was still staring at her phone, but trying not to smile. He could tell, and it made him happy.

"I bet you do."

"I'm anxious to show them to you."

"Is that right?"

"Anytime you want, Minx."

He pulled into the airport parking lot, waving briefly at John, but not rolling down his window to invite further conversation today. What little time they had, he wanted to spend alone with Jane.

He cut the engine and stared out the windshield, waiting for her to say something.

"Okay," she said.

"Okay, you want to come see my covers?"

"No. Well, yes. But, no." She looked down, swallowing, and she shifted her phone from hand to hand, nervously. "I need to ask you something."

"Anything."

She looked down and swallowed again before raising her eyes to his. Hers weren't playful; they were serious and nervous; maybe trying to be brave—he couldn't tell yet. Instinctively he knew that whatever she was about to say, he wasn't going to like it.

"Just for now…could we…put this…" she gestured with her hand back and forth between them, "…on ice?"

He could feel his face falling. She was only in Montana for a week. The last thing he wanted to do was put anything "on ice" where she was concerned. He sat back, turning away from her, focusing his eyes on the terminal in front of them.

"Can we do that?" she whispered.

No, we can't. This is real to me. I don't want to slow down or, or—

"Why?"

"I think it would be for the best."

The best? No, Jane. The best would be you in my bed tonight or me in yours. Anything else is not *the best.*

The disappointment he felt almost knocked the wind out of him; made him feel like a teenager who'd just been refused by the girl he'd gotten up all of his courage to ask to the prom. Lars kept his eyes down. He didn't want her to see the hurt there.

"I like you." Her voice was more emotional—lower and softer—when she added, "You know I do."

She was making everything so goddamned complicated and it didn't need to be.

"And it's been so great getting to know you and spending time with you, but now it's—it's, um, time for me to go to work. I need to concentrate on Samara and the shoot. And I need you to do whatever it is you, you know, need to do…without feeling like you owe me anything."

Need to do. Like screw your cousin, apparently.

He looked at her, angry now.

"I don't want to get together with your damned cousin! I'm not that—Aw, hell, what's the point? You haven't heard a word I've said." He huffed in frustration before starting again. "I *don't* owe you anything, Jane. But, I felt like this"— he mimicked her hand motions back and forth between them—"was special…was maybe the *start* of something special."

She gulped, looking away from him.

"I'm *not* Ben Abaz, but you're pushing me away— pushing *this* away—for no good reason. You're shutting this down, but just for the record, I don't want to shut it down. I want to give it a *chance*." He tilted his head to the side, and his brows furrowed as he softened his voice. He tried one more time. "I know you've only known me for a couple of days, but Jane…"

He looked at her face, which reminded him of a mannequin—plastic and apathetic, calm and professional— and he let his voice trail off. Her eyes didn't water with tears, and she didn't flex her jaw. Her face was blank as she stared at him, void of any of the disappointment he was feeling. At the growing ache in his heart a painful realization manifested itself in the front and center of his brain, blinking in neon, unable to be ignored: *She's blowing you off. And you need to stop accepting her excuses for why.*

He leaned back from her and swallowed the lump in his throat, wanting to wince but biting the side of his cheek instead. No. She didn't get to see how much this hurt him.

Suddenly, he felt angry. Really angry. He hadn't been looking for her; he had been minding his own business. She walked into his life with her curly hair and raspy voice, big green eyes that couldn't stop looking at him, and now she was walking out. And it hurt. More than he ever could have guessed.

His words were low and hard-edged when he finally spoke again. "You want to break this off? Fine. But don't call it taking a break or putting it on ice. Just call a spade a spade and tell me you're not interested, Jane. Tell me you don't want this. Tell me you don't want me. Tell me—"

Jane's phone buzzed loudly on her lap.

"It's for the best," she whispered. "She's here."

CHAPTER 6

How she had managed to remain impassive in the van was beyond her. The coping skills she had picked up as Sara's assistant must have been more finely tuned than she realized, because inside, she was weeping from the pain of giving him up and setting him free. But she knew in her heart that there was no other way.

She had hurt him; his voice had been angry by the end of their conversation and he had barely looked at her since they had entered the terminal—hadn't met her eyes even once or said a word to her. The loss of his warm, playful teasing was painful and she already felt raw from the chafing and aching of her heart. *It's for the best*, she reminded herself gently. *His anger is better than his pity or his rejection,* both of which were practically guaranteed.

She and Lars were waiting at the end of the escalator side by side when Jane saw Sara and Ray step onto the top step. She fought the urge to grab Lars, kiss him with every bit of passion and despair in her heart and tell him she was wrong—*I don't want a break, I want you!*—and greet her cousin with the words, "He's MINE. You CAN'T have him." But she knew that wasn't the smart move.

The smart move was to wait it out, agonizingly, and see if Lars meant what he said, see if he could possibly withstand

Sara, not because he owed Jane anything, but because it was his own personal choice. That's the only way it would matter. The only way she would believe it. She had to admit her heart felt tragically, cautiously hopeful, in spite of her speech in the car. In that small sliver of space that already belonged to him, she desperately hoped that Lars could meet and get to know Sara, but—somehow, somehow, somehow—choose Jane.

"Janie!" Sara exclaimed in a breathy, delighted voice, three steps from the bottom of the escalator, as Ray hung back, talking on his phone.

Jane looked up from her thoughts and her breath caught for an instant, as Sara offered her most beautiful, beaming smile. There were times that Jane was still blown away by the beauty of her cousin, even after a lifetime of knowing her.

Looking at Sara was like looking at a wonder of nature: a blooming rose, dappled with mist, at the height of its exquisiteness; the perfect reflection of a mountain in a still pool, majesty mirroring majesty; the clouds when the sun sets, ablaze in reds and oranges and impossible lavender. That was Sara. You stood in awe of nature's bounty when you beheld her impossibly beautiful, heart-breaking perfection; it almost hurt to look at her and once you did it was almost impossible to look away. Jane had never known a day of her life without Sara, but she still stared, stunned that such natural perfection in another human being actually, well, *existed*.

Sara pushed her large, expensive sunglasses up on her

head and Jane noticed that she had put makeup on, something she generally didn't do when traveling.

"Janie! I missed you *so* much!"

Okaaaaaaaay. We're doing the "loving relatives" bit.

Jane hadn't seen that coming. Sara must have decided she *really* wanted Lars. "Loving relatives" was an act Sara generally reserved for world-class photographers and other industry giants with soft spots for Jane. It was Sara's way of disarming them: by showing them how much she loved her drab little cousin, Jane, of whom they were already fans. *We both love Jane, so naturally we'll love each other too!*

Sara was casually elegant in simple black sandals, a straight black column skirt in soft cotton that undulated against her body with every step, and a long-sleeved gray t-shirt, deeply scooped, showing off her magnificent collarbones, hugging her pert breasts underneath. She wore several silver bangles on her elegant wrist and a simple necklace of braided silver and corded brown leather around her swan-like neck. Her dark hair was long and loose, parted in the middle, falling in shiny, lustrous, touchable waves.

She held out her willowy arms and giggled as Jane stepped forward, wrapping her in an expensive-smelling embrace. Then she stood back, putting a long, tapered, manicured finger under Jane's chin. "Mmmm. Look at you, my sweet little cousin. I could just eat you up."

Then softly, leaning down until her lips almost grazed Jane's ear. "Introduce me to him. *Now.*"

Jane stepped back, taking a deep breath, and sighed, looking up at Sara and forcing a small, painful smile.

"Flight okay?"

"Mm-hm," Sara breathed, eyes narrowing just a touch when Jane didn't immediately offer up Lars.

She put an arm around Jane's shoulders and turned, as if surveying her kingdom. Zeroing in on Lars, she feigned surprise, all wide eyes and voluptuous smile. "Well, now. Who in the world is *this*, Janie?"

Jane turned to Lars, who stared back at Sara, his face inscrutable.

"Lars Lindstrom," he said. "Tour operator."

Sara looked him up and down, lazily, suggestively, her eyes smoldering. As her gaze trailed back up his body, meeting his eyes again, Jane noticed Lars's lips tilt up in a small smile.

Jane forced herself to watch. She forced herself not to react. She reminded herself that she'd seen it all before: What man wouldn't be flattered by this sort of undiluted attention from a world-famous supermodel?

"Lars," she said. "This is my cousin, Samara Amaya."

Samara put out her hand, and Lars took it. "Miss Amaya. Welcome to Montana. Good to meet'cha."

"*Miss Amaya*? Oh, no, no, no," she purred, clasping his hand. "We're going to be friends, Lars. Good friends. It's *Samara*."

"Samara," he repeated, still holding Samara's hand, still smiling at her.

Suddenly Jane couldn't bear to watch anymore. She ducked out from under her cousin's arm and left them alone, turning to Ray, who enfolded her in a warm embrace.

He whispered in her ear, his snarky twang welcome: "Miss Thang looooove her cousin…when it suits her purpose. And what a purpose. He is dee-*viiiiine*, honey."

Jane leaned back, and Ray scanned her face, wincing. "Ooooo! It's like that? You got it bad for him, huh, Miss Jane Mays? Well, Ray-Ray's here now. We'll work it out, girl."

Yeah, right. She glanced over at Lars and Sara, who bantered back and forth in what appeared to be flirty conversation. Miserably, she turned back to Ray.

"How was she on the flight?"

"'Ray do this, Sebastian do this'. You know how she gets. But, honey, I just put on my mask and say 'You wreck my beauty sleep? I wreck your beauty'. Bassy didn't get off so easy."

Jane looked up to see Sebastian step cautiously onto the escalator, wobbling under the poorly distributed weight of several bags. Two leather bags on one shoulder that appeared to be slipping down his arm, plus another bag on the other shoulder, and two shopping bags in each hand.

"Poor Sebastian!"

"He charges a lot more than I do, honey. *He* can help with the ever-lovin' bags."

Ray looked over at Sara with a sour expression on his pursed, shiny lips. Jane's glance followed only to find Lars laughing at something Sara was saying. He was eating out of her hand and Jane's heart twisted.

"Look away, sugar," advised Ray. "We'll see what we can do about that."

Jane turned her back to them, looking back at Ray

glumly, but was soon accosted by Sebastian, who practically fell on top of her with a desperate whisper.

"*She. Is. A. Monster.*"

Jane shook her head at Sebastian, warning him to button it up. They were all in unspoken agreement in their disdain toward Sara, but both men knew better than to be overt in their dislike. Sara was their bread and butter; they'd do well to keep their true feelings carefully concealed.

"Let me help you," said Jane, taking two of the shopping bags from Sebastian and hefting one of the three leather bags onto her own shoulder so that he could mop his forehead with the sleeve of his silk shirt. "*Goddamn it*, Jane. She just *left* everything on the plane. Just got up and walked off like the Queen of Sheba. And *you...*" He pointed one stubby, neatly manicured finger at Ray, scowling.

Ray put his sunglasses on languorously, smirking at Sebastian. "Girlfriend *know* better than to ask Ray-Ray to carry her stuff. Boundaries, Bassy. Build some ASAP."

Then he turned and sauntered over to introduce himself to Lars.

Jane smiled at Sebastian sympathetically. Six hours next to Samara was more than anyone should have to endure. Carrying her mountain of baggage through several terminals must have been the breaking point. She smiled at him gently.

"Sorry it was a bad trip."

"Well, at least you're here now, Jane. No more leaving us three days early. We *need* you back at home, especially with Laney down." He readjusted the luggage, beads of sweat sliding from his temples down his cheeks.

"Any intel on that? On when Laney might be back in action? And—hey!—how was the weekend? You never sent me a run-down."

"I visited Laney on Saturday afternoon, Jane. Brought her some chicken matzoh soup. She looked awful. Could barely speak." Sebastian combed his fingers through his thinning hair, trying to compose himself. "The MoMA was tame enough."

"What about the vodka launch on Sunday night? She sent me boob shots." Jane raised an eyebrow at Sebastian.

"Wild after-party at the Mondrian."

"Anything I need to know?"

"Nah." He shook his head. "Press wasn't there."

"Did she meet anyone?"

"Some kid from one of the newer boy bands."

"Please tell me he was over eighteen?"

"Barely, but yes." He looked sheepish. "Laney's better at screening these guys than I am."

Jane nodded. "No harm done, I guess. I would've seen something on Twitter by now if she'd gotten herself in trouble. Any checked bags?"

He rolled his eyes at her. "Whadda*you* think?"

I think Lars is going to need a bigger van.

She turned to see if the baggage claim belt had started spinning yet and had a quick flashback to her own arrival three days ago:

Miss Mays?

Mr. Lindstrom.

Lars. Yeah.

She looked at Lars, who was chuckling at something Ray was saying. Ray gesticulated madly, and then put his manicured hands on the hips of his sea-green, slim-fit jeans, pretending to pout. Sara chuckled prettily whenever Lars glanced her way, but otherwise shot Ray daggers, clearly wishing to have Lars all to herself. Jane watched as her cousin gestured to a coffee kiosk, then looped her arm in Lars's. As they sauntered away, Ray looked back at Jane and shrugged.

Thanks for trying, Ray.

Jane was already a speck in Lars's rearview mirror.

Just as she had predicted.

***

Lars had to admit two things:

One, despite Jane's warnings, Samara was incredibly warm and charming which,

Two, wasn't what he had been led to expect.

Jane had painted her cousin as a real dragon-lady, but he was finding Samara to be sweet, funny, disarming, and—yes, as expected—the most beautiful woman he had ever seen up-close in his entire life. It wasn't a matter of opinion. That Samara Amaya was undeniably gorgeous was an empirical fact.

Tall, with a tiny waist, voluptuous breasts, and a pert, rounded ass, she was eye-catching. But add to her figure, her face: rosy red lips, pillowed and feminine, and lavender eyes fringed with thick black lashes. She was utterly stunning in every way, and like any other red-blooded man, it was impossible not to notice.

Being attracted to her wasn't optional; as Jane had—more or less—predicted, it was inevitable.

That said, he didn't *want* to be the sort of fickle guy who made decisions by his attraction to a beautiful woman. He was better than that. As he'd repeatedly promised Jane, he *wasn't* that guy. A terrible person could come in pretty packaging. It's just that Samara didn't seem so terrible. Not yet, at least.

Besides, Samara's attention was a balm to Jane's rejection.

Jane didn't want him. She'd barely said a word to him since they left the parking lot after her "ice" speech. Aside from politely asking for his help recovering the bags from baggage claim, and giving him the claim tickets, Jane had kept her distance after introducing him to Samara. She didn't touch his hand as she handed him the tickets, or wink or smile or call him "Just-Lars" or anything. It was almost like last night, like the last three days, never even happened. It was like he was just "the help" now, and it hurt like hell.

He grumbled as he sat down in his seat, fumbling with his keys, feeling distracted, confused, because last night, holding Jane in his arms? He could have sworn that—

"Is this…okay?"

He jerked his head up, surprised to find Samara sitting next to him in the passenger seat of the van.

"I thought we could get to know each other better."

Used to having Jane sitting beside him and perhaps even hoping for a few minutes of conversation with her while they drove back to Gardiner, his heart sank a little, though he worked hard to conceal it by offering Samara a bright smile.

"Sure. Of course. You can sit wherever you want to."

"Great," she purred.

As he started the engine, however, he glanced in the rearview mirror and caught Jane's eyes for a second. She turned away quickly, her face cool and unreadable. He breathed through the sharp wave of pain he felt from her rejection, then turned to Samara, giving her a flirty smile.

If I'm going to be hurting, then she can hurt a little too.

"What kind of music do you like, Samara? Radio's all yours."

"Funsies!" She leaned forward and turned it on, only to wrinkle up her nose when the Beach Boys started singing. She turned to him with a pretty cringe. "Ugh. Oldies? No, thank you. Mind if I change it?"

We don't like the same music, he thought, but shrugged good-naturedly. "Not at all. Find something you like."

"*This* is my jam!" She smiled, finding a pop station. "Okay if I turn it up a little?"

"Whatever you want."

"Say that again," she whispered, grinning up at him.

Feeling a moment of guilt, he glanced in the rearview mirror before merging onto the highway and caught Jane's eyes again. Her face was impassive, but she looked away quickly, and he couldn't help feeling like he was somehow betraying her by sitting next to her gorgeous, captivating cousin.

No. Screw that. She doesn't get to make me feel guilty. This is

160

what she wanted. Anyway, what am I supposed to do? Make Samara Amaya go sit in the back?

"Whatever you want," he repeated, and she giggled in response, clapping her hands.

"You're adorable!" she declared. "So! I ran into Gisele at the Mondrian on Sunday night and when I told her I was shooting in Minnesota, she told me to watch out for lions and bears." She laughed again, and it was such a high-pitched, breathy, tinkly sound, he couldn't help comparing it to Jane's hoarse, raspy tone. *For first cousins, they couldn't be more different.* "Now, Lars, there aren't any lions and bears where we're going, are there?"

Wait a second. Did she just say *Minnesota*? "Um...your friend's been misinformed, I think. There aren't any lions in *Montana*. Not like the kind in Africa. I mean, there are *mountain* lions, but we call them cougars."

"Cougars! Oh, my God! That's *so* funny!"

"Why's that?"

"Because...that's what you call..." That tinkly giggle again, accompanied by the clinking sound of her bracelets as she gestured to him. "You know...um, oh, never mind. This is *fascinating*. Keep talking, Lars."

"Well, uh, cougars are the biggest cats in Yellowstone. And yes, Miss Amaya, there are bears—"

"No more *Miss Amaya*!" she scolded, reaching over to caress the muscles on his bare forearm from the elbow to his wrist then back again. "*Samara*. We're going to be *good* friends, remember?"

A shiver went down his back and goose bumps rose up

on his arm beneath her fingers. It was a reaction to being touched, and not one that he could help, but it made him feel fickle all the same. *Wildlife. She's asking you about wildlife.*

"Ahem, there *are* bears, however, um, Samara. Grizzly, brown, black—"

"You're so big and brave," she interrupted. "Promise you'll keep me safe? Protect me with your life?"

"We're very careful with the talent that comes through," he replied, clearing his throat.

"Well," she murmured, "I am a *very* talented girl."

He glanced at her and she giggled again, reaching into her bag for something. After digging around for a moment, her head snapped up and she bellowed, staring straight ahead: "JANE! WATER!"

Lars jumped in surprise, turning his head sharply to Samara, thrown off by the sudden change in her tone. In a split second, she'd gone from adoring client to demanding harpy. A bottle of water appeared on the bolster between Lars and Samara, and she grabbed it, unscrewing the top and taking a big gulp before turning back to Lars.

"My throat is just *so dry* from that flight." She tilted her head to the side, coyly, and grinned, wetting her lips with her tongue and lowering her eyes. "Now, tell me more about the cougars in Minnesota. Then maybe I'll tell *you* about the ones in New York. Deal?"

He nodded, trying to ignore the uncomfortable feeling that the space between Samara and Jane might be more of a minefield than he could handle.

***

Jane tried not to look at them, sitting side by side in the front seats.

She could hear a low buzz of chit-chat, but Sara had purposely turned up the music to muffle their conversation. She touched Lars's arm and Jane fought the deep, screaming instinct to leap over the seat and grab a handful of her cousin's glossy black hair and slam her pretty face into the dashboard.

Sara was an accomplished flirt, very good at showing men the side of her that they most wanted to see, and hiding the real—immature, demanding, selfish—person that Jane knew her to be. But the reality was that men wanted Sara when she *wasn't* flirting; they still wanted her when she was being disgusting, being impossible. When she turned on the charm, they were putty, and from what she could gather, Lars was no different, quickly succumbing to her cousin's charms. Jane looked out the window despondently.

Buzz, buzz. She reached for the phone in her back pocket.

Don't let it get to u, girl.

Ray was texting her from the seat beside her.

Jane glanced at him, but he was still, as if quietly enthralled by something he was reading on his phone, his body mostly turned away from her toward the window.

She wrote back: *Can't help it. Hurts.*

Now, I know u didn't fall for him that hard.

Might have.

Jane. Have u lost ur ever-loving mind?

Yes. Clearly.

U gonna let her have him?

Like I have a choice.

Always a choice, sugar.

Jane breathed deeply and leaned her head against the window, putting her phone under her leg where it buzzed twice more in quick succession. She ignored it and Ray stopped texting.

She'd be lying if she said that she didn't look for the words *I'm not that guy* in her head, but they were getting softer and softer now. It was just a matter of time before he made a move on Sara, before she lost him for good.

Well, Jane, at least you didn't sleep with him this time. At least there's that. A few kisses will be easier to forget.

She closed her eyes, her fingers reaching up on their own to touch her lips gingerly, rubbing them like she was putting on lip gloss. It had only been a few hours ago that she woke up beside him and he leaned over to kiss her lips good morning.

Always a choice, sugar.

Jane looked up to the front seat in time to see Sara clutch his arm again, playfully, and then she said something that made them both laugh.

No. No there isn't a choice. There never is.

The only "choice" had been to let him go.

She comforted herself that at least she'd gotten that right.

***

By the time Lars pulled up in front of the cottage, he was starting to feel very, very confused.

Aside from the time she had barked the word "WATER" at Jane, Samara was charming and funny, telling her own silly stories and listening to his. Not to mention, she gave new meaning to the word *beautiful*. What man could sit next to the supermodel, Samara Amaya, for an hour and a half, chatting with her and making her laugh, and not get a little high on the attention?

"Lars? Lars!" He looked in the rearview mirror, yanking the keys out of the ignition.

Jane had been explaining the accommodations to Samara, Sebastian and Ray, and Lars was so lost in his thoughts, he didn't realize she had finished speaking and was waiting for him to open the doors and help with the luggage. He nodded at her and jumped out of the van, slamming the door behind him, angry with himself for getting distracted.

He walked around the back of the van to open the sliding door first. Sebastian stepped out, stretching, then Ray, then Jane.

Jane stood half-crouched in the doorway, her battered Red Socks cap covering her curls and her mossy eyes flat when they met his. Lars put out his hand and it stung a little when Jane hesitated before taking it. But when he touched her, sliding her hand into his as she had last night when they danced to "Woman," a fierce longing for her clenched his heart, stronger and more visceral than any emotion he'd felt sitting beside Samara Amaya for ninety minutes.

Do you feel it too, Jane, this tremendous chemistry between us?

When his eyes skimmed back up to her face, he saw the confusion there, but something else too: compassion, maybe? Or pity? Dropping her hand like it was on fire, he backed away from her, feeling hurt. *You don't want me? Fine. But I don't need you feeling sorry for me, Jane.*

"Janie, darling! We don't have all day!" Samara called from the front seat.

Lars turned his back on Jane and moved to open Samara's door. She swung her legs out of the door in one elegant, pivot, reaching out her hand. Lars took it, offering her a wide smile.

"Thanks," Samara winked at him, lacing her fingers through his, and with a small note of disappointment, Lars realized that touching Samara's hand was nothing like touching Jane's. For all of her sexiness and beauty, he felt…nothing.

"Jane. Janie!" she cried, looking at her cousin with delicately furrowed brows. "How strange! My cell phone has *four bars* here. Didn't you say there was no service here? Wasn't that why you couldn't write back to me?"

"Oh, well, like I told you, we got that fixed. I'll, um, I'll have to call the governor and thank him for working so quickly to make sure you're comfortable," Jane answered, glancing at their laced hands for a pregnant moment before looking back at her cousin. "When I told him *Samara Amaya* was coming to *Minnesota*, he said he would *move mountains* to get cell service here in time. I heard some machinery last night and voila! Mountains were moved. Just for you." She turned to him, her expression salty. "Lars, did you hear? Gardiner has cell phone service now."

Everything she'd said, in such a deadpan voice, was so

absurd, he couldn't help smiling at her. "Go, Minnesota!"

Samara looked back and forth between him and her cousin with narrowed eyes, uncertainty passing over her pretty face before she smiled brightly and shrugged.

"What a relief that you were able to take care of it, Jane. Such a capable little mouse. What would I do without you?"

Lars noticed that Samara didn't say much as Jane showed her around the cottage. She nodded, her face unreadable but for the occasional tight smile she offered Lars as Jane pointed out the improvements that had been made in time for her arrival.

Now, Samara wasn't exactly jumping up and down with delight, but she certainly wasn't yelling or screaming or carrying on in protest either as Jane had led him to expect. No tantrums. No throwing things. No prima donna behavior whatsoever.

Hmmm. Lars started to wonder how much of Jane's complicated relationship with Samara was based on pure and simple jealousy. Samara was strikingly lovely, confident and charming, while Jane was smarter, sharper and more down-to-earth. Maybe Jane had some seriously bitter feelings about being the girl-next-door beside her drop-dead-beautiful cousin?

Had Jane set up Samara, purposely implying that she was difficult to put her cousin at a disadvantage in his eyes? None of what Jane had implied about her cousin appeared to be true. Samara seemed like a genuinely nice person, especially for a celebrity. It made him feel a little disappointed in Jane, and a little protective toward Samara.

Lars couldn't account for the disconnect, and there were really only two reasons: either Jane was jealous of Samara and had misrepresented her, or Jane had told the truth and Samara was hiding her true nature. But, Lars, who had just spent two hours in her company, didn't see how that was possible, which meant that he had to consider the possibility that Jane, whom he had liked so much based on *who* she was, wasn't really who he thought she was at all.

***

Jane watched out the cottage window as Lars pulled away to take Ray and Sebastian to the Best Western. After that, he'd go back up to Bozeman to pick up the rest of Sara's team, who were coming in on a later flight. It was unlikely Jane would see him again today. Her shoulders slumped with exhaustion and sorrow.

She could already feel the change in him, the confusion, the migration from liking her to liking Sara. The way he had pulled back from her after offering her his hand, running to do Sara's bidding. He was still angry at her for breaking things off between them, but he was backing away from her too. She could also read the puzzlement in his eyes, and she was sorry for that. The thoughts he must be having and the feelings he was trying to process would be difficult and conflicting for him, but she had seen it all before, and she knew that he would resolve them in Sara's favor. She was a modern-day siren, and no man could reject the spell Sara was capable of casting. There were no exceptions.

Jane sighed as the van drove out of sight, a cloud of dust the only visible reminder that he'd even been there at all.

"*Are. You. Fucking. Crazy?*"

A glass flew by Jane's head and smashed into the wall beside her. She jumped, her heart thumping with shock. She had noticed Samara's tight-lipped assessment of the little cottage and knew she was unhappy, but Jane hadn't braced herself for her cousin's first tantrum. She turned to face Sara, who stood across the room with her hands on her hips, her pretty face red and snarling.

"I will *not* stay here, Jane, in this *fucking* rickrack *hovel*. Fix this. Now."

Jane took a deep breath to calm herself, blinking at the shards of glass on the floor. "I can't. We're in the middle of nowhere. There's nowhere else to stay unless you want a hotel room."

She squatted down, picking up the larger pieces of broken glass first. She'd need to see if there was a vacuum hidden somewhere in the small cottage. Sara liked to go barefooted.

"I don't stay in *fucking* motels, and I *refuse* to stay in this, this, Kozy Kabin SHIT HOLE." She pointed at Jane. "You are *enjoying* this, you little bitch."

"I assure you, Sara…I'm not." Jane crossed to the kitchen, opened the garbage can, and threw the pieces in. *Rise above it, Jane. Rise above it.*

"Don't you *dare* talk back to me. You fucking are if I *say* you are, you worthless piece of shit." Sara leaned over the kitchen counter, eyes bulging, and nostrils flared. "Tell me this, Jane: What the *fuck* were you doing out here for three days if *this* is what you have to show for it?"

"Unpacking your bags, taking photos of your locations, getting groceries for you…" …*falling for Lars, seeing fireworks, feeling fireworks…*

Jane turned to rinse her hands in the sink, but Sara had already seen her face. She sidled up alongside Jane, her eyes boring into Jane's head. She leaned forward until Jane felt her cousin's breath on her ear.

"You can't have him, Janie," she hummed. "You know that, don't you?"

Jane stared at the water running over her hands. She didn't feel any physical pain, but she must have nicked herself on some glass because she saw some red streaks swirl down the drain.

"How do *you* like it?" asked Sara. "A little taste of your own medicine…cousin."

Jane turned off the water and turned, standing with her hip against the sink as she stared back at Sara. This was familiar territory, though it had been a while since Sara had lodged this particular attack.

"I never took anything away from you, Sara," said Jane softly.

"Fuck you." Sara raised one perfect, delicate eyebrow. "You took *everything* away from me."

Tears filled her eyes, as she remembered the awful day she'd been told that her life as she knew it was over: that she'd have to move to Boston to live with her uncle, aunt, and cousin.

She'd visited with her father's brother and his family

every summer, of course, but she was unprepared for the impact of seeing her uncle's face after her father's death. His face, practically identical to her father's, had been so familiar, so beloved, such a relief. Looking into his eyes was the only thing that comforted Jane, and made sense in a world that had tumbled down around her. As a ten-year-old orphan, she had bonded fiercely to her uncle Mays, staring at his face unobserved for long moments, quietly pretending that he was her father returned to her. And her uncle, who grieved terribly the loss of his brother, tried to treat Jane as much like his own daughter as possible. That was a problem for young Sara, of course. She'd never forgiven Jane for "stealing" her father.

"I had nowhere else to go," whispered Jane. "I was ten years old."

"Poor little Janie," Sara cooed, running the back of her hand over Jane's cheek. "Poor little orphan. Plain Jane, my poor, pathetic, unloved, little cousin."

Something snapped inside of Jane and she reached up and took Sara's wrist, firmly moving it from her head. "I may have the *distinct* misfortune of being your cousin. And I may be plain and little. But I'm *not* pathetic—"

"And not that little," Sara mocked under her breath, wrestling her wrist out of Jane's grasp and massaging it.

"—and I'm *not* unloved," she added, twisting the knife. "Your father loves me *like his own*. You know that better than anyone, *Sara*, don't you?"

Her comment hit its mark soundly and she watched as Sara raised her head slowly, eyes narrowed, her lips in a tight thin line.

Jane's heart skipped a beat and her face flushed. *Where had that sudden backbone come from?* Jane knew she *had* a backbone, but rarely did it surface in reaction to her cousin. Almost never. She had made it a point to treat her position with Sara with as much calmness, professionalism and forbearance as possible because she knew it was what her uncle expected from her. But, it felt so wonderful—and so liberating!—to strike back, she could feel one of several small, tight threads binding Jane to her cousin…snap. The relief of it made her quiver, almost made her sigh.

Looking up, Jane shivered, taking in Sara's flinty expression, and while she didn't regret her words, she braced herself for a slap, either actual or rhetorical.

Unexpectedly, Sara's face neutralized before her, but her voice was a low, spiteful whisper when she spoke. "You can't have him, Jane. Lars, the tour guide? He's mine. You know *that* better than anyone, don't you?"

Jane clenched her jaw, blinking at her cousin, hating her with every cell in her body.

"I tell you what, sweet, little cousin," Sara continued, "if I have to stay here in this shit hole, you'll have to stay here too. On the couch. In case I need you." She smiled at Jane before turning on her heel and heading back to her bedroom. When she got to the bedroom door, she looked back at Jane and winked. "Front row seat for you, Janie. Hope you packed your earplugs."

***

I hate her.

IhateherIhateherIhateher.

Jane took a deep breath and plopped back down on the couch. Her phone buzzed and she fished it out of her back pocket, glancing at it.

If Miss Thing gets on ur last nerve, come find me at the Ritz.

Jane couldn't help a soft chuckle. Ray must be settling into the Best Western.

Lars would be headed back up to Bozeman by now to pick up the rest of Sara's team. Jane would walk over to the hotel to make sure they were all settled in and up to date on tomorrow's schedule. The *Trend* people were coming in today too, but they were renting vans at the airport to drive themselves to Gardiner. Anyway, Sebastian would coordinate with them; Jane was only responsible for managing Sara's team.

I'll be by later, she wrote back to Ray.

For the remainder of the afternoon, Jane busied herself finalizing shoot details on her phone, verifying that Sara's on-location trailer had everything she needed and avoiding her cousin as much as possible. Mercifully, Sara stayed in her room, smoking cigarettes and watching TV.

Jane had to get out of the stifling closeness of the cottage, so she took a short walk around the four cottages, peeking in the windows of the other three. They were rough shells compared to the one Sara was staying in: the walls and ceilings weren't finished, and the floors were concrete slabs. Pipes jutted out from the walls without fixtures and electrical wires went nowhere. It made Jane realize how much work went into fixing up Sara's cottage in the week or two before her arrival.

Jane thought of Lars's face the first time he showed her the cottage and how she had laughed out loud, insisting that Sara would throw a fit when she saw it. And she had, of course, but only after Lars had gone.

Jane hated herself for breaking things off with him. She hated herself for not being strong enough to roll the dice and see what happened, for not being confident enough in his words and intentions to believe that he might actually want her. But with all that giggling and touching on the ride from the airport, Lars was probably already falling for Sara, just as Jane had predicted. Not that knowing it would happen made it hurt any less.

Looking out at the meadow where she and Lars had seen the bison, she felt a terrible heaviness squeezing her heart. It felt like a million years ago. Waking up with him in her bed this morning felt like a million years ago, too. Like a different life, in which she was a different person: the cousin that was worthy of a beautiful man's love. Somewhere in the universe—even if the odds were a million to one—that scenario must exist, right? Somewhere? At some point in time?

Suddenly, as Jane envisioned herself as the unlikely victor over Sara, a sudden, awful thought occurred to her:

What if Lars is the million to one exception?

What if, given the choice, he would have chosen me?

Would he have been true to me, if I had just let him make his own choice?

She caught her reflection in one of the picture windows

as she passed by an empty cottage, and stopped to look at herself. She looked like a short, dumpy high school boy. Average height, baggy clothes, baseball hat. Shoulders rolled forward. Head down. Defeated.

What if Lars is the exception? she asked herself again.

She took off her baseball cap, folded it in thirds and shoved it in her hip pocket. She ran her hands through her curls, until they stayed back off her face. Her face was hazy in the glass, which made it easier to see the *Felicity* thing he had alluded to. She tilted her neck to the side, and caught the twinkle of diamond studs in her ears.

She took off her sweatshirt, straightened her back and tied it around her waist. Underneath she was wearing a simple V-neck t-shirt, and underneath that, the sheer black bra she'd been wearing last night. She couldn't bear to take it off yet.

Twisting back and forth, checking herself out, she noted her long neck and attractive profile, and even the way her curls caught the sunlight. They had some golden highlights, no doubt from being outdoors more than usual over the past few days, and the unexpected glimmer of color surprised her, pleased her.

She glanced down at her jeans and wrinkled her nose. They were shapeless, awful baggy things that she had worn in college when she was fifteen freshman pounds heavier. She could do better.

Always a choice, Sugar.

She sighed, staring at her reflection.

Was it really that simple? To make a choice and stick to it?

Her doubts still plagued her, but since finding the gumption to stand up to Sara, she found they were softer and less resolute.

No, Jane could never compete with Sara in looks, but she could do better than too-big jeans, glasses she didn't really need and a shapeless sweatshirt. Not to mention, looks weren't everything. Jane had other gifts, other talents. For starters, she had a better personality than her cousin. She was smarter and funnier. She was kind, compassionate and empathetic. Less self-centered, and more selfless.

She thought of Sara's spitefulness: the way she was going after Lars not just because he was hot, but because she suspected Jane was interested in him first. It was such a shitty thing to do—something that one woman should never do to another, especially if they were family.

Jane gritted her teeth and narrowed her eyes at her reflection before heading back to Sara's cottage.

Maybe I can't have him in the end, but maybe making the decision for him wasn't the right move either.

***

Jane waited until after Sara had eaten dinner and settled herself in the bath before she walked back into town to speak to the crew at the Best Western.

The crew always bonded like a family on these editorial shoots, and Jane was always glad to see everyone assembled in one room; she appreciated their camaraderie. They met in the small conference room off the hotel lobby, and after exchanging hugs and greetings, they sat around a small table going over the shoot schedule. Jane reminded them to be alert, prompt and efficient, and to do whatever it took to make Samara Amaya shine. She also reminded them that most of them would be fired over the next two days, but that they shouldn't worry. Jane herself had lost count after being fired dozens of times in the first six months of her employment.

"You all know she doesn't mean it. She's just stressed. So, take it with a grain of salt and keep doing your job unless you hear from me, okay?"

"Girl, we all know the drill. Here's what I want to know. Is there a pool going yet on how long it takes her to get the Viking into bed?" Shanelle, Samara's hairstylist, stood beside Ray, sucking down a Diet Coke.

Jane rolled her eyes. "Really, Shan?"

"He is *fine*, honey. Mm-mm-mm."

Ray nudged Shanelle in the side. "Why you pushing me, Ray-Ray? Don't be *pushing* me around, now."

Margot, Sara's stout, cheerful costume mistress, gave Shanelle an air-high five. "If I was sixty pounds slimmer…"

"Girl," purred Ray, looking at Margot over his sunglasses, "you all sorts of foxy, sexy, fine just the way you is."

Margot beamed at Ray, absentmindedly playing with her fingers, which seemed bereft of a needle and thread whenever she was without them.

"No bets, folks. Let's just keep our focus." Jane turned to Franco. "She's going to need you in the morning. Tai chi at seven-thirty, and I got everything you need for her morning shake."

Franco's muscular physique was further accentuated by his perpetual uniform: a crisp white t-shirt under an expensive, navy blue Dolce and Gabbana tracksuit, and he owned those threads with the same aloof professionalism with which a financier wore a thousand-dollar tailored suit and tie. Everything about the over-groomed, handsome, Italian trainer screamed *confidence*. He'd only started working with Sara over the summer, but she was already dependent on his health regimen and vigorous workouts, insisting that he join them on shoots longer than two days, which was fine with Jane. The harder the workout, the more amenable her cousin.

"Thank you, Jane," he said in his mildly accented English, the ever-present trace of flirtation in his tone.

"We all done here, Superstar?" asked Ray, winking at her. "I need me some *Brokeback Mountain* action. Some of us want to go find a local martini attached to a local cowboy."

"Well, good luck with that," said Jane, wondering where exactly Ray thought he was going to chase down a martini in Gardiner. If anyone could, however, it was Ray. "Let's keep it to *one*, though, okay? Plenty of time to check out the local color this weekend while Samara's in Jackson Hole. Franco, you're going with her. Sebastian, you too. You two will share an adjacent suite. She'll have her own."

The Amangani at Jackson Hole was one of the most exclusive resorts in the country; Sara's suite alone cost $1,300 per night, and the one Sebastian and Franco would share cost $975 per night. The Amangani had a spa, workout facility, fine dining, boutiques, and every amenity a world-class pain in the—um, *supermodel* could ask for.

"I assume you'll be staying with her ladyship, Jane?" Sebastian typed the details into his calendar.

Yes. Yes, she generally stayed with Sara, on a rollaway somewhere unobtrusive so she could be available to her cousin, if needed.

I hope you packed your earplugs. Sara's evil warning skittered through Jane's mind.

While she had no idea if Lars would actually end up in Sara's bed, the chances were decent. *I'll be damned if I have to lie on a nearby rollaway listening to them. No. Absolutely not. I refuse.*

Without any warning, Jane felt a second of those tight threads snap apart inside of her. Another tie that had bound her in servitude to her cousin was broken, and a shutter of relief passed through her, making her sigh then chuckle softly with the pleasure.

"Um…no. I won't be going," she murmured. It felt exhilarating to utter the words, even as she ignored the uncertainty that accompanied them. Sara would be pissed not to have Jane at her beck and call.

Five sets of eyes were glued to her face when she looked up. Jane gulped, feeling her cheeks flush at this brash act of insubordination to her cousin.

Ray slowly lowered his sunglasses.

Sebastian looked like he might weep.

Margot looked at Shanelle and Shanelle looked at Margot, then back at Jane, wide-eyed, at a total loss.

The only person who seemed unaffected by this news was Franco, who simply stared at Jane, mildly amused.

"You're not…coming?" whispered Sebastian.

"No, I'm not. I'm going to…um…" Jane tried to organize her thoughts. *What am I going to do?* The answers came swiftly: turn off my cell phone, play euchre, sleep in my own room at the Best Western, and be a normal, regular person who isn't anyone's slave for two days. "I'm going to take a few days off. A little vacation. *Sara* can go without me."

Ray's eyes were as wide as saucers, and Sebastian adjusted his glasses, looking apoplectic, but Franco nodded at Jane with respect, his brown eyes thoughtful as he stared at her.

She smiled at all of them with more confidence than she felt. "So, Franco and Sebastian, if you need anything from me between now and Friday afternoon, please let me know. I won't be available next weekend."

They were still staring at her in silent shock, so Jane lifted her chin and asked, "Anything else?"

Amongst murmurs of no and dazed shaking heads, she buckled her backpack, and slung it back over her shoulder.

"Great. Then I'll see you all tomorrow. Remember, it's a shoot day. Bring your A game!"

Ray approached her as the others headed back to their rooms.

"So, I was just wonderin'…what did Miss Thing say about this *vacation*?" He used air quotes around the words vacation, his brown eyes unblinking.

Jane took a deep breath and let it go slowly. "She doesn't know yet."

"And when, 'zactly, are you planning to share this

glorious news with her?"

"I thought the last minute would be best." It occurred to her that she hadn't told the crew to keep it quiet until then. "You think she'll hear about it from anyone else before then?"

"Janie." Ray smiled at her sadly. "You jump on the tracks and push us out of the way over and over again. Ain't *no one* in this crew gonna say *nothing* to her. I know it ain't your strong suit, but you *can* trust us, Janie Mays."

"Thanks, Ray," she murmured, squeezing his arm in gratitude.

"You got it. And on that note, I'm off to find greener pastures." He slid his sunglasses back over his eyes as he headed out the door in pursuit of a man with a martini.

"Jane."

She turned around to find Franco standing behind her, his hands by his sides and his expression thoughtful. When he spoke, Jane realized his usual flirtatious tone was missing, replaced with a respectful baritone.

"*Mi sorprendi*, Jane. You, ah, surprise me tonight."

She and the handsome Italian trainer had never spoken much to one another aside from organizing workouts for Sara. "I'll pay for it, though, won't I?"

"Maybe." Franco nodded at her. "But-a…maybe not. You don't know this, but I have a sister. Back in Italy. She's, ah, *sorellina*, ah, younger. A quiet girl. But, ah, when she have enough of the big brothers, she finally push back to us. The thing about pushing back, Jane? You have to-a mean it. You have to-a stick to it. Yes?"

Jane stared at him, then nodded in agreement.

He patted her on the shoulder, as she imagined he would his little sister. "It's good you find a little spirit, Jane. *La Samara?*" His face transformed as his eyes darkened and his mouth curved slightly in what might have almost passed for a seductive grin had his voice not lowered to a soft growl that was more predatory than sexy. "*Lei non sa che cosa ha bisogno.*"

Jane cocked her head to the side in question. "What does that mean?"

"She don't know what she needs," he translated, holding Jane's eyes for a long, uncomfortable moment. Then, he turned his back to her, sauntering out of the room without another word.

Unsure of what to make of such a statement, Jane filed it away and concentrated on what he'd said just before: *You have to mean it. You have to stick to it.*

Walking back to Sara's cottage, Jane felt the growing change in herself and embraced it. Even knowing she was going to go back to Sara's to sleep on a hard couch wasn't enough to dim her spirits. She'd made a strong decision, a good decision, and she intended to stick with it.

Jane didn't know what in the world was coming over her, but she could feel a shift inside of her, as though she was reclaiming herself, refusing to be mistreated any more.

When she looked up, she was surprised to find herself passing the Prairie Dawn, and she slowed down, stopping to peek in the window of the coffee shop, her heart leaping with relief to see Nils and Lars sharing a table in the back.

She was sure Sara would have called him, by now, demanding *company* after her bath…but maybe she hadn't been able to track him down. Or maybe Lars had actually ignored her call. Jane stared at him through the glass, watched his face as he grinned up at his older brother then rubbed the stubble on his jaw with his calloused fingers. *Or maybe he'd even said no*, whispered her heart.

I'm not that guy.

It was a one in a million chance, she reminded herself, but couldn't help watching him unobserved for a few more quiet, precious moments before turning into the darkness and walking back to Sara.

CHAPTER 7

An early morning knock on the cottage door surprised Jane, and she reached for her phone on the coffee table in front of her. 7:10 a.m. Too early for Franco, who wouldn't be here for another twenty minutes, or Lars, who wasn't expected until eight-thirty. She could tell Sara wasn't up yet—she would have awakened Jane to make coffee.

Jane shook her head to scatter her dreams and put on her glasses, swinging her jean-clad legs over the side of the couch as the mystery guest knocked again. She had slept in her clothes, forgetting to pick up a pair of pajamas from her hotel room and too tired to walk back and forth to the hotel again once she'd reached the cottage last night. She ran a hand through her hair and padded to the door.

She was surprised, and completely delighted, to find Maggie on the doorstep, holding a cardboard tray of coffee cups.

"Maggie!"

"Heya, Jane. Brought coffee. That okay?"

"More than okay! A friendly face. You have no idea…"

"Goddamn it, Jane!"

Maggie's eyes flew open, and she craned her neck in the direction of Sara's voice. Jane cringed at Maggie, mouthing the word "Sorry!" as she peered over her shoulder at her cousin, who wore only a black camisole and black panties on her perfect body.

Sara glared at Maggie from over Jane's shoulder, narrowing her eyes and scowling. "It's fucking *early*, Jane. I still had fifteen more minutes to sleep, that I fucking needed, but no! I am fucking awakened by the sound of you and… and… and this *person* blabbing in the doorway! And I can't find my *goddamn* lip balm."

"Sorry, Sara," Jane muttered.

"My name is *SAMARA*. Don't *fuck* with me this morning, Jane. *Who. Thefuck. Is. This?*" She flicked her fingers at Maggie like she was shoo-ing away a fly.

"This is Maggie," said Jane. "And she's kindly brought us coffee. Do you *want* coffee?"

Sara pursed her lips, asking in an imperial whisper, enunciating her words carefully, "Where the *fuck* is my Burt's Bees Island lip balm, Jane?"

"Calm down. I'll find it for you. *Do. You. Want. Coffee. Or. Not?*" She enunciated her words just as carefully and bitchily as Sara had.

Sara approached Maggie. "Do you *own* a clock? Do you *know* how early it is to be knocking on someone's goddamned door?"

Maggie's eyes were so wide, Jane thought they might pop out of her head.

"Stare much?" Sara blew a raspberry at Maggie, and Maggie was jolted out of her trance. "Which one is my latte? Did you at least get my *fucking* coffee order right, Jane?"

Maggie tapped on the lid of one of the four cups, her

finger lightly trembling.

"Thank, Christ." Sara grabbed the coffee off the tray then sauntered back to her room, booming, "Burt's *fucking* Bees!" in her wake.

Jane turned back to Maggie, whose mouth and eyes were frozen open in shock, and offered her an awkward smile. "She's not a…morning person. Come on in?"

Maggie shook her head. "No, thanks."

"I'll come out, then. Just give me a sec?"

Maggie took a ragged breath and nodded, backing away from the door.

Jane followed Sara to her room, where she found her cousin on the bed watching MTV, ashing her cigarette into the plastic top of her coffee cup. Her room was already a complete mess, clothes strewn everywhere, magazines spread out on the bed, smoke drifting toward the ceiling. Jane raised both windows, watching the smoke make a hasty escape into the cool morning air. She opened the drawer of the bedside table, grabbing four different lip balms, and depositing them in front of her cousin without a word. She took the empty glass tumbler next to Sara's bed and switched it out for the plastic cap, which she carefully threw in the garbage.

"Franco won't like it that you were smoking," she said.

"Shut up, Jane. I'll shower before he gets here."

"He'll smell it."

"What about the words 'shut up' wasn't clear?"

"Do you need anything else?"

"*Do you need anything else?*" Sara mimicked. "No. Get out."

Jane's new backbone considered telling her cousin to go screw herself, but she thought of Maggie waiting outside and wasn't anxious for another showdown with Sara in earshot of her new friend. She backed out of the room, closing the door behind her.

Returning to the living room, she shrugged into her jacket and found Maggie outside, leaning against the hood of her car, the other three coffees sitting next to her.

"Are you okay?" Maggie looked at Jane, her eyes wide with concern.

"Oh, yeah." Jane nodded, wrapping her arms, crossed, around her chest. "She's just—"

"A roarin', flamin' slag."

"Um…yeah. She is." Jane giggled. "You've got a way with words, Maggie."

Maggie's accent thickened appreciably with disdain. "I wouldn'a believed it if I hadn'a seen it with me own eyes, Jane. So bonnie, but what a gob! Is she *always* like that?"

Jane shrugged. "Sometimes worse. Sometimes better. She doesn't like the cottage. She doesn't like waking up early. She doesn't like me."

"How do you handle it? That—that *abuse*?"

"It pays the bills."

"It's disgraceful."

"I'm used to it."

"Well, that's a bloody shame, Jane."

"It is what it is. I don't have—I mean, Sara and her folks are all the family I've got. When my uncle asked me to help her in high school, I wrote a few essays for her. When he asked me to help with her career, I signed on as her assistant. I couldn't say no to him."

It felt good to unburden herself to Maggie, but in truth, she'd done a lot more than write a few essays. She'd essentially handled her homework and Sara's, and when Sara got special permission to take her final exams at home so that schoolwork wouldn't interfere with her modeling commitments, Jane had helped with those too.

Jane *always* acquiesced whenever her uncle asked for help on Sara's behalf. It was impossible for Jane to say no to him. When she looked into the beleaguered eyes of her dead father in her uncle's beloved face, she'd say yes to just about anything.

Maggie cleared her throat and Jane looked up at her.

"It's none o' my business, Jane. But, I think it's *time* to start sayin' no." Maggie picked up the tray of coffee. "Didn't know what you liked. Cappuccino's there. Black coffee here. With milk and sweet there."

Jane picked up the black coffee and sipped, savoring the rich, bitter warmth.

"Thanks, Maggie."

Maggie checked her watch, then grimaced. "I've got somewhere to be, but I have a few minutes. Have time for a story? About how I ended up here?"

Jane nodded, closing her eyes, enjoying the morning sun on her face, the cool, fresh air, the soft burr in Maggie's voice, hopeful that MTV would prove compelling for at least another ten minutes, or until Franco arrived.

"My aunt Lily bought the Prairie Dawn, years and years

ago. She was me mum's eldest sister, and she trail blazed here to Montana in the 70s, after readin' about Yellowstone in a magazine. Left her family and went on a grand adventure. Married a month later to a man she barely knew but loved with all her heart. Opened a tea room the month after that and decorated it with books when the library in Big Sky closed down. Within a year, her new husband died of exposure durin' a winter hike, and she was left alone. And for twenty-some-odd years she ran the Prairie Dawn. Everyone knew her, everyone loved her, and this town became her family, her life.

"Five years ago, she wrote to me mum. She was sick and she knew she was dyin', but she was too far gone to go back to Scotland. She asked if my mum would come and take over the café, but mum didn't want to leave Scotland. But I did. So, I came here to do for her until the end and inherited the cafe. This is my home now.

"I left my family, Jane. Left them all behind, and it doesn't mean I don't love them…it means I had to make me own way, just like Lily did. I won't tell you it wasn't scary. It was, at times. There are—" Maggie paused, biting her lower lip for a moment before finishing. "There are still times it scares me that I could lose what I've built here because I love it so much. But it didn't fall into my lap. At some points—at *many* points—I had to choose it. I *chose* the life I wanted."

"You're saying I should quit my job and find a new life?"

"I asked how you handle that kind of abuse. You gave

me some song and dance about family. That's *not* family, Jane, how that she-devil just spoke to you. I dinna know what it is, but it's *not* family." She took a deep breath and let it go slowly. "You dinna seem happy, Jane. And if you're not happy, then aye, it's time for a change. It's time to choose the life you want, not just tolerate the one you have."

Maggie was several years older than Jane, and Jane had a sudden fantasy of what it would have been like to have a cousin like Maggie instead of a cousin like Sara. Older, wiser, kinder. Maggie wouldn't have been threatened by ten-year-old Jane because she would have been in college; she would have come home on her breaks and told Jane about her boyfriends and professors and—

"You're daydreamin' now. Hopefully of a life that doesn't include *that* piece 'o work." Her sour expression gentled and she smiled at Jane, tilting her head to the side. "How're things with Lars?"

Jane winced, lifting her cup to her lips and sipping slowly.

"Paul said he saw you two nippin' at the park on Monday night before the fireworks."

"It wouldn't have worked out." Jane said softly, looking meaningfully at the cottage before taking a bitter sip of coffee. "I broke it off. I told him I needed time, but it was really just letting him go, saving him the trouble of having to break things off with me once he met her and—"

"Wait a bleedin' moment. You're not sayin'—I mean, Lars doesn't—Jane, does Lars have an eye for that…that…" Maggie's face was getting flushed and indignant.

"I don't know. But Sara wants *him*. I know that for sure…which means it's just a matter of time before they…" She shrugged, feeling miserable. "He certainly seemed captivated with her yesterday, and she's…she's gorgeous. You saw her."

"Aye! An' *heard* her too!"

"Well, she's not like that around him. Sara's very good at showing a different face to different people. To him, she's beautiful and adorable, fawning all over him and hanging on every word. He'll never see the side of her you saw. She'll make sure of it. She'll be charming."

Maggie lifted the tray off the hood of her car, opening her car door and putting the cups gently on the passenger seat. "She's charmin' and I'm English. We'll just see about this, Jane. She's puir trouble and no mistake."

Maggie bussed Jane on the cheek before getting into her car and rolling down the window. "The Prairie's closed all day tomorrow, but we'll still have euchre tomorrow night! I expect to see you there, Jane. Tell that witch to go t'the devil if she doesn't like it!"

***

Lars wasn't surprised to see Maggie walk into the Lindstrom & Sons office with coffee. She came by now and then when the Prairie Dawn was quiet.

"Good morning, Maggie May!" said Lars's father in greeting.

"Heya, Mr. Lindstrom. I had two extra coffees and dinna want them to go to waste. I figure you can fight over 'em." She put the tray holding two cups on Karl's desk and winked at him.

Nils looked up from a transportation schedule he was reviewing, and Lars could practically *see* the sparks fly between his brother and the redheaded barista, but per usual, Nils did nothing about it.

"Pop," said Nils, still looking at the schedule. "You remember I'm taking a vacation day tomorrow, right?"

"Yup. Lars'll handle the talent and I'll drive the others. Where're you—"

"Did you want the other coffee, Nils?" interrupted Maggie.

"Sure," he said, standing up. "What'd you bring?"

"Leftovers. Jane, the wee, sweet lassie took the black one. The *pain in the arse* took the latte. There's two left."

"The—the *what*?" Lars stood up from the loveseat in front of his father's desk, staring at Maggie's back.

Maggie looked around at Lars with a meaningful purse to her lips then glanced at his father.

"Oh. Sorry, Mr. Lindstrom. The *talent* took the latte," she amended, smiling sweetly at Mr. Lindstrom. She glanced back at Lars. "The smokin', screamin', cursin' pain in the arse of talent who treats our Jane like rubbish. That one."

"Are you talking about *Samara*?" demanded Lars, crossing his arms over his chest. The same Samara who was so easygoing and funny in the van yesterday? Who liked the cottage far more than Jane thought she would? Who didn't have a negative word or glance for anyone the entire time Lars was in her company?

"Aye. The very one."

Nils, still standing by the tray of coffees, searching Maggie's face. "She screamed and cursed at *you*, Maggie May?"

Maggie took a deep breath and tapped her index finger on her chin, considering. "Aye, she did. She snarled, 'Do ye own a clock?' at me, and she asked, 'Stare much?' She blew a raspberry at me face and then she said, 'Did ye at least get me feckin' coffee right?' Oh, wait. I guess she actually said that last part to our Jane."

Nils furrowed his brow looking at Lars. "I don't like it. I don't care if she's talent or not. She has no cause to curse at Maggie. I don't care who the heck she is."

Maggie smiled at Nils, her face softening. "Dinna worry for me, Nils. Jane got the brunt of it, poor lass."

Lars wasn't sure what to make of this new information, but he didn't like it. Suddenly Maggie turned to him, pulling at his arm. "Come for a walk to the Prairie Dawn, Lars. I'll make you a coffee, too. Whatever you like."

"Yeah, uh…okay."

Maggie grinned at Nils for a second, then turned and headed out the door, with Lars falling into step beside her.

"Can't figure you two out to save my damn life," said Lars, glancing at her. "You and my brother."

She crossed her arms. "I dinna want to talk about Nils. Brother or not, it's none of your business."

"Fair enough."

"No, wait. I take it back. I *do* want to say somethin' about Nils. He never offered me anythin' but friendship. Never led me down the garden path. Never kissed me in public, at the park, durin' the fireworks, in front of the whole town. Never—"

Lars interrupted her with a soft growl. "Now who's sticking her nose in someone else's business?"

"I am."

"Well, Miss Smarty-Pants, you don't know what you're talking about. *She* broke things off, Maggie, not me. She's not interested. I promise you she's not. She said as much yesterday and barely looked at me after. Blamed it on work. Blamed it on her cousin. But, come on, I know when I'm being blown off. I know when I'm being let down easily. *I* do it often enough."

"If you think that's a blow off, you're daft, Lars. You're a bloody fool."

"Am I?"

"You are."

"Well, thanks for that. Great talk. I think I'll head back to the office and get my own cup of crappy coffee."

Maggie put her hand on his arm. "I dinna mean to rile you, Lars. And you're right: I dinna know all the details of what passed between you. But you wouldn't believe what she puts up with, our Jane. Her cousin is a bloody nightmare."

Lars took a deep breath and huffed softly.

"Jane pushed *me* away. Not the other way around. And Samara? Well, I hate to break it to you, but, Samara's gracious and warm, as beautiful as she is charming."

"You're callin' me a liar?"

"No! Not at all! But maybe you took their exchange out of context, Maggie. You know, cousins are like siblings.

They can be rough on each other. It's not our business to judge them."

"Och! Ye think I'm judgin' them unfairly?' Aye, of course. Now, I'm rememberin' all the times ye lads called yer Jenny a *feckin' bitch*. Sure. Of course."

Lars bristled even hearing the words come out of Maggie's mouth. No way, no how any of the Lindstrom men would use that kind of language in conjunction with their sister. It was unthinkable.

"You're saying that's the sort of language Samara and Jane used with each other?"

"Not with *each other*. One *uses* it. The other *takes* it." They had arrived at the Prairie Dawn and Maggie stopped, her hand on the door, looking up at Lars. "Will you do me a favor, Lars? Keep your eyes open. She's not who you think she is, this Samara Amaya. Dinna be taken in by a pretty face and pretty ways."

"Is that what this is all about?" asked Lars. "You don't like her because she's pretty? I'm surprised at you, Maggie."

Maggie's brow furrowed as she stared at him, as stunned as if he'd slapped her. For a minute he thought she might tell him off for the accusation in his words, but her face softened in concern.

"I'm your friend, Lars. I'm tellin' you two things: One, there's a wicked, dark side to this Samara character. And two, if you like our Jane, dinna give up on her yet. There's a lot more goin' on between those two than you know."

She patted his arm gently then opened the door. Lars trailed behind her feeling frustrated and confused.

Maggie had no reason to lie to him. She was a trusted family friend. But he couldn't reconcile the picture she was painting of Samara with the engaging young woman he had met yesterday. And he wasn't about to base his opinion of her on hearsay, even if the source was trusted and well-intentioned. Maybe, as he had suggested, the cousins used rougher language with each other than either he, or Maggie, was used to. Maybe it only seemed abusive, when it was just part of their family banter.

It still bothered him quite a lot that Jane had broken things off without giving him a chance to weigh in on the decision—his anger toward her was strong and authentic. He'd genuinely liked her snappy retorts and funny observations, pretty green eyes and soft brown curls. Despite how different the cousins were in appearance, he didn't want Jane any less after meeting Samara. He liked her as much this morning as he had while waking up beside her yesterday morning. Jane had felt organic in his life, like a missing puzzle piece. There was strength and certainty in how easily he had fallen for her; in how comfortable and right and *hot* it felt being with her, in how *possible* she felt to him.

But she'd made her feelings clear: She didn't trust him, she didn't want him, and her decision to force him from her life had hurt him deeply. If anything, Samara's enthusiastic attention to him offered a balm to that pain.

Maggie asked what he wanted, and Lars ordered a black coffee with a shot of espresso, leaning with his back up against the bar as the early morning sun streamed into the windows of the Prairie Dawn.

Don't give up on her yet.

Maggie's worlds circled round and round in Lars's head.

He just wished Jane had given him a reason not to.

***

Maybe it's time to start sayin' no.

Jane *wished* she had said a big, old-fashioned "no" to riding with Sara and Lars this morning, but Sara was making a point. She had called the Lindstroms, insisting that she and Jane wanted to ride separately from the rest of her team, which meant that while Mr. Lindstrom drove the rest of the crew in the van, Lars had been forced to pick up Jane and Sara in his truck.

They all had to sit together in the front seat, and Sara spent the entire time pressed up against Lars, asking him about the other celebrities he had met over the years, while Jane busied herself with her phone or stared out the window. It was a singular type of torture to overhear the conversation as Lars told her cousin animated stories, leaving Jane out entirely. The only upswing was that it solidified her decision not to go to Jackson Hole, and even helped fortify her courage to break the news to Sara. Her challenge now was to keep the news to herself for as long as possible so that Sara's mood on the shoot days wouldn't be affected.

Let's just get through Wednesday and Thursday first.

Friday will be here soon enough, and I'll tell her I won't be going.

When they got to the Sheepeater Cliffs, Jane jumped out of the truck before Lars even opened his door and watched from a distance as Sara insisted that he show her to her trailer, personally. Lars had looked back at Jane, giving her an inscrutable look, but Jane looked away, heading to the *Trend* people to get an idea of how they wanted to start the day. She ignored the ache of longing in her heart as she watched Lars walk away with Sara.

You knew how this would go, Jane, and you protected yourself as best you could.

No regrets this time.

***

Shoot days were always heavy on employee casualties.

They started early, ended late, and everyone had to be on their toes, from Sara and her crew to the photographers, stylists and assistants from *Trend*. Losing focus could mean losing the perfect light, the perfect shot. The pressure to do everything flawlessly was relentless until the day was over, and it was up to Jane to keep Sara's team on their collective game.

Sebastian was the first to be fired, quickly followed by Margot, then Shanelle. Margot and Shanelle were rehired when Sara realized she couldn't finish her hair on her own, and she needed to be sewn into one of her outfits. By midday, Sebastian was mopping his sweaty forehead, nervously pacing back and forth in front of Sara's trailer, and Jane asked herself for the hundredth time why he always wore silk when it didn't breathe well.

"Sebastian, invest in some linen," she quipped.

"Very funny, Jane. See how *you* feel when *you're* fired."

"Oh, I've already been fired twice today."

"JANE! WATER! NOW!" Sara screeched from her trailer.

"But, obviously, it didn't stick." She punched Sebastian playfully on a silken arm. "Chin up, pal. She'll retract it by dinnertime."

Trend's stylist, Amy, pulled Jane aside as she approached the Kraft table for a bottle of water. "She going to be ready soon, Jane?"

"Makeup's done. Hair's almost done. Margot's sewing her in. You know Samara."

Amy rolled her eyes. "I know *of* Samara. All I really *know* is you, Jane, and you make things easy, kid."

Jane grinned, grabbing a water bottle as she gestured to the landscape. "I love the concept for this shoot, by the way."

The shoot concept was "Go Green: Transformed by Nature" and the story was that Sara was an edgy girl from New York exploring a national park for the first time. The shoot would start with edgy, urban clothes shot against the stark beauty of the basalt columns, which meant to mimic the chrome and steel in Manhattan. Then, gradually, Sara's clothes, hair and makeup would morph into a more natural beauty as the landscapes became more lush and colorful behind her, until she was completely transformed by the park in the final shots by Yellowstone Lake, almost one with the nature that surrounded her.

Today's shoot had Sara's black hair in a slick ponytail styled high on her head, harsh, futuristic black, white and grey tones in her makeup, and monochromatic sets of clothes and accessories. When Jane had last checked on her, Shanelle was getting the ponytail perfect and Margot was sewing Sara into a black cropped jacket which she wore over a long grey skirt with black military-style lace-up boots.

"I'm wondering if three changes today was too aggressive?" asked Amy. "We're only on the second and it's already two o'clock."

"Don't worry," said Jane, "Samara's a pro, and the light looks great."

Amy looked at the sun. "Can't have the sunset on the cliffs. The warm light wouldn't work. Needs to be cold and stark."

"It'll be okay. Sun sets later here." Jane smiled at the nervous stylist, putting her hand gently on the other woman's arm. "I'll go hurry things along, okay?"

"You're the best, Janie."

Jane headed for Sara's trailer, noticing that Lars's truck, which had left the set for a couple of hours, was back. One of the backup generators that fed power to the strobes had failed, and he had been sent back into Gardiner to get a new one from the local hardware store. She wondered when he had gotten back.

"WATER! NOW!" The sweet sound of her cousin's lilting call broke through her reverie, as Jane headed back to Sara's air-conditioned trailer.

"Amy's getting antsy." She put the bottle of water on the small vanity table beside her cousin.

"Useless," Sara muttered, picking up the bottle and taking a careful swig so she wouldn't ruin her makeup. "Hurry up, Margot. I bet if you had to eat a bowl of chips instead of sew my jacket, you'd move your fat ass a whole lot faster."

Margot leaned in toward Sara and bit the end of the thread. "All set."

"Ugh! I hate when you do that. You think I want your big fat lips touching me? I'm not a lezbo, Margot. Think again." As Margot backed up into a corner of the trailer, Jane saw tears in her eyes. Oblivious, Sara apprised herself in the mirror. "Good, I guess. Took you long enough."

"You look great," Jane offered, looking over at Margot sympathetically. "Great job, Margot."

"Whatever, ass-kisser." Sara glanced over at Jane. "Did you pack my purple lace Vicky undies?"

You mean your favorite one-night-stand undies?

"Yep."

"When we get back, put them out for me. I want them for tonight."

"Is that right?"

"Mmm." She smoothed a nonexistent stray hair and pursed her lips, then turned from the mirror looking at Jane. "Lars is coming over later."

Jane wanted to clamp her eyes shut against the tears that suddenly brightened her eyes, but she didn't. She felt them water, but otherwise kept her face as neutral as possible. "Anything else?"

"Mmm. Champagne."

"Already in your fridge."

Sara smiled at Jane sarcastically. "Always so efficient."

Margot held out a pair of sleek, black leather gloves. Sara slipped them on, then pumped her fists twice to stretch them a little.

"And plan to take a hike from, uh, eight to ten. That should be enough time for us to, you know…unless you *want* to listen." She patted Jane's cheek with one gloved hand, making a pouty face. "Aw, Janie. It was coming at you like a freight train, little cousin. You were smart to get out of the way. You always were the smart one."

Sara flounced out the trailer door to take more pictures with Margot following behind. It slammed shut and Jane found herself alone.

Lars is spending the night with Sara.

She caught her reflection in the vanity mirror and sat down gingerly, looking at her face. She was still wearing the same clothes she had on yesterday and hadn't had a chance to shower yet today. She looked rumpled, sad and tired, watching tears pool in her shiny eyes. Her lip quivered as a wave of self-pity overcame her, and she ground her teeth together to keep from crying. She took off her cap, running her fingers over the tattered, used-to-be-fuzzy, red "B" lovingly, remembering the cap perched on her father's balding head. She hung it on the side of Sara's mirror and ran her hands through her hair, bowing her head, still willing the useless tears not to fall.

***

Lars stood at a respectful distance from the photographer, assistants, and equipment, watching Samara pose in front of the basalt columns of Sheepeater Cliffs.

She looked like the powerful heroine of a futuristic science fiction movie: leather boots and leather gloves, with a skimpy black jacket that showed her taut abdomen and a flowing grey skirt that moved and swayed with the breeze of the day. She struck pose after pose without complaining, taking direction from the photographer, and giving him exactly what he asked for.

"Pout, Samara!"

"Now, sexy. Make me want you, darling. That's it. That's it. Stunning."

"Surprised. No, not over-the-top, just a little."

"Show me bored, but keep it alive. Beautiful, darling."

Lars realized, with some admiration, that she was very good at what she did, and it was fascinating to watch her face change completely on a dime at someone else's request. It took skill and talent.

Lars was still feeling confused about Maggie's warning from this morning, but couldn't reconcile her description of Samara with the warm, accessible person he met again today. She sat in the front seat of the truck next to him on the way to the shoot, asking him questions about other celebrities and sharing inside information about them.

He liked her stories and her funny comments, the way she made him feel as she touched his arm, giggling and flirting. She was a little forward, yes, but she made him feel desirable and worthy after being dumped.

Glancing away from Samara, he caught a glimpse of Jane with her arm around a large woman's shoulder, sitting on the steps of Samara's trailer. The woman seemed pretty upset, and Lars could tell that Jane was trying to cheer her up. Seeing her so kind and unguarded after two days of cool, professional Jane instantly reminded him of the Jane he'd gotten to know when she first arrived, and he was surprised to feel his unresolved feelings for her surface so quickly.

I didn't want to put things on ice, he thought. *I wanted to give us a chance.*

Suddenly recalling her singing along to "I Go to Pieces," he felt his face soften as he watched her. But his eyes quickly narrowed as he remembered her "ice" speech, and he stalked away—away from Jane and the trailers and the photo shoot, toward the woods, where he could think.

Lars had had a meeting with his father and brother this morning before setting out to pick up Samara and Jane, even before Maggie arrived with coffee and attitude.

"Nils and I been doing some talking, *Midten* and here's the thing…we make a lot of money on these cele'berty gigs, and Nils here thinks you're up to the task of taking 'em over. Nuts to bolts, top to bottom. Talent comes to Yellowstone, they deal with you. It would be your slice of the pie."

Lars had smiled at his father, looking back and forth between him and Nils. "I've been waiting for this, Pop. I been trying to show you I'm ready to take on more."

His father's weathered face broke into a grin. "Son, your biggest strength has always been your love of Yeller. I always knew that. Your mamma and I could barely get you in the house at night when you were a little'un. So, I tell you, I been hesitant to turn over the business side to you. I figure you're the best guide and tracker we have. Makes no sense to have you behind a desk. But I also see the talent likes you, they respond to you, and you seem a heck of a lot more comfortable with 'em than me or Nils. So…"

Lars looked at Nils, who stood beside their pop with his arms crossed stoically. "You've earned it, little brother. Just see this one through, and we'll draw up the papers for Lindstrom Elite. It'll be an off-shoot of the regular tourism business, fifty percent under your control, twenty-five each for Pop and me."

"What about Lindstrom & Sons?" Lars asked, pushing his advantage.

"What about it?"

"Well, I figure Erik's gone now. It's just the three of us. I think my share of Lindstrom & Sons should go up a little bit too."

Nils looked at his father, who cleared his throat.

"Well, Lars, what're you thinking?"

"If I have fifty percent of Lindstrom Elite? Well, I guess forty-forty-twenty would be fair, Pop. I think I deserve it."

"Even with Lindstrom Elite in your pocket?"

"In *half* my pocket. And working with difficult types."

His father looked at his watch, then back up at Lars. "I gotta do that pickup at the Best. How 'bout you come on back tonight. Nils, you too. We'll finish this conversation and get the numbers worked out."

Lars nodded.

His father shrugged into a navy-blue fleece jacket embroidered with the Lindstrom & Sons logo, then turned back to Lars. "Lot depends on this here assignment, though, Lars. You gotta prove to us that you can handle these types, and there's no time like the present, son."

Lars nodded again, watching his father leave the shop, heading over to the lot to pick up the van. He had grinned at his brother who raised his eyebrows at Lars.

"Driving a pretty hard bargain, *lillebror.*"

"I think I've earned it, Nils."

"I guess we'll see."

Finally. It was the chance Lars had been waiting for; the opportunity to move onward and upward in his life, make a little more money, have a little more control over his work and family's business. A lot was riding on this job, and Lars would do whatever it took to be sure it all went smoothly.

He turned back toward the shoot to see the crew break into applause. Samara's agent and Jane helped her negotiate the ragged rocks in front of the cliff, and lead her back to her trailer. She'd be changing into the third of three outfits now.

Part of Lars wished he could throw a pack on his back and escape into the woods, spend the day under a canopy of trees, tracking a bear or wolf pack, or even just be on the lookout for elk and moose. There'd be a lot less time for hiking and exploring while he was getting Lindstrom Elite off the ground. He imagined that there were stacks of paperwork to do when crews like this one came into town. All of the rentals, the hours of work, the shuttles and pickups, and all of the add-ons. He leaned his elbow against the sign that read "Sheepeater Cliffs" with a short blurb about the history of the cliffs, considering how his life would change. He wouldn't have nearly as much time for the park anymore.

But, getting ahead takes a little personal sacrifice, right? Don't complain you want more responsibility and then balk when it's offered.

Samara's glowing report was the key to proving to his father and Nils that he was ready for this new venture, and their confidence in him was warranted. He headed back to see if he could be useful; he wasn't going to let this opportunity slip through his fingers.

CHAPTER 8

Distracted by his thoughts, Lars bumped into Jane on his way back toward the trailers.

Literally.

Walking quickly in opposite directions, both with their heads down, hers slammed into his chest as they collided. She stepped away from him quickly, but his breath hitched for a second, surprised to find himself so close to her. When she looked up, her eyes slammed into his, and he felt the impact in the very tips of his toes, which curled inside of his hiking boots.

"S-Sorry," she whispered.

"It's okay," he answered, fisting his hands by his sides. "Heya, Jane."

He told his mouth to smile at her, but it didn't. It couldn't. He was hurt and angry, and he hated it that his body still responded to her when she'd made her disinterest in him so clear. It was humiliating to feel so much for her when she could walk away from him so easily.

"Heya, Lars," she answered, sliding her eyes away. They rested on the ground for a moment before she took a deep breath, glancing at the vibrating phone in her hand. "I was coming to find you, actually. Sara wants to see you."

His entire body deflated. She wasn't looking for him, as

his heart was clearly hoping. She was just on an errand for her cousin.

Without a word, he turned toward Samara's trailer, surprised when Jane fell into step beside him.

"Lars...I, um—" she started in a soft, raspy voice, and he looked down at her curly head, ordering his hands to stay fisted by his sides and not reach for their promised softness.

"What? What do you want from me?" he demanded, his voice brusque and angry. His heart pounded behind his ribs, and an uncomfortable lump formed in his throat as he stopped walking to face her.

She looked up at him, raising her mossy-green eyes to his. They were so instantly familiar to him, the perfect shade of downy, velvet green such that he'd seen a million times on the trunks of trees at the Bleached Cliffs. He longed to see tenderness in her eyes—anything, *anything* that would give him hope, that would tell him not to give up on her.

"N-Nothing," she murmured, staring down at the ground.

An unfamiliar anger rose up within him, making him feel mean. "I've been meaning to tell you, Jane...you were right. Your cousin's amazing."

Her neck snapped up and she flinched as though he'd slapped her, her sweet lips dropping open in an "o" of surprise. An almost-inaudible whimper of pain escaped from her throat as she took a jagged breath and held it. After blinking several times, she exhaled softly, her shoulders drooping as she nodded, hurrying past him.

Over her shoulder, she called, "Don't keep her

waiting."

He knew he had hurt her, which, he had to admit, made him feel terrible and slightly gratified at once. Why should he be the only one suffering? He ran his hands through his hair, watching her retreat, half considering chasing after her, grabbing her, dragging her into the woods, and kissing her until she admitted that whatever was between them was not even close to over, and *deserved* a second chance. But her quick walk away from him had turned into a run, and she had already disappeared.

"*Damn it*," he snarled under his breath, clenching his jaw and finally unfurling his fisted fingers.

Sighing deeply, he closed the distance to Samara's trailer, knocking once before stepping inside the dim, cool trailer, and pulling the door shut behind him.

At the sight before him, his mouth fell open. He swallowed, his heart pounding, his blood rip-roaring like molten lava through his body. What he was looking at was totally inappropriate, but he couldn't look away.

Samara sat on a stool with her back to him in a purple lace bra and matching thong. The twin globes of her mouthwatering ass rested, bare and inviting, on a velvet stool, and her dark hair just reached the flimsy clasp of her bra.

She caught his eyes in the mirror as he walked in, then swiveled to face him. He could make out her nipples through the filmy fabric, dark and taut in the center of her perfect breasts. As he stared, they puckered into impatient points, fighting against the gauze that trapped them.

"Hi," she whispered, looking teasingly down at her breasts before raking her eyes up to his. "Thanks for…coming." Placing her hands on either side of her breasts, she pressed them together. "You like?"

He cleared his throat and gulped, unable to look away, unable to process a coherent thought with the near-deafening pounding of his heart in his ears.

She looked him up and down, slowly, deliberately, stopping at his groin and licking her lips. "Because I know I do."

Samara giggled as she stood up, reaching for his hand, and raising it to her breast. She molded his palm around the perfect orb of purple lace, and moaned softly.

"Kiss me," she whispered.

His mind shot back, with alarming clarity, to bumping into Jane outside, to the terrible hurt on her face when he'd mentioned Samara.

If you do this, he thought in a flash of certainty, *it's over. Whatever was possible with Jane will be impossible. She will never forgive you if you do this, Lars.*

Samara wound her arms around his neck, stepping up on tiptoes to reach his lips. His hand still rested, where she'd placed it, on her breast, and her nipple hardened against his palm.

She will never forgive you. Never.

He blinked, sliding his eyes to the woman before him: Samara Amaya, by all accounts one of the most beautiful women alive, was standing in front of him in panties and a bra and he was…

—he slid his hand away from her breast and reached up with both hands to disentangle her arms from his neck—

…refusing her.

With unswerving conviction Lars faced the truth:

I don't want Samara. I want Jane.

And I'm not going to do anything that would jeopardize a possible second chance with her.

"I'm sorry," he mumbled. "I'm not…I mean, I don't want…"

Samara blinked at him, her lips parting in shock as he placed her hands by her sides, then dropped them, stepping away from her.

Suddenly the front door of the trailer opened with a blinding flash of sunlight, and Margot stepped inside, pulling the door shut behind her. Realizing almost immediately that she wasn't alone, her face registered surprise, her eyes sliding to Samara's scantily clad figure before sliding back to Lars.

"GET OUT!" screamed Samara. "Don't you know how to *fucking* knock?"

"Sorry! I'm so…sorry. I d-d-didn't know…" The large woman turned awkwardly in the small space, trying to open the door to leave. "I didn't realize—"

"Now you do. I'm busy. Get out. NOW…*dear.*"

She growled the endearment through bared teeth, but it wasn't enough to offset her tone. Her voice, which was generally so light and carefree, was laced with…with what? Impatience? Yes. And frustration. And something else too. Menace? Surely not menace.

"I'm—I'm so sorry for interrupting you, Miss Amaya.

So sorry," mumbled the woman as she finally got the door open.

"Remember to knock next time," said Samara in a singsong voice, waggling her fingers at the woman in farewell.

As Margot closed the door, Lars turned back to Samara, who sat back down in front of her vanity, taking out the ponytail and running long fingers through her inky black hair.

"Well that ruined the mood, huh?"

Could she have misunderstood what had just happened between them? Margot hadn't interrupted anything. Lars had been in the process of turning down Samara's offer when Margot entered.

"Shoot day," said Samara. "Lots of pressure on the poor dear. She's so fat, the heat's probably getting to her. Probably Jane too."

Lars stood by the door, anxious to leave, waiting to be dismissed, and incredibly glad that he'd had the willpower to—*Wait. What?*

"Jane?" He didn't realize he said the words aloud until Samara tilted her face away from the mirror to look up at him.

"She's always been *chunky*, but she didn't use to be so *fat*."

"Jane's not fat."

Samara chuckled, brushing her hair in long strokes. "Oh, you're so sweet. No wonder she has a crush on you."

"A crush?"

"Her eyes follow you around like a puppy dog." Samara turned back to the mirror. "I'll speak to her. Tell her to back off. She uses her dead parents as an excuse to glom on to everyone she meets. It's very awkward. Especially for me. What can I do? She's family. I was practically forced to let her work for me. But I'll have a word with her."

Lars was starting to feel awkward, all right. But it had nothing to do with Jane.

"Please don't do that," he insisted. "Jane's been great. You don't...you don't need to talk to her."

"Well, okay. But if you change your mind, tell me. Pathetic little thing. Well, not *so* little, huh?" She smirked, catching his eyes in the mirror. "Anyway. Enough about Jane. I want to talk about you...and me."

She bunched her shoulders like a coquette and giggled as she turned back around to face him. "Sorry we got interrupted. Why don't you come over tonight? I have a bottle of chilled champagne in the fridge! We can pick up where we left off?"

...at me rejecting you? Well, that'll be fun.

No part of Lars was tempted by Samara's offer, but the promise of Lindstrom Elite literally *rested* on her satisfaction and approval. He wasn't about to whore out his body to a woman he didn't want, but he did need to be delicate about her feelings. He had no interest in offending her.

"Wow. That's tempting," he said, still standing against the door. "But I have a meeting tonight."

Out of the corner of his eye, he caught sight of something: Jane's beat-up Red Sox cap hung limp and forgotten over the corner of Samara's vanity mirror.

Samara followed his eyes.

"That's not mine," she said, pursing her lips in disgust. "Ratty old thing."

"No. It's Jane's."

Out of nowhere he had a sudden flashback to Jane straddling him on the bed in her hotel room. He had barely had the self-control to demand she tell him to stop or go. All he had wanted to do was throw her on her back and bury his body in hers, quench his thirst, requite his longing—

Samara's voice forced him back to the present.

"Ugh. It was her dad's so she takes it everywhere. It smells." Samara rolled her eyes before grinning at him. "So… tonight isn't good?"

"I wish I could," he lied, "but I have to work tonight."

"*I'm* your work this week, aren't I?" She tilted her head to the side, straightening her back, thrusting her chest out toward him. The back of her hand ran lazily across her chest, finally resting above her cleavage.

Strangely, the battered little cap hanging on the side of the mirror had more allure for Lars than the supermodel coming on to him. He simply wasn't interested in her.

Maggie's words flitted through his head, making more sense now. He didn't like the way her costume assistant had appeared so terrified. He didn't like the way Jane had turned into an automaton as soon as Samara had arrived, and what's more, as much as he was still hurt by Jane's rejection, he didn't like the way Samara was talking about Jane either.

"You're my client, yes. But I'm afraid my meeting

tonight can't be canceled." He didn't want to make her angry, so he smiled and softened his refusal. "Sorry about that."

She smiled, mollified. "Of course. Tomorrow night instead?"

Again, he didn't want to outright refuse her, but he had zero interest in spending additional time with her. Furthermore, he needed to get out of this trailer. It was getting claustrophobic.

"We'll see," he said noncommittally, opening the door to leave.

Samara cleared her throat, reaching for Jane's cap, eyes narrowed. "Send Jane in, would you?"

He stepped outside, taking a deep gulp of fresh, clean air, and trying to get his head around what had just happened: Lars Lindstrom, one of the biggest playboys in the Yellowstone area, had just turned down the advances of supermodel Samara, because he couldn't get Jane, *who'd rejected him*, out of his head.

"I'm going to start drinking," he muttered, putting his hands on his hips and staring up at heaven.

"Champagne?"

He turned to find Jane standing behind him, likely referring to Samara's intended rendezvous. She knew Samara's plan for him to come over tonight and drink champagne? Of course she did. She wanted him to be free to do what he needed to do, right? *God, this whole situation is so fucked up.*

"No, Jane. I have to work tonight." His words were

clipped, curt and angry.

But something inside of him softened instantly as he heard her soft intake of breath in a surprised gasp.

"You…said no?" she whispered.

He watched her cheeks flush pink with an unguarded, pleased expression that widened her eyes and turned up her lips in the slightest smile. The afternoon breeze moved her curls, and he wanted to reach over and wrap one around his finger. Amazement continued to play out over her face as her brows knitted in wonder or confusion, and she held his eyes, her lips still and soft.

Suddenly, touching a curl wouldn't be enough; his heart hammered with emotion as he stared into her eyes. He wanted to grab her, seize her lips with his punishingly, unforgivably. It felt like a million years since being in her bed Monday night and he was angry that he still wanted her so much. Angry that he had just turned down guaranteed sex with a supermodel because he didn't feel about Samara the way he felt about Jane. He was angry with her for making him feel discarded and he was especially angry…

…because as he gazed into her eyes, he felt hope that they could still work out. And he hated himself for hoping.

"She suggested tomorrow instead," he said.

Her eyes narrowed on his like lasers, blazing and hot, and as he stared at her, a smile spread across his face and he sucked in a satisfied breath. Despite all the work she'd put into making him think it was over for them, her eyes told him *everything* he needed to know; everything he'd been *longing* to know for two long days as she ignored him.

No woman looked that way at a man she didn't want.

He exhaled in a bemused chuckle, and raised his eyebrows, nodding, holding her eyes.

"Well, well. Look at you, Minx. "On ice," my ass."

Then he sauntered away, his body hotter and more excited for Jane than it had ever been for any woman, at any time, ever before.

Thank God he had turned down Samara.

He wasn't giving up on Jane, after all.

***

Jane watched him walk away, feeling confused and bewildered. She couldn't remember any man ever turning down a night with her cousin. Men moved heaven and earth for a moment alone with Sara.

My God, Jane thought, feeling a nervous giggle bubble up from deep inside, *how did Sara take it? Did she just stand there, dumbstruck by his refusal?* Jane didn't recall scratch marks on Lars's face, so maybe her cousin had been too stunned to react. She shook her head. *Good Lord, the rest of the afternoon is sure to be unpleasant now!*

But somehow that didn't matter. A grin spread across her face as Jane's heart thumped wildly, desperate to believe that Lars could be the exception, as he'd claimed. More than anything—anything at all in the whole world—Jane wanted to believe that it was possible for someone to want her, someone who she wouldn't lose, someone who would belong to her. So that she could finally, after seventeen long years, feel like she belonged to someone once again.

After losing her parents she was frightened to hope.

Losing Ben didn't help either. Her tender heart barely dared to feel, and she had resigned herself to a life full of work. But, now, here was Lars. Who may or may not have a date with Samara tomorrow night, but had turned down a date with her today.

She remembered the facts laid out in her freshman statistics class: Consider an experiment that can only yield one result. The probability of the result is 99.9 percent, but there was always 0.1 percent existing for chance, for anomaly, for the possibility of random phenomena.

A random phenomenon. Could Lars Lindstrom be the 0.1 percent? Could he have meant it when he told her *I'm not that guy*? Could he actually be—

"JANE!"

Jarred from her thoughts by the melody of Sara's dulcet, loving voice, she truncated her thoughts, shook her head and stepped inside. Sara was sitting at her vanity in purple underwear, a cigarette hanging from her lips as she wielded Margot's heavy silver cutting scissors, which flashed like lightning in the dim light of the trailer.

Jane stepped closer, her eyes widening in horror as she realized what her cousin was doing.

"What are you—NO! No, Sara! Stop! Please! Stop!" Jane ripped the scissors away, throwing them across the trailer. Whimpering in pain, she gathered up the cut-up scraps of faded, beat-up canvas from her cousin's lap and clutched them to her chest. Tears of outrage burned her eyes and a desperate cry of sorrow escaped from her throat. "How could you? How *could* you, Sara?"

Tears trailed down Jane's cheeks as she stared at her cousin in disbelief. She felt the jagged-cut edges of the old fabric against her fingertips as she cradled the pieces of the beloved cap in her hands.

The old baseball cap had been Jane's version of a security blanket, a tangible reminder of summer Saturdays enjoying a baseball game with her dad at Candlestick Park before she was forced to move from San Francisco to Boston as an orphan.

It reminded her of happy times, of feeling warm and loved; it didn't smell like her father's head anymore, and it didn't look as it did when he wore it. It had faded and frayed from so much use and handling, but she loved it—it was her most treasured thing, and now it lay broken in her hands, in pieces.

"You unbelievable fucking bitch," Jane murmured, shaking her head back and forth and backing away from Sara.

And just like that, the third of those threads snapped inside, untethering Jane even further from her hateful cousin.

Sara had the decency to look sheepish.

Maybe she knew she had overplayed this hand. She shrugged as she stubbed out her cigarette, speaking gently. "C'mon, Janie. I was sick of that dirty old thing lying around. It was…distracting. I'll buy you a *new* hat. Any hat you want."

"I don't *want* a new hat…" Jane leaned against the door, examining the pieces in her hand. Sara had severed the brim from the cap, and then cut the cap in three large pieces, but the front piece that held the red, once-fuzzy B was still intact. Jane took the other three pieces, and gently lowered them into the garbage, then put the B into her back pocket. When she looked back up at Sara, her eyes were cold.

"I should quit right now and leave you here by yourself."

Sara's eyes widened in panic. "Now, Jane. Don't be rash. I'm sorry I hurt your little hat—"

"I'm *not* going with you to Jackson Hole this weekend," Jane growled, low and furious.

Sara looked surprised, then tilted her head to the side, trying to be charming, cajoling. "Janie, come on…"

"No! I'm *not* going to Jackson Hole with you. That's final. And I'm staying in my own hotel room for the rest of the shoot. I can't bear to be near you."

Sara chuckled lightly, shifting nervously in her seat. Her voice was smooth, careful. "You better step back, little cousin. Sorry about your hat, but you'll stay with me as planned."

"No, Sara. I *won't*. And that's final."

"*Watch it*," Sara warned, her voice like the crack of a whip, but Jane held her eyes without flinching. She didn't lower her glance, or back away. She stood there, locked in a showdown with her despicable cousin, violet eyes to mossy green, until Sara finally looked away.

"Fine," Sara conceded tightly. "Have it your way. You know what? You need to cool down a little anyway. A couple days off will do you good."

Jane turned her back on Sara, moving to the door. "I'll

send in Ray and Shanelle first."

"You do that, Janie. You do that for me."

***

Lars was surprised when Jane asked to be dropped off at the hotel that evening on the way back from the shoot. He noticed that neither of the cousins was very chatty, both occupied with their phones during the ride and only answering his questions with a word or two.

As they got to the cottage, Samara climbed over Jane, who sat stiffly in the seat, refusing to move over or look at her cousin. "Send Sebastian over, Jane."

When Jane didn't respond, staring straight ahead in steely silence, Samara thanked Lars for the ride, but slammed the door a touch too hard as she got out of the truck, stomping alone to the front door of her cottage.

Jane didn't seem okay. She seemed withdrawn and deeply sad. As angry as he felt with her, he couldn't bear to see her like this.

"You okay, Jane?"

"Mm-hm," she murmured.

Lars turned the truck around, heading back into town. "Music?"

"N-no, th-thanks," she said, sniffling softly.

He heard her voice catch and it made his heart catch.

He'd never seen her like this. He'd seen her cool and aloof, distant and professional, even sad, but this was different. He remembered his sister Jenny's face in the days after their mother had died. He recognized in Jane the kind of pain that rose from grief. He wanted to reach out to her, but he didn't want to be rejected by her again.

"*Is* everything okay, Jane?"

"It will be," she murmured in a thready voice, looking out the window, away from him. After a moment she turned to him. "Would you mind getting Sebastian and bringing him over to Sara's place?"

"Sure. I'm glad to help. Whatever you need."

"Thanks," she sighed, returning her eyes to the window.

They drove in silence until he pulled into a parking space at the hotel. Surprised she didn't immediately jump out of the truck to get away from him, he tried again.

"Would it help to talk about it?"

She rolled her neck away from the window until she faced forward, resting the back of her head on the seat back with tears brimming in her eyes, looking straight ahead. She bit her lower lip, and her raspy voice was low and muffled when she spoke. "Do you ever feel like things didn't turn out the way you expected them to? Like, you're on the wrong path?"

"Are *you* on the wrong path?"

"I don't know. I don't see any others," she whispered, and he could tell she was stifling a sob.

How he wanted to open his arms to her, draw her to his chest, help her to know everything would be all right. But he had no right to touch her. It might only make things worse for her, and certainly for him.

"Look harder, Jane. You're smart. You'll find your way."

She turned to him, eyes watery and wide, and in his

whole life, he'd never seen anything—nothing at all—as beautiful as Jane Mays's green eyes. Tears spilled down her face in rivulets, fat, round drops, one after another, as she gazed at him, looking completely miserable. He couldn't help himself anymore. He reached over and brushed them away gently with his rough, calloused thumb.

"How can I help?" he asked in a whisper.

"You can't. I have to figure it out for myself." She smiled sadly and then leaned away from him, swiping at her eyes. When she looked back over at him, her eyes were softer than they'd been in days, and it felt like hope to him. "Thank you for being so kind to me, Lars. For making a terrible day not quite so terrible at the end."

He turned his face slightly, taking her hand in his, grateful when she didn't pull away, grateful to be sitting beside her, for the light touch of her skin against his. His heart leapt just to be alone with her once again, and he knew as certainly as he knew his own name that he'd made the right decision today in turning down her cousin.

There was only Jane for Lars.

She slid her hand away and took a deep breath, opening her door. Before she hopped out, she turned back to face him.

"Thanks, again. See you tomorrow?"

He nodded as she closed the door behind her. He didn't trust himself to speak.

And just like that…he didn't feel angry or sad anymore. It didn't matter that she had pushed him away a few days ago, and it didn't matter that she had once claimed they were better off without each other.

Because in his heart, he knew the truth: they were better off together, and he was going to figure out a way for them to be together.

***

Taking Sebastian to Samara's only took a few minutes, and then Lars stopped at home for a quick bite before heading back to the Lindstrom & Sons office. His pop was on the phone when he got there, and Nils was finishing a sandwich at his desk.

"*Ja*, Jenny-girl, that's fine. Tell Erin her *morfar* can't wait to see her! Ha ha. She's a smart one. Travel safe, Jen. Tell Sam to get you here in one piece. You too. Bye." He smiled at Lars, putting the receiver back in the cradle. "Can't wait to see that Erin."

Lars smiled back at his father. "I know, Pop. Me too."

"She's a beauty, like her *mamma*. Can't wait to hear her start talking!"

"Going to be confusing when the twins call you *farfar*." In Swedish, the word for grandfather was dependent on whether you were speaking to your mother's father or your father's father. *Morfar* for your maternal grandfather, and *farfar* for your paternal grandfather. So, while Jenny's daughter would call him one name, Erik's daughters would call him something different. "When are they getting here?"

"Saturday for lunch. You'll come to the house?"

"*Ja, Pappa*. Of course. I can't wait to see the girls again. And *Minste* and Kat."

"Your *mamma* and me? We have three boys, and one

girl. Your sister and brother? They give me three girls. How 'bout one of you settle down a give me a grandson? Even things out a bit!"

Nils didn't look up, but Lars chuckled. "No pressure, Pop."

"With the right girl, *Midten*. Like Katrin for Erik. Maybe like Maggie for our Nils…"

Nils grunted and cleared his throat, looking annoyed.

Lars passed on the chance to tease him further. "Too bad Katrin didn't have any sisters."

"What about this New York girl?" asked his father. "Maggie likes her lots. And Nils. And Paul."

"Paul?" His voice was so harsh when he said his friend's name, it didn't even sound like him.

"Sure. Paul says she's a great girl."

"She is."

Lars didn't like this one bit. He thought back to the concert in the park when Paul seemed so chummy with Jane. Paul wouldn't make a play for Jane, would he? He could see how Lars felt about her, couldn't he?

"He sure got over Jenny quick."

"Lars! Jen's been gone almost two years. Married with a child now. It's good for Paul to move on."

Like hell he'll move on with my Jane.

Over my dead body.

He looked up at his father's twinkling blue eyes, and knew his father was reading his face like a book.

"Huh. Well, if it's like *that*, son, you'd best do something about it, eh? Sooner than later, I think."

"I guess I'd better at that."

But that was the problem. He *wanted* to spend time with Jane, but he wasn't sure how to go about it.

Why was she so sad, and how could he help make it better?

He needed a way to spend time with her away from her cousin. He wondered if he could convince Jane to stay behind in Gardiner for the weekend while Samara headed to Jackson Hole. His family would be in town for the twins' baptism, yes, but half of his family already loved Jane and he knew the rest would be just as warm. He'd have to think about it, try to come up with an excuse good enough to get her to consider staying.

Suddenly he frowned. And he'd have to be sure Paul got out of the goddamned way. If Paul wasn't aware that there was something between Lars and Jane, it needed to be made crystal clear and no mistake.

Nils stood up from his seat, gesturing to the round table in the front window where they often sat with clients, planning adventures or tours.

"Guess we should get to it?"

They each took a seat at the table, ready to hammer out the future of Lindstrom Elite.

CHAPTER 9

As Thursday wore on, Jane just kept reminding herself, *Get through today; she's gone tomorrow. Get through today; she's gone tomorrow.*

They were at Old Faithful, and for once it wasn't Sara who was slowing down the shoot, it was Old *UN*Faithful, which hadn't blown its top in over an hour. Since wait times were anywhere from ninety minutes to two and a half hours, it could still be a while before the jet of hot, steamy water erupted into the sky again.

Sara sat in her trailer pouting, kept company by Sebastian since Jane was keeping her distance. The sky was clear and the sun was high, but the air around them was filled with moisture from the geyser's steam and there was no way Sara's hair and makeup would last through the heat of the late afternoon. They had gotten a great set of two shots in the morning, but now they all cooled their heels waiting. There were other geysers nearby, but none of them had the awesome height and power of Old Faithful, so they waited for the intense bubbling to begin, when they would hurry Sara from her trailer over to the flat rocks in front of the geyser for the second shoot.

Jane sat in a director's chair next to Ray, counting down the minutes until the shoot was over for today and she could go back to her motel room and then to the Prairie Dawn for euchre.

Ray turned to her, nudging her elbow to get her attention.

"Honey, I have *got* to know where this magical, stiff backbone came from, because you know your Ray-Ray likes anything magical and stiff!"

Jane turned to Ray, who had lowered his sunglasses to peek at her.

"I don't know." She shrugged, popping a lollipop between her lips. "I guess everyone has a breaking point."

"And yours shoulda been in Madrid when she screamed BITCH at you loud enough to wake up the dead at three o'clock in the a.m., drunk off her bony ass from too much Cava."

"Nah. That was already months overdue," she said, remembering Cairo.

"Things gonna change when we get home, Janie?"

"I think they're gonna have to, Ray."

"Now, I know you ain't talking about leaving us, because you would not break Ray Cartier's tender heart."

"That wouldn't be my first choice…but Sara may not have room for the new me."

Ray put his sunglasses back on his head and leaned back, sighing in the warmth of the sun. Jane looked toward the parking area and saw Lars leaning against his truck, like an actor out of a western movie, impossibly masculine with his cowboy boots, jeans, polo shirt and cowboy hat. What a long, boring day for him.

As much as she would have loved to spend the day leaning against his truck next to him, and as much as her spirits soared yesterday when he turned down Sara, she still didn't trust that they were out of the proverbial woods. She thought about the conversation she had overheard this morning that made her hopes take a significant dive.

She'd come up behind Sara and Lars sipping coffee near the Kraft table, and unseen, she'd eavesdropped on their conversation.

"About tonight…" she heard Sara say.

Lars had looked at her quickly. "Hmm?"

"How about this weekend instead? Know where I'm headed tomorrow?"

"Jackson Hole, right?"

"Mm-hm. But I could use some company, Lars. You. Me. At the Amangani. Infinity pool. Gorgeous dinners. Amaaaaazing bed. Pick up where we left off yesterday? Hmmm?"

Jane's heart was hammering. *Pick up where we left off yesterday? What happened yesterday?* Jane had assumed that Lars turning down a night with Sara was the extent of their interaction, and her stomach rolled over uncomfortably at the thought that they'd possibly gotten physical in her trailer.

"Tempting," he had murmured.

"Mmm. Speaking of that bed, I am a very creative girl."

"Hmm."

"Promise." Sara ran her fingers lightly up and down Lars's arm. "Say you'll…*come*? I'll make it worth your while."

"I'll, um…I'll definitely consider it."

"Yay," she exclaimed, clapping softly.

Jane couldn't see his expression from behind, and without looking at his face, she couldn't figure out the context of their conversation. She watched as he threw back the rest of his coffee then tipped his hat to her, walking away.

Though his answers to Sara leaned towards unenthusiastic, Jane's stomach had flip-flopped, making her feel nauseous. She didn't know what to think—was he going to Jackson Hole? And more importantly, had they fooled around yesterday?

Damned if she'd ask. She couldn't. She wouldn't.

Jane stepped up beside her cousin to pour herself a cup of coffee.

"That Lars walking away? How was last night?"

"Rescheduled to tonight. Don't worry about me, Janie."

"Oh, I'm not worried about you, snake."

"Still mad at me. How boring."

"Almost time for the shoot, Sara."

"God, I hate it when you call me that."

"Get used to it. I'm not calling you anything else anymore," said Jane, taking a sip. "I know who you are, Sara Mays."

"Really can't say I like your attitude on this shoot, Jane. For God's sake, have a funeral for the fucking hat, and get it over with already."

Jane glanced at her cousin's face and was surprised to find some guilt there…or was it shame? *Human emotion. Huh. Well, there's a first for everything.*

"It was my dad's."

"I know. God. You wore that thing to bed every night for years."

"You remember that?"

Jane was surprised. They rarely talked about their shared childhood. It was uncomfortable to recall a time when they were—more or less—equals.

"Of course I *remember*. I'm your *cousin*. We shared a room, dumbass."

Jane had a sudden flashback to one of her first nights living with the Mayses. She had woken up in the middle of the night crying, as she often did, arms outstretched, reaching for...for...her parents? For someone to comfort her?

Suddenly, Sara had pulled back the covers of Jane's bed, pressing her small body into Jane's empty, aching, open arms. Jane had clasped them around Sara, tears spilling into Sara's black hair in the darkness. Sara's arms had encircled Jane, and the cousins had fallen back to sleep without a word, face to face, holding each other until morning.

After that night, Jane never woke up crying with her arms outstretched again, and she felt grateful to Sara, who had never acknowledged the incident, and even denied it years later when Jane reminded her of it. *That never happened. You were dreaming, Jane...*

But Jane hadn't been dreaming. It was one of the only times she ever remembered Sara showing her any real tenderness after her parents' death, and even now, more than ten years later, it confused her.

Jane had reached into her back pocket and rubbed the fuzzy, red B. "I still don't understand why you did it."

"Christ, I said I was sorry. Can you *please* stop pouting?"

"No. It was a really, really shitty thing to do. I can't forgive you yet."

"Well then…you know what? Fuck you, Jane. Fuck you and your stupid, fucking hat. I'm not sorry anymore. I'm glad I did it."

She'd chucked the rest of her coffee on the ground in an angry splash then turned on her heel and stomped away.

Ray sighed beside her in the sunshine, adjusting his sunglasses, bringing Jane back to the present. He gestured at the geyser with a hot-pink manicured finger. "When is this thing going to blow its wad already?"

"Charming, Ray."

"You know me, doll. Prince Charming. The blacker, gayer version."

Jane chuckled.

"Speaking of Prince Charming, how's it going with Mr. Hot Cowboy Man?" He gestured to Lars. "And what the heck are you doing here with me when you should be talking to him? You know Miss Thing have to have her AC. You got that boy all to yourself for once."

"It's confusing," Jane confessed.

"Well, I don't know why. He hasn't jumped into bed with her yet. Don't barely go near her."

"He's supposed to go to her place tonight. And…she asked him to go to Jackson Hole."

"You ask me, you're giving him a reason to say yes."

That stung. Jane hit Ray on the arm. "Be nice."

"*You* be nice. Ray-Ray just sittin' here, soakin' up the sun and you hit him."

"He didn't say no."

"What?"

"Samara asked Lars to go to Jackson Hole and he didn't say no."

Ray turned to her and lowered his glasses again. "Did he say *yes*?"

"He said he'd consider it."

"Then you take my word, honey. He done said no."

"How do you—"

"Now, you know your Ray know a thing or two about the boys, right?"

Jane cracked a grin, nodding.

"Then you go give that cowboy some honey, Miss Janie Mays. Give him a reason *not* to go to Jackson Hole."

"But what if I go talk to him, and he's wonderful, and I fall for him, and none of it matters…and he ends up going with her, after all?"

Ray took a deep, long-suffering breath and sighed loudly. "Now we gonna talk, honey. You ready to listen up?"

Jane nodded.

"One? You already *fell* for him, girl. You can deny it all you want, or avoid him all you want or whatever other fucked-up little reindeer games you gonna play all you want, but I know you fell for that cowboy and you know it too. So, we just gonna be straight about this, and you know bein' *straight* with this here Ray-Ray is a rare goddamned thing, so respect, okay?"

"Okay," she said, unable to hold back a smile for her friend.

"Two…you ain't even *tried* for that boy. You done thrown up your hands without even puttin' up a fight. You ain't given him no chance to show you nothing. Just sulk all around here convinced he gonna let you down. Well, seems to me you're *making sure* that he gonna let you down. You want a chance? Then damn, girl, take one!"

Jane took a deep breath, nodding at Ray's good advice.

"And three…turn on your brains and look around. If he *want* Miss Thing, where would he *be* right now?"

Jane smiled at him. There was no one in the world like Ray Cartier and she adored him with all her heart.

"Her trailer?"

"Ding, ding, ding. Gold star for Miss Janie Mays. Her trailer. And *where* is he, pray tell?"

"Hanging out by his truck by himself."

"She wins again! Now, honey, you go give him some sugar. But first…" Ray took a tube of something out of his back pocket, grabbed Jane's chin and swiped it on her lips. "Mm-hm. That's better. When you gonna let Ray-Ray do you a makeover?"

***

Lars had been watching Jane talk to Samara's makeup artist, trying to figure out how to approach her about this weekend.

More and more, he stayed on the periphery of the action. The longer he spent with these modeling folks this week, the more he felt like a fish out of water. As much as he appreciated the chance his father and brother were giving him, the more he thought about it—the waiting around, the difficult personalities, the insane demands, the endless drama—the more he missed the simplicity of taking good, normal folks out to discover and enjoy the park. After years of wanting more responsibility, more to do, he was getting what he wanted: a chance to shine with a new endeavor. He wished it felt organic to him. He wished it felt like a better fit.

He thought about his favorite tour groups in the past, all of which had included long hikes, phenomenal views, coming across something special like a family of grizzlies or an eagle's nest. Normal, everyday people who had saved up money to see something awesome at Yellowstone, and he helped make that dream come true for them. So much of this particular job just felt silly.

Jane was the only exception to all of the nonsense that accompanied this group. She was uncharacteristically straight-shooting and down-to-earth for a city girl working with a celebrity. But she was so guarded; so damn untrusting and complicated, he didn't know what to do with her. If she wouldn't give him a chance to prove he wanted her, how was he going to show her?

He flicked his glance to Samara's trailer. There was no way in hell he was going to Jackson Hole. He didn't much *like* Samara, but most importantly, his extended family was coming into town, and family was family: it trumped everything else in the life of a Lindstrom and that was that. Not to mention, Lars wanted a real chance to reconnect with

Jane, and he was only going to get that chance while Samara was out of town.

So, Jackson Hole was out of the question for myriad reasons, but he wanted—he *needed*—to remain in Samara's good graces too, so he was stringing her along. That felt wrong too, and it bothered him. He just didn't know what else to do.

Lars looked up and was surprised to find Jane walking over to him. She had gotten rid of those baggy, shapeless jeans today and was wearing a pair of fitted jeans that actually showed she was a woman with some pretty appealing curves. She had rounded hips, not just slack skin over bones, and a nice waist that tapered in. His big, calloused hands had just about spanned the hot, smooth skin of that waist when he'd held her on his lap in her motel room.

She had taken off her sweatshirt from this morning to reveal a breast-hugging black tank top underneath that skimmed the top of her jeans, giving a peek at the soft white skin underneath when she bent or twisted a certain way. Lars had been watching, as surreptitiously as possible, and every time he got a slight look, his fingers tingled, recalling the satin warmth of that skin. She looked simple and chic with black sandals and those dark red toes that had distracted him so much on Monday night, and her days in the park were giving her some nice color; even her brown curls had picked up a little gold from the sun. She wasn't wearing her cap anymore, he noticed, enjoying the way her curls moved with her steps. He couldn't see her eyes because she was wearing sunglasses, but her lips were rosy and slick and his body tensed in response to her as she came closer; needing her, missing her, excited that she was *finally* seeking him out.

She sidled up to him, then pivoted, leaning back against the side of the truck beside him, her elbows resting like wings along the side with one foot raised, resting against the rubber of the back tire. She didn't look at him, just stared straight ahead, standing beside him with a lollipop between her lips.

He readjusted his body just enough that his arm grazed her elbow, and he felt it in his gut, how much he wanted her.

"Are we allowed to say hello?" he asked, referring to her ice pact.

She glanced up at him, putting her sunglasses on top of her head.

"Hello," she answered, that low rasp making his galloping heart beat even a little faster.

"Hello."

"I have two questions for you, Professor."

His breath caught at her use of the nickname. "Go for it."

"Are you going to Jackson Hole this weekend?"

He wanted to concentrate on Jane, but he was distracted by something out of the corner of his eye, which drew his attention away from her. He barely heard her question, turning his head toward the spitting, bubbling geyser. *Didn't anyone notice?* The bubbling and steam had started.

"Wait! Don't they realize—?"

He sprinted toward the photographer, yelling, pointing at Old Faithful. Everyone straightened up, jolted by his alert and Samara was rushed out from her trailer. Ray touched up her makeup as Lars helped her take her position in front of the roar and thunder of the steaming column of water.

He backed up, adrenaline still pumping, eyes wide as he watched in admiration as they got the shots, and impressed with Samara for making the most of the three or four minutes she had. Whoever she was in her personal life, she was a professional when it came to her job. He was fascinated watching her pose, watching the assistants scurry around with fans and strobes, and the camera clicked like crazy while the photographer barked instructions against the fury of water.

He took off his hat and scratched his head, caught up in the excitement of the moment, leaning against the guardrail watching. As Old Faithful stilled and sputtered, Jane and Sebastian accompanied Samara back to her trailer, and that's when it occurred to him.

CRAP! Jane. Wait. What was her question? Something about Jackson Hole? *Oh, no.* Did she think he was headed to Jackson Hole this weekend? *Shoot.* He knew it had probably taken a lot of courage to ask him that question, and he had basically run away from her the moment the words were out of her mouth. He needed to fix this.

Now wasn't a good time. She would need to help Samara get undressed, and looking around, he realized that everyone was packing up to go back to Gardiner. He'd have to wait until tonight.

First chance he got, he'd head over to the Best Western and lay it out for her.

***

Margot placed the clothes back on hangers and hung them on the bar at the back of Samara's trailer as Shanelle brushed her hair out. Jane busied herself straightening up the trailer, finding Sara a pair of jeans and a t-shirt to change into now that the shoot was finished for the day. She felt awkward about how the conversation had ended so abruptly with Lars, and she still didn't have her answers.

"Um, Jane?" Jane turned to Sara, who was shrugging into her t-shirt. "You're pretty unhinged lately and I was thinking you could use a couple days off to get your head straight. I won't be needing you this weekend. I've arranged my own…um, *delicious* company for Jackson Hole. You'd just be in the way."

Jane's first reaction was to roll her eyes; Sara was purposely making this announcement in front of Margot and Shanelle to assert her control over Jane. *Whatever.* Sara didn't know the crew had heard it from her first on Tuesday night. *Day late and a dollar short, Sara.*

But wait…Delicious company.

Was she talking about Lars? Jane looked down, absently stroking the soft kid of the gloves she was holding. Sure, she'd overheard them this morning, but Lars hadn't confirmed that he was interested in joining Sara for the weekend.

"Fine," she murmured, a sick, unsure feeling growing in her stomach.

Don't ask, don't ask, don't ask!

"Who's, um, joining you?"

Shit, Jane.

Sara turned to Jane and smiled her prettiest smile, managing to look innocent and surprised at once before chuckling lightly. "Well, Lars, of course."

Jane furrowed her brows in confusion as her face fell. *How? When?* Had Sara cornered him and somehow managed to get a "yes" out of him?

"Really? I thought—"

"You thought what, Jane?" Sara stood up in front of Jane with her hands on her hips and turned to Margot. "Margot. Tell her what you walked in on yesterday. Go on. Tell her."

Margot had her back to them, arranging a blouse on a hanger, but she turned to face her boss, letting it fall to her side. Her brows furrowed and she swallowed as she looked at Jane, who read her fleshy, baleful face like a book. Whatever Sara was alluding to was true.

"Tell. Her. Margot." Sara's voice was firm and insistent. "Just tell her."

"I-I don't know if I really saw anything…"

"Yes, you do, you fat piece of—" Sara took a deep breath. "Just tell her, dear. Exactly what you saw."

Margot tilted her head to the side, grimacing at Jane.

"It's okay, Margot," Jane whispered, eyes trained on the chubby woman's face.

"I walked in on them…um…alone together. They were—"

"—making out," supplied Sara. "And what was I wearing Margot?"

"Bra and panties."

"Uh-huh. 'Cause the rest of my clothes had already been torn off my body. And if the hippo here hadn't interrupted us...well, Janie, use your imagination. I'm sure you know what would've happened next."

Jane's heart was beating so fast, her chest hurt. Her eyes glistened with tears, but she wouldn't allow them to fall. Breathing was another story. Had Sara given Jane a roundhouse kick to the gut, the wind wouldn't have been as effectively knocked out of her.

Lars had hooked up with Sara? Kissed her polluted, treacherous lips? Touched her with his gentle, calloused hand? It was so heartbreaking and so humiliating, she didn't know which emotion to latch onto first.

"Oh," Sara cooed, reaching out a hand and taking one of Jane's, "look at you, so sad. But, you'll get over it. You always do. *So strong.*"

She squeezed Jane's hand then dropped it, and it fell limply at Jane's side. And just like that, the fourth of those tiny threads deep inside of Jane snapped with an almost audible *twaaaang* sound and Jane knew that she was nearly untethered. Almost free of this viper, this cancer, this awful, terrible life that she so hated.

"Yes," she whispered, sorrow making her voice raspier than usual. "I *am* strong."

Shanelle put her hand on Jane's shoulder but Jane shrugged it away, her eyes burning. She leaned down until her face shared the mirror with Sara's, and she gazed into her cousin's eyes.

"I'm leaving."

"What? N-not for good!" Sara exclaimed.

Jane tilted her head to the side, regarding her cousin with tired, glazed eyes, unable to form the words to answer her. *Something is not better than nothing when the something is hateful, horrible you.*

She backed up without promising she'd be back tomorrow, and walked out of the trailer door, slamming it behind her. Beelining to the *Trend* van that was about to pull out of the parking area to take the magazine crew back to Gardiner, she tapped on the door and Amy slid it open.

"Room for one more?" Jane asked, blinking back tears.

"Sure, Jane." Amy nodded, raising an eyebrow as she probably made the connection that Jane wouldn't be riding back with Sara or the rest of her team.

Jane climbed in, taking the empty row in the back for herself, and the van started back for Gardiner.

Once she was settled in the back seat, scrunched down, head turned to look out the window, only then did her heart drop completely as the first tears fell. She winced, and her bottom lip trembled, so she covered her mouth with her hand and let the silent tears fall at will. The *Trend* folks either noticed and left her alone, or simply didn't care. Either way, no one bothered her.

He had caved. He had caved, after all. Turns out you *are* that guy, Lars. Just like all the rest of them. You *are* that guy.

Thank God you didn't sleep with him, she thought, trying to look on the bright side.

Shut up, Jane. The man of your dreams is spending the weekend with your cousin. His beautiful lips kissed hers. His hands were on her body. There is no bright side.

There. Is. No. Bright. Side.

She must have looked like an idiot asking him whether or not he was going to Jackson Hole. No wonder he had run away from her at the speed of light. After last night—his kindness to her as he dropped her off—she'd allowed herself to hope. What an idiot she must have looked like today. She didn't know what was worse: the humiliation of finally letting down her guard a little only to be blown off, or the reality that he was finally lost to her.

Her phone buzzed in her pocket.

You are totally unhinged. Do I have to pack myself for JH? -S

Jane stared at the text, considering the option of telling Sara to go fuck herself, then wrote back a more civil message instead.

Yep. -J

When the van pulled up in front of the Best Western, Jane hurried to her room, texting Maggie that she didn't need a ride to the Prairie Dawn tonight since she wasn't out at the cottage anymore. She would shower and change, and head over to the cafe after she'd had a long, well-deserved cry in the shower.

Her heart was in pieces.

He was lost to her.

***

Lars was anxious to get to the Best Western and find Jane.

He'd seen her leave Samara's trailer and run over to the *Trend* van for a ride home, and while he'd been initially concerned as he watched her, he remembered that the cousins weren't getting along. She was probably just avoiding Samara. Still, a feeling of unease fell over him; he didn't want any more misunderstandings between them, and by not answering her questions, it was possible she'd think the worst.

Samara, however, had other plans, which were thwarting Lars's intention to get to Jane. On the ride back to Gardiner, she kept talking about the hotel in Jackson Hole, and shared how much she was looking forward to getting to know him better. He needed to get out of it and was starting to feel desperate.

"How about some music?" she asked.

"Sure," he replied, groaning inwardly as he recalled her love of pop music.

She rolled the dial until she found a very loud, very angry song, and turned it up.

"You like Pink?" she asked, putting her wrists together in front of her, and moving her body to the rhythm of the music. "Do you *love* this song? Oh my God, she's so strong! I met her at a club last month and she is *awesome!* I work out to this."

Lars glanced at her moving sexily in the seat beside him, in rhythm to the loud song. It was absurd to even compare this ride with any of the drives he'd taken with Jane, who'd softly sung along to beautiful love songs beside him. Damn, he missed Jane. He needed to get to her and answer her question about Jackson Hole with a resounding no. It was the perfect opening to try to get her to stick around this weekend.

The song ended after three or four minutes and Samara yelled, "YES!" fanning her face and turning to Lars, "Water! I need water! NOW!"

"Um, I think the rest of the water went in the Kraft truck at the end of today."

"Well, that's *not* so helpful, is it?" She continued fanning herself, annoyed. "So, I guess you'll have to stop for water somewhere."

Stop for water? "Um. We're in the middle of the park. There's nowhere to stop. There's nothing between here and Gardiner. But we'll be at your place in thirty minutes or so…"

"Seriously? I'm *thirsty!*" she whined, sighing strenuously. "*Fucking* Jane. This is *her* fucking fault."

"Whoa…pardon?" Lars wasn't accustomed to women using that sort of language; he had no recollection of his mother or sister ever using the F-word. He remembered his conversation with Maggie when she'd insisted Samara's language had been, er, *spirited*. Well, yet again, she'd been right. It occurred to Lars that Maggie had probably been right about everything and he owed her an apology.

"Jane. Jane, my cousin. Short, plain, grouchy, dumpy…ringing a bell? If she were here, I'd have some goddamn water. Instead, she's being all…" Samara lowered her voice cartoonishly, mimicking Jane's raspy tone. "I'm not coming to Jackson Hole. I'm taking a vacation."

Lars was about to say something on Jane's behalf when Samara's words registered. He whipped his head to face her. "*What?*"

"Yeah! She's not fucking coming because it doesn't suit her. Do you think Pink's assistant takes a fucking vacation when she's needed? I doubt it. But you hire family, you get screwed."

He told his brain to ignore her language and focus on her meaning.

"So...Jane's not going with you this weekend."

"No, and good riddance. We'll have a much better time without her." She lowered her eyes and licked her lips. "Can't wait to get you stripped down on that bed...I am going to ride you, cowboy, like..."

Lars didn't hear anything else she said, although he was careful not to show Samara how pleased he was by the news that Jane would be in town all weekend while she was away. He occasionally nodded in response to the colorful picture she was painting of them in bed together, while mostly ignoring the tawdry details.

All that mattered was that Jane was staying and she'd be here all weekend! He was ridiculously happy to hear—

"Whoa!" He was so distracted by his thoughts, he didn't hear whatever led up to Samara's hand in his lap, firmly grasping at his crotch, boldly trying to massage him through his jeans. "Hey! Cut it out!"

He jerked her hand out of his lap, trying to keep the truck on the road with one hand on the wheel. The truck shimmied into oncoming traffic, and Lars looked up just in time to slide back onto his side of the road and avoid a collision.

He pulled over to the side of the road, cutting the engine and turning to Samara.

"Not okay, Samara," he said.

"Umm, have I missed something here? I'm *throwing* myself at you, and honey, I don't usually have to work this hard."

"Then stop trying."

"What? Why?"

Her hand reached for his lap again, but he grabbed her wrist.

"Samara. Stop."

She snatched her hand back, eyes narrowed, a sneer on her pretty mouth.

"Do you…not want this?"

Lars swallowed. The simple answer was: *No, I don't. I want your cousin.* But he couldn't say that to her. She'd have him fired, his father's company would lose the revenue from the job, and his chances at Lindstrom Elite or a third share in Lindstrom & Sons would be up in smoke.

"Samara. Don't be crazy. Any man would want to be with you."

She stared at him for a moment before exhaling loudly.

"Then what is the problem?" She spoke deliberately, separating and enunciating her words.

He was at a total loss. He couldn't reject her, but there was no way he was fooling around with her again. He needed a reason…a good reason…

"I have a condition…um, a rash," he blurted out. *What? What are you saying? What are you doing?* "Down there."

"Wh-what?"

"Yeah. A rash." He cringed. "It's uh…red and bumpy…from the, um…the heat, and…I think I should let it…um, clear up first."

"You have a *rash*. On your…"

She gestured to his lap with a finger.

"Uh-huh. Yeah. It's not pretty."

She looked at him, her nose curled up in disgust, as if she'd seen something distasteful. She looked at the hand that had been groping his lap, and wiped it on her jeans. "Is it…contagious?"

"No. No, no, no. I have…um, medicine for it."

"When's it going to be better?"

"Like, um—" *I definitely don't want to go to Jackson Hole with you, so…* "—a week? Or so?"

"Oh."

"I was, um…hoping it would clear up in time, you know, to join you. That's why I didn't, um, give you an answer about this weekend. But I think it's probably best if you go without me."

Samara shrugged, but Lars saw a little color in her cheeks. He didn't know if she was buying his lies or not, and he knew she wasn't used to being rebuffed. At all. Ever. She sat up straighter, pushing her breasts forward. "So…you're turning this down?"

"Only 'cause I have to, you know, for *your* sake. For your, um…health. And safety."

She tapped one fingertip against her lips, staring at him. It was a slim, tapered finger, with a red fingernail so slick and shiny and beautiful, it looked wet.

Her efforts to be seductive, however, were utterly in vain.

He didn't want to sleep with her, now or ever, and to avoid doing so, he was willing to make up a pretty outlandish—and, let's face it, completely disgusting—personal reason to get out of it. He'd certainly been flattered by the attention she paid him that first day, and there's no doubt she was beautiful. But she was also an immature, foul-mouthed, demanding, pouting brat. He pitied the guy who ended up with her.

Not that he needed a reminder of how Jane made him feel, but he got one last night when he held Jane's hand, and again today as she walked over to talk to him by his truck; he could barely think straight when Jane was around, he wanted her so much. And, as it turned out, he was about to have a whole weekend of open road with that someone else. Damn skippy, he was going to make the most of it.

Samara took a deep breath and sighed, taking her phone out. "Maybe I should tell *Trend* to find a more...*willing* tour operator. I like shoots to be fun. I don't think this is working for me. I don't think *you're* working out, Lars."

Wow. Was she *threatening* him? Terrific.

She was fumbling with her phone, her thumbs moving fast, ignoring him. He heard it ding like she was sending messages. For all he knew, she was texting the *Trend* folks to axe the Lindstroms from this job. Screwing up his own personal career was one thing; affecting his family's livelihood was another matter entirely. He had to buy time. He had to figure out a way to keep her happy until Monday. If he could, he'd still have the weekend with Jane, he'd still get his promotion, and by Monday Samara-the-Terrible would be gone.

"Samara," he said, as low and sexy as he could muster for her, reaching out to put his hand on her thigh, "I could always come track you down in New York. Come stay with you for a weekend."

She turned to him slowly, a catlike smile making her pretty face mysterious and dangerous at once. "You'd do that for me? Come all the way to New York? Give me a night to remember?"

He didn't love lying, but a small lie now could give him the overall outcome he desired.

"Absolutely. I promise a night you'll never forget."

"I like the way you're touching me right now, Lars."

"Tip of the iceberg, baby."

"What will you do to me, Lars?" she asked.

"Whatever you want," he answered, grinning at her, though he wished like hell he could move his hand away.

He felt sick to his stomach even hearing the words coming out of his mouth. But he thought of Jane, of how terribly he needed this weekend alone with her. He knew he could turn things around if he just had this time with her. And while he also knew that promising Samara anything was fundamentally a bad idea, bad ideas were all he was coming up with in a pinch.

For now, he needed Samara to go, Jane to stay and Lindstrom & Sons to keep this job. Apparently, making sexy promises to Samara was the only way to get all three.

"Deal, Lars," she agreed, her voice silky and firm.

"Deal, Samara," he winked at her, gratefully moving his hand back to the steering wheel, keeping his face impassive while he wondered if he'd just made a deal with the devil.

He turned the key in the ignition, but nothing happened other than that grating, crunching sound. He turned it again and again, but the engine wouldn't turn over.

No, no, no, not now!

He glanced at Samara, who raised her eyebrows at him.

"Sometimes it's temperamental. We'll give it a moment," he said, but when he turned the key again, he didn't even get the grating sound. Nothing. Nada. It was dead, and he banged on the steering wheel, angry and frustrated, because it meant three things:

One? He'd have to flag down a car to get them back to Gardiner because his phone didn't have a signal this deep in the park.

Two? He'd have a very thirsty, very unhappy Samara on his hands for a little while, and he really wasn't excited for that, nor how unprofessional it looked for them to be stranded in Yellowstone.

Three? He'd need to come back for the truck and get it towed back into Gardiner. His shoulders slumped.

He wouldn't get to Jane for hours.

***

A long, hot shower and a change of clothes had helped…a

little.

Jane still felt crushed by Lars hooking up with Sara, and his decision to accompany her to Jackson Hole, but after processing the initial surprise, it would have been disingenuous to claim total shock. She had felt sure from the beginning that Lars would eventually choose Sara over her. It had just taken a little longer than Jane had anticipated and in those extra days, recalling his sweetness, a fragile hope had taken root in her heart.

She walked along Main Street in Gardiner toward the Prairie Dawn, feeling the heaviness in her heart. *At least I have a quiet weekend to get over him. I'll be fine when he returns with her on Sunday.*

Or would she?

Jane had to admit that of all the men she had met in her adult life, Lars had certainly seemed different. Casually unaware of his own good looks, loving the same outdated music she did, quick with playful banter, making her fingers and toes curl with how good it felt to have his lips on hers.

I admit it. I thought there might be a chance with him. I thought he might be the exception. I wanted him to be the exception.

The pain of admitting her own failed hopes made her eyes threaten to tear up again. The pathetic reality was that Jane Mays was such a terribly lonely person to be. No parents, no real family except for a quasi-loving, overly-demanding uncle who prioritized Sara's needs over Jane's. Her only friends were Sara's personal staff; her life was a series of work-related appointments and interactions with people who wouldn't care less about her if she wasn't attached to her cousin's name.

The ache of her loneliness swept over her, and she took a deep, shaky breath, unable to find a cheerful thought to assuage the pain of Lars's rejection.

Oh, Jane, she thought with some surprise and regret and huge amounts of sympathy for the pathetic realization she was having. *Did you think you could be like Maggie's aunt? Come to a strange, new place, find real love and start a new life? Did you think that could happen for you?*

I think I sort of did, she answered, and then she admitted the truth that she had kept hidden from herself, and certainly from Lars. *Yes, I did. I hoped.*

"Smarten up," she said aloud, quietly, under her breath. "You know better."

She opened the door of the Prairie Dawn and saw her friends waiting at a table in the back.

"Jane! You're here!" said Paul as Maggie waved her over to the table.

"I'm here," she answered, glumly, glancing at the empty chair. "Where's Nils?"

Something undefinable passed across Maggie's face as she glanced at Paul, before she offered Jane a tight smile. "I don't know if he's coming. Had to go get Lars."

Just his name. Just his name made her ache.

"Go get him? Is everything okay?" Jane asked, hating herself for wondering.

"I guess he and your cousin broke down on the way back to Gardiner," said Paul.

And that's all it took for her eyes to fill completely with

tears.

She stared down at the table, miserable, unable to conceal it from her new friends. She had promised she wouldn't cry any more after her shower, but she couldn't help it. They had probably pulled over to make out, unable to keep their hands off each other. She remembered the sweetness of his lips on hers just a few days ago and felt the tears well up and spill over the corners of her eyes. She stared at her hands folded on the table. She couldn't bear the sympathy or kindness she knew she would see on their faces if she raised her head.

"You okay, Janie?"

She shook her head back and forth slowly no.

Paul reached over and put his hand over hers. "You want to talk about it?"

She shook her head again and reached up to wipe the tears away, grateful that they didn't force her to talk. They just gave her a moment, sitting in respectful silence beside her.

Finally she took a deep breath and sighed, looking up at them and wiping her nose with a proffered napkin. "I'll be fine."

"Jane, sometimes things might look one way—"

"Paul, I know you're trying to be nice, but gosh, I don't want to talk about it."

Jane switched her glance to Maggie, who had been conspicuously silent.

"Can I just say one thing?" Maggie asked.

Jane exhaled noisily, rolling her eyes, then nodded once.

"He cares for you, Jane. He didn't want to break things off with you. I know that for true."

"Well…" Jane looked at the table, refusing to let Maggie's words make her second-guess her choices. Lars and Sara had been inevitable from the start. "He got over me pretty quick either way, so it really doesn't matter anymore. Now can we *please* talk about something else? How was *your* day?"

"What do you mean by that?" asked Maggie, searching her eyes.

Jane shrugged, a little taken aback. For the first time since she arrived, she realized her friend was acting strangely. Preoccupied. Jumpy. "Just wondering if you had a good day."

Maggie twisted the claddagh ring back and forth on her finger. "Busy. Up to Billings and back for an appointment."

"Is that a long drive?" asked Jane.

Maggie looked flustered and without answering, she turned to Paul, changing the subject. "How's, um, how's Miss Mystic?"

"She's good."

Jane smiled at him, swiping the last bit of wetness from her cheeks. "From that grin, I'd say better than good. Did you tell her you're coming?"

"I did."

"And?"

"She's getting used to it."

"Huh." Her hackles rose at the thought of some Connecticut girl playing around with a man as nice as Paul.

"I hope you're being careful."

"Careful?"

"I just don't want to see you get hurt."

"I haven't felt like this since…" His voice trailed off.

Maggie tapped the table twice to get their attention. "Now don't you go all murky too!"

"Nah. No regrets, Maggie. I don't love *her* like that anymore."

"Who?" asked Jane. "Love her *who*?"

He looked at Jane. "Jenny. Jenny Lindstrom."

"Another Lindstrom breaking hearts? Is there no escape from that family?" Jane cried.

"Not in Gardiner," said Maggie, giving Jane a sympathetic smile of her own.

"Well, we're quite a threesome," Jane observed. "Forget coffee. We should get some vodka. Drown our common sorrows."

Paul piped up. "You two drown 'em. I'm over my Lindstrom. Got Mystic on my mind now…"

Speaking of Lindstroms, the front door opened, and Nils trudged in, locking his eyes with Maggie immediately and heading for their regular table.

"You're here," Maggie murmured, almost as though she couldn't believe it, and Jane could have sworn her friend's eyes were watering as she looked down at her half-finished coffee like it was the most fascinating thing in the world.

Boy, she was acting funny tonight. Jane made a mental note to ask her what was going on later when Nils and Paul were out of earshot.

"I'm here," he said softly, staring at her bowed head like he wasn't sure if he should go or stay. Finally he flicked his glance to Paul. "Did you deal yet?"

"We were waiting for you. Everything okay?" Paul slid the deck toward Nils as he put his coat on the back of his chair and sat down beside Maggie.

"Long day. Finally get back to Gardiner and I have to pick up Lars and drive Miss Amaya back to her cottage. Then I got to pick up that nervous, sweaty fella from the motel and take him over there to keep her company. These famous types sure are a lot of work." He looked up and caught Jane's eyes. "Uh. Sorry, Jane. No offense. Present company excepted."

"Oh, I'm not famous, Nils. No offense taken. Samara Amaya's a terrible person. Say whatever you like."

Paul glanced at Jane nervously then went back to sorting his cards. Maggie still hadn't looked up from the table, and though she'd slid her cards from the center of the table to the edge in front of her, she rested her hands on the pile, making no move to sort them, like she was frozen, or waiting for something to happen.

"How's Lars?" Jane asked, flicking her gaze up to Nils.

"Fine. But his truck's dead for now. Arranged for a tow. He won't be back in Gardiner for a while."

"Poor, disappointed *Miss Amaya*," Jane observed, dryly.

Nils looked up at Jane. "How's that?"

"She'll have to wait for this evening's company."

"What's that got to do with Lars?"

"Lars is screwing my cousin," Jane offered matter-of-factly.

"I guess that'd be his business if it were true."

"I guess so. And it *is* true. We could be family one day, Nils. My cousin. Your brother."

"We could be family one day, I guess. But it won't come about like that."

"Why not?" asked Jane.

He looked at her square in the eyes, and she saw the compassion there. Whatever she said didn't matter; he wouldn't rise to the bait. He wouldn't spar with an injured thing. He spoke firmly but gently to her, and it shamed her a little bit.

"There ain't no chance on God's green earth that Lars is sleeping with that woman."

"Really?" challenged Jane, loving Nils for letting her be angry without pushing back too hard, hating him for not letting her pick a fight when she wanted one, and further hating that his words made her feel a glimmer of hope. "My information says otherwise."

"Then your information's bad, Jane."

"Is that right?"

"That's right."

"And why is that?"

Nils folded his cards in a neat pile and folded his hands on top of them, in almost a mirror image of Maggie beside him.

"Because Lars is taken with *you*. And if you're taken with someone…if you feel that they—in fact—*belong* to you…" He shifted toward Maggie, who still stared down at the table in front of her. Jane watched, mesmerized, as he leaned his face toward Maggie's ear, speaking in almost a whisper, "…it's *impossible* to let them go."

Maggie lifted her eyes slowly and looked up at Nils, her mouth opening softly in surprise, as she held Nils's gaze with a primitive, aching intensity.

The energy between them was like a force field, magnetic and exclusive. Jane knew that the decent thing to do would be to give them privacy by looking away, but she was utterly captivated by the scene playing out in front of her.

Maggie's face grew increasingly pink under Nils's unwavering scrutiny, and Jane saw her clench her jaw twice, but it was her eyes; large and shimmering green in her face, that broke Jane's heart as they searched Nils's face for the answer to some unasked question.

Finally, Maggie looked away from Nils, blinking her eyes rapidly and biting her lower lip. She didn't say a word as she stood up and headed out the back door without looking back.

Jane could barely breathe, waiting to see what would happen next. She shifted her gaze from the back door to Nils, who stared down at the table, nostrils flaring, his breathing audible to Jane, who watched him in tense, fascinated silence. He finally stood up, scraping his chair loudly across the floor as he grabbed his coat. Shrugging into it without a word, he followed Maggie out the door.

Jane watched until the back door slammed shut, then

turned, with wide eyes, to Paul, who stared after them like he was in shock.

"What just happened?" Jane whispered, flustered and uncertain, and a little bit excited too. She was positive she'd witnessed something humongous, but she had no idea what it was.

"Well, I'll be damned." Paul beamed at Jane, and then laughed aloud, shaking his head as if in shock. "I definitely don't think we're playing euchre tonight."

Paul picked up his cards and threw them into the center of the table.

Jane gave Paul a wobbly smile.

"Coffee?" she asked, taking his cup. He nodded and she went up to the bar for two fresh cups. When she returned, he was still staring at the table with a bemused smile.

"I'll be damned..." he muttered again, glancing at the back door of the café then beaming at Jane.

"Okay. You have to school me here, Paul, because I am in the dark. What. Just. Happened?"

"I wouldn't have believed it if I hadn't been here. This is the sort of stuff legends are made of, Jane. I'm serious."

He picked up his coffee and took a sip. "Okay. Ready for this? Family tree time. You gotta follow me here, Janie. Listen carefully.

"Jenny, who I used to have a thing for, is Nils's sister, married to Sam. Ingrid is Jenny's best friend, who's married to Sam's cousin, Kristian. Kat is Kristian's sister, also Sam's cousin, married to Erik, who is Nils and Lars and Jenny's brother."

"Oh, for the love of Pete! Don't you people ever marry someone from out of town?!"

"Like Miss Mystic?"

"Don't distract me."

Paul chuckled. "Here's another way to look at it…Jenny's a Kelley, but she was a Lindstrom. Kat's a Lindstrom, but she was a Svenson. Ingrid's a Svenson, but she was a Nordstrom."

"Clear as mud, Paul. Clear as mud."

"Jen, Ing and Kat. Let's just call them the Lindstrom Ladies."

"Now you're talking."

"Okay… There's always been another Lindstrom Lady, but only unofficially, because the brother she belonged to hadn't claimed her. Well, he had, sort of. No man in town was going to make a play on Maggie Campbell while Nils Lindstrom lived and breathed. Only one ever tried and failed, because even though there was nothing spoken between those two, everyone knew. Everyone *knew* they were meant to be."

"Go on," she urged breathlessly.

"Nils pretty much fell in love with Maggie at first sight, I guess…three or four years ago now. We all knew it. Even Nils knew it, not that he ever did a blessed thing about it, really. After a year or so, Maggie caught on too. But somehow, he never managed to make a real move on her. Mr. L…he started inviting Maggie to Thanksgiving and Christmas, and she became a good friend to Jenny too. Nils and Maggie became great *friends*, as you can see…"

Jane nodded, taking a sip of her coffee. "But nothing ever happened? In all that time?"

Paul shook his head. "I've had my suspicions, but no, I don't believe so. His brothers and sister tease the living daylights out of him. But he never budged. Almost like since we were all watching and waiting, he got stage fright or something. Kept Maggie in the friend zone, and then it became a bad habit, I think."

"And Maggie was okay with that?"

"Maggie told me once, just a few months ago, actually—after way too many beers on May Day—that there were only two moves left that Nils could make: He could 'bed her or wed her', but anything else would be a waste of her time."

"Whew! She *told* you that? Did she ever tell *him* that?"

"I think she must've. I forgot my wallet at the bar that night, and he walked her home. And Janie? She was three sheets to the wind. Could have said anything. And I have to say…sure sounded like he was answering a question for her tonight."

"Yeah. It was decision time. Go time." She smiled at her friend. "So…wedding bells…or…?"

Paul shrugged, and then chuckled. "Damn if I know, Jane. Still can't believe it happened. Literally *just* happened."

"Maybe it's nothing. Maybe she walked home, and he…"

"She went home all right. She lives upstairs." Paul pointed to the ceiling and Jane couldn't help but look up and wonder what was going on up there.

"Then he…"

"…was a man on a mission." Paul nodded. "Sure *looked* like he followed her home."

Jane smiled at Paul then giggled nervously. "So, right now, up there is the, um, the first time they're, um—whew. Well. I have to go wash my brain so I stop thinking about other people doing…um, *that*."

Paul chuckled, shaking his head. "Wow, the Lindstroms are going to be in a tizzy this weekend…if they find out."

"Well, I'm certainly not telling anyone." Jane put her elbows on the table, cupping her chin in her palms, leaning toward Paul. "What's this weekend?"

"Big doings. Erik and Kat's twins are being christened."

"Too bad Lars won't be here for it."

Paul took a deep breath and sighed. "I don't know where you're getting your information, Jane, but Nils was right. It's not good."

"He's going to Jackson Hole with my cousin."

"No chance, Janie. Not with the whole clan coming into town. That's just not Lars. He wouldn't miss it. Not for anything."

"Well, Sara's not just *anything*. She asked him this morning, and he said he'd consider it. Then she told me later that he was going with her."

"Time will tell, I guess." Paul shrugged. "I know you said you don't want to talk about it, Jane, but you and Lars…"

"Lars and I aren't…"

"Yeah, Jane. Yeah, you are. I saw you two together."

"He *made out* with her, Paul," Jane whispered this,

looking down at the table, eyes burning all over again.

"What?"

"Yeah. Someone else saw and told me. It happened."

Paul stared at her hard, then looked down at the table. "Doesn't add up, Jane. I *know* him and it doesn't add up."

"Please don't give me hope," she murmured, raising her glassy eyes to him.

"Aw, Jane." Paul took her hand and squeezed it, smiling at her gently. "'*Her hope is treacherous only whose love dies with beauty, which is varying every hour*'."

"What does that mean?" she asked sadly, shaking her head back and forth in misery.

"It means hope can only hurt you if you affix a huge feeling like love to something fickle like beauty. But Lars isn't fickle. No matter what you've been told. No matter what you think you know. No matter what someone claims to have seen. I've known him for years, and he's solid. I care about you and I'm telling you: I think it's okay for you to hope."

He leaned forward and kissed her cheek then leaned back with a gentle smile.

Jane squeezed his hand back and sighed, wondering how he could possibly be right.

"You know, it's probably selfish of me to say so, Janie, but I hate to think of you leaving Gardiner. Sure wish you could find a reason to stay here with us."

Me too, Paul, she thought wistfully, thinking of Maggie's Aunt Lily, thinking Gardiner would be the perfect place for a fresh start if she had a good reason to stay. *Me too.*

CHAPTER 10

By the time Lars had finally showered, changed and walked to Jane's motel room last night, she was gone, so he walked up the street to the Prairie Dawn to see if she was there. Looking in the window, he'd seen her at a far table with her back to the door, and Lars had placed his hand eagerly on the door handle to go inside and talk to her.

But then something stopped him: he realized that Maggie and Nils weren't there and there was no trace they *had* been there.

He moved back to the window next to the door, trying to get a better view. Two people, two coffee cups, a neat pile of playing cards. Leaning forward and cupping the glass with his hands, he realized that Paul was holding Jane's hand. He swallowed, cringing against a sick feeling in his gut, then watching with dread as Paul leaned in toward Jane's face the way you do when you're kissing someone. When Paul leaned back, he smiled at her gently, like a man who really cared about a woman.

Lars turned away, nauseous and limp, backing down the steps of the café onto the sidewalk, and turning in a daze toward home.

Holding hands? Kissing?

It couldn't be. It couldn't. Paul wouldn't do that to him.

He'd seen them at the park together on Monday, right? Paul *knew* that Lars was into Jane. He stumbled along, feeling blindsided and confused, when something awful occurred to him; Jane was under the assumption that he and Samara were hooking up. If she'd shared that information with Paul, it was fair for Paul to assume that Jane was now…available.

He clenched his fists at his sides and his pace picked up from a bewildered stumble to a walk and then to a run, until his lungs burned, and he was home in half the time it usually took to get there. His eyes teared up as he unlocked his front door, but he blamed it on the run and the chill of the evening. Nils's upper floor of the house was dark and quiet, and although baring his heart to his older brother wasn't something Lars had ever done, he would have considered doing so tonight.

She had rejected him and turned to Paul.

And it hurt like crazy, because he'd thought—he'd desperately *hoped*—that he and Jane would have another chance.

Goddamn it!

Lars's life has been pretty uncomplicated up to now.

His feelings had never confused him or otherwise disrupted the solid contentment that pervaded his life. He felt love—real, deep, true affection—for his family and close friends, and he was generally well-liked by folks in Gardiner. He was a good son and brother, a hard worker, a loyal friend, and a trusted guide. The most important thing in Lars's life was his family, and second to that was the earth inside of Yeller, and after that was everything else, which balanced out fine for a complete, uncomplicated life that felt good and full.

Until now.

Meeting Jane had changed things for him in myriad ways.

Mostly because if he walked away from Jane, or otherwise lost her, his life wouldn't be complicated, nor would it ever again feel full.

Jane was complicated. She was distrustful, skittish and insecure on one hand, and a sassy, witty, smart-ass on the other. She had lost her parents and a man she thought she loved, which had only compounded her flaws, and she lived her life in the shadow of a cousin who was neither gentle nor loving when Jane needed gentleness and love. She was good at her job but didn't like it, and while she liked photography, she had relegated it to a hobby. He sensed there was a deep well of love in her heart to give, a warmth and playfulness he had seen and felt. But, if she wouldn't take the risk of opening her heart, it could never be shared.

And yet without his permission or blessing hers was the face the earth had turned to him, to whom he felt bundled and bound, as surely as he did to Yeller, as surely as he was a Lindstrom, and he didn't know what to do if he couldn't have her—if she wouldn't, or couldn't, belong to him. He longed for the good and full, uncomplicated life he had always known, but after knowing her—the twinkle in her mossy, earthy eyes, the rasp of her deep voice, the unexpected way she made him laugh out loud, how the mere touch of her hand made his blood boil and rush—that satisfying life might be forever elusive without Jane Mays in it.

All of these thoughts floated round and round in his head all night long, invading his dreams, stealing his peace, complicating his heretofore uncomplicated life, and leaving him utterly exhausted in the morning.

And so, after the worst night's sleep of his life, during which his subconscious and ego ran laps, and his conscious mind woke up swearing off women forever, Lars woke up alone in his bed. He showered and dressed, and with his truck in the shop for another day, he started his walk back into town to get the van and do his pickup at the Best.

Although there was nothing he would like less, though little else he longed for more, he would have to start his day seeing Jane.

***

Friday had finally arrived, and Jane woke up for the last day of the shoot feeling a mix of emotions.

This evening would start her first weekend-vacation in years, which should have made her feel as light as a feather, yet her mind was heavy with thoughts of Lars. It was impossible to discount what Maggie, Nils and Paul had each said last night, in their own way, about Lars. She liked them and felt the good intentions behind their words as they all insisted that Lars had genuine feelings for her…and further, Paul, whom Jane realized she had even grown to trust in the short time she'd known him, had gone so far as to say her heart would be safe with Lars.

Despite her feelings for Lars, which grew deeper and

more intense hour by hour, she didn't know how to reconcile her friends' gentle and encouraging advice with Margot's grudging admission about what she'd seen. Jane's feelings—inconvenient and unwanted though they were— dominated her heart to the point of intense distraction. Her heart demanded she reconcile these accounts today. She would need to muster the courage to talk to him, *regardless* of Margot's confession, *because* of her friends' insistence on his constancy.

After showering, she pulled all of her curls back into a pert little ponytail and secured the stray wisps with some bobby pins, briefly admiring its cuteness before getting dressed. One thing Jane had learned during her week in Gardiner was that fall came quickly to Montana. September morning temperatures hovered in the low 60s, so she opted for the slim-fit jeans she had picked up at the only clothing shop in Gardiner and the same black camisole and green cardigan sweater she had worn on Monday night.

With Sara handling her own bags for Jackson Hole, Jane didn't need to be anywhere quite yet. The Lindstroms wouldn't be by to pick up the crew for about half an hour. Deciding to take a morning walk on her own, she stopped at the lobby coffee kiosk, pouring herself a to-go cup before heading out onto the misty, quiet, early morning sidewalks of Gardiner.

As she walked along, she turned her thoughts to the end of the conversation she had with Paul last night. She hadn't consciously thought about staying in Gardiner, but after Paul mentioned it, she couldn't get it out of her head.

Stay in Gardiner. She had to admit, the thought was compelling.

Leave New York and Sara behind.

Leave her mediocre relatives and a job she hated.

Stay in Gardiner, which fit Jane like a glove, with people whom she'd come to treasure over the course of the past week; people who she thought could be real, lasting friends to her.

She had substantial savings from working for Sara and would easily be able to set herself up for a couple of years at least, especially if she lived modestly. She could take pictures of the park and send them to magazines and galleries back east to see if she could establish herself as a reputable nature photographer, maybe even finance her own coffee table book of Yellowstone photography.

Just stay. Just stay like Maggie's Aunt Lily and make Gardiner her home.

But when she thought of Lars, she realized it wasn't that simple. She couldn't just stay; things were complicated by their...their...whatever it was or had been, between them. He'd think she was staying for him, chasing after him, after he had rejected her. They'd want to avoid each other, almost impossible in a very small town, meanwhile placing people they both cared about in the middle of their awkwardness.

It was impossible. No matter how fine a fit Jane and Gardiner might be, there was really only one invitation that mattered to her, and despite their previously scalding chemistry, she sure didn't imagine Lars asking her to stay in her immediate future.

The misty morning, no doubt resulting from the longer, cooler nights that signaled the coming fall, gave her walk a little extra atmosphere as dreamy swirls of cloudy air veiled everything in mystery. The streets were mostly empty, so she couldn't have missed the tall figure who approached her purposefully, mostly concealed by the swirling fog.

She froze in her tracks, gasping softly, bewildered by his sudden appearance, as if it should be impossible that Lars Lindstrom was suddenly standing before her, actualized from nothing but vapor.

She heard, rather than felt, her coffee cup slip from her slackened fingers and crash to the ground beside her in an ungraceful splatter.

He had broken stride at her unexpected appearance, gazing into her eyes with disbelief as he closed the scant distance between them.

Jane sighed with involuntary pleasure watching him. He was so beautiful, materializing out of the mist like magic, so familiar, and yet so devastatingly impossible, her heart wouldn't let her look away even though her mind acknowledged the sharp and shredding certainty that he didn't belong to her. Surely, he would walk by her, without a glance, without a word, and vanish into the otherworldly gauze of mist behind her, elusive and unobtainable.

But he didn't walk by.

He stopped in front of her, the heat from his body startling her as she stared—helpless, undone—at his chest, unable to move, holding her breath.

"Jane," he breathed, low and fierce, in disbelief or anger or surrender. Her eyes fluttered closed against the anguished mosaic of feelings she heard in the way he said her name. Her aching heart took comfort in the desperate intensity she heard in his voice, because she recognized it, and she longed to answer it by sharing the strength and depth of her own struggles.

If her chest didn't feel so physically tight from the force of her heart thumping against her gasping lungs, which grounded her in reality, she may have believed she was still asleep, still dreaming. She had been holding her breath, but she released it in a sob, gasping for another gulp of air quickly, wild not to break the moment. It felt unreal, like a spell; too fragile, too dreamlike to be *possible*.

The backs of his fingers caressed her chin before lifting it, and when she opened her eyes, she caught hold of his, which were…shattered. And not just that…betrayed. *Betrayed.* His shoulders moved up and down with the force of his breathing, and his face contorted, searching hers frantically.

Jane had only one thought that she embedded unconsciously in her gaze:

I am yours.

His eyes widened, briefly reading hers, and without warning his lips descended, furious and punishing. His teeth clashed against hers as he growled into her mouth, his corded arms imprisoning her against the wall of his chest as he slanted his mouth over hers again and again. Desperate to touch him, she writhed against him like a wild thing, pushing at him, desperate to loosen her trapped arms from the cage of his body.

Still kissing him, struggling free, she moved her hands up to his face, her cold fingers settling on the feverish ridge of skin under his eyes. She felt him flinch beneath her palms, and he sobbed into her throat, his fingers curling in defeat on her lower back.

She quieted his despair, cradling his face in her small white hands, her gentleness a ballast to the rawness of his fury. Moving her lips against his with a slow, soothing rhythm, she tenderly coaxed his tongue to love hers, to stop fighting.

As he surrendered to her, he seemed to lean into her compassion with exhaustion, in gratitude. She felt his passion shift from anger to tenderness and slid her hands into his hair, arching her body against his, melting into him, at his mercy even as he acquiesced to her.

Settling into the kiss, neither able nor willing to break away from the other, they moved lightly to the rhythm of their beating hearts, clasped to one another as the mist swirled around them. Lars's hands finally uncoiled and he held her as gently as he would something precious. Jane gradually lowered her hands from his face until they laced at the back of his neck, as she would if he belonged to her.

After a while, she drew back, tucking her head under his chin, which she felt on top of her head as his arms tightened around her.

"Jane," he sighed, in a broken whisper, and she tilted her head to look up into his eyes. They were fraught—still hungry, but also mired in injury, which confused her because *she* was the injured party between them. She lowered her hands from his neck and his arms went slack, letting go of her, stepping away.

"Lars?" she murmured, her body still tingling, still reeling, her brows furrowed in confusion and frustration.

"You're killing me…you're…" He shook his head, looking down. "I can't do this, Jane."

"*I'm* killing *you*?" Her mouth opened and she shook her head. "I don't understand."

"I'm sure *Paul* could help you figure it out."

"Paul?" *Paul? What does Paul have to do with this?* "Paul! What are you talking about?"

"I saw you."

"Saw what?"

"Don't play games with me!"

"*Me play games*? That's rich! How *dare* you!"

"How dare *I*? How dare *you*!"

"You're not making any sense," she snapped.

"Neither are you!"

"I'm…I'm leaving. I have things to do."

"Good! Go already!"

"I will! I'm going!" She pivoted and started walking away, but he grabbed her hand as it swung back and jerked her back up against his body. In one whip-fast motion, he placed his hands firmly on her hips and leaned down with unerring precision, sealing his lips over hers, demanding, branding. And too brief. As he drew back from her, his eyes flashed and glinted like jagged glass sweeping sharply over her face.

"I'm getting the van. I'll pick you up in twenty minutes," he growled, his hands still holding her hips.

"Fine," she spat, frowning at him. "I think you should quit kissing me."

His lips twitched up and he leaned down one last time, brushing his lips against hers with an agonizing, almost unbelievable, gentleness that made her knees so weak, she swayed when he released her without a word or glance, and walked into the mist.

Jane took a deep breath, filling her lungs, turning her neck to watch him go, utterly confused by what the heck had just happened, and praying to God it would happen again.

***

Goddamn it, Lars, what is the matter with you?

He poured himself a cup of coffee at the kiosk, waving hello to the front desk clerk, and sat down in the lobby, waiting for Samara's team to gather in the lobby. If he hadn't gotten such a rotten night's sleep, he wouldn't have been up so early...he wouldn't have left so early...he wouldn't have bumped into—

Damn it, Lars! He had been so wound up over her, wanting her, feeling rejected by her, to suddenly see her walk out of the mist had been an occasion for which he was wholly unprepared. He meant to walk right past her, without a look, without a word, but he was drawn to her like a magnet, and somehow found himself standing in front of her.

But it was her eyes that had propelled his mouth onto

hers.

Her eyes that told him some part of her still wanted him, whether she was with Paul or not. He was so angry at her, so hurt, he had grabbed her roughly up against his body, slammed his lips down on hers so mercilessly, their teeth had clashed.

Damn it, damn it, damn it!

When she fought against him, pushing at him, it struck him that his behavior was deeply inappropriate. He had loosened his grip so she could pull back, and smack him good across the face. So feeling her small hands reach up to caress his face had shocked the hell out of him, and his whole body had reacted to her tenderness; all he wanted to do after that was show her how much he liked her, how much he wanted her, how fine and dear and irreplaceable she was to him.

Even after that kiss ended, he couldn't bear to let her walk away, so he'd grabbed her back, held her for an extra stolen minute, almost smiled when she told him to stop kissing her, because even as she said the words, her body didn't back them up by making a move to leave his arms.

Damn it anyhow! You shouldn't have done that!

He was angry with himself, and with her, and more confused than ever. He *knew* what he saw last night. He saw Jane and Paul sitting alone, holding hands, Paul making cow eyes at Jane, and leaning in so close to her face, he was either kissing her or inspecting her pores. And while, no, Lars had to admit he hadn't actually *seen* the lip-lock, there was little doubt in his mind as to what had happened between them.

So how come Jane had been so indignant? And why did it make him feel like maybe he had jumped to some hasty conclusions based on circumstantial evidence? He sat back in his chair taking a deep breath and letting it out in a forceful, frustrated sigh.

"That bad?" He looked up to see Margot, the portly costume person, standing in front of him.

"Aw. Women!" He shook his head, standing up. "No offense. *A* woman. One very exasperating woman."

"Miss Amaya?" she guessed.

He shook his head. "Jane."

Margot looked down at her coffee, her lip trembling. "I'm so sorry, Mr. Lindstrom. Miss Amaya made me say it. I wouldn't make trouble. I hate that she made me."

"Wh—" Lars cocked his head to the side, watching her. "Wait a second. What are you talking about?"

Margot's anguished expression doubled, and her shoulders fell.

"You kissing Miss Amaya in her underwear. She made me tell Jane."

Lars closed his eyes, his nostrils flaring in anger and frustration as he realized what Margot was saying. "Samara made you tell Jane that you saw us kissing."

Margot swallowed, nodding nervously.

"But we weren't kissing," he said.

"Oh," said Margot, biting her lip. "Well, I said I saw you and Miss Amaya alone in the trailer and Miss Amaya was only wearing her underwear. Maybe she said the part about you kissing, or—"

"What else did she say?"

"Oh…well, she said you ripped off, um, her, um clothes. And she said you were going to, um, pick up where you left off when you got to Jackson Hole."

Lars nodded at her, trying to keep his simmering fury under control.

"She said I was going with her to Jackson Hole?"

Margot nodded.

"Anything else?"

Margot shook her head no, looking sorry.

"Hey, Margot," Lars asked, and she looked up at him. "You didn't do anything wrong. In fact, I think you helped things. I know you did. Thank you."

Her eyes brightened. "Jane's the best, Mr. Lindstrom."

"I know it," he answered, offering her an encouraging smile.

Her words this morning suddenly made a lot more sense, and Lars was determined to set things right today.

***

Taking a seat in the very back of the van, Jane stole glances at the back of Lars's head as they drove out of town, using the quiet time to try and figure out what exactly was going on between her and Lars.

This kiss they'd shared this morning had been intense, passionate perfection, but the emotions swirling around it— propelling them to one another so fiercely—were so much messier and hard to divine.

She shivered, raising actual goose bumps all over her

body, remembering the demanding way he'd claimed her on the misty sidewalk, how much she'd liked it. She knew he was angry with her, but she was okay with that, because she was furious with him too. And somehow, in the midst of that mutual rage, she'd wanted so badly to comfort him, to connect with him, and by gently touching him, she had felt his anger segue to tenderness, and it had filled her heart to know that the feelings between them were still so potent, so real.

No matter what happened between Lars and Sara in Jackson Hole, there was a certain satisfaction Jane felt in knowing that there was still some serious heat and emotion between her and Lars. Sara hadn't won. Not entirely. Lars had met Sara, and—most likely—made out with her, but he still felt something real for Jane, and that made her, strangely, happy.

Not to mention, Nils and Paul had vehemently denied Lars's interest in Sara.

The intensity of this morning's kiss and his friends' refusal to believe Lars and Sara were together was making Jane start to question things.

Was he going to Jackson Hole or not?

Was he into Sara or not?

Frowning as she recalled Margot's admission yesterday, Jane tried to remember the specifics of what Margot had seen. She'd walked in on Lars and Sara alone, and Sara was only wearing underwear. But Jane realized that *Sara* had supplied most of the details about how physical she and Lars had gotten—about kissing and touching each other. Those tidbits hadn't come from Margot, but from Sara. And it was definitely possible that Sara was lying, because she lied whenever it suited her purposes, and hurting Jane was one of Sara's reasons for living.

Jane rested her head on the glass beside her as they drove under the Roosevelt arch and into Yellowstone.

What exactly had Margot seen?

Because, as Ray pointed out yesterday, Lars wasn't acting like a man obsessed with Sara.

And Paul had been so insistent that Lars would never leave Gardiner while his family was coming to town, and Jane had never actually heard Lars accept Sara's invitation.

What did Lars mean this morning when he'd cried, *I saw you!*

Saw *what?* What would make him so angry? So…jealous? She hadn't hung out with any men except Ray, who was gay, and…Paul. Paul, with whom Jane had shared coffee in the café last night after Maggie and Nils went upstairs. Could all of that teeth-clashing, growling anger possibly have been about Paul?

Looking into the rearview mirror at just the right time, Jane's eyes slammed into Lars's, and she could feel it in her gut, in her heart, in every cell of her body: unfinished business. He slid his eyes back to the road, but Jane felt it as surely as the noon bell in every western movie…a showdown was coming.

***

Samara wore her hair in a complex arrangement of loose braids with a garland of white flowers, soft, natural makeup, a short, floral peasant dress in a gauzy fabric with a brown suede belt and high-heeled brown suede sandals. Lars couldn't imagine her looking more different than she had on the first day of the shoot when she was in black, white and grey with sharp, angry makeup and black leather combat-style boots. She looked soft, luscious and innocent, neatly concealing her *true* nature, which he now knew to be scheming, lying and vicious.

Sitting next to him on the way to the shoot, Samara had been unable to engage him in conversation, because Lars had nothing to say to her, and was even less eager to listen to her stupid nonsensical chatter, and her annoyingly high-pitched giggle all the way to Yellowstone Lake. Thank God for his imaginary rash. Since this job was essentially completed after today's shoot, with the exception of airport transfers on Monday afternoon, Lars would not be spending an extra second of his time with her, and he certainly wouldn't allow himself to be caught alone with her ever again.

Jane was another matter. He wanted to spend every available second alone with her from now until her plane taxied away, and if there was any chance he could convince her to stay for a few extra days, he'd press his advantage. He wouldn't think about goodbyes right now; right now he just wanted to get things with Jane back on solid ground. He didn't care if she'd kissed Paul, as long as she wanted to be with him now, and he'd tell her that the first chance he got.

She looked over at him from where she stood watching Samara, and his lips turned up. Jane's cheeks flushed as she turned away.

Whenever you're ready, I'm waiting for you, Jane Mays.

As if she read his mind, she sauntered over to where he stood by his truck, like a déjà vu from yesterday, before Old Faithful started erupting.

She stood in front of him, hands on her hips, and pushed her sunglasses on top of her head. Squinting up at him, she took a deep breath and let it go slowly.

"Hi."

"Heya," he answered.

"Sara says you're going to Jackson Hole with her."

"I'm not."

He watched a slow smile tilt her lips up, and she even let out a tiny chuckle as her mossy eyes searched his. He could tell she was pleased, and it made his heart hammer with pleasure of his own.

Suddenly her face clouded over.

"You kissed her."

"That's not what happened."

"What *did* happen?"

"What happened with you and Paul?"

"What are you *talking* about? Nothing!"

"Jane, I saw you last night at the Prairie Dawn. I was walking to the Best Western to talk to you, and I saw you two through the glass. You weren't playing euchre, that's for sure."

"Maggie and Nils—"

"I don't want to hear about Maggie and Nils. I'm talking about you and Paul. I saw a whole lot of handholding. And then, I saw him lean forward and—"

"On the cheek, Lars! He kissed me on the cheek, like a brother or a friend. He was comforting me."

"Huh," he scoffed. "Didn't seem brotherly to me."

"This from the one who ripped my cousin's clothes off."

He flinched, then shook his head in disgust. "You actually *believe* that?"

"Someone saw her standing in her underwear with your lips on hers. You tell me."

"My lips were nowhere near hers and besides—"

"JANE! WATER!"

She looked over at her cousin, then quickly slid her eyes back to him.

"Are you with Paul or not?" he demanded.

"Are you with Sara or not?" she shot back.

"JANE! WATER, NOW!"

Ready for a costume change, Samara stood a few yards away with her hands on her hips, staring at Lars and Jane with daggers in her eyes.

"I have to go," Jane muttered.

"We're not done," said Lars, watching as she turned around to go help her bratty cousin.

***

The whole crew clapped enthusiastically as Sara finished the last set of photos, and she made a pretty curtsy, blowing kisses at the photographer before heading back to her trailer to change for her weekend of relaxation.

Jane had asked Lars to transfer her bags to the smaller van that Mr. Lindstrom would drive to Jackson Hole, while

Lars would drive Jane and the rest of the team back to Gardiner. Tomorrow morning, Ray, Shanelle and Margot would be driven to the airport for their flights home, and Jane would leave on Monday with Sara, Franco and Sebastian when they returned from Jackson Hole.

Leave on Monday.

Her heart clenched at the thought of leaving Lars.

Shanelle braided Sara's hair in a requested French braid, and Margot finished hanging the last of the shoot clothes.

One of *Trend*'s people would drive the trailer back to the rental place in Bozeman and ship the designer clothes back to New York.

Sara took her time changing, and finally, it was just Jane and her cousin left in the quiet of the trailer as Sara finished dressing in jeans and a designer sweatshirt for her ride to Jackson Hole.

"Jane…" Sara started, gently, and Jane's head whipped up at the unfamiliarity of the tone. "I'm worried about you."

Jane rolled her eyes at Sara, but didn't move from where she stood, across from her cousin.

"You're staying behind, and Lars is here, and I know you like him…but, I don't think he is who you think he is, or who you want him to be."

"You're mistaking me for someone who gives a shit about your opinion."

"Fine, Jane. Have it your way."

Jane put her hands on her hips. "Okay. What? What are you trying to say?"

Sara cleared her throat, leaning into the conversation.

"Okay…so you know he was kissing me yesterday, right?"

Jane stared at her cousin, pursing her lips. No, she didn't know that. She didn't feel like she had the whole story.

Sara raised her eyebrows. "Oh. Okay. You're not sure about that, huh? Even though Margot—"

"Margot didn't see you kissing him, Sara. You said that. She didn't, and besides…it's just not adding up."

"What isn't?" asked Sara, narrowing her eyes.

"He hasn't stayed at your place once. He isn't going away with you. I don't know…I feel like…maybe he *doesn't* like you. Maybe he actually likes…*me*."

Sara's mouth dropped open, staring at Jane with a wide, mocking smile. "YOU? Are you *crazy*?"

"God, you're such a bit—you know what, Sara? I don't want to talk to you anymore. Your bags are packed. Mr. Lindstrom's waiting. Have a nice—"

Jane turned to leave, but Sara jumped in front of the door. "There's something you need to hear."

"Sara, get out of my—" Jane tried to reach the doorknob behind her, but Sara quickly pressed the voice memo app on her phone, choosing a voice recording dated yesterday.

"Listen."

Jane rolled her eyes, but stopped to listen.

"Samara, I could always come track you down in New York. Come stay with you for a weekend."

"You'd do that for me? Come all the way to New York? Give me a night to remember?"

"Absolutely. I promise a night you'll never forget."

"I like the way you're touching me right now, Lars."

Jane jerked her eyes to Sara's and to her shock, and Sara nodded. "Keep listening."

"What will you do to me, Lars?"

"Whatever you want."

Jane's stomach rolled over, and she threw up a little bit into her mouth then swallowed it back down.

"Deal, Lars."

"Deal, Samara."

Sara hit the stop button and shoved the phone in her back pocket.

"I recorded that yesterday."

Jane stared at the floor of the trailer as her heart raced and her fingers grew cold. Her whole body trembled, and she regretted that she didn't insist on leaving before hearing that conversation, which would be very difficult to erase from her memory. It was his voice. They were his words. Sara had used his name in every sentence, which meant she had recorded this conversation on purpose. Jane doubted that Lars even knew she had a recording. It didn't matter.

The familiarity with which he spoke to Sara, the fact that he was obviously touching her as the recording was made, the image of them—

Jane clamped her eyes shut against the images assaulting her and, feeling faint, reached forward to steady herself by placing her hand on the door by Sara's shoulder. After a moment, she felt Sara's arms encircle her as they had so long ago, and Jane was pulled into her cousin's embrace. Suddenly she was ten again and, seduced by the comfort Sara was offering, Jane rested her cheek on her cousin's bony shoulder, wetting her fleecy sweatshirt with the tears from her silent sobs as Sara ran her hands soothingly up and down Jane's back. It felt so good to be held, to be held lovingly by someone who was her blood, her family.

"You can't leave me now," Sara whispered. "Come to Jackson Hole."

Yes. Yes, I will. I will go with you. You're my cousin…my family…

She drew back, about to nod yes…when she caught sight of Sara's eager, expectant violet eyes. Panic was retreating now that Sara was so close to getting what she wanted most of all: a contrite, grateful Jane, back at her beck and call.

With blinding illumination, Jane felt the last of those tiny threads inside break with an unforgiving, irrevocable snap, and she knew she wasn't going anywhere with Sara.

"You knew how I felt about him," she murmured, staring at her cousin as she would at a monster. "You knew from the start."

"Janie…"

"It doesn't matter if you kissed him or he kissed you. And that conversation you just played for me? That doesn't matter either. Not where you and I are concerned." She reached up, pushing a wisp of Samara's dark hair back behind her ear.

"You win. You win, Sara." She tilted her head to the side with a resigned grimace. "And I…I quit."

Jane heard Sara gasp as she reached around her and

pulled the door open against the dead weight of her cousin's stunned body. Stepping out into the sunshine of the late afternoon, she saw one of the *Trend* vans pulling out, headed back to Gardiner, and she ran for it. They stopped and opened the door for her, and just like that:

Jane was free.

***

Sitting in the van, Lars had been waiting for Jane to finish up in Samara's trailer so he could drive the crew back to Gardiner, so it surprised him to see her sprint from Samara's trailer to the *Trend* van and hop inside. Since Samara was headed to Jackson Hole in a different van with his father, he couldn't blame the last-minute change on a rift with her cousin. This time, he had to assume Jane was avoiding *him*.

He may have gotten her back up a little bit during their little spat about Samara and Paul, but it didn't seem like the sort of deal-breaker that would make her avoid riding back with him. Huh. She had come from Samara's trailer. Samara. Samara had done something, he was sure of it. He needed answers and he knew where to find them.

"Folks," he started, speaking to Ray, Shanelle and Margot, "I need to speak to Miss Amaya for a moment before we head back to Gardiner. I'll be right back."

Despite his previous pledge never to be caught alone with Samara again, he needed to understand what had just happened with Jane. He knocked on her trailer door.

"Back so soon?" she asked, opening the door.

Lars shoved the door open, and Samara stepped back as he entered the trailer and slammed the door behind him.

He put his hands on his hips, staring at her, his face concealing nothing.

"What just happened with Jane?"

"You know…you're cute, Lars, but you're not that cute."

"Neither are you."

"Fuck you. Nobody talks to me like that. What're you? Some tour operator in some shit hole, backwater town? I don't have to answer to you."

He stood against the door, arms crossed over his chest. "You *will* answer to me. And you *will* tell me what you just said to upset her."

"Me?" She snorted. "That's a laugh. It wasn't *me* who upset her, cowboy."

"Then who?"

"Boy, are you dumb."

"You're a woman. That's the *only* thing keeping me from smashing my fist into your face."

"Don't threaten me."

"You are a *despicable* person. I know you lied to her, made up some story about me ripping off your clothes and kissing you, but I didn't initiate that encounter, nor did I enjoy it."

She stared at his crotch for a long second. "Yeah, right."

"Why do you want to hurt her so badly? What in God's name did she do to you?"

"SHE TOOK *HIM* AWAY FROM ME!" she bellowed with such rage, Lars winced in shock, as if she had taken a swing at him and connected.

"What? *Who?*"

"My father," she snarled.

Lars's head was spinning. "Jane went to live with you because her parents were killed in a car accident."

"She took him away from me. He loved her more."

"No surprise there." He knew it was cruel. He didn't care.

She stared at him with a furious half-smile on her face then fished her phone out of her back pocket. "You think *I'm* a monster? *I'm* not the one who just broke her in half."

She tapped on two buttons and he furrowed his brows for a moment, trying to figure out what he was listening to. Then he realized. He was listening to himself…propositioning Samara in the truck last night on the side of the road. He thought she'd been texting *Trend* to fire the Lindstroms, but she'd had other devious plans, apparently, and had been recording their exchange. When he raised his eyes to hers, he knew they must have been murderous because she physically stepped back, away from him.

"You recorded that? Yesterday when we were talking?"

"Just in case I needed it."

He nodded, revolted that he was alone with her, repulsed by her, unable to see anything beautiful in her anymore.

"And you played it for Jane just now."

Samara jerked her head in a satisfied nod.

"How'd that work out for you?"

Samara took a deep breath, straightening her back and her neck, looking at him with cold, angry eyes. "She quit."

"Huh," he exclaimed, smiling a little in spite of himself. "Well, thank God for small miracles."

Her nostrils flared, and she narrowed her eyes, staring at him, holding her phone tightly, the old-fashioned silver microphone on the screen adding the smallest bit of ambient light into the darkened trailer.

He turned away from her, unable to take a good, deep breath, wanting like hell to get as far away from Samara Amaya as possible. He'd gotten the information he'd come for.

How to fix the damage now? Damned if he had a clue.

He turned the knob to leave but her voice stopped him.

"You really wanted Jane more than me?" Her voice was small like a child's, like she was about to cry.

"I only *ever* wanted Jane," he answered with his back to Samara. "It had nothing to do with you."

Then he stepped outside, closing the door behind him, walking back to the van. He'd known from the start that winning Jane's trust would be hard.

Thanks to Samara, now it looked impossible.

CHAPTER 11

Jane's eyes burned with tears and a huge lump crowded her throat.

She'd been so looking forward to her weekend of freedom, and after kissing Lars this morning and hearing him admit that he wasn't going to Jackson Hole, a whole fantasy had taken root in her mind. For a few sweet hours, she imagined herself spending the weekend with him.

As she lay despondently on her motel bed, in the same place and position where Lars had held her on Monday night, she winced, wrapping her arms around her body. Thinking about Sara and Lars together made her feel sick. Why had he kissed her in the morning mist if he was planning "a night to remember" with her cousin? She couldn't think about it anymore. It was making her crazy.

So, on to the next mess.

She had quit her job.

Finally. And while part of her felt like dancing around her motel room, the other part was feeling slightly terrified.

Jane's uncle was going to be very upset with her; he would certainly try to pressure her to return to Sara's employ. Could she hold up against the pressure this time, as she hadn't been able to before? She pictured his face, her father's face, asking her to give Sara another chance, and her resolve weakened. Then she fished the fuzzy B out of her back pocket and held it in front of her eyes, feeling her strength return as she shoved it back into her pocket. Nothing and no one would entice her to ever work for Sara ever again.

Where are you going to go, Jane? And what are you going to do?

She knew she couldn't very well stay in Gardiner, but nowhere else sounded right either. She'd always dreamed of returning to San Francisco where she'd grown up, but it would be lonely. She could go back to Boston, find her own apartment in Cambridge, look up some of her college friends, and see if she could explain things to her aunt and uncle. Or she could return to New York, where she had solid business contacts…or did she? Would anyone work with Jane Mays when she wasn't attached to Samara Amaya?

Jane massaged her aching head, seeking her mother's voice from long ago. *Ice cream, sweet baby Jane. That's the answer to everything. We need some ice cream.*

"I wish it were that simple," she muttered softly, missing her mother with a longing that tightened her chest and made her feel breathless. She sobbed and laughed at the same time. "Ice cream, huh? Okay, Mama."

Jane sat up and wiped away the tears that had fallen as she lay on the bed. She stood up and rooted through her wallet for a few dollars, then looked around the room for her cap before remembering it was gone. She sighed, missing its comforting presence—one of the many things she wished she hadn't lost this week.

***

Jane opened the door of the grocery store and picked up a basket, strolling over to the produce section.

Some vacation. Starting in the grocery store staring at a hill of grapefruits.

She picked one up, enjoying the feel of the cool, smooth-bumpy rind under her fingertips.

"So, yesterday…you had a question for me…"

Her fingers squeezed in reaction to his voice behind her, the fingernail of her thumb digging into the tough peel unconsciously, and extracting a sharp, bitter-smelling mist. She turned around slowly to find Lars standing by the oranges, basket hanging from his elbow. He was impossibly handsome in cowboy boots, dusty jeans and the same white polo shirt embroidered with "Lindstrom & Sons" that he'd been wearing when he kissed her in the mist this morning.

By the time her eyes slid to his face, she realized he'd watched her eyes ascend from the boots up. He raised his eyebrows, smiling. "Take a picture, Minx…"

"…it lasts longer," she whispered.

"Your voice slays me, Jane."

"So, you didn't go, after all. To Jackson Hole." She held the grapefruit between both hands, her fingernails still digging into its waxy skin.

"I told you I wasn't going."

"You told me a lot of things."

"I haven't lied to you."

"Then you're lying to someone else."

"That is absolutely, one-hundred-percent true."

"Why should I trust you if you're lying to her?"

"Because she's impossible." He ran a hand through his short blond hair. "Because you find yourself in an impossible situation with her, and say whatever it takes to get out of it. Even if words were never cheap to you before, you use them, you...you...you say anything. Just to get away."

Everything he said was relatable to Jane. More than once Sara had put Jane in a position that required heavy duty lie-telling, and it was never a comfortable place for her.

I like the way you're touching me right now, Lars.

It hurt to remember the recording, and Jane blinked back more tears. "Why should I believe you?"

"Because I'm telling the truth."

"So says a liar," she murmured, looking up at him with tired eyes.

He cringed and exhaled audibly, looking away from her for a second before seizing her eyes again.

"Can I fix this?" he asked.

"I don't know," she answered, fingernails extracting more bitter spray.

"You're murdering that grapefruit."

"I'll buy it," she said.

She stared at his light-blue eyes, wishing she could silence her heart, which pleaded with her to find a way to believe him, to trust him, to keep him.

"I was—" she started then stopped, swallowing the lump in her throat. "I was wrong about Jackson Hole. About you going."

"I was *never* going. For the record. Never. I never said yes to that."

Jane nodded. "She said you were."

"I know." He tilted his head to the side. "She was my client. It was my job to keep her happy. You don't keep a supermodel happy by offending her."

But how far did he actually go to keep Sara happy? That's what Jane really needed to know.

Tears flooded her eyes, and she tore her gaze away from him, looking down at her feet. "She played...um, a conversation for me...that you two had, and—"

"I know. I went to her trailer and made her play it for me after you left."

Her eyes darted back up to his face and he reacted to the distress he saw there, wincing again. He raised his hand, as if to touch her, and then drew it back, swallowing like it hurt.

"What do you mean?" she asked. "How did you—"

"I went to see her after I saw you run from her trailer to the *Trend* van. I asked her what she had said or done to upset you. She played the recording for me."

Tears slid down her cheeks. "You were touching her when she recorded that."

He nodded. "I had my hand on her leg."

She swiped at her eyes, embarrassed to feel fresh tears fall.

"She was threatening to fire my father, to remove us from the job and refuse payment. God, Jane, please—"

"Did you sleep with her?"

"What? NO! No. Absolutely not!"

"Were you...naked with her?"

"Jane, no! No, no…I was never naked with her. Never even close."

"But, you touched her."

"Once. Once on the leg when she made that recording. The leg. *Nowhere* else, Jane. I swear to God. That other time? When she invited me into her trailer? She only had underwear on, and I was totally caught off-guard…she…she took my hand and put it on her breast, then she pressed her body against mine and was about to kiss me, but I pushed her away, just as Margot walked in…"

Oh, God, how she wanted to believe him.

"Convenient."

"Truthful."

"Skeptical."

"Frustrated!" he growled through clenched teeth, taking a step closer to her. He ran his free hand through his hair, tousling it again. His face was sharp with irritation. "Jane. All I ever wanted—from the beginning—was you."

Me.

She only had a moment to enjoy his words, because two simultaneous thoughts scattered them: the first was that she could tell he was telling the truth, and the second was that he had just used the past tense. She swallowed and turned around, facing the grapefruits, unable to bear the intensity in his stark, silvery-blue eyes. She let the mangled grapefruit in her hand roll dejectedly into her basket as her eyes filled with more embarrassing tears.

"And now?" she whispered.

"Now?"

"You said that all you ever *wanted*, was me. Past tense."

Feeling his breath on the back of her neck was the last thing she expected, and her eyes shuddered closed, her free hand curling into a fist.

"Jane. I am *still* not that guy, but *damn,* you are making it hard on me," he whispered close to her ear. She felt his fingers push the damp curls off the back of her neck and his lips brushed the hot, throbbing skin hidden there. She would never look at a grapefruit the same way again. "You walked away from me. You *pushed* me away. I didn't initiate anything with your cousin, and when she did, I pushed *her* away. And that conversation you heard? That was me getting out of going to Jackson Hole so my family wouldn't lose this job." His lips skimmed her skin softly, gently. "I didn't know how to turn her down without being fired."

Jane had to admit…his explanation made a lot of sense. Facts and events clicked into place organically, and she could finally see how everything had happened, regardless of how it looked. He kissed her neck again then put his hands on her shoulders, turning her around to face him.

"Jane…just give me the weekend. Give me three days: three days to show you how I feel…and, and if you don't believe me, if you don't trust me—if you still think I *ever* wanted Samara Amaya more than I wanted you, I'll drive you up to the airport in Bozeman on Monday and I'll never bother you again. Three days, Jane. Please."

Jane was so sick and tired of letting old fears of pain and abandonment hold dominion over her heart. Just as she had let fears of being alone keep her bound in servitude to her ungrateful, unkind cousin, she was allowing the fear of rejection to keep her from finding some happiness with Lars. It was time to grow up. It was time to realize that taking a fall wasn't the end of anything. She had, in fact, already fallen several times this week. Fallen for Lars...fallen when she let him go...fallen when she thought he was with Sara...fallen when she thought she had lost him. The more Jane fell, the more she belonged to him, as if the key to finding her way— to finding *him*—was to keep falling, and to stop protecting herself.

"Okay," she murmured.

"Okay?" he asked, with a surprised half-smile that tugged on her heartstrings.

"Okay," she said, with a little more backbone and a small smile of her own. "I don't have anywhere else to be."

"I heard," he answered, raising his eyebrows at her. "You quit."

"Yes, I did."

Jane realized she'd been holding her breath and she let it out in a rush, staring at Lars, as her smile grew. She put the back of her unoccupied hand to her cheek and felt the dry heat there, wishing her racing heart would slow down. Her wish had come true, after all: they were going to spend the weekend together.

"Come over tonight," he suggested, his eyes, filled with hope, scanning hers.

"I have to get ice cream first," she answered, and his face broke into a pleased grin that made her insides turn to jelly.

He walked down the aisles with her and then to the cashier. He hurried ahead to open her door for her as they approached his truck.

"Do you need anything from your room?" he asked.

She turned to him and shook her head slowly, unaccountably nervous. Too much change at once. She was on vacation. She was unemployed. She was spending the weekend with Lars.

"You'll drive me back to the hotel later?" she asked.

"If you want, Minx. You're in charge."

Seated side by side, he lowered the visor on her side, and just grazing her shoulder, he took out a disc, slipping it into the CD player. As he pulled out of the parking lot, Ricky Nelson's voice filled the cab, singing "Traveling Man."

Jane turned to him with a smile. "What a great choice."

"Yeah?"

"I love this one."

"Me too."

"It's…magical… *'and in every port I own the heart of at least one lovely girl…'*" She sang along quietly.

"Magical?"

She shrugged. "Kind of. Isn't it?"

"I don't know if it's…*magical.*"

"Okay, Professor, then why do *you* love it? A girl in every town? A honey in every port of call? That how you roll?"

"Are you crazy? *Way* too much work. One's all I need." He grinned at her.

"Random phenomenon," Jane murmured, shaking her

head.

"What?"

"Unlike every other man in the world, you *don't* covet the lifestyle of a philandering playboy."

"You make things too complicated, Jane. It's a good song. I like it. Makes me happy. Can't that be enough?"

Jane didn't answer. She wasn't totally sure of what they were talking about now. She looked over at him in the dim light of the truck. His blond hair gleamed like polished silver in the setting sun. Her fingers itched to reach over and tousle the front, run her hands through the—

"Take a—"

"—picture. I know. You gotta get a new line."

"I want to ask you something."

"Okay."

"So…my family's coming into town tomorrow. My brother Erik and his wife Kat are having their twin girls christened at our church here on Sunday. Anyway, we're definitely a bunch of rowdy, overwhelming Swedes, but I was wondering if you'd come with me to the luncheon tomorrow and the christening on Sunday."

Jane turned to look at him because she wanted him to see her eyes, because he deserved to see how much his invitation meant to her. "I'm really flattered…but, your family doesn't want some stranger tagging along with you, do they?"

"You don't know them. They're a more-the-merrier type of crowd, and besides, I know they'd love to meet you. They adopt people. Look at Maggie…look at Paul…they'll be there too. *I'd* love for them to meet you, Jane."

It reminded her of something her mother used to say: *Won't you come into my garden? I would like my roses to see you.*

The idea of spending a weekend with a family, anyone's family, was so tempting, Jane almost couldn't think clearly. Since losing her parents, the thing she missed most in her life was that feeling of belonging to someone. She ached to say yes, but she was wary of getting too attached. They'd only committed to spending a weekend together. Jane was still leaving on Monday.

But why not go, Jane? Why not enjoy this weekend with him? Why not just say…

"Yes. Okay. I mean, sure, I'd love to."

He broke into a grin, letting his breath out and holding her eyes as he parked the truck in his driveway. "I was so nervous to ask you."

"Did you think I'd say no?"

"I hurt you."

"You explained everything. And she is…impossible."

"One more thing: do you think we could *please* not talk about Samara this weekend?"

"Sounds perfect to me," Jane said. "Hey…I just remembered something—"

"What? You're going to my nieces' christening with Paul?"

"Now *that's* something we're going to need to talk about," she said. "You know, I'm not the only one with trust issues, Lars."

"Fine. Then, please just tell me…what's going on with

you two? What did I see?"

"I don't like unwarranted jealousy, so I'm not answering this question again. Got it?"

He nodded, holding her eyes.

"You sure?"

"Jane!"

"We're friends. *Friends.* Nothing else. He kissed my *cheek* last night. He was trying to cheer me up because I thought you were going to Jackson Hole with my cousin and Paul knew I had feelings for you. He talked to me about the woman he's met online, and I talked to him about you." Her lips tilted up a little and she looked at him tenderly. "He gave me hope. He said my heart is safe with you."

"He's right." He smiled at her. "That's my goal for the weekend, Minx. For you to trust me."

Jane took a deep breath but crossed her legs toward him. "Got your work cut out for you, Professor."

"I'm a hard worker. I care about you."

"You barely know me."

"I know everything I need to know, Jane Mays." He took a deep breath, looking away from her, gesturing to the house in front of them. "So…this is my driveway. That's my house. You're in charge, so we can stay here in my truck chatting all night if you like, or we could—"

"I'll come in."

***

It was taking all of his self-control not to kiss her or touch her, but he didn't trust their footing yet and he meant it when he said that she was calling the shots. He couldn't afford to make any mistakes with Jane right now, so he was fully prepared to follow her lead. He walked around to her side of the truck, offering his hand to help her climb down.

"Hey, before I interrupted you…you were about to say something. Something you remembered. What were you going to say?" he asked.

She laced her fingers through his as they walked up the porch steps. Her hand was soft and warm, and it felt ridiculously good to have it back in his. He looked down at their interlocked hands. Flat-out sexy.

"The grizzlies."

The grizzlies. She wanted him to take her to the park.

Through the haze of his lust for her, it occurred to him that this—right now, right this second holding hands with Jane in his driveway staring into her eyes while the sun died behind them—was a *perfect* moment. And he never wanted it to end. He thought he had a grip on his feelings for her, but suddenly he knew they were deeper than he had realized. If it didn't feel so damn good, it would have been sobering to pinpoint the second he knew that he was just about gone.

"Want to see 'em tomorrow?"

"Will you take me?" she asked, bright eyes twinkling up at him.

Anywhere, Minx. I'll take you anywhere.

"Yeah. Tomorrow morning. Early."

"How early is early?" she asked, as they walked up the steps and he unlocked the door that led into his living room.

"So early it'd be smarter for you to just stay over." He meant for this to be playful, but his voice, full of hunger for her, came out gruffer and more serious than he intended. He shut the door behind him, and as his eyes adjusted to the darkness, she dropped his hand.

Damn it, Lars. You overplayed that hand. Don't push h—

He could barely see more than the outline of her head and shoulders in the dim light, but feeling her hands on his chest made his breath catch. First just her fingers, flat against his pecs before she slid them up to his neck. He took a shallow breath as she pressed the base of her hands flush to his jaw, fingers resting cool and light on his cheeks. Reaching out, he found her waist, and then lowered his hands to her hips, pulling her up against his chest. He knew that the back of the sofa was just behind her, so he stepped forward. When she bumped up against the upholstery, he slipped his hands under her backside and lifted her, so she was perched up in front of him. He stepped forward once more, between her legs, and his blood raced south as he felt her legs rise, brushing against his thighs until she locked them around his waist, behind his back, pulling him as close to her as possible. She reached up to wrap her arms around his neck, pulling him down to her until his lips made contact with hers.

He wanted her. God, how he wanted her.

His lips slanted over hers again and again until they matched perfectly, their tongues touching, licking and stroking gently. He found the edge of her flimsy little shirt and lifted it up over her head, until there was nothing between him and her skin but her bra and his polo shirt, which he pulled up and off one-handed, breaking contact with her for only a second, before finding her lips in the dark again.

He ran his palms up and down the smooth, warm skin of her back, finding the clasp of her bra and dispatching it quickly. She loosened her arms from his neck so that he could slip it down, listening to the whisper of it hitting the hardwood floor.

He ran his palms up and down her bare back, sighing into her mouth, blood rushing like lava to his groin as his chest pressed—*skin against skin*—into hers for the first time. Her soft breasts were crushed against the hair of his chest and his heart beat relentlessly, a riot of feelings wreaking havoc on his body, in his head, and in his heart.

She tore her lips away from his and he heard her voice as if through gauze, "Wait. Lars, wait."

Lars bent his head to her shoulder, pressing his lips to her soft, sweet-smelling skin, then dragging them along her collarbone to the base of her throat where her pulse fluttered in a tiny alcove. He rested his lips there with his eyes closed, fingers still running slowly, reverently, up and down the smooth planes of her back.

"Lars," she whispered.

Finally he raised his head and leaned back to look at her.

His eyes had adjusted to the soft twilight flooding the room from the windows and he could just make out her face: red lips, tendrils from her little ponytail loose around her face, wide eyes tender and soft as they gazed up at him.

His arms were still wrapped around her as she perched

on the back of the sofa, and she felt small and warm in his arms, which were dark and tan against the white skin of her waist. Trying to slow down his heart was impossible. This wasn't enough. This wasn't nearly enough. He wanted her. All of her.

"Lars," she murmured again in her throaty voice, reaching up to touch his cheek with her palm. "There's no rush. We have all night."

All night. He glanced down between them, where her breasts pressed against his chest. The impulse to kiss his way from her neck to her waist, loving every spot of skin in between, was almost unbearable.

All night. It was more than he had hoped for. He took a deep breath, trying to calm down. She was calling the shots and if she wanted to slow down, he wouldn't pressure her, no matter how much he ached for her. He nodded, sighing loudly, maybe even a little sorry for himself.

She pulled back a little, her arm folding across her chest to cover the tips of her breasts. Her feet hit the ground and he leaned down, feeling around for her shirt on the floor. She slipped her arms through the straps, wiggling it over her head as he leaned over and turned on the lamp beside her. Her hair was disheveled, and her lips were just a little puffy.

He groaned, wondering how he was going to make it through tonight if she didn't want—didn't *need*—what he was hoping for.

"All night, huh?"

She gave him a half-smile, flicking her eyes to his waist, to below his waist where they rested for a moment with amusement before returning to his face. She bit her upper lip, trying not to grin and failing wildly.

"Yeah," he confirmed, looking down at the prominent bulge in his jeans, then back up at her teasing face. "Yeah, that's the way it is. You're *killing* me, Jane."

"Sorry. I got carried away." She stepped away from the couch, and stopped trying not to grin. She beamed at him. "Self-control, my fine Swedish friend. I'm barely in the door and we've already gotten…distracted."

He leaned back from her, crossing his arms over his chest and couldn't help but notice how her eyes widened as she stared at his chest. Her mouth opened slightly and she licked her lips, her face concealing nothing. "I—I mean…sorry for staring. That is just…*unreal.*"

Lars chuckled, raising his eyebrows, before snatching his shirt off the ground and throwing it on over his head, ruining her view. "And…off limits, apparently. Remember: self-control, Minx."

"Duly noted." She tilted her head to the side, sighing with a little moan. "Seriously, though, don't give me a song and dance about working out. That's gotta be Viking genes or something."

He chuckled at her, shrugging, feeling ridiculously pleased. "Partially genes…plus hikes. Climbs. Free weights. I can think of some other aerobic activities I wouldn't mind adding to the roster…like, immediately."

"Like, what?" she rasped with a teasing grin.

"Like, in my bed."

"Like, with a partner?" She leaned up against the couch,

staring at him, then bit her lower lip slowly. His eyes darted to it and he actually felt his body sway toward her like he was drunk.

"*Killing* me, Minx," he repeated, straightening up.

The room was quiet, and they stood before one another, eyes locked, a little stunned, maybe, both seeming to need a minute to process what was happening between them. Lars reached out gently and put his arms around her, and Jane wrapped her arms around him, leaning her cheek on his chest under his chin. They stood there together for a while, not moving, not kissing, not speaking, just holding each other.

Finally Lars leaned back to look into her eyes.

"Nothing feels as good as this, Jane," he whispered. "Nothing ever has."

Jane smiled, but he thought he saw some sadness creep into her expression before she rested her cheek back on his chest and answered, softly,

"Agreed."

***

Lars hadn't expected a dinner guest, but he always kept the fixings for *våfflor*, or Swedish waffles, on hand. Jane sat up on the counter beside the waffle iron, heckling him as various 60s songs played on the kitchen CD player.

"It is a damn shame you've never tried *Svensk våfflor*, Jane. We need to remedy your embarrassing lack of culinary experience."

"By making waffles in an electric waffle iron?"

"Yes, *smärta i nacken*, in a waffle iron."

"What does that mean?"

"Literally? Pain in the neck," he answered, ending with a chuckle and winking at her.

"How much Swedish do you know?" she asked as he added batter to the iron and gingerly closed the top.

"Good bit. Enough to get by."

A glop of batter oozed out the side and he caught it with a spatula before it dripped onto the counter.

"Tell me more words."

He glanced at the iron between them, which seemed okay for now, and leaned one elbow on the counter, grinning at her.

"Okay. Let's see…*Värdefull.*"

"Means?"

"Valuable…precious." He took a deep breath, tilting his head and gazing at her. "*Härlig.*"

She raised her eyebrows.

"Lovely," he murmured.

She grinned at him, happy. "More, please."

"*Lita på mig.*"

She tilted her head to the side in question.

"Means you can trust me…well, literally it means you can *rely* on me. But, it's the same thing."

"Is it?"

"Yeah. I'm never going to lie to you again, and I'm not going anywhere, Jane. *Jag lovar dig.*"

Her eyes widened at the word "lovar" and she drew back a little, sitting ramrod straight on the counter. She swallowed, looking nervous. "*L-lovar?* What's *that* mean?"

"Calm down." Lars smiled at her discomposure. "*Promise*. It means, *I promise you*, not…"

"Whew! Got nervous there…"

"Nervous?"

"Yeah, I mean…it sounded like you were saying…"

He raised his eyebrows, smirking to conceal the unexpected disappointment he felt to hear her say that. It's not that he was ready to tell her he loved her, but his feelings for her had definitely grown beyond mere affection. He knew it. He could feel it. They were rushing, bounding, hurtling toward love.

He looked down and shrugged, shaking off his disappointment. She was here with him, wasn't she? In his house, in his kitchen, staying the night, giving him a chance. *Don't rush things, Lars. Be patient with her.*

"Lars." He looked up and her face was soft, maybe even a little worried. She gave him a small, cajoling smile. "One more?"

Lars nodded, looking down, thinking. When he looked back up, Jane's eyes were wide, waiting for him to say one last thing in Swedish. His thoughts were still barreling in one direction, and he couldn't just hit a switch to detour them or turn them off. There was only one phrase circling in a loop in Lars's head, and once he thought of it, he couldn't think of any others, so he said:

"*Jag är förälskad i dig*, Jane." *I am falling in love with you, Jane.*

"Means?" The bell on the waffle iron dinged loudly between them, making Jane jump a little.

"Means the *våfflor* are done, Minx. Ready for something sweet?"

***

Idiot! Jane took a plate of waffles covered in some sort of Swedish jam that was unfamiliar to her and stayed perched on the counter as he leaned beside her, eating in silence.

Great job, Jane. You could have offered a hard cringe or vomited or something just to add a little extra repulsion to your reaction to the word lover which wasn't even the word lover!

She wished she could go back to the moment and just smile at him, raise her eyebrows, stay silent…*anything!* Anything but her stupid stumbling, bumbling response that shut him down and didn't come anywhere close to expressing her true feelings.

"These are great," she offered.

He nudged her thigh with his elbow. "Told you."

"Where'd you learn to cook?"

"My *mamma*. She was a great cook."

"I don't know if my mother was a great cook. I don't remember." She took another bite of the cakey waffle covered with crimson jam. "What's this again?"

"*Sylt Ligon.* Ligonberry jam. It's—"

"Swedish. I am learning that you are very Swedish."

"And here I would have thought a smart girl like you would have picked up on that already. My name being Lars Lindstrom and all…"

"Big difference between having Swedish blood and having a Swedish life."

"Just wait 'til tomorrow, Minx. You'll think you're in

Stockholm."

"I can't wait." And she couldn't. How long had it been since Jane had spent time with a real family? Not counting awkward holidays with the Mayses where Sara sulked around whining about how *boring* it was to be home, she couldn't actually remember.

"Hey," Lars looked at her, eyes alert, tilting his head. "Do you hear that?"

Jane listened, but she didn't hear anything. He took her empty plate and put it in the sink, turning down the music. Then she heard it: the muffled, but unmistakable, sound of a woman's light laughter.

"Where's that coming from?" Jane whispered.

Lars nodded, pointing a finger at the ceiling.

"Who's up there?"

"Nils. And…"

"Maggie."

Lars whipped his face to Jane, shaking his head back and forth fast. "Nah. He's liked her for years, but they haven't—you know, they haven't…"

"Umm…" Jane bit her bottom lip, trying not to smile.

"What do you know?" he whispered, ice-blue eyes teeming with questions.

Jane slipped off the counter and took his hand. "Where can we talk?"

"Tell me now!"

"I'm not going to tell you the whole story whispering in your kitchen when they're right above us doing *that*."

He turned and pulled her through the kitchen, back

through the living room—Jane sighed as they passed the sofa—into a hallway, pushing open one of three doors. She assumed the other two were a bathroom and spare bedroom, because she knew instinctively that she had just entered Lars's bedroom.

Jane took a deep breath. She had never seen such a big bed in her life. It dominated the room. A dark brown leather frame with a simple, but imposing, dark brown leather headboard in three sections, each section corded with more dark brown leather. It was simple and elegant, but also a strong, masculine choice. There were three pillows against the headboard, and it was neatly made with a plush, butter-colored comforter.

She looked away from the bed, taking in the rest of the room: neat as a pin with navy blue walls and dark brown chair railing and crown molding. A bureau with a large mirror sat opposite the bed and had a framed black-and-white picture of four young children in skiing gear, lined up from tallest to shortest, and Jane knew instinctively that the second-tallest child was Lars, posing on the slopes with his brothers and sister.

There was a comfortable leather reading chair in the corner with a bronze lamp behind it. Lars crossed the room to turn it on and the room was suddenly bathed in a warm, honey-gold glow. He watched her from the doorway, seeming to realize that the energy between them had shifted as they stepped into his bedroom. He cocked his head to the side, gesturing to the chair.

"Do you want to sit?"

Jane would be eternally grateful to him for not patting the bed and asking her to join him there, instead giving her a moment to adjust to her surroundings. She nodded gratefully and crossed the room, sitting down, curling her legs under her. He sat on the corner of the bed, watching her with those Arctic-blue eyes, slightly amused, his lips trying not to tremble.

"Seriously, Jane. Did you think I was going to jump on you or something?"

She grinned, settling back in the comfortable chair. "It wouldn't be the first time, Professor."

"It definitely won't be the last time, Minx," he promised.

She saw it on his face, the way he suddenly shifted from playful banter to hunger, but instead of pushing things, he looked down, sitting up straighter, composing himself. "But, right now, I have to hear this news…"

"They can't hear us in here?"

Lars shook his head. "We made sure our, um, bedrooms weren't on top of each other."

Jane gave him a sardonic look. "To control the noise from the traffic?"

"You flatter me, Jane. You definitely flatter my brother. I can count the number of times he's brought a girl home on one hand. If he's been getting regular action, he's been getting it somewhere else."

"Sure as heck got it somewhere else last night," Jane declared, grinning.

"Okay. Talk, Minx. Now."

"Well, I don't exactly know what happened…but, we were all sitting together, and Nils dealt the hands for euchre. And I…I said that I was surprised Nils hadn't driven you to Sara's cottage, since you were sleeping with her." Jane cringed, looking down. "S-Sorry."

"That's all behind us now," he said gently. "Tell me the rest."

"So, Nils said that it was impossible that you were with Sara, because you were into me."

Lars nodded at her, smiling. "He got that right."

"Anyway, then he said something like…if you belong to someone, you can't let them go. Something like that. And when he said that last part, he was only looking at Maggie. Like, whispering it to her, almost. And Paul and I just stared at them with our mouths open."

"Nils said this? My brother?"

"Yes! And, then, um…well, Maggie just stared at Nils. Hard. Intense. Just…eye to eye. And he just stared back. And then she got tears in her eyes and jumped up and left out the back door. She didn't say anything. Just left. And Nils…I could tell he was upset—like, *really* upset, like, I could hear him breathing, he was feeling so intense about it. And then he got up and followed her."

***

Damn, Nils. Did you finally make a move? He knew that Nils wasn't around when he got back from the Prairie Dawn last night, and come to think of it, he didn't actually remember hearing Nils come home at all.

"Wow. Sounds like I missed a lot!"

317

Jane grinned at him, adorably small in his massive leather reading chair. He loved seeing her in his space. He hoped he'd have many more opportunities to see her in his space, comfortable, settled in. *Stop getting ahead of yourself. Focus. Nils. Mags.*

Jane went on. "Paul said he thought Maggie might have given Nils an ultimatum in the spring, and last night was sort of the moment of truth…"

Paul again. It rankled him, but he knew it would really upset Jane for him to continue questioning Paul's role in her life, so he kept his face impassive.

"Did *Paul* have the details of this so-called ultimatum?" *Seems to have the details on everything else going on in my family's life.*

"Uh-huh. Yep. He said that in May, Maggie got real drunk at a party or something and told Nils he had two choices—he could bed her or wed her, but anything else would be a waste of time."

"I don't recall a wedding in the past couple of days, so that would mean…"

Jane pursed her lips, trying not to smile. "Uh. Yeah. Already had to banish the image from my brain once. Please don't stick it in there again…"

He smiled at her, unable to ignore the double entendre.

"Stick it in there? Jane! I'm shocked!"

Her shoulders started shaking with laughter. "I didn't mean it like that—"

"Thinking about my brother like that!"

"Wrong brother," she murmured, holding his eyes.

The entire vibe in the room had shifted with two

words, the air heavy and thick between them. He noticed the faint movement of her breasts with her breathing, which he could just make out as heavy and slightly ragged, as she cast her gaze down uncertainly. He half expected her to retract the words, but she didn't, which he loved.

"You think about *me* like that?"

"No," she deadpanned, looking up at him, head tilted sardonically. "*Erik*."

"Kat sure wouldn't like that."

"Yeah. I don't think Kat's got anything to worry about, Lars."

"Well, I wouldn't want to disappoint you, Minx, if your heart's set on—"

"Do you generally disappoint?" she volleyed back, low and direct.

"Not that I know of."

She licked her lips and bit her lower lip, killing whatever was left of his self-control. She looked up at him from under lowered lashes and the frank challenge in her eyes was his undoing. He had to have her. Now. But it had to be on her terms, so he gave her a choice.

"The chair or the bed?" he asked, his voice gravelly.

"Bed," she answered, holding his eyes.

Her simple answer was so hot and he was so amped up with wanting her, it took every ounce of self-control he possessed not to leap up, swoop her into his arms, and throw her back down on his bed. He reached out his hand to her and as she stood up, he pulled her to him until she stood between his legs. He stared at her breasts, which moved with her breathing, only hidden by the thin, clingy fabric of her shirt.

She tilted his chin up to face her, looking deeply into his eyes.

"What does it mean?" she breathed.

"What?"

"What you said before in the kitchen. Yahg are…"

"*Jag är förälskad i dig?*"

"That one," she whispered, nodding slowly.

Her eyes said she was ready to hear it, even though she'd indicated before that she wasn't. Her eyes, that were painted with the same brush God had used on the greenest parts of Yellowstone, searched his, and he remembered his promise never to lie to her. He put his arms around her waist, lacing his hands on the small of her back, so she couldn't run away after he said the words.

"It means I'm falling in love with you, Jane."

She didn't look surprised or shocked, or like she wanted to cry or like she wanted to run. Her lips tilted up the barest bit, and she stared at him, nodding slowly, almost imperceptibly.

"Is that right?" she rasped, placing her hands on either side of his face and lowering her lips to his.

***

Jane rested her head over his heart, her palm flat over the damp, cooling skin of his chest, studying the way the moonlight filtered in through the slats of his venetian blinds, in stripes of light across the dark blue wall behind the leather chair.

Her leg lay wedged between his, and her breasts were flattened against the hardness of his chest. One powerful arm lay draped over her back and his other hand lazily brushed back the hair from her face in slow, gentle strokes, grazing the shell of her ear with every caress. His heart pumped under her ear—it sounded like life, if life could be simplified to one single perfect sound.

She closed her eyes, reliving the gentleness and control of his powerful body hovering over hers as he searched her eyes, making sure that she wanted him, that she was ready for him. She had pulled his head down to kiss her, and he had let go, inching forward to bury himself inside of her. She still didn't know how he was able to pace himself, control himself, when his body was so obviously ready for her from the moment they walked through his door. He was slow and patient with every step of their lovemaking, and in the end, he ensured that she was on her way to bliss before meeting her there. They climaxed at the same time— something Jane had never experienced before—and the sweetness of it, the completeness of it, made her eyes flood with overwhelmed tears, trailing silently into her hair as he held her.

For almost as long as Jane could remember, loneliness had been her constant companion. And now suddenly, for one blistering, beautiful moment in his arms, Lars had given Jane something heretofore unknown in her adult life; a taste of what it would feel like to be cherished and wanted, to belong to someone else. If being with Lars like this—her body moving rhythmically with his, her heart beating in tandem—could be distilled to a drug, she'd be an instant addict. But they hadn't made each other any promises, and the heartbreaking certainty of her impending departure made the miracle of their connection almost too much to bear.

"You asleep, Jane?" he whispered.

She pressed her lips to his skin before returning her cheek to the warmth of his chest. "Nope."

"Are you okay?"

"Yep."

"That was…intense."

She couldn't answer. Her eyes welled with more tears.

"Your hair's wet," he said gently, tenderly moving his fingers through the curls behind her ears. "Why are you crying?"

She swallowed the lump in her throat, owning the reality that one weekend with Lars Lindstrom wouldn't possibly be enough for her, even though it was all she had. She would be ruined for anyone else. For the rest of her life, she was ruined.

"It surprised me," she murmured, blinking rapidly as she touched her lips to the skin of his chest again.

"You've never…?"

"Not like that. Not at the same time. Not…"

His hand reached out gently for her chin, tipping it up so she was looking into his eyes.

"Jane, I *want*—"

She couldn't read his expressive eyes in the dim light, but she could tell they were glistening with emotion as he bit his bottom lip then released it, taking a deep breath and sighing.

"What?" she asked, softly. "What do you want?"

Lars put his hands under her arms and dragged her slowly up the length of his body until they were nose to nose. She could feel him, hard and long against the apex of her thighs, where longing pooled.

"You."

"Again? Already?" she whispered, her face breaking into a smile.

"A million times again," he murmured. Then he reached up and placed his hands on either side of her face, pulling her lips down to his.

***

Later, as she slept soundly beside him, he answered the question she had asked. *What? What do you want?*

What he *wanted* was to see her fall for him as hard as he had fallen for her.

What he *wanted* was for her to stay.

Nothing complicated. It would sound like this:

His voice saying, *Jane, I want you to stay with me, and not leave Gardiner, and move into my house with me, and sleep in my bed every night, and let me make love to you over and over and over again.*

And her voice saying, *Okay.*

Just like that. Simple. Straightforward. Even obvious. The only right answer to a multiple-choice question.

She was curled up beside him, and he could feel the heat of her breath on his neck as she breathed deeply in sleep. He cradled the back of her head in his hand, her curls threaded through his fingers. He had almost lost her this week, but she was somehow—miraculously—recovered to him. And now that he knew what it meant, how it felt, to join his body with hers, to feel her heart beating against his, her legs open to cradle him between them, finding completeness so intense that he cried out from the pleasure of it. He couldn't lose her again. He couldn't know what it felt like to have her sleep beside him and then say, *Goodbye, Jane. Keep in touch.* It was impossible. It would, as Samara had said about Jane, break him in half.

He intended to ask her to stay. Indefinitely. But he feared two things: the first was timing. He didn't want to do anything to jeopardize their weekend together by asking her too soon. The second was that he didn't actually know what her answer would be, and the possibility of her refusal leveled him to the ground. She had only lived in big cities: San Francisco, Boston and New York. Her life was full of exotic travel and glamorous adventures…and even if she didn't work for Samara anymore, surely she wouldn't be able to leave that life behind completely. Surely Gardiner wouldn't be enough.

If it would break Lars in half to lose Jane, the other half of Lars would break if he left Yellowstone behind. He believed that everything good about who he was and what he was, in his life and in his heart, was because Yellowstone owned something deep inside of him, which lost, like a compass without a magnet, would leave him ungrounded.

He drew strength from the very earth in the park, the music of its beckoning call in his ears at all moments throughout the day. He had learned courage and prudence from his awareness of everything wild and unpredictable that lived and lurked in every corner and crevice, patience and faith from bearing witness to the shifting seasons. He knew his personal definitions of certainty, hope, respect, tolerance, mercy and dignity had come into his life through days in the park, through lessons learned there, and moments found there. His bond was strong and true, tethering him to the sacred place that was Yellowstone.

He closed his eyes, sighing. They weren't mutually exclusive; Lars could have Jane, if Jane would stay. With a leaden heart, he knew that if Jane wouldn't stay, he would have to say goodbye to her, and it twisted his heart to even imagine it. For the first time in his life, the only time, he resented the hold of his park on his heart, even as he couldn't deny it and couldn't abjure it either.

He leaned back and looked at her sleeping face, her red, swollen lips, and curls that fringed the delicate shell of her ear. Overwhelmed by the intensity of his feelings for her, the sheer force of his longing to have her remain in his life, he felt a wave of deep emotion fill his heart like a tidal pool until it overflowed. It was as simple and certain as the green of her eyes, or the softness of her skin, or the heat of her smaller body beside him right now, or anything else that was real and true and wholly uncomplicated in his life:

Lars wasn't *falling* in love with Jane.

He was already irrevocably, terminally in love with her.

CHAPTER 12

Lars drove Jane back to her hotel early in the morning so she could shower and change, and he arranged for his father to handle Ray, Margot and Shanelle's ride up to Bozeman for their flight back to New York. A park excursion trumped making an airport transfer any day, and Lars seemed delighted to get out of one in lieu of the other.

"Your dad didn't mind?" Jane asked, as they pulled into the still dark hotel parking lot.

"Nah. Park comes first. Unwritten rule."

"Even if I'm not a paying customer?"

"Even then."

She grinned at him and purred, "Grizzlies."

"If we can find 'em." He unbuckled his seat belt and slid over to her, putting his hands on her face and kissing her gently. "Best night of my life, Minx."

She beamed at him. "It wasn't half bad."

"Room for improvement?"

"Can't see how…but practice *does* make perfect."

"You're gonna get me all hot again."

She pecked his lips and unbuckled her seat belt, looking back at him one more time. He was too gorgeous with his blond bed head and lazy, tired eyes. He was tired because of her. The thought made her breath hitch as images of their night together rushed in, surrounding her.

"I'll be back in an hour. Six sharp," he said, sliding back to his seat and buckling up. "Coffee?"

"I'd love it. Thanks," she said, grinning at him.

She slipped into her dark, quiet hotel room and stood with her back against the door for a moment, listening to his truck drive away. Then she hugged herself and giggled, jumping onto her bed with an elated shriek. The last time she'd been alone in this room, she'd been curled up on the bed weeping after hearing that horrible recorded conversation, sure that Lars was lost to her. *What a difference a day makes.*

And a night.

"Lars," she breathed his name aloud, as she had over and over again last night, and lowered her arm, taking a deep breath. She didn't want to shower yet. She could still smell him on her body.

She stood up and looked at herself in the large mirror that spanned the bureau across from the bed, and she barely recognized herself. She was stunned by how pretty she looked. Her lips were rosy and bee-stung from so much kissing, her cheeks had a light tan, and her eyes were luminous in her face, deep green, as if transformed by...by...what?

Staring at herself, she realized, with a startling clarity, that at some point over the past week, she'd probably had an opportunity to turn back, to walk away, to give up. Whether she hadn't recognized the opportunity at the time, or had ignored it entirely, she hadn't taken it. And now it was too late.

Jane placed her fingers on her chest gingerly and felt the strength of her pumping heart recklessly declaring to whom it now belonged. She tilted her head and smiled at her reflection, at the pretty girl in the mirror, because despite having nothing in her life until now with which to compare the depth and strength and ferocity of her feelings, she instinctively knew.

She was falling in love with Lars Lindstrom.

***

After a quick shower, she put on the slim-fit jeans she'd bought at the boutique in Gardiner, and made a mental note to go back there later today to see if they had anything she could wear to church tomorrow. She couldn't very well attend a christening in jeans.

She threw on her cream t-shirt, making another mental note to do a quick load of laundry at Sara's cottage, or she'd have nothing clean left to wear. She shrugged into her brown suede jacket. It would be chilly in the park this morning.

She pulled her damp curls back into another cute ponytail, securing the loose ends with a few pins. Her lips were still rocking a pretty rosy glow, so she swiped on some lip gloss pilfered from Sara's trailer leftovers. When he knocked on her door, she was ready. She picked up her backpack, which she had loaded up with her camera, various lenses and filters and threw her sunglasses on top of her head.

Lars was leaning up against the doorframe, oozing so much raw masculinity she almost rolled her eyes. "Aw, come on. *Really?*"

It was ridiculous that he was this hot. She looked him up and down slowly, with unapologetic candor, finally meeting his eyes with a grin. *Your bed, Cowboy. Later.*

He smiled back at her, flashing straight white teeth, the tan skin crinkling around his Arctic-blue eyes. He was wearing cowboy boots and jeans again, of course, but instead of his regular polo shirt that he wore for work, he had on a grey t-shirt under a long-sleeved, button-down shirt in a navy and grey plaid, which was open, unbuttoned. Over that, he wore a weathered, tan, canvas barn jacket with a dark brown leather collar that just grazed his neck, and a tan cowboy hat over his silvery-blond hair.

"*Seriously?*"

"What?" he asked, turning slightly to place his hands on the frame over her door and hang there innocently, extending his arms and flexing his chest muscles in front of her, blocking the entire doorway with his body and grinning back at her.

He was so adorable, she chuckled.

"Look at you, all proud of yourself."

"What do they say? If you've got it, flaunt it?"
"Oh! And so modest!"

He lowered his arms, crossing them, his eyes twinkling. "I'm just teasin'."

"I've only seen you in work clothes. In your polo shirts."

"Yeah, this is more…me."

She shook her head, wishing she could compose

herself. He looked like the cover model for a "sexy cowboy" shoot. All he was missing was a lasso over his shoulder and a horse in the background.

"Well…it works."

"Does it?"

She stepped forward until she was almost touching him then raised her eyes to his face.

"Yeah." She placed her palms on his grey t-shirt and his muscles flexed under her hands. "We're never going to make it to the grizzlies at this rate."

"Screw the grizzlies," he growled.

He held her eyes as he put his hand on her neck, his fingers resting on the hairs at the nape of her neck, his thumb brushing her cheek in front of her ear softly. As he pulled her gently toward him, she rose up on tiptoes to meet him, closing her eyes as his lips touched hers. She moaned against the heat, the jolt, the swirling inside, fingers curling on his chest. He adjusted and readjusted his lips until they were molded full and flush to hers, slightly parted, moving rhythmically.

His free arm encircled her, his other hand moving against the contours of her neck, kneading the warm skin there, the rough pads of his fingertips gently grazing her hot, eager skin and delivering a sharp sweetness that made the muscles in her back flex, arching her into his body. Finally his lips moved from her mouth, grazing her cheek to her ear as she leaned into him, surrounded by his smell, his taste, the urgent sound of his breathing as his teeth tugged gently on her earlobe.

She gasped an *ahhhh* sound which ended in a moan from the back of her throat, surprised by the sharpness of his teeth and the way her insides turned to jelly at the unexpected bite. She leaned her neck to the side and his hat fell to the floor as his forehead finally rested under her ear, on her pulse, bowed in supplication or prayer, or just…heaven.

His chest moved rapidly under her fingers, she could feel the insistent thumping of his heart. She slowly opened her eyes, raising her hands to his face, and gently pushed him back, away from her neck so that she could read his eyes.

He didn't smile at her. He looked at her, and she read *vulnerable* and *overwhelmed* on his face, all signs of cocky teasing gone. The fierce tenderness in his eyes had to be a mirror of her own. She had a name for her own feelings, and last night he'd given the same name to his. They were falling in love with each other, and it was too soon and too much and it should be impossible after knowing one another for only a week, but staring back at his face, into his beautiful blue eyes, she knew that it was happening and there was nothing—*nothing*—that either of them could do about it now.

"Jane…" he murmured, the sound of her name on his lips imbued with hunger, with tenderness, with longing.

And that was the moment she realized it; she trusted him. No man looked at a woman like that if there was room in his heart for any other woman. Her heart was safe with him.

She pulled his head back down and pressed her lips to

his, sweeping her tongue over the seam of his lips until they opened for her. He wrapped his arms around her again, his hands curling into fists against the suede that covered her lower back, pushing her closer and closer to him, as if she could never be close enough. Her fingers played with the short blond hair behind his ears and she felt him shiver, heard a strangled groan released from his throat, felt the evidence of his arousal increasingly unmistakable against her belly.

If they didn't stop now, they were going to end up on her bed in a matter of minutes.

She turned her head gently away from him, positioning his forehead against hers, eyes closed, trying to catch her breath. She could smell coffee light on his breath, just as she had tasted it a moment ago.

"Grizzliesssss," she breathed, wetting her lips and smiling as she opened her eyes.

He leaned back from her, grinning. "Damn, Jane. *Every word* with that voice. I could listen to you all day."

"Grizzliesssss," she said, again, trying for lower and breathier, but couldn't pull it off because she started giggling. "And good, 'cause that's the plan."

"You're goofy this morning."

"I'm happy this morning," she answered, readjusting the bag on her shoulder, and straightening the sunglasses that threatened to slip off her head after so much kissing.

"Is that so?" He leaned down to pick up his hat and backed out of the doorway, watching as she pulled the door shut behind her.

Jane thought of last night and this morning and today and tomorrow…

"That's so."

***

Lars wasn't sure how she'd feel about him making her a mix CD like a high school crush, but if the look on her face was any indication, the hours of work it had taken to put his favorite 60s songs on a CD and print a picture of grizzlies for the inside cover of the jewel case were well worth the effort.

"You made me a mix? When did you have time? It's like we're going steady, *Just-Lars*!" Always a little sassy, but he could tell she was pleased as her cheeks colored pink and she touched the picture gingerly with her fingertips, and it made him feel awesome.

"Tuesday night. After you broke things off. I was feeling sad."

"So you did something nice for me?" She tilted her head, smiling at him tenderly.

"I couldn't stop thinking about you, Jane. I had to do something."

She took the CD out of its case and slipped it into the player.

"I wasn't sure what you'd want to listen to, so I put some of my favorites on…we'll see what you think."

As the familiar strains of the Del-Viking's "Come Go With Me" filled the cab, Jane turned to him and beamed.

He'd done well.

She started singing along softly, legs crossed toward

him, occasionally looking at him with that sweet smile, bright green eyes taking in the scenery as they flew under the Roosevelt Arch into the park as he'd done a thousand times before.

Last night wasn't enough and this morning with her wasn't going to be enough, either. For that matter, nor was the combination of today and Sunday and Monday, unless he had all of the days after that. He *had* to figure out a way to convince her to stay.

He picked up his coffee cup and took a deep, bracing sip, wishing he could just enjoy these moments with her without worrying about the future. He had no right to expect a future with her—hell, he'd only known her a week—but she had insinuated herself so deeply into his heart over the course of a few days, it hurt, *really hurt*, to think about saying goodbye.

He thought about his sister Jenny. Jenny met and fell in love with her husband Sam over the course of a single weekend a couple of years ago, so no one could tell Lars it was impossible to feel this much, this fast.

He knew it was possible. He just hadn't seen it on his radar.

And he didn't exactly know what to do about it.

***

Lars said it would be another half hour before they passed Mount Washburn, and from there, another ten minutes until they got to Lower Hayden Valley where he'd recently found the mama grizzly and her cub, not far from the wolf pack.

"Lower Hayden's probably our best bet for seeing any

334

wildlife," he added. "Even if we don't see the grizzlies, good chance we'll see elk, buffalo, coyote…but, maybe we'll luck out. Unusual for the wolves to be in the valley this time of year. They generally head to the mountains for the hunting and don't come back until October or November."

He had been quiet for a while once they started their drive, introspective maybe, and Jane had listened to the music, looking out the window. But, after a while, he was *so* quiet, Jane almost worried something might be wrong, so she was relieved when he started talking about Yellowstone again.

Jane could listen to him talk about the park forever. There was a confidence in his knowledge that she found incredibly sexy. She reached for her coffee cup and took a sip, glancing at him. "How'd you learn so much about Yellowstone?"

"Mostly just grew up here. My father bought the tour business from an old mountain man back in the 80s. John Cooper led tours out of Gardiner ever since he returned from World War II, but he was getting on in years, and so my pop bought him out. Old Coop didn't have much of a business, really, mostly just took fishing parties out for catch-and-release fly fishing."

"What's catch-and-release?"

"Oh, man, you are a city girl," he chuckled, glancing at her. "Catch-and-release means you let the fish go. You don't keep it or cook it."

"Doesn't it have a…a thingy in its mouth…"

"Does it have a hook in its mouth? No. You take the

hook out.”

“And it swims away all torn up and bleeding?”

“You use a barbless hook, pull it out gently and throw ‘em back in.”

“But, it’s in pain…”

“Jane, those diamonds in your ears? How’d you get them in there?”

“Oh, my ears are pierced.” *Comes the dawn.* She smiled at him. “I see.”

“Doesn’t really hurt them. They get back out there looking all tough, find a friendly little girl fish who’s all impressed, have little fish babies…better than ending up on a spit or skillet.”

She grinned. *He’s so uncomplicated.*

“Do you catch and release?”

He glanced at her askance. “Right now I prefer catch. Release has me a little worried.”

“Are we still talking about fish?”

“I hate it that you’re leaving on Monday, Minx.”

Me too. Jane’s breath caught in her throat. But, telling her that he didn’t want her to go wasn’t the same as asking her to stay.

“We weren’t even supposed to have today,” she murmured. “Odds were that one of us should have been in Jackson Hole this weekend.”

“I like our odds.”

“Me too.”

“I like…us.”

“Me too.”

"Jane…would you ever consider, um… I mean, what's your plan? Now that you've quit working for Samara?"

She shrugged, shaking her head. "I don't know. I don't have a plan yet. That's the truth."

"You'll stay in New York?"

"My apartment's there. All of my stuff."

"Right, but…are you going to *live* there?"

"I just—I don't have an answer to that question yet. I quit yesterday. I have to figure out what comes next."

"Okay." He settled into his seat, and his shoulders drooped, as if he was backing off from something.

He wasn't trying to ask her to stay in Gardiner, was he?

Now, don't go jumping to conclusions or trying to see what you want to see, Jane.

"How much longer until we're there? At…what was it—Hayden Valley?" she asked, trying to steer the conversation back to the park.

"Ten minutes. Not much more. It'll be a lot of waiting. But, I promise we'll see something. We've got about two hours to see what comes along. Promised my pop I'd—*we'd* be at his place by noon."

"Why not 'dad'? What's with 'pop'?"

"Nils called them *Mamma* and *Pappa,* so we all did."

"I bet it was great to be one of four. Nicer than one of one."

"It had pluses and minuses, I guess. I don't know any different. I sure wouldn't trade it."

"You want kids?" She regretted it the moment the words came out of her mouth and cringed. *Argh! Jane! The kiss of death question for any fledgling relationship!* She glanced at him sheepishly and his face was merry, so he must have caught on to her discomfort.

"You offering?"

"You're incredibly inappropriate."

"You're incredibly adorable…"

"Quit teasing me." She grinned at him. "Just answer the question, Professor."

"Umm. Yeah. I definitely want kids. You?"

"Yeah," she answered wistfully. "More than one. It's lonely being an only child. I wouldn't want that for my kids."

"I always thought I'd have three or four."

"*Three or four?*"

"I could be happy with two," he amended quickly.

This kept happening in their conversations: they'd start off talking theoretically about something, and then without warning, she'd sense that they had somehow segued from theory to reality. She decided to try something. She took a deep breath.

"Okay, then let's have two."

She wasn't sure if he'd play along or get freaked out. She waited, her heart beating faster, tingling with anticipation, wondering if she had overplayed her hand or if he'd…

"Two it is," he finally answered smoothly. "Any names picked out?"

"Swedish, maybe. Like their *pop*. Nothing trendy."

"Agreed." A smile turned up the corners of his mouth. "Except I don't know any Swedish names."

"Then I'll buy you a book and we'll lie in bed and I'll pronounce them all so you can decide what you like."

"Good plan. Where will we live?"

"Why not build our own house?"

She sighed. "A house. I haven't lived in my own house in a long time. I've been a guest in someone else's since I was ten."

"Then let's go crazy and make it four bedrooms, just in case I can convince you to have a third. I helped Erik build his house, I guess he can help us build ours."

"Free labor! Even better!" She giggled, glancing at him, though her chest was starting to tighten.

"Staying in Gardiner okay with you?" He glanced sideways at her, grinning.

"Absolutely."

"Lots of family coming and going, though."

"I haven't had much family in my life, so I'll make up for lost time by adopting yours." Her throat started to feel thick, but she couldn't stop. "Church wedding?"

"Is there any other kind?"

"Weekends in Yeller?" Her eyes burned.

"I'd have to insist."

"Just like this one," she murmured, her smile fading.

"Just like this one," he whispered, pulling over into a parking area that looked out over an expanse of green meadow.

What had started off as silliness was making her feel dizzy because in such a short span of time, she'd described everything she always wanted: a man she loved, a home of her own, babies and family, church and Yellowstone. She realized that she wasn't kidding; she was articulating her ultimate fantasy under the thin guise of teasing. She suddenly felt like the emperor in the children's story who realized he was naked, and she wished she could cover herself.

She was in love with him.

In love with him.

She didn't want to go back to New York. She didn't want to go anywhere. She wanted to stay with him forever and build that house and have those kids.

But he hadn't asked her to stay, and she didn't know how to protect herself from taking the biggest fall yet if he didn't. After all, the only thing more painful than not getting what your heart wanted, is imagining that you could have it in the first place. It was sheer foolishness to let herself get carried away.

***

"Mrs. Lindstrom?" he teased. But then he glanced at her and saw her face. He furrowed his brows together in confusion. "Jane? Jane, are you okay?"

"Foolish," she breathed softly, not necessarily to him. She seemed to be lost in her own thoughts.

He looked out the window so she wouldn't see his face fall. The mood in the truck had plummeted in an instant, and he wondered if she was slipping away from him, reviewing what a life stuck in Gardiner would look like, and deciding she wanted none of it.

Sure, come live with me in some small house my brother and I build, surrounded by crazy Swedes coming and going all the time, in this tiny town, and have a bunch of kids with me, and wander around a gigantic national park every weekend.

She was, essentially, a city girl. It must have sounded like hell to her. And all the while, the thought of Jane in his life permanently had sounded like heaven to him.

"We're here," he mumbled, his heart heavy. "Maybe get your camera ready."

***

Two hours later they headed out of the park. Jane had gotten some good shots of grazing wildlife, although none of the elusive grizzlies. They'd seen moose and deer, elk and bison. No grizzlies in sight.

Not to mention, the playful mood between them hadn't been restored since they'd lost it, and as they headed back to Gardiner to have lunch with the Lindstroms, Jane wished she knew what to say or do to recapture the lightheartedness of the morning.

"Tell me about your brothers and sister," Jane urged. "Paul told me a little, but I'd love to hear about them from you."

"Well, there's Nils, who you know. Me and Erik. And Jenny."

"Interesting how you grouped yourself with Erik."

"Huh. I didn't even realize I did."

"You're closest to him?"

"I don't know. I guess," Lars said, drumming his fingers along to the Shirelles singing "Baby, It's You."

"I love this song," Jane said, glancing at him and grinning. "...*I can't help myself, when baby, it's you. Baby, it's you.*"

341

And finally that got her a little smile from him.

"So, Nils. What do you think the story is? How come it took so long? Him and Maggie?"

"Now, that, I may have some insight on that. There was this girl in high school. Years ago. I mean, Nils is thirty-three—"

"How old are *you*?" She blurted out. All this time, Jane had imagined Lars in his mid-to-late thirties and Nils edging up toward forty.

He looked at her, smiling, curious. "How old do you think I am?"

"I-I thought about thirty-six."

"Thirty-six!" He ran a hand through his hair. "Do I look thirty-six?"

"Clearly I'm not a good judge."

"Jane! I'm thirty."

Thirty. Wow. No wonder he was so…energetic. She grinned at him.

"What are you thinking about?"

"I'm not telling."

"You owe me one after thinking I was thirty-six."

"Okay, fine. I was thinking that you are very youthful…in bed."

Lars threw back his head and laughed. "Like…adolescent or…"

"Or," she confirmed.

"Oh, so we're talking about stamina."

"Actually we're talking about Nils."

"Damn, Jane." He shook his head back and forth,

almost unable to keep his eyes on the road. "You get me so hot."

"I aim to please," she said quietly. She couldn't stop smiling either. He was just so fun.

"You succeed."

"Nils!"

"Right, right, okay. So, before I was so rudely interrupted, I mentioned that he's thirty-three. Anyway, there was this girl in high school. His year. Veronica Olsen. She was gaga for Nils, and he had it bad for her too. They were hot and heavy senior year, but after graduation, she moved away to Missoula. Nils got this forestry internship for the summer up near Missoula to be close to her, but he came back at the end of the summer and he was…different. I don't know how to explain it. He never talked about her again. Never. I've still never heard her name pass his lips.

"After that, he never dated much. I'm pretty sure he had a thing with this girl Missy Branson for a while, but I don't even know what that was. Friends with benefits, I guess? Missy wasn't the type of girl you get serious about. Anyway, speed up ten years, and Maggie blows into town, all sassy with this thick Scottish accent, and she looks a lot like Veronica. A petite, good-looking redhead. The one time I mentioned the similarity to Nils, he told me we'd have a problem if I ever mentioned Veronica's name again. So, years go by, Maggie's patient…and one night my girlfriend, Jane, is hanging out—"

"Ah-hem," Jane interrupted him. "Wait a sec. Can we go back a few steps, Professor?"

Lars grinned at her. "Sure. Which part do you want to go over?"

"You said that years went by and then one night…"

"Oh, the part where my *girlfriend,* Jane, is hanging out with—"

"Yep. That's the part I'd like to review."

"Any objections?"

"Just some clarification."

"I'm falling for you like crazy, and after last night…well, 'girlfriend' is as good a word as any to tell you that I only want to be with you."

She shrugged. "Well, I guess…"

"You guess what?"

"I'll be your girlfriend."

"Thank God. You know, since we already planned out our future."

"About that…"

He nodded at her, feeling sheepish. "Foolish, I know."

"No. I shouldn't have said that. About it being foolish. I didn't mean the fantasy was foolish. Not at all. It was sweet. I just…things feel like they're moving fast between us. Sometimes I feel like I've known you forever and other times I feel like it's been a minute. And I don't want to slow down, but it still makes me a little nervous."

"Jane."

"Lars."

"I have no interest in hurting you."

"I know, but—"

He pulled over under the Roosevelt Arch and looked at

her. "Listen to me, Jane, because this is the truth. I'm not going to hurt you. Not now, not ever. If anyone gets hurt between you and me, it'll be me. Not you. I promise."

"You can't promise me that."

"I just did."

She unbuckled her seat belt and slid over to sit next to him, staring ahead at the expanse of prairie in front of them before turning to him and lifting her eyes to his.

"I'm falling for you too," she whispered.

"Aw, Jane," he murmured, searching her eyes tenderly before closing his and lowering his lips to hers.

CHAPTER 13

Lars's father had set up two picnic tables in the front yard of his property, which had a direct view of Yellowstone and the mountains beyond. As Lars parked the truck Jane recognized Mr. Lindstrom at a grill near the picnic tables talking to Maggie, and sighed in relief. It was good to see a familiar face amidst all of the blond Lindstroms filling Mr. Lindstrom's front porch.

Lars looked over at Jane. "You ready?"

She took a deep breath, smiling for him. "As ready as I'll ever be."

He hopped out of the truck and opened her door for her, holding her hand as they approached his father's house.

"Lars!" A tall, blond man who looked a lot like Lars jumped up from where he was sitting on the porch steps and rushed to greet Lars and Jane.

"*Minste!*"

Lars let go of Jane's hand to embrace his brother, clapping him on the back. Jane watched as these two hulking blond men had a brief but touching reunion, wondering what it would feel like for one person to be that glad to see her, let alone a whole porch full. Lars put his arm around her shoulders, drawing her up against his side.

"This is Jane."

"Heya, Jane."

"Heya, Erik." She smiled. "I didn't think you guys would look so much alike."

"Ugh!" Erik cringed, hitching his thumb over at Lars. "Are you saying I look like him?"

"*Minste* is just sore he's the baby."

"Jenny's the baby," countered Erik.

"Jenny stands alone," said Lars, looking over Erik's head.

"Yes, she does," said a tall, striking, blonde woman, who approached the brothers with a wide smile.

"Heya, Lars," she said softly.

"Jenny-girl." What a different reunion now. Jane watched as Lars enfolded his sister gently in his arms, careful not to wake up the blonde baby sleeping on her shoulder. "Aw…look at Erin."

"Nothing nicer than a sleeping baby," said Jenny.

"This is Jane," he whispered, reaching for Jane's hand again.

"Heya, Jane. You guys don't have to whisper. She's out like a light."

Another blond man, with slightly redder hair, came up behind Jenny, putting his arms around her waist, and Jenny leaned back against him.

"Want me to take her, Jen?" he asked in her ear.

"No, I'm good. Sam, this is Jane. Came with Lars."

Sam stuck out one hand from around Jenny and Jane shook it.

"Hey, Jane."

"Hi, Sam."

Another woman, blonde and petite, approached them, holding a blonde baby in the crook of each elbow. *This must be Katrin, Erik's wife.*

"Oh," sighed Jane, "They're so tiny!"

"They're a handful," said Kat Lindstrom, raising her eyebrows at Erik until he took one of the babies from her, transferring the little girl to the crook of his own elbow instead.

"You look good, Kat," said Lars, winking at his sister-in-law.

"Watch it, Lars," said Erik, giving his older brother a sour look then softening as he glanced at his petite wife with pure love in his eyes.

"Thanks, *Midten*," Kat said, coloring pink as she kissed Lars's proffered cheek. "It's good to see you."

She turned to Jane. "I'm Kat, by the way."

"Hi, Kat. I'm Jane."

"Oh! So, you're *Jane*." Kat smiled warmly, touching Jane's arm with her free hand and winking at Lars. "Paul's told us all about you."

Lars huffed beside her and she felt his fingers tighten around hers.

Jane looked over at Maggie, who stood beside Mr. Lindstrom at the grill, then caught sight of Nils, sitting with Paul at a picnic table. She had expected to see Nils and Maggie canoodling, but it seemed that they were keeping their distance from each other instead. *Hmmm.*

"He called you 'Lars's Jane'," added Jenny.

Jane looked up at Lars, as if to say, *See? I told you that you had nothing to worry about.* His expression softened to a grin as he winked at her, shaking his head softly.

"Lars's Jane is going to go say hello to Paul."

Kat took her arm with her free hand. "I'll come!"

***

Lars watched them go, feeling a stab of jealousy as Jane sat down next to Paul at the picnic table, across from Nils. Lars clenched his jaw, narrowing his eyes, and put his hands on his hips. He didn't have any reason to be jealous, right? Jane was with *him*. *His* girlfriend. Not Paul's. His. Lars's Jane.

He was suddenly distracted by Erik's sharp elbow in his side. "Whoa, brother. That's Paul. Our *friend*. Your *best* friend."

"Yeah. I know. But he likes Jane."

"Not like you do, Lars," said Jenny, with a touch of humor in her tone. "Besides, Jane seems likable."

Erik clapped Lars on the back. "He's into some girl online. From Connecticut, of all places. Talking about going to see her, even. I don't think you have anything to worry about."

"Yeah, I know. It's just…it's new, you know?" He turned to Erik, glancing down at the baby in his brother's arms. "Who's this?"

Erik twisted his neck around to get a better look at his daughter's face. "Heidi."

"Heya, Heidi," Lars whispered, touching her tiny hand. "You did good, little brother."

Erik raised his eyes, not about to be distracted by

pleasantries. "So…*Jane,* huh? I just about fell over when I heard you were bringing a girl."

"She's not a girl, not like one of the park girls."

Jenny glanced over at Kat and Jane flanking Paul on the picnic bench, and rolled her eyes at her brothers. "Please, no stories about park girls today. I highly doubt Kat and Jane would appreciate hearing about your wildcatting days, boys."

Sam winked at Lars from over Jenny's shoulder, grinning. "Someday you two are going to have to tell *me* all about it, though."

"Sam Kelley, do not encourage them."

Sam pressed his lips to Jenny's neck. "Leave 'em alone, woman."

"So…" Erik prompted, rolling his eyes at his sister and shaking his head in disgust. Erik had lived in close proximity to Jenny and Sam for a while after they were first married, and had told Lars many tales of Jenny and Sam not being able to keep their hands off each other. While Erik found this incredibly gross, Lars, who was more laid back, just sort of shrugged. *Good for Jenny-girl. That's what marriage should be like. That's what I'd want mine to be like.*

He glanced up at Jane again then shrugged off his premature thoughts.

"So what? She came in last weekend with a magazine crew. Assistant to Samara Amaya, who also happens to be her cousin."

Jenny raised her eyebrows. "*The* Samara Amaya, the supermodel….is *your* Jane's cousin."

"Yup. Anyway, me and Jane hit it off from the start.

Her cousin's a total bi—" He looked at Jenny and for a moment it was like looking at his mother. He chose a different word. "Well, she's a rhymes-with-stitch, and Jane quit her job yesterday. So…"

Sam interjected. "Jane quit her job?"

Lars nodded. "Yeah. I haven't asked her yet, but I want—I want her to stay."

Erik's mouth dropped open. "Seems kind of quick."

Lars's eyes connected with Jenny's and she tilted her head the way all the Lindstroms did, covering one of Sam's hands with one of hers and smiling gently at Lars because she understood, because she knew.

"Shut up, Erik," she said, tender eyes only for Lars. "It happens when it happens. Fast, slow, doesn't matter. You can't control how you fall for someone."

Jane and Kat had moved to the white-painted porch and Jane was holding baby Dagmar on the swing, chatting with Kat, who sat on her left, with Maggie on her right. Lars watched as she leaned down and brushed her lips on the sleeping baby's forehead then turned to Kat, smiling at something she said. It was as though she'd been part of his life, his family, forever. She fit in every bit as well as he'd hoped she would, and his longing for her to stay doubled, tripled, multiplied to such a degree, he started to wonder—in a very real way—how he would handle his disappointment if she wouldn't stay, and how in the world he'd ever get over her.

"It happened, Jen," he whispered, his yearning heart full of love, laced with worry. "I already fell."

***

"She's going to be hungry in a little bit. You don't mind holding her a little longer, Jane?" asked Kat, who wanted to go inside to warm up a couple of bottles.

"Not at all!" sighed Jane, who was finding she loved the warm weight of the baby in her arms, which sort of surprised her, since she'd spent almost no time around children in her life. Actually, it was probably being surrounded by a family—people of all ages from Mr. Lindstrom to baby Dagmar—that felt so poignant, so inclusive, so good.

Kat winked at Jane and Maggie then headed inside, followed swiftly by Erik, who—in Jane's opinion—handed Heidi off to his father rather quickly and suddenly to join his wife.

As the screen door clanked shut behind Erik, Jane turned to Maggie and grinned. "Well," said Maggie, laughter in her voice and wide green eyes merry. "I guess we can figure out what's goin' on in there!"

"Probably the same thing that was going on at Nils's place all weekend," said Jane, peeking up at her friend with a sassy smile.

"Och! You're so fresh, Janie!"

"Am I right or am I right?"

"Can you keep a secret?" asked Maggie, eyes dancing.

"Yes! Of course!"

She forgot she was holding the baby for a moment and lurched closer to Maggie. Dagmar shifted in her sleep, one eye fluttering open as Jane held her breath. Thankfully, she settled back into sleep.

"Well, so can I," whispered Maggie with a chuckle.

Jane looked over at Nils, who sat beside his father on the picnic bench, across from Lars and Paul. Jenny and Sam hovered by the edge of the table, all of them laughing at something Mr. Lindstrom had just shared. Lars was taller and blonder than Nils, a little less stocky and more athletic. He looked up at her suddenly, his face brightening just for her, his smile changing just slightly from familial to sexy, as he bit his bottom lip. Jane's heart fluttered as she turned back to Maggie.

"Looks like I wasn't the only one." Maggie grinned at her teasingly, but her voice was serious and warm when she continued: "He looks happy. So do you."

"It's still new," said Jane quietly.

"What ended up happenin' with your cousin?"

"He refused her."

"Did he, now?"

"He did."

Dagmar stirred again, and Jane transferred the baby to her shoulder, briefly wondering how much time she had before the child started wailing for her bottle. She rubbed the infant's back instinctively, hoping to give Kat and Erik a few more minutes together.

"Your aunt Lily…" started Jane, and then thought better of her question. She'd only known Lars for a week. He wasn't going to ask her to stay in Gardiner. That would be crazy. Staying would be crazy too, even if he asked. You didn't meet someone, fall in love with them and decide to stay with them over the course of a week, did you? Of course not. Crazy.

"Mmmm?"

"I've been thinking about her."

"What've you been thinkin', then?"

"That she was very brave. But she moved here for an adventure."

"Not a man," said Maggie perceptively.

Jane turned to look at her. "Would it be crazy?"

Maggie shrugged. "Sometimes you have to take a chance on crazy. Maybe crazy could be the best decision you ever made. Maybe crazy would change the entire course of your life."

"Like your Aunt Lily coming here," said Jane.

"Aye. And me too. You'd be surprised, Jane, by the decisions I've made."

"Like what?"

Maggie glanced at Nils again, then sighed and shook her head. "We're talkin' about you."

"It should be impossible for me to care about him this much in such a short amount of time."

"Bollocks," said Maggie. "Nothin' is impossible when it comes to love."

They both looked over at the Lindstroms as they broke into another round of laughter.

"Do you know how Jenny met Sam?" asked Maggie.

Jane shook her head no.

"They met and fell in love over a long weekend. But Sam was from Chicago and Jenny from here. Worlds apart. They tried to stay away from each other. They couldn't."

"Couldn't?"

"They were meant to be, Jane. Once you know it, it's no good to fight it." Maggie looked over at Nils again. "Not if you belong to someone. Not if you're sure."

"Why won't you tell me about you and Nils?" Jane asked, as Dagmar finally let out a howl for her bottle.

"That's a story for another time. Och, Janie, it's a book all in itself. And nothin' close to what I was expectin'."

Kat suddenly appeared at the screen door, hair mussed and cheeks flushed, Erik close behind, holding two bottles, and looking very satisfied. Jane stood up, handing the baby to her mother amidst a flurry of embarrassed thanks. Jane watched Erik peck his wife on the cheek with a knowing smile before heading down the stairs to give his father the other bottle.

Babies sleeping and howling, siblings laughing, friends and family on a swing or around a picnic table. Everything about the Lindstroms' version of family was foreign to Jane, and everything about it felt more right and more perfect, than anything else she'd ever known.

Crazy was sounding better and better.

***

Maggie had agreed to loan Jane a dress for the christening, so she left with Maggie after lunch, and Lars promised to pick her up in half an hour.

"Stay and visit with your family," she encouraged him, her heart leaping as he stared into her eyes with hunger.

"No chance, Minx. I'm picking you up in thirty minutes."

A shiver had run down her spine with the unspoken promise in his words and as she exited the Prairie Dawn half an hour later with a dress draped over her arm, all coherent thoughts dissolved into a pool of lust. Leaning against his truck in cowboy boots, jeans, a t-shirt and cowboy hat, Jane couldn't have conjured a more perfect-looking man with witchcraft. And just looking at him made every sensible thought she ever had in her entire life fly out the proverbial window. He flicked the brim of his hat and grinned at her.

"Ma'am."

"Who? Me?"

"Ain't nobody else here." He looked her up and down lazily before meeting her eyes again. "And weeeell, I'm new to this here town. I was hoping to meet someone who could…show me around."

Jane widened her eyes innocently then batted her lashes, pressing her free palm to her chest.

"I'm not sure I can help you, mister. I'm new here myself."

"Aw. I bet your husband wouldn't like it anyhow, you takin' up with a newcomer like me."

She held up her hand, wiggling her fingers. "Oh, no! I'm not married."

"My lucky day!"

"Maybe I have a boyfriend."

"Well, then he's a fool to let you out of his sight."

"Huh! You think I'm the type of gal who'd ride off into the sunset with any old cowboy who caught my eye?" She tilted her head to the side, biting her index finger gently between her front teeth.

He missed a beat in the conversation distracted by her finger in her mouth. As he licked his lips, she saw his pupils dilate a little.

"Caught your eye, huh?"

"Could be."

"I'm not any old cowboy."

"Is that right?"

He stepped forward, putting his hands on her hips and leaning down to position his lips on the sensitive skin behind her ear. His warm breath made her eyes close and her knees turn to jelly. He nipped the soft pillow of her earlobe and she shuddered before he whispered low, "That's right."

After a second, she realized that he had leaned back and she was standing there like a dope with her eyes closed. She opened them to his grinning face.

"So, what're you up to now?" he drawled, darkened eyes still managing a twinkle.

"Haven't got a plan right this minute, Cowboy. You got any ideas?"

She flicked her glance to right below his waist, then back up to his eyes, a smile playing on the edges of her upturned lips.

"Oh," he answered, his voice low and sexy, "I've got one. Pretty big one."

"Maybe you can…*fill me in* at my hotel?"

"Damn, Jane," he said, grinning, as he opened her door and helped her into the truck. "Just…*damn*."

***

An hour later they lay tangled together in Jane's bed, the late-afternoon sun casting her motel room in a warm, honey glow. For Lars, who had never been in love, he could barely remember what his life had looked like before Jane walked into it a week ago. Moreover, he couldn't bear to think about what it would look like without her in it.

"You going back for dinner?" Jane murmured.

"Promised I would. Come with me?"

Jane's cheek rested on the soft blond hair of his chest, and he felt her take a deep breath before shaking her head back and forth on his chest.

"I'll be there tomorrow. You should have some time with them on your own. Without me. Anyway, I think I'll go to Sara's. I need to start packing her up for Monday."

"*Sara's*? You don't work for her anymore."

"I wish it were that simple," Jane sighed.

"It's pretty simple, Jane. You quit."

"Yes, but, I can't just—I mean, I can't *not* pack her up."

"Why not? Last I checked, she's an adult." His words didn't sound casual because he couldn't keep the edge out of his voice.

"She's also my family. I can soften the blow of quitting by helping her pack up."

"Well, I hope you don't expect her to thank you for it."

"Hey," she leaned up on his chest, looking in his eyes. "What's your stake in this?"

"My *stake*?"

"Yeah. You're giving me a hard time. I mean, why do you care if I pack up Sara or not?"

"I care about *you*. I don't like seeing you pushed around."

"Which is why it's smarter for me to do it today while she's gone."

"Which is why it would be smarter for you not to do it at all."

"Okaaaay. Coming on a little strong here, Lars."

"Strong? She treats you terrible, but you're going back to—"

"I never said I was going back. I'm just packing her up."

"You say *packing her up*...but, it's like a gateway drug—"

"A *gateway* dr—"

"—next thing you'll be getting her water. After that she'll get you to go to the airport with her, and suddenly you'll be sitting next to her on the plane, writing her emails and taking her calls and—"

Jane pushed off of his chest, sitting up cross-legged and crossing her arms, which not only hid her breasts from his view, but made it clear she wasn't feeling very happy with their conversation.

"I don't like this."

"Well, I don't like seeing you mistreated." He pushed back to sit against the headboard, staring at her, crossing his arms too.

"You think I'm so weak? I'd just go back to her? Just like that?"

"I think she's crappy family, but she's the only family you've ever known. So, yeah, I think she's a weakness."

Her eyes filled with tears and she breathed through her nose, tilting her head back. He watched her blink several times rapidly and swipe at her eyes, and it took everything in him not to reach for her, not to comfort her. But, damn it, he loved her, and he would do anything to keep her here, even if that meant hurting her a little so she would see things the way they were.

When she looked at him again, he knew she *was* hurt. Her voice was raspier than usual, and not in a way that was sexy, but in a way that was holding back tears, and he hated himself for it.

"You know what, Lars? You have your dad and three siblings still living. You have a brother-in-law and a sister-in-law and a bunch of nieces and some adopted friends, and I bet you have a slew of cousins, aunts and uncles somewhere nearby too. I saw you all today. You have this big, beautiful, loving *family*. You have something I've never even dared to dream of having.

"You didn't lose your folks when you were *ten*. You had your mom until you were in your *twenties*. You watched TV shows with her. She taught you how to make waffles. Do you know what I'd give for memories like that? You've lived in one small town your whole life with a handful of people you've known your whole life, with an amazing family and a job you love.

"Well, I don't have an amazing family or a job I love, but I have Sara and her parents. That's it. Three people in the whole world. So forgive me if I want to try to mend fences a little bit before she leaves, but our lives are *very* different, so I'll thank you *not* to judge me."

"I'm not judging you, Jane. I just don't want you to be Samara Amaya's grateful doormat." *Whew.* It even hurt to *say* the words. He knew he was pushing her, *really* pushing her, now.

She recoiled as if he'd slapped her. She gasped, pulling the comforter around her, covering herself, finally staring at her hands in her lap.

"Is that how you see me?" Her voice was small and broke a little.

He couldn't bear it anymore.

"Jane," he breathed, low and desperate, reaching for her.

"No." She stared at him, her eyes glistening, and her jaw taut. "Please answer me."

He winced, shaking his head.

"No," he breathed. "You're funny and strong and smart. Adorable. Beautiful. You're the most interesting, fascinating, teasing, infuriating woman I've ever known. Ever. How do I see you? God, Jane. You'd run if you knew."

She stared at him, eyes wide and watery.

"They're *not* all you have," he whispered in a furious rush.

"What does that mean?"

"Sara and her parents. They're *not* all you have."

"Yes, they are, Lars. I don't have any other—"

He reached out, putting his hands under her arms, and in one quick move, he pulled her onto his lap, cradling her against his chest before she could protest. He wrapped his arms around her as her face shifted from confused to indignant, as though she was trying to decide whether or not to fight, to escape him. He searched the green eyes so close to his face, the (*right now, sad and angry*) green eyes he loved so much.

"They are *not* all you have." He swallowed, holding her eyes. "You have me."

She had been tense and awkward in his arms, but now she softened and relaxed, staring back at him with her mouth slightly open, her eyebrows furrowed.

"I'm all in, Jane. I've never felt like this, ever before. Not for anyone. I'm all in."

He looked at her mouth, and then back up at her eyes, which were so conflicted, so confused, he almost wished he could stop talking and just kiss her and make love to her and reassure her that way. But Jane was someone who had never felt the sort of belonging that he had taken for granted his entire life, and if he wanted Jane, he was going to have to be extremely clear.

"Jane…" His heart was racing, and he swallowed against the lump in his throat. "I want you to stay. I want you to stay in Gardiner. With me."

She took a hitched, audibly ragged breath and held it, staring at him, before finally releasing it in a sob that shook her shoulders, and made her crumple forward. Her forehead fell into his neck, and her arms, which had stayed crossed over her chest as he held her, loosened until they fell limply into her lap. He tightened his hold on her, cradling her in his arms, and let her cry.

She finally lifted her head to look at him, and it broke his heart a little, to see her looking so young and undone.

"You okay, Minx?"

She sniffled, staring at him. "You do? Want me to stay here with you, I mean?"

"I do. Whatever's between us, I want to give it a chance. I want you to stay, Jane." He shrugged and smiled, a man who couldn't account for the depth or speed of his feelings, but knew their truth, nonetheless. "I know Gardiner's not exactly the epicenter of the world…but maybe it would grow on you. You could stay a while and see what you think."

"I love Gardiner. I love"—her voice trembled with emotion as she dropped her eyes—"the idea of staying with you. But are you sure? You sure you won't regret it? Some girl you barely know, complicating your easy life…"

"This *isn't* complicated, and I know you a lot more than barely." He smiled at her, one arm releasing her back so a calloused thumb could swipe away her tears. "I want you to stay with me, Jane. It's as simple as that."

***

And just as those threads had snapped to release her from Sara, she felt a new one knot, behind her ribs, under her heart, binding her to Lars even more indelibly than she'd ever been bound to her own flesh and blood, and she heard herself whisper:

"Then I'll stay."

His eyes closed slowly, as she imagined they would if his body was cold and tired, and he slowly entered a hot, waiting bath. As though those three words from her mouth could offer him that much comfort, that sort of pleasure. While they were closed, she placed her hands on his cheeks, and leaned forward to touch her lips to his. A feather touch at first—light and gentle, a kiss to seal a promise. And he let her kiss him, still and waiting.

She leaned back and looked at his face, the silver stubble of his beard, his blond lashes still on the delicate skin under his eyes, his cheekbones so tan and high. Gazing at him, she heard the words in her head *I love you, I love you, I love you, Lars*…she felt them in her heart and she knew their truth in her soul, but she couldn't say them.

The strange and simple fact was, since her parents had died, Jane had never actually said those words. To anyone.

As much as she wanted to say them to Lars, her lips didn't form them, no sound came from her throat to propel them, and she realized that she wasn't ready to hear her voice say them again after so many lonely years. Holding them close to her heart was safe. Keeping herself safe was all she knew. Sharing them would mean that her gasping heart would be filleted—laid open to any wound, any harm, to any loss. To grief.

Jane loved Lars. She knew she did. But saying the words would mean he knew it too.

Instead, she threw her leg over his lap, straddling him, and watched as his eyes opened, surprised, then electrified in a liquid second. He wet his lips with his tongue, his eyes darkening, staring into hers with hunger, with certainty.

"I want you, Jane."

And with one, swift move, he repositioned her on top of him, impaling her, sinking into her, claiming her body just as surely as he'd claimed her heart.

***

"You're going to be late," Jane murmured, her voice thick and drowsy against his chest.

Lars, who sat comfortably against the pillow-padded headboard, sighed. He looked at the clock radio on the bedside table. 5:52.

"I'll be a little late, then."

"I don't want you to be late," she said, moving her fingers slowly across his chest as though she were writing in cursive.

"Then come with me."

"I really do have to pack up my cousin. At least get started."

"It worries me," he admitted with a sigh.

"Why?"

He took a deep breath, running his hand through her curls, realizing how delicate they were, occasionally snagging on his rough skin.

"I know you said you'd stay, but Gardiner's no San Francisco or Boston or New York. I'm worried you'll realize you've made a mistake. I know—I mean, I know we haven't known each other that long, but I don't *like* what my life looks like without you in it, Jane. And I don't want some brutal, long-distance relationship because that'll kill this. It's too new for that. I have to come to you, or you have to stay with me."

Jane leaned on his chest and caught his eyes. "Lars, I already said I'd stay."

He put his hand on her cheek, looking at her face, loving her as he had never loved anyone. "I know."

"I *want* to stay."

"After living in all those amazing places?"

"They *are* amazing," she conceded. "But not one of them has Lars Lindstrom. And he's *more* amazing."

His heart contracted and he leaned forward to kiss her lips gently. "Happy."

"Handsome."

"Beautiful."

"Crazy."

"Adorable."

"…late."

"You trying to get rid of me?"

"Nope. But I want your family to like me. I don't want to be the girl that blew into town and stole you away."

"You're stealing me either way, Minx. I'm yours."

Jane smiled at him, running her hand through his hair. "They don't need to know that yet."

"Truth be told, I'm not just stalling for you, although you are worth stalling for…"

"Other distractions?" she asked, raising an eyebrow.

"You said before…I've lived in one town my entire life with a big family and a job I love…"

"And…"

"And I *don't* love my job. Not the way it's gonna be, anyway."

"What's going to change?" She put her head back down on his chest and he went back to stroking her hair.

"I love Yellowstone. A hundred percent. I love being in there. Tracking, hiking, camping. I also love leading tours—taking regular, normal people into the park and showing them something awesome. That look they get?" He smiled. "Like you, with the bison? Man, that feels good. We get these people coming in from all over the world, and they've used their life savings for one big trip. And they come to *me*. They *trust* me. And I take them fishing or hiking or camping. And...they see what *I* see, and then, they *have* that. That experience. That memory. That's what I love."

"So, what's the problem? That's what you do, isn't it?"

"Sort of. Maybe not for long, though. My dad and my brother want me to start this new company called Lindstrom Elite. More jobs like your cousin, movie stars, TV crews. People willing to pay a lot for personalized service while they're visiting. More Samara. Less average American Joe."

"More lucrative?"

"Probably."

"You don't want it," she murmured, and her smile was so tender, he wondered what it was about their conversation that had softened her face so dramatically. He tilted his head, distracted by how beautiful she was, smiling up at him.

"I don't think so," he finally answered, shaking his head. "Nah, that's not true. I know I don't. Like I said before. I just want to be a really good tour guide. Maybe help the yahoos now and then."

"The yahoos?"

"Rangers. If they need help tracking or something."

"Well, I don't see the problem. You know what you want. Tell your dad and Nils you don't want Lindstrom Elite. Tell them what you want."

"Oh, is that all there is to it, Minx?" he asked, grinning down at her curly head, loving her, loving that she was in his life to listen to him, to talk to.

"Pretty much, *Just-Lars*. Unless you want to keep doing something that doesn't make you happy."

"So says the girl who just quit her job who's going to go do her old job tonight."

"I'm not going back, Lars. I can't think of anything that would make me go back. I'm staying. I'm yours."

Even though he was already late…

Even though he needed to get to his father's house and she needed to get to Sara's cottage…

Even though they'd already spent all afternoon in bed…

Even though neither of them had actually said 'I love you'…

His heart exploded with happiness with her simple reassurance—*I'm yours*—and he pulled her up to kiss him again.

CHAPTER 14

Jane smiled at herself in her hotel room mirror, turning around twice to admire the way Maggie's dress fit her body. It was a simple sheath dress of light wool plaid with a black patent-leather belt at the waist. When Jane had commented on the pretty blues and greens in the plaid, Maggie had tilted her head, giving Jane a sad smile and sharing that it was called a Campbell plaid.

"It's my clan plaid, Jane, such that I'd wear to a weddin' or a christenin' like tomorrow. But, since I'll not be goin', you wear it for me, aye?"

Jane had tried to convince Maggie to join her, reminding her how much the Lindstroms would miss seeing her, but Maggie had declined demurely, sharing it was best, for now, if she didn't attend. Jane wanted to press her for details, but Maggie was entitled to her secrets, so Jane let it go.

Maggie had been kind enough to loan Jane black patent-leather wedge heels with a peep toe that showed off two of her red toes, and a string of pearls to wear around her neck. When she had tried on the outfit for Maggie, her friend had sighed.

"Ye're nae Scottish, Jeannie? Och, lass, ye could be leavin' fer t'kirk on Sunday mairn, ye're sae bonnie." Jane had widened her eyes at Maggie's thick accent and Maggie had giggled softly, which made Jane feel relieved. "Dinna ye ken what ye're Maggie's sayin', ye bloody Sassenach?"

Jane had smiled at her friend, at a total loss.

"I'm sayin' you look lovely, Jane. Proper Scottish."

Jane had washed her hair then run gel through her curls, using a thin black, plastic headband to keep them back. Her diamonds glistened in her ears and Jane had put on a full face of makeup, using supplies she borrowed from Sara's cottage yesterday with skills she'd adopted watching Ray a thousand times.

And the result was amazing. Jane didn't know if it was quitting her job with Sara, a little magic in Maggie's tartan, or simply putting some effort into her appearance, but she didn't look anything like herself. She was completely transformed and stared at herself in amazement. Gone was Plain Jane Mays and in her place was someone new, someone reborn.

She breathed deeply, her heart fluttering as she remembered waking up in Lars's bed this morning. He'd been facing her, still asleep, and she had gazed at his face for half an hour before he woke up, remembering his tenderness when he made love to her during the night. Sleeping like spoons, naked and warm, she had shifted in her sleep, rubbing up against him, stirring them both into a realm somewhere halfway between wakeful and asleep. Without a word, he had moved his hands to caress her breasts, and she had shifted her body to welcome his hardness, needing to feel him moving inside of her again.

They had peaked at the same time and as Jane had cried

out in release, she felt Lars's breath, hot and urgent on her neck, as he whispered something in Swedish.

And then she knew, staring at herself in the hotel mirror. No job, nor dress, nor makeup could have engineered such a transformation. Jane was looking at a woman in love. Desperately in love. And it was time that Lars knew.

She stared at her lips in the mirror then closed her eyes, focusing on his face in her mind, even as her body trembled with the import of the sacred words that hadn't passed her lips in fifteen long years. Finally, finally, finally….

"I love you," she breathed, almost a whisper at first, and then stronger, "I love you, Lars."

She opened her eyes, her smoky eyes with long, thick, dark, made-up lashes, and said it one more time, deeper and slower, and strong: "I love you, Lars."

And then she smiled at the girl in the mirror who looked a little like the Jane Mays she used to know.

***

With fifteen minutes left until Lars was picking her up, Jane decided to get a cup of coffee at the kiosk in the lobby and check out. She looked around the very average hotel room, and knew she would forever remember the moments she spent with Lars in this room. She felt grateful. She felt happy.

She put her lipstick and phone in the simple black patent-leather purse she had borrowed from Maggie, put her camera bag on her shoulder and locked her hotel room door behind her, a packed bag in each hand.

Her phone rang just as she had finished checking out, and her heart sank like a stone as she saw who was calling.

Don't answer!

But she had to. Her heart may not have been tethered to Sara anymore, but there was one person in the world from whose affection and regard Jane would never be able to detach herself. She took a deep breath and pressed Talk.

"Hello?"

"Good morning, Jane." His familiar voice made her wince with love, with longing, but her shoulders rolled forward, suspecting the reason for his call.

"Morning, Uncow."

Jane had called her uncle "uncow" for as long as she could remember—long before her parents had passed away, when the two families spent every summer at a family resort in Cape Cod. She couldn't pronounce the "l" sound as a child, and everyone thought her mispronunciation was so adorable, they had encouraged it long after her tongue stopped twisting. She had never called him anything else.

"How's Montana?"

She tightened her jaw as her fingers turned cold and her stomach flip-flopped uncomfortably.

"Fine. Good."

"I'm not going to play games with you. What happened between you and Sara? She said you quit?"

Jane's unoccupied hand clenched into a fist, her nails biting into her palm. "Yes. I – I did."

"Jane! What were you thinking?"

"We're not…um, getting along that well, Uncow. It's

been a tough shoot, and I think Sara needs—"

"Jane, Sara needs you. She is your family. Practically your—your sister. Frankly, I'm shocked by this selfishness. I'm appalled."

Jane cringed, her face contorting as she sat down on a bench outside of the lobby as he continued. The disappointment in his voice was almost unbearable.

"Family looks after each other. Family takes care of one another. I can't believe I have to say this to you, of all people, Jane! I took you in when my brother died. I honored my responsibility to him. I cared for you like a daughter and I haven't asked much of you in return, because family doesn't expect payment. Family helps one another because that's what families do. Sorry if you don't like it, but family doesn't quit when the going gets rough. That's when family has to stick together, Jane."

Her face felt hot and she knew it was red. She could feel a bead of sweat break out on her upper lip, despite the cool morning.

"Jane? Are you listening to me?"

"Y-yes, Uncow," she whispered, her chest tight. She imagined the sick sound of metal on metal, manacles clanking shut on her wrists as he went on.

"Now, I am asking you to go back to New York with Sara and give her a little time. You are the glue that holds Sara together, and walking away from her is very cruel, Jane. Need I remind you that you had no job and no income before Sara took you on? Conversely, her career was a mess without you. You *need* each other. You cannot just walk away from her when it pleases you. Go back to New York and see if you two can work things out, or at least help her find a replacement—"

Jane's heart dropped and tears bit the backs of her eyes. *I'm not going. I'm not leaving him.*

"Please, Uncow," she whispered. "Please, I can't."

"*Can't?* Mayses don't say *can't*, Jane. *Can't* is just the…"

"…opening bid," she responded, by rote, in a daze, her heart in anguish.

He paused. "Now, you listen to me, niece…I'm asking for your help. I'm *asking* you not to say no to me. I'm insisting on it."

She straightened up, thinking of Lars. "But, I've…I've met someone, and he's—"

"I heard all about that. Some tour operator in Montana? Be sensible, Jane. You've known him for a week. Sara is your family. You cannot possibly be choosing him over your blood. The girl I know—the child I *raised*—is smart and sensible, which are two of the many things about her which bring great joy to *my* heart, and *would have* brought great joy to my brother. Anyway, if your feelings for him won't last through a few months apart, I suppose you will have learned something of value about the depth of your…*feelings.*"

They are not all you have…You have me.

"I already told him I'd stay."

"Then tell him you've changed your mind. Tell him you are a person of character who loves her family and doesn't let them down willy-nilly. Tell him that they took you in when you had nowhere to go and your *uncow* is not asking for very much."

I want you to stay.

Then I'll stay.

"I can't."

"You *will*, Jane!"

She had never heard her uncle's voice so sharp and angry. The tears she'd been holding back slipped from her eyes.

"You *will*, or we will have *nothing* more to say to one another, you and I. Nothing more. And I will *not* welcome you back to our family. I will assume you have turned your back on us, and I will take similar measures." He paused. "Am I understood? Am I *understood*, Jane Mays?"

A life without Uncow. A life never being able to see her father's eyes staring back at her again. She couldn't lose her uncle. It would be like losing her father all over again.

"Yes, Uncow," she whispered, her heart shattering into painful shards, puncturing her soft insides, making it difficult to breathe.

"Your aunt and I will come down to the city on Wednesday night for dinner, and we'll work this all out. We'll speak to Sara and impress your value upon her so she eases up on you a little. I know she can be a…handful. But, deep, deep down she cares for you, Janie. She needs you. It's all going to be okay. You're a good girl, Jane. Travel safe. Goodbye, now."

Jane stared at her phone in shock, in disbelief, for several seconds after her uncle had hung up. She was startled by the lobby doors opening and jumped, watching as a father and his young daughter walked out holding hands, the daughter clutching a hot-pink fishing pole that leaned up against her shoulder. The little girl grimaced at Jane and Jane raised her hands to her tear-stained face. She hurried into the lobby and bee-lined for the bathroom.

She rested her hands on the cold marble counter, staring down at the sink before her, trying to catch her breath, and silent the infighting exhausting her brain.

I am not going back to New York. I'm staying with Lars. I love Lars.

But, if you stay, you lose Uncow.

If I go, I lose Lars.

Maybe not. Maybe he'll wait for you. If you stay, losing Uncow is guaranteed.

How long will he wait for me? They'll try to trap me into staying there forever.

You don't know that.

I can't go. I can't leave him!

But, you cannot *lose Uncow. You already lost your mom and dad. You* cannot *lose him too, and that's final.*

She looked at her face in the mirror. Her perfect makeup job was a wreck. She took paper towels, wetted them and tried to even out the tear lines. She opened her loaner purse and freshened her lipstick.

Her face, which had looked so fresh and happy only ten minutes ago was now worried and worn. She smiled at herself in the mirror, but it quickly faded. It was going to be an awfully long day if Jane couldn't smile for more than two seconds, and Lars was certainly going to pick up on her sadness. He was much more perceptive than most men, something she loved about him.

Her despair overwhelmed her. She would be swallowed up by Sara's needs, Sara's schedule, Sara's life…and Lars would have girls coming and going from the park. Girls who wanted to touch his beautiful body. Girls he could look to for comfort as he got over Jane.

How could their week together hold up over a few months apart?

She knew his feelings for her were true. Hers were too. But Jane was a realist and such a new love probably wouldn't withstand the distance. As Lars had observed last night: long distance would kill it.

Still, if she wanted to have both her uncle and Lars in her life, going back with Sara and staying on with her for a little while longer seemed like the only way. She could try to talk to her aunt and uncle and explain that she wanted a new life; she could try to reason with them. Maybe she could train Laney as more of an assistant for Sara; heck, Laney might even be a better fit for Sara than Jane was. And then when she returned to Lars, she could have him without losing her uncle.

Even as these desperate thoughts circled in Jane's head, they were underscored by the cruel and harsh reality of the situation: if she left Lars after committing to stay, feeding into a fear he had already shared with her, she would almost certainly lose his trust, and eventually, his love.

She heard his voice at the front desk, asking for them to call her room and she tried to smile at herself one more time.

You have to believe this right now because there is no other option, Jane:
You will survive the distance and you will come back to him.

She nodded once at her reflection then swallowed,
smiling her brightest smile as she opened the door and
stepped into the lobby.

***

Lars watched Jane, who was sitting on the porch swing
again, bouncing Erin on her knee as Jenny talked animatedly
beside her.

He couldn't put his finger on it, but something didn't
feel right as the day wore on. She looked beautiful—when
she had come out of the lobby bathroom, his mouth had
literally dropped open, she looked so stunning. Her dress,
her shoes, her beautiful face and soft hair. She looked every
bit as lovely as her exotic cousin, in her own fresh-faced way.

She had taken his hand, smiling, and they'd headed to
church together, sitting in the same pew he sat in with his
family for most Sunday mornings of his life. She smiled and
commented at all of the right places, helping to lay out the
lunch at his father's house and taking one of the girls when
Kat or Jenny needed a hand.

No one else would've noticed.

But Lars noticed.

Jane was quiet. She didn't banter, even when he baited
her. He caught her several times looking distracted, far away,
then quickly composing herself when someone spoke to her.
When he took her hand throughout the day, she had been
the one to drop his first. Especially when he had shared with
his family at lunch that Jane was staying in Gardiner, she had

looked down nervously first, before raising her eyes with a careful smile. A smile that didn't reach her eyes.

Lars thought he may have been reading into things, but it almost seemed like she was avoiding him. Oh, she was working hard to act normal, but she wasn't, and he could tell.

He played with the heart-shaped keychain in his pocket. It had a copy of his house key on it, and he had intended to give it to Jane tonight so that she could start coming and going to and from his place after checking out of the hotel this morning.

But he couldn't shake the increasingly uncomfortable feeling that something was wrong. He had seen a variation of this behavior before. Last Sunday when she'd gotten businesslike with him and Tuesday when she'd broken things off with him; both times she had backed away from him. Both times she was letting him go or protecting herself. So, what was this, then? A sickening feeling started rolling around in his gut and he knew. Letting him go. Protecting herself.

He sucked in a breath of air and held it, concentrating on it so that his eyes wouldn't water with the force of his disappointment. It was suddenly as clear to him as the park on a sunny day.

Jane wasn't staying, after all.

***

As the sun started to set, Jane hugged Jenny and Kat goodbye, and was surprised when each of the Lindstrom men embraced her too. She kissed the babies on their foreheads and tried not to wince with unexpected longing when Jenny waggled Erin's hand and said, "Bye-bye, *Tant* Jane."

Everyone had giggled and Jane had done her best to look surprised and amused, even as her broken heart bled. She had let them all believe that she was staying in Gardiner and hated herself for deceiving them. *Tant* Jane. *Maybe if you stayed, one day you really would have been Tant Jane.* But her decision was already made, no matter how much it hurt.

She had purposely tried not to be alone with Lars for most of the day. Knowing she had to leave him tomorrow was proving almost unbearable. Not to mention, spending hours appearing normal and happy while her heart was in turmoil was unbelievably exhausting.

She could feel the façade coming down now that they were alone. She had hoped to have one last night with him. One last happy night together without worrying about tomorrow, but she knew it was going to be impossible. She could barely keep the tears from falling.

They rode to his house in heavy, fraught silence and he turned to her as he pulled into the driveway.

"Do you want to go back to the hotel instead?" he asked quietly, staring straight ahead.

"No." Her voice broke when she answered.

He turned to look at her and she could see the pain on his face. "What's the point of coming in, Jane?"

He knew. How did he know?

A fat tear rolled down her cheek as she gazed at him.

"I love you," she rasped in a whisper. "That's the point."

***

I love you. That's the point.

It was like the wind had been knocked out of him. It was the last thing he expected to hear. He hadn't buckled up for the short ride from his father's house to home, and he lurched across the seat, grabbing her into his arms, burying his face in her neck as hot tears gathered in his eyes, threatening to fall.

Is that what this was all about? Saying 'I love you'? For the first time all day, he took a deep, relieved breath.

"Oh, God, I thought…I thought…"

"You were right," she answered in a broken voice, her arms around him, her chin on his shoulder.

What? What did she say?

He leaned back, staring at her glassy eyes, confused.

"I can't stay." She swallowed, looking as miserable as he felt. "My uncle called this morning. He wants me to go back with her."

He had been holding his breath, and now he exhaled, letting go of her, running his hands through his hair. He gave her a hard look, angry with her, angry with this situation.

"But you told him no, right? You told him to go to hell, right? You're staying. You're staying with me."

He looked at her face and his heart twisted, like a knife gutting him from the inside out.

"He asked for a little time," she said in a small voice. "He reminded me about the responsibility of family. Think if it was Jenny or Nils or Erik. What would you do?"

He closed his eyes against the pain of what was

happening. She said she would stay and now she was leaving him. She was going back to New York.

"Lars. Lars, look at me. Please look at me." He looked up at her, biting his lip against the unfamiliar sting of tears in his eyes. "It's not forever."

"I hate to state the obvious, Jane. But we've only known each other for a week."

"What does that have to do with anything?" Even though she knew it had to do with *everything*.

"We needed time to build this. We've already had a shaky start with Paul and Samara between us. We needed clear road. We needed time together."

"I love you. A few months isn't going to ch—"

"A few *months*!"

"—to change that. We'll build while I'm away. We'll build when I come back."

"We can't build while you're away and there's no guarantee that you'll come back," he shot back, leaning away from her. His voice was a shadow of its normal self. "You're going back to your life, Jane."

"*You're* my life," she whispered.

"Right," he said dryly, swiping at his nose.

"You *are*. But, he's my uncle. He's all I had for so long. He was the one who loved me. He kept me from falling into the chasm. He stood between *them* dying and me *wanting* to die. I *owe* him."

"You shouldn't *owe* family like that. He doesn't own your life just because he honored a promise to your father, Jane. That's not how things are supposed to work."

She hung her head and wept, the unfairness of it all crashing down on her. She had never loved anyone as she loved Lars…and here he was. Hers. Someone who *belonged* to her. Someone who wanted *her* to belong to him. She felt as if she was being ripped away from him in the most painful, unbelievable way. After this weekend she never wanted to wake up without him again. Their time apart stretched before her like eternity.

He slid over beside her, pulling her close to him, his cheek against hers. He inhaled raggedly. "I don't know what will happen, Minx. Once you get there. Once you're at home again. This could all change in your head—feel more like an infatuation and less real than it really was. Than it really is. I just want you to come back." He finished simply, "I want *this*. Come back."

She started sobbing again, so relieved by his words, she clung to them desperately, even as she suspected he didn't actually have much real hope. She held on to the back of his neck, shuddering from the onslaught of emotions. "I'll come back…I promise."

He kissed her hair and down her neck, then caught her lips in a hungry, longing kiss, holding the back of her head with one strong hand, his other hand on her hip, keeping her close to him. When he stopped kissing her, he leaned his forehead against hers, his eyes closed. She knew he was upset. Terribly upset, even, and she remembered his words under the Roosevelt Arch: *If anyone gets hurt between you and me, it'll be me. Not you. I promise.*

It made her want to weep that he'd been right. It wasn't

that she wasn't hurting too, but she was making a choice that was hurting them both.

She leaned back from him, tilting her head to the side as he often did, memorizing his face with an urgency she hadn't felt before. She didn't want to sacrifice another moment to despair while she was still with him, while he still belonged to her for a few more hours.

"We still have tonight," she murmured, placing her hand on his face.

He turned his head to kiss her palm. "Stay with me?"

"I checked out this morning. Where else would I go?"

His face shifted the slightest bit from sad to…well, still pretty sad.

"I could go stay with Paul."

His lips twitched.

"Or Nils."

More twitching.

"Or your dad. He's a good-looking man…"

He was definitely biting back a smile now.

"Nah. I already made my choice," she drawled in the gravelliest murmur she could muster and watched as his eyes changed. "Let's go to bed. And just stay there."

Without a word, he pulled her out his truck door, up the porch stairs, into his house, through the living room, down the hallway, into his bedroom, into his arms and into his bed, just as she had asked.

***

"Tell me about New York, so I can picture you there."

He lay naked on his side, his head only slightly raised,

pillowed on his bent elbow, looking at her. She exactly mirrored him, so that they were face to face, but they didn't touch, as if by mutual, unspoken agreement. Their bodies had been in almost constant motion for over an hour, touching, loving, clinging to each other. They were cooling down.

They hadn't mentioned her leaving since the truck, and Jane stared at him, sensing the strength of his feelings being thrown off his body like heat. Sadness. Anger. Confusion. She had tasted them on his lips, felt them even when his body was fused to hers.

"You don't have to ask that."

"Okay." His eyes dropped hers. "Fine."

She stared at him, disappointed that he didn't ask again, then swallowed, trying not to cry. "Will you come and see me?"

"Like, for a weekend? I don't think so, Jane. I think— don't get me wrong; I *would* come, if it was where you wanted to be. If it was somewhere you loved and I needed to learn to love it too, I'd come find you in New York. But you were ready to give it up. I don't think you love your life in New York, I think you love your uncle. And I *don't* love your uncle, because I think he's trapping you into a life you don't want for the sake of his selfish child. And I am *angry* with him that he doesn't see that, or sees it, and still does it."

"You're angry at me too."

"Yes," he answered simply, capturing her eyes again. Cold, angry.

He took a deep breath and held it for a beat, then let it

385

out slowly, and she felt it on her lips, on her cheeks, on her neck.

"If I come to New York, it makes it easier for you to stay there. I don't want to make it easier, because I want you here with me. Because I think you want to be here with me, and I want to support *that* plan, not some other plan that has you leaving for all of the wrong reasons. Anyway, I don't want a weekend, Jane. It would just mess with my head. It definitely wouldn't be enough. I want you back when you're all in. When you're ready"

"I *am* all in. I *am* ready."

She watched a litany of emotions walk across his face, ending in disappointment.

"No, love. No, you're not." He turned and sat up, swinging his legs over the bed putting his back to her. "I'm getting water. Do you want some?"

"No, thanks," she whispered and watched as he padded around the bed and out of the room.

Jane rolled onto her back, staring at the ceiling, and felt a tear fall out of the corner of her eye and roll into her hair. She didn't reach up to wipe it away. She closed her eyes against the assault of her feelings.

You're making a mistake. You're making a mistake. You're making such a big mistake.

The right decision shouldn't hurt this much. Shouldn't feel this wrong.

She raised her hands to her face, letting the fleshy pad of her palm press hard into her burning eyes. She revisited her uncle's words: *We will have nothing more to say to one another.*

Nothing more. And I will not welcome you back to our family. I will assume you have turned your back on us. But if she went back she could settle things to Sara's satisfaction and earn her uncle's approval. She could return to Montana with a free and peaceful heart.

She thought through what the next few months would look like. A week to settle back in…another two or three weeks to convince Laney to step up to be Sara's full-time assistant… another two or three weeks of on-the-job training…and one last week to pack up her apartment and ship her things. Two months. Two months and she'd be able to keep her uncle happy. She could come back to Lars after Thanksgiving. No, she'd have to stay for Thanksgiving. Crap, and Christmas was always packed with shoots. If Laney wasn't ready yet, Jane would have to stay on a few extra weeks. After New Year's, then. She could come back in January. Well, as long as Laney was ready for New York Fashion Week at the top of February. Jane would need to be sure she could handle that…or maybe Jane could go back to help. Just for that week. Or maybe it would be best to return to Montana after Fashion Week. Mid-February.

Five months. Like an albatross. Five months.

She ground her teeth together and turned onto her side, away from where Lars had been lying beside her, toward the door and raised her knees to her chest, wrapping her arms around them. The stark reality of the situation leeched hope out of her heart like a syringe. No matter how strongly they felt for one another now, what they had was way too new to make it for five months apart. Especially if he wouldn't come to see her.

It hurt her when he said that he wouldn't come. But what he said had made grudging sense to her. She didn't love her life in New York, and she understood why he didn't want to support her decision to return to it. She was only going back out of obligation, because she didn't see a better alternative.

Could she live without her uncle? Could she turn her back on him? Could she refuse him, begrudge him a mere five months of her time? Just because the timing was bad for her heart?

Jane swallowed against her confusion and increasing hopelessness. No matter which decision she made, she would hurt and disappoint someone she loved.

Lars stalked back into the room, depositing a glass of water on the bedside table beside her, then squatting down beside the bed until he was eye-level with her.

"Heya, Minx."

"Heya, Lars."

"Don't go."

"I'll come back."

"Don't go."

A tear rolled over the bridge of her nose, and he caught it with his calloused thumb, raising the thumb to his mouth and pressing the wetness to his lips.

"Move over," he whispered.

***

He stroked her curls off her forehead, loving the weight of her head over his heart, hating how long it would be until he felt it again. His still-racing heart throbbed with yearning, his mind desperately tried to find a loophole that would allow her to stay. Nothing in his life had ever felt as intimate, as visceral, as satisfying, as making love to Jane. Letting her go went against everything he felt, everything he wanted.

But she was leaving. In a few hours. He couldn't shake the aching sorrow of her impending loss. His mind kept circling back to it.

"What will you do?" she whispered. "While I'm gone?"

"Is there anything I can do to convince you to stay?"

"I have to do this. I have to try to make things right with him. How can I convince you I'm coming back?"

He stopped playing with her hair and laced his hands behind his head. "You can't, Jane."

"If Sara's friend Laney will take the job, I can start training her immediately. Maybe I can come back for a weekend in November once she's found her footing."

"November." He didn't realize how much he'd been pinning his hopes on her return until he heard her say the word November. He had assumed that when she said she'd go back for a little while, she was talking about a couple of months. Now, she was talking about a *visit* in November. "Jane, when you talk about coming back, what's the timeframe? *When* will you come back?"

"I don't know for sure…it depends on how quickly I can find a replacement and train that person…and then—"

"*When, Jane?*"

She leaned up on her elbow. "The earliest would be after the New Year. F-February."

He nodded at her, quickly, silently, holding her eyes. He knew they must look angry, furious even. "Five months."

"I think so," she whispered.

She stared at him with those huge green eyes, and he could see her hope, her longing, beseeching him to wait for her, to trust her. He wanted to reassure her. He wanted to lift her up onto his chest and hold her and tell her five months was nothing, but he couldn't do that. Five months *wasn't* nothing and he couldn't act like it was.

"What are you thinking?" she asked him, stricken.

"I'm wishing…I wish…"

"What?" She reached up and wiped her wet cheeks with the backs of her hands.

I wish you'd tell your uncle and cousin to go fuck themselves. I wish you'd realize that people wait a lifetime for what we found over the course of a week. I wish you'd see that something this new and this tender needs our protection. I wish you'd see that I will love you enough that you will survive saying goodbye to them and we will figure out how to win them back together. I wish you'd stay. Damn, Jane, I just wish you would stay.

"I wish things were different."

"Will you—" Her voice broke. "Will you hold me?"

He wished he could say no, but he couldn't. He loved her. He lowered his arms from behind his head and put them around her, pulling her back up against his heart, where he wished she could stay far longer than tomorrow. He held her in heavy, desperate silence long into the night until they both fell asleep.

CHAPTER 15

He hadn't made love to her since last night before they fell asleep and was unusually quiet as they woke up. He didn't reach for her. He barely looked at her. He finally swung his legs over the side of the bed with his back to her.

"I can't take you to Bozeman, Jane," he said softly. "My father or Nils will have to do it. I—I can't. I can't watch you walk away from me."

"Please come and visit me in New York," she asked in a timid whisper.

She watched as his shoulders slumped and his head bent forward. She heard him sigh, and he looked at her from over his shoulder, furrowing his brows, then looked away.

"Have to shower."

While he showered, she dressed, folding Maggie's things neatly into a plastic laundry bag pilfered from the hotel. Hopefully she'd find a moment to return them before leaving today.

"I hate the way we're leaving things," she muttered, sitting at his kitchen table as he made them coffee. Each time he moved, she could smell his soap or shampoo or deodorant. Whatever it was, it smelled like him and made her want to cry.

"*You're* leaving things, Jane."

"I'm hurting as much as you are."

"I highly doubt that. You could make a different choice."

She winced. "You're not even trying to understand. You're being really mean."

"*I'm* being mean? That's rich."

"If you want to hurt me, it's working."

He squatted in front of her, putting his hands on her knees, and she looked up into his sad face, focusing on his tight lips. She watched as he clenched and unclenched his jaw before meeting his eyes.

"I don't want to hurt you, I…I…" He looked away, shaking his head.

"You what?" she asked softly, her eyes watery with tears.

"It's *killing* me that you're leaving. And it makes it worse that you don't want to. This thing between us, Jane, it's special. I've never, ever felt like this before. Never." He swallowed, looking down at his hands on her knees, and she covered them with hers. She watched as he turned his hands, so they were palm to palm with hers. "I know you say it's not for long, but I feel like this is it for us. I'll drive you to your cousin's, and you'll leave, and you'll be gone. This'll just become a memory, and eventually we'll get over each other, but in the meantime, it's going to hurt."

"I'll come back," she whispered, squeezing his hands.

He lifted his eyes to hers, and she saw the pain there, the sadness and confusion. She hated herself for what she was doing to him. She leaned forward and he tilted his head to meet her, sealing his lips over hers with precision, with perfection.

As they pulled into the parking area in front of Sara's cottage, Jane had turned to him. "Think about coming to see me. I know you don't want to. But I want you to. I'm going to get out of there as soon as I can."

He took a deep breath and it was shaky as he exhaled. He sniffed through his nose, but he didn't look at her.

"I'll miss you," she continued, unbuckling her seat belt and sliding closer to him. "I'll miss everything."

"Yep. Me too." His voice was ragged, and his tone was clipped.

She slid a little closer, facing him, wishing he would turn to her. "Wait for me."

He turned to her and her chest hurt from the ache in his glassy eyes. "I'm not good at goodbyes, Jane."

She swallowed and nodded, placing one hand on his cheek and pressing her lips softly against his as tears coursed down her cheeks. She leaned back from him, sliding toward the passenger door, putting her camera on her shoulder.

"I love you," she whispered to his stark profile, which stared straight ahead, and she thought she saw him nod almost imperceptibly through the blur of tears.

Standing alone in front of Sara's cottage, Jane wiped her eyes, watching his truck pull away, watching him go.

I'll come back. I'll come back.

She swallowed, her eyes burning from sadness and worry and lack of sleep, her body aching from use, her heart raw from regret. Her head raced as the finality of her decision set in, and she closed her eyes against the pain of knowing that there was no guarantee she would ever see him again.

You're making a mistake.

The words ran through her head on a loop like one of the news feed screens in Times Square, and she felt the pulling in her heart, the terrible pull to race after him and never let him go.

She stood in the dusty parking area in front of Sara's cottage and watched until she couldn't see him anymore. Until he was gone.

She took a deep breath, and in the quiet of the morning she heard music playing—classical music. From inside Sara's cottage. *That's unusual.* Sara hated most music except pop, and this wasn't just classical. It was...opera. She wiped at her eyes, then fished the key out of her pocket and trudged to the door, letting herself in, curious to find out why Sara was listening to opera.

Jane opened the door and her jaw dropped to the floor.

Sara stood in the kitchen, barefoot, in jeans and a simple white t-shirt with her hair in a ponytail, her back to Jane. She stood at the stove, moving something around a frying pan with a wooden spoon, and Franco sat on a stool at the kitchen bar watching her.

Now, Jane had known Sara her entire life.

Jane had *never* seen Sara cook. Anything. For anyone. Not a piece of toast. Not microwave popcorn. Nothing. If it wasn't made by someone else, ordered as takeout or unwrapped and eaten, Sara didn't want it.

"I don't-a like 'em burned, so keep 'em moving like I show you, *Dolce*." Franco sipped a cup of something then noticed Jane out of the corner of his eye. He turned his face to her without a word, a broad, confident smile showing his white teeth. He put his index finger to his lips, beckoning Jane with his other hand.

"I won't burn them. I'm being careful, Franco."

"Turn around, *Dolce*. Say hello to-a Jane, then finish my eggs, eh?"

Sara turned to face Jane and smiled pleasantly, if not enthusiastically. "Oh. Hi, Jane."

Jane's bags slipped off her shoulders into a noisy heap on the floor. Sara had no makeup on, nothing. But Jane had never seen her look so beautiful, so young and radiant and happy. Not ever. Not since she was a very little girl.

"Eggs, S." Jane watched as Sara smiled at him then nodded once, moving the eggs around the pan. His soft Italian accent made the "S" sound like a caress, like, "Ehhh-sah."

"M-morning," murmured Jane, wondering if she'd suddenly been transported to an alternate universe in which Sara was a pleasant, caring, nurturing person who was— apparently—adept at taking direction from her beefy trainer on making eggs for his breakfast.

"Jane, you want espresso? Eggs? What can we offer you?" he asked cordially.

Jane blinked at Franco, trying to get her head around the meaning behind his words. Was *Sara* going to make her eggs? Coffee? "No! I mean, no, thank you. I mean, I'll help myself."

"As-a you like." He gestured to the coffee machine then picked up his phone, scrolling through messages.

Jane took a cup out of the cupboard and poured herself a coffee. She backed up, flicking her eyes back and forth between Franco and her cousin, waiting for one of their heads to pop off to reveal short-circuited wires underneath.

She watched as Sara picked up the pan and awkwardly pushed the bright yellow pile of scrambled eggs onto a plate. She opened several drawers before finding a fork, and then she placed both items in front of Franco, smiling at him eagerly, thrusting out her chest and rocking slightly on her bare feet. He didn't look up from what he was doing on his phone for a good ten seconds, holding up one thick index finger, telling her to wait. Which she did. Jane forced herself to blink. When he finally looked up, he smiled at Sara tightly, with a curt nod of approval, and then he picked up his fork and began to eat.

"So…um, how was Jackson Hole?" Jane asked, wondering if she had missed the news about aliens abducting tourists from the Amangani over the weekend.

"S, you tell—a your *prima* how you like the Jackson Hole."

Sara turned to Jane and Jane noticed a slight hint of annoyance that she was being directed to make conversation with Jane. *Being directed*. Why? And why in the world was she complying? What the hell was going on between these two?

"It was fine, Jane. As it turned out, I didn't need you after all. In fact, you would have just been in the fucking way and I—"

Franco looked up from his eggs, shaking one finger back and forth, reminding her in a singsong tone. "Ah, ah, ah. Civility, S."

He spoke slowly but firmly. It sounded like "Cee-vee-lee-tee, Eh-sah."

Sara looked at him, wide-eyed, and then took a deep breath, as though re-setting herself. She turned back to Jane, speaking through a sigh.

"It was fine, Jane. Thank you for asking."

Franco leaned his head to the side, opening his palms, and sighed. His voice was a purr as he nodded slowly at Sara. "Ahh. Like-a that, *Dolce*."

Sara's eyes were heavy, and her mouth was parted in…in what? Pleasure? She took a deep breath, closing and opening her eyes like a porn star, and a smile spread across her face. Catlike. Sexy.

Franco ignored this frank display of arousal and finished his eggs, finally sliding the empty plate forward to Sara, who took it and placed it in the sink.

Jane blinked again and realized she had been holding her breath as she observed them.

"Franco," started Jane, having seen just about enough to feel a little worried and a lot confused. "Can I have a private word with my cousin?"

"*Sí*. Franco needs a shower." He turned to Sara, his eyes intense and narrowed. His voice was low and sexy, almost a whispered growl. "Civility, S. Come and join me when you done."

Sara stared at him, nodding, her ponytail bouncing up and down. Jane saw her nostrils flare as her eyes followed Franco across the room until he closed the bathroom door behind him.

"Sara!" Jane whispered. "For fuck's sake!"

Her cousin turned to her in a daze then took a deep breath, composing herself. For the first time that morning, Jane could see traces of the old Sara. The pre-Jackson Hole Sara.

"What?" Sara demanded in an annoyed whisper.

Jane took her cousin's arm and pulled her to the far corner of the living room by the windows, away from the bathroom where they could hear the shower running.

"What the *fuck* is going on with you two?" Jane demanded.

"We…connected."

"You *connected*," Jane repeated. "What does that mean? Did you connect over a brain transplant?"

"I don't know if you would understand," Sara sighed.

"Try me."

Sara smiled, and The Cheshire Cat had nothing on Sara's salacious grin. She flicked her eyes over to the sofa, where Jane saw a pair of handcuffs, a black silk scarf, a riding crop and assorted other latex "toys" in brightly colored shapes and sizes. She gasped, mouth open, turning her face back to Sara.

"Oh. My. God."

"Don't be so goddamn provincial, Jane!"

"Is he *forcing* you to—?"

"Don't be absurd. No one forces me to do anything. I'm Samara Amaya, jackass."

"You mean you…*want*…things…to be…like *that*?"

Jane raised her eyebrows, still trying to get her head around the fact that her bitchy, domineering cousin was almost certainly playing a willing Submissive to her trainer's Dominant. Bossy, mean, selfish Sara was Franco's submissive. She couldn't have been more shocked if aliens *had* abducted Sara. She still wasn't discounting the possibility.

"Not that you *deserve* an explanation, Janie. But, it just…*happened*. I was unpacking, and he came into my room to see if I wanted to loosen up with some yoga stretches. I yelled at him to find me a goddamn bottle of water, and he said that if I ever spoke to him like that again, he'd shove the goddamn bottle of water up my ass and he'd make sure I begged him for more. I raised my hand to slap his face, and he grabbed my wrist and yanked me up against his body. I thought about screaming but he was kissing me so hard, my arms were pinned behind my back…everything was so angry, and so hard, and I was so wet, and then I just…surrendered." Sara's eyes were wide and luminous, dilating as she spoke, her breathing heavier as she remembered. "I swear to God, Janie, I came while he was kissing me. No one's ever…I mean, I never knew—"

"Okay! Stop, please." Jane put her palms up and averted her eyes. But, as grossed out as she was by the details, Jane couldn't deny that she was also fascinated. "Wait. Knew what?"

"How it feels to play rough. To let someone else be in

charge." She smiled at Jane from under heavy black lashes.

"Like *that*?" Jane glanced at the handcuffs and riding crop again.

"Oh, little Janie. That's just the tip of the iceberg. He's so strong. So demanding. He *needs* so much; he *wants* so much. I want to keep up. I never know what's next. I don't want to disappoint him. And it's, like, shocking and *a-m-a-z-i-n-g*. I don't want it to—"

"Enough!" She didn't know how to make sure Sara was safe without hearing the gory details. "Are you sure you're *okay* with this?"

Sara's voice was wistful, far away as she looked out the window. "It's like…it's like being a little girl again."

Jane cringed, then looked away, at a total loss for words.

"Don't be disgusting, Jane. I don't mean anything perverted by that. I didn't know what I needed. But he's so strong and he's so in control, it's like being taken care of by someone who knows exactly what's best for me, and when I please him…" She sighed, her glance flitting longingly to the bathroom door. "…he pleases me."

Jane's nose wrinkled like she'd smelled something sour, leaning back from Sara, still trying to get her head around this change. She thought she had seen everything, but she had never seen this side of Sara, and honestly, Jane wasn't sure if she was ready for it.

"Your body can't be marked up," Jane blurted out.

In an instant the old Sara returned. "Oh, Jane! You're such a goddamn goody-two-shoes peasant. You think I'd let him do that? We have a *safe word*, for chrissakes. I'm not a moron. And I see your simple-minded face, but it's not...*dirty*. If it's, you know, what *I* want, and what *he* wants, there's nothing wrong with it. So, to answer your stupid, fucking question, yes, I'm okay with it." She took a deep breath and touched her neck, slowly, languorously, in thought. "He makes me feel free. I know it sounds weird, but he makes me feel safe, Jane. I haven't felt safe in a long, long time."

Since you were nine years old.

"S!" They heard Franco call from the shower.

Sara looked at Jane, her face flushing with anticipation. "Gotta go. Don't worry about me, little Janie."

She watched Sara close the bathroom door behind her, then practically fell to the couch, pulling her sweatshirt over her hand to push the "toys" away with a disgusted grimace. As loud moaning noises emanated from the shower, Jane took out her phone and glanced at it. She had an hour until Mr. Lindstrom arrived to pick them up and Sara certainly didn't need Jane.

Jane had just enough time to get to the Prairie and back. She could return the borrowed dress and say a quick goodbye to Maggie.

***

Lars was anxious to get to the park and get the hell away from any reminders that Jane was leaving. He swiped at his burning eyes again, refusing to cry like a little kid or a woman. But he ached from the pain of it. To be so close to having someone you wanted in your life only to lose her…only to watch her make the decision to walk away.

He pulled into an available parking space and slammed his truck door shut. He threw open the glass door of the small office and stood in front of his father's desk without offering a greeting or pleasantries. Mr. Lindstrom looked up and smiled then returned his attention to his computer, putting up his index finger.

Lars didn't feel like waiting. He put his hands on his hips. "Pop, just stopped by to tell you I'm quitting. I can't do that drop-off today and I—"

His father took off his reading glasses, turning in his chair to give Lars his full attention. "Whooooa, *Midten*. Slow down. Come in and talk to me."

"You or Nils have to do the drop-off."

"That's fine."

"And I'm not doing it anymore." He plopped down in the loveseat across from his father's desk, fingering the brim of his cowboy hat. "These city folks. These talent jobs. No more."

"No one said you had to. Thought you liked working with talent." Mr. Lindstrom furrowed his brows at Lars, tapping his lip with the stem of his glasses.

"I don't. I don't like it. I won't do it anymore."

"Am I wrong to ask if there's more to this than—"

"Jane's not staying." He tossed the hat on the glass table in front of him and ran his hands through his hair.

"Ah." His father folded the glasses gently, placing them carefully beside his keyboard.

"She said she was, but now she's not. She's going

home. Some obligation to her uncle, staying with a job she hates working for that bitch instead of—"

"Language, Lars."

"Sorry, Pop. She's says it's temporary, but I know it's not. She said she'll come back, but come on…" He tightened his jaw, hating the way his heart twisted as he boiled down everything to a few final sentences. He picked up his hat, studying the brim again. "Doesn't matter. I only came by to say I'm quitting. I can't do Lindstrom Elite. I know that's what you want, and I can't do it. So…"

"It was a suggestion, Lars. An idea. Not in stone. You don't have to quit."

"I think I do, Pop. I'm not an equal part of this business."

"How do you mean?"

"I own ten percent."

"What would make you happy?"

"Thirty would be fair."

"You don't handle management, son."

"I could, Pop. I haven't been given a chance."

"Maybe you haven't at that."

"I have ideas too. Wildlife tours. Adventure tours. Camping, hiking. More of that. I could come up with some new ideas."

"I'd like to see 'em. And we can make some changes. You're integral to our success, Lars. Part of the reason I started my own business was so that I could be my own boss. I don't answer to anyone but you boys, and you don't answer to anyone but me and Nils. You're a few years younger, always seemed happy just being a guide. I didn't want to push you to take on more."

"Well, I'm ready."

"Then we'll figure it out. No need to quit. You don't want talent jobs? Nils can take 'em for a while. Heck, we can turn 'em down if we want."

A huge lump had formed in his throat as his father acquiesced to his requests. It didn't help. It didn't help the ache inside to know that Lindstrom & Sons would be reorganized. The pain was still there, twisting, throbbing.

He fingered the brim of his hat with his eyes down. If he looked into his father's ice-blue eyes and saw love there, he might start to cry, and he couldn't bear the humiliation of bawling in front of his father.

"I liked her an awful lot, Pop," he whispered. "I might've fallen in love with her."

"Might've?"

Lars shrugged, blinking his eyes rapidly and swallowing again.

"*Jag älskar henne.*" *I love her.*

"Thought as much when you walked up with her for Saturday lunch. Looking like the proudest man in the land because of the hand you were holding."

"Yeah," he murmured, remembering her small, white hand against his massive, tan one as they danced to "Woman."

"She know that?"

"I didn't actually say the words…"

"Probably should've, son."

Lars nodded. He probably should've, but what good would it have done? She had already made up her mind to go.

"Maybe she'll come back as she says."

"No guarantees now."

"Lars, wouldn't have been any guarantees if she'd stayed either."

"But she would've been *here*. We would've had a chance."

"And now?"

"Feels like we don't."

His father sat back in his chair, folding his fingers under his chin. "Sounds like giving up to me. Makes me wonder how my son's defining 'love'."

"What else am I supposed to do? Follow her to New York?"

"I don't have an answer for you. But we don't live in covered wagon days. Last I checked, airplanes fly to New York from Montana. Don't they?"

"You're saying visit her?"

"I'm saying airplanes fly to New York."

"You're saying not to give up."

"I'm saying airplanes fly to New York. Full stop."

"It sucks." Lars swallowed, nodding. "She likes it here. She wanted to stay. She was the one, Pop. The only girl I ever met who I hoped would stay. Only city girl I ever met who not only considered it, but seemed to want it."

"Sounds like a girl who's worth waiting for."

"She's so goddamned complicated."

"Lars—" he warned, his tolerance for cursing at an end.

"Yessir." Lars nodded his head in apology.

"Love isn't simple or cheap, son. That's for certain." He leaned his elbows on the desk, and Lars looks up at his father, at those ice-blue eyes that were the same as his. "But, once you find what you want, there's nothing really left to say. Your mamma? Half the time that woman drove me crazy. Still would've died for her. You know, her kin didn't want me for her. They were book-reading people, like your mamma. I was from the earth, like you…"

Lars watched his father's eyes look away, far away, distracted, remembering.

"It was complicated, Pop?"

"She was worth it," he whispered with feeling.

His father took a deep breath, and gave his son a sad smile. "I hope *I* was. Spent our whole life together keen to be worthy of that woman."

Lars stared at his father, not knowing what to say too moved to say anything.

"I'll do the drop-off," Mr. Lindstrom said, tilting his head to the side. "Headed to the park?"

"Thought I would."

His father nodded and Lars stood up to go. His father's voice stopped him, but he didn't turn around.

"Lars? Sometimes you have to lean into 'complicated'. Show it you're not going anywhere. No matter what."

"Yes, sir," Lars whispered, letting the door close behind him.

***

"Paul will be sorry he missed you, lass."

Jane took another sip of her coffee, remembering the first time she'd come in, looking for a cup of warmed milk. It seemed like so long ago.

"I'll be back, Maggie."

"So you say."

Maggie gave Jane a brief smile then busied herself rinsing mugs in the sink under the counter.

"Hey, you believe me, don't you?"

"Do you really want to hear what I think?" Maggie looked up, wiping her hands on her apron, and Jane nodded, although she wasn't sure. Maggie looked downright angry. "Jane, I dinna mean to speak harshly, but I feel strongly that…you should get yer head outta yer arse."

Jane's eyes flew open and she leaned back in her seat, shocked by Maggie's tone and demeanor. Her accent sure got thick when she was mad.

"M-Maggie!"

"There's a man. A good man who wants to take a chance on you. And you want to take a chance on him. And neither of yous got a thing standin' in your way. Doesn't work out? Nothin' ventured, nothin' gained. If it does? You've found the love of your life, ye wee lucky thing. But then you tell me that you're not stayin', after all. You're leavin' him. You're goin' back to New York, with your skag cousin, to a job you hate, like a scared school lass, because your uncle yelled at you. Do I have all that right, now, Jane?"

Jane nodded, stunned.

"Then I hope Lars can find a *grown woman* once ye go."

Jane's face fell and she nodded, feeling miserable.

"Och, Jane." Maggie said gently, walking around the bar to sit down on the stool beside Jane and put her arm around Jane's shoulders. "You haven't a mum to tell you this, so maybe I'm bein' too harsh with you. But, lass. Comes a time when you leave childish things behind. And when the man you want, wants you back, you don't leave him behind. Not for anythin'."

"But, my uncle…"

"Blast yer selfish family. So, he'll be a wee bit mad at ye, Jane. Maybe for a day, maybe for a week, maybe for ten years. Who can tell? But Lars'll have his arms around ye for comfort. We dinna live our lives for our parents. At some point, we bid them farewell. And if they try to hold on, it's on us to pull away."

"You're brave," said Jane. "You come from a long line of adventurers."

"You could be brave too, Jane. Take a risk. Take a chance."

Jane swallowed, wishing again that she'd had an older sister like Maggie.

"I don't want to leave him, Maggie."

"Then dinna leave him, Jane. Stop makin' yer life so bloody complicated." She put her palm to Jane's cheek and Jane could smell the ground coffee beans, comforting and warm. "Stop gettin' in your own way, lass."

***

When Jane arrived back at the cottage, Mr. Lindstrom was there, packing up the back of the van and securing several pieces of luggage to the top. Sebastian sat inside the van, and Jane assumed that Sara and Franco were still inside.

"Almost ready, Jane. Your cousin all set?"

"I'll get her, Mr. Lindstrom."

Sara and Franco stood in the middle of the living room, kissing like they were the only two people in the world. In spite of herself and without a shred of jealousy for her cousin's new affair, Jane couldn't help the overwhelming surge of loneliness that crashed over her.

You're making a mistake and it's almost too late.

She cleared her throat.

"Ah-hem. We're ready whenever you are."

They didn't stop kissing immediately. They took their time finishing, and finally Franco released Sara, stepping back from her. "*Dolce*, S. You please me."

Jane looked down at the floor, uncomfortable to be a third wheel to such intimacy, but she didn't want to keep Mr. Lindstrom waiting. And she needed to get the hell out of Gardiner before she changed her mind.

Jane sat beside Mr. Lindstrom in the front seat, while Franco and Sara shared the first seat with Sebastian, who was asleep within minutes of leaving Gardiner. Franco had advised Sara to let him "have-a the silence" for the duration of the ride and she complied by nestling into his side, pulled next to his body by one massive, tan arm and promptly fell asleep beside him. When Jane looked back, Franco winked at her.

"It's-a good, Jane, S and me," he whispered, glancing at Sara then back at Jane. "And-a you give me the idea."

"*I* did?"

"When-a you say you not coming to Jackson Hole, I think…how's-a S going to take that? Then she take it, and I think…maybe she don't want to be in charge of everything. So, I be a little rough with her, see what she say." He kissed his fingers and opened them in celebration, grinning at Jane. "Sure enough. The tigress just a kitten under all-a the yelling. Except when I *want* the claws."

She held up her palm. "Got it. Good, um, good for you two. Got it."

She turned to face front in her seat. When she looked back again, Franco's eyes were closed, and he rested his head on Sara's.

Jane glanced at Mr. Lindstrom, at the father of the man she loved. She didn't know what to say. Surely, he knew what had happened between them. Surely his words for her would be as bruising as Maggie's. He had a right to them.

"Mr. Lindstrom?" she started in a small voice.

He glanced at her.

"I just want you to know that I love him."

"Saw you together on Saturday and again yesterday. I believe you."

"Do you think he'll wait for me?"

"He's a man, Jane. Waiting's not our strong suit. But, if I know my *Midten*, he'll try like hell to hold on."

Mr. Lindstrom adjusted and readjusted his hands on the steering wheel, as if he had something on his mind, then he turned to Jane.

"You know what the saddest word in the world is,

Jane? In the whole world?"

Jane shook her head.

"Regret."

"Regret," she whispered.

"Saddest word there is. Try to live without regrets, girl."

Regret. Jane thought back to the last time she made this ride to the airport last Tuesday. They had danced together and spent the night before holding each other, and she had broken things off the next morning on the way to the airport.

She had wasted Tuesday, Wednesday, Thursday and some of Friday missing him, wondering about him, falling in love with him. She had wasted time instead of making the most of every minute she could have had with him. She regretted it.

And suddenly, she wished she could turn back the clock and have those days back, have those nights back, spend those nights wrapped in his arms, touching his face, loving him.

Today is Monday, and you're leaving him today. Next Monday you'll be sitting in a cab or on the bus in the middle of midtown traffic, and you'll ask yourself: Why did I leave him? Why did I let him go? Why did I waste time flying back to New York when my heart was beating in Montana?

The saddest word in the world is regret.

She thought of Maggie's Aunt Lily. Of Maggie's words from earlier: *When the man you want, wants you back, you don't leave him behind.*

Because if you do, you will regret it…maybe for the rest

of your life.

All morning she had heard the words in her head: *You're making a mistake. You're making a mistake.* And then she knew—it was true. Jane's decision to leave Sara's employ had been the *right* decision, because it was about self-respect. Her decision to take photos of Yellowstone, perfect her craft, and start a new profession had been the *right* decision, because it was about nurturing her gifts. Her decision to stay with Lars had been the *right* decision, because it was about love. The only bad decision she had made, for all the *wrong* reasons—obligation, fear, pressure, loneliness—was to go back to New York.

She looked down at her lap, feeling the quickening of her resolve until her decision was made, and this time, it was in stone. It was final.

Jane was staying in Montana.

She would have to call her uncle and tell him. He might hang up on her. He might try to strong-arm her into going back. Certainly Sara, who had to be behind her father's directive, would raise hell. And she might lose them for a while. Maybe even forever. But something wasn't better than nothing, after all. And something like life she knew with the Mayses certainly couldn't hold a candle to the potential of a life with Lars.

Jane turned to Mr. Lindstrom, her heart lighter and more resolved than it had ever been in her life.

"Mr. Lindstrom?"

He turned to her; eyebrows raised.

"After my cousin gets on that plane without me, I'm

going to need a ride home, if that's okay."

He smiled at her, his tan, wrinkled face crinkling with pleasure.

"Well, Jane. Can't think of anything I'd rather do than get you there."

***

Mr. Lindstrom offered to handle the baggage check-in and Franco went to find some herbal tea for Sara. When she protested that she'd prefer a latte, he put his hands on her hips and lowered his mouth to hers, hard at first and then softer, until she seemed more pliant in his arms.

"Franco don't-a like the caffeine for you before we go flying, S. The tea be better for you."

Sara had smiled at him and nodded. Jane still felt stunned by the change in Sara, but also fascinated that what it took to tame Samara Amaya was something no one, including her parents, had ever tried: a firm hand. Franco didn't seem to care that she was beautiful. And what was it Sara had said? She felt safe with Franco in charge. *Safe. Hmm.*

Sara started into the terminal after him, but Jane grabbed her arm and pulled her over to a bench under an awning on the sidewalk near the SkyCab, pulling her cousin down beside her.

"Jane, what are you doing? We have to check in."

"Remember what you said before at the cottage? About how Franco makes you feel safe?"

"Yeah. So, what?"

"You've never felt safe...not since you were nine. Not since your uncle and aunt died and your cousin moved in

413

with you, and your whole life changed."

Sara's face clouded over, hardened. "And?"

"Your whole world changed. So did mine. But everyone felt sorry for me, focused on me. No one felt sorry for you." She paused for a second, trying to connect with the human being behind her cousin's fucked up façade. "You didn't always hate me, Sara, did you? Do you remember that one night? That night you held me? You crawled into bed with me and held me?"

"I don't have time for this." Sara's eyes flashed and she started to get up, but Jane grabbed her arm, making her stay.

"Do you remember when you got in bed with me? Do you remember that night?"

"You're being tedious."

"Just tell me if you remember!"

"Yes! Yes, okay? Yes, I remember! You cried every night. You were so fucking sad. You were reaching for someone and I was the only one there. Yes, I remember. Are you happy now?"

"You loved me, Sara." Jane winced, holding back tears. "We loved each other. We did. Why do you hate me so much now?"

"I don't hate *you*, stupid! It was never about *you*. I only ever wanted *him*. I didn't want to *share* him, Jane. You needed so much. *Too* much. He wasn't *your* father! He was mine! But I lost him."

"I didn't have anyone else."

"Which made me a bad person for resenting you. Selfish, unhappy Sara who should be grateful for what she has, and is a terrible person because she isn't. She's beautiful and her parents are alive and well. And it's true…my dad didn't die. But I still lost him. I still lost him, Jane, every bit as much as you lost yours." Sara swiped at her eyes angrily. "I just wanted my family back to the way it was, but I wasn't allowed to be sad because *you* had the market on sad. And I wasn't allowed to resent you, because *you* were an orphan. But I became an orphan too. Just in a different way. Sara took a deep breath then breathed out in a hiss, fanning her eyes to keep from crying. "Goddamn it, Jane. You are the trial of my life."

Jane stayed silent beside her cousin, processing Sara's pain without resenting her for it.

Sara finally clasped her hands in her lap and turned back to her cousin, speaking softly, rapidly, unable to look Jane in the eyes. "Lars never made a move on me. He came to my trailer and I was already in my underwear. I *threw* myself at him. He didn't kiss me."

"I know."

"And that recording? I was basically blackmailing him. I said if he didn't make me happy, I'd have him fired. He only said all of that stupid stuff about coming to New York to buy time. He never would have followed through. He doesn't care a thing about me."

For a second, just a brief, sweet second, Jane had a vision of what life could have been like for the cousins, and she realized, if she left Sara now, that someday, somehow, that vision might come true.

"I'm not going with you, Sara," Jane whispered, looking

at her cousin's lovely profile. "I'm not leaving him."

"You're staying here?" she asked, and if Jane wasn't mistaken, a flicker of hope brightened Sara's eyes.

"I am."

Sara bit her lip. "Until my dad forces you to come back, Jane. He's going to be—"

"Furious. He made that clear. He probably won't talk to me for a while." Jane shrugged, still staring, glassy-eyed, at her cousin's face. "Maybe forever."

"Not forever, dummy. God, you are *so* dramatic." Sara rolled her eyes, standing up and readjusting the unfamiliar weight of her own carry-on bag on her own shoulder. "Your *uncow*—that goddamn, *stupid* name that I hate—" She took a deep breath and refocused. "He'll cave, Jane. Eventually he'll miss your boring chats about world news and books and art and shit…and he'll break down, give you a call, check in to see how you're doing…"

"I don't think so. He's going to be very angry with me for a very long time."

Sara made a disgusted noise, crossing her arms and sighing loudly again. She tilted her head to the side, pursing her lips.

"You're so fucking annoying, Jane. Look at you. Look at that miserable face. You know what? You're useless to me like this anyway. I can't have you representing me if you're going to be all sad and depressed and…and blotchy. Bleccch. You may as *well* just stay here. I don't want some useless, mopey assistant following me around." Sara picked a nonexistent piece of lint off her t-shirt. "So, you're fired. I'm promoting Laney. It's *my* choice. Not yours."

Jane searched Sara's face and Sara tried not to smile as she took her phone out of her back pocket and dialed, waiting a moment for someone to answer.

"Hi, Daddy, it's Sara. Yeah, we're at the airport. Yeah, she's here. Well, thanks for making it happen, but here's the thing…I changed my mind. I fired her. Yes, Jane. Who else? No, I don't want her to come back with me. Because I don't want her to be my assistant anymore. I want Laney. *Laney.* Well, I thank you for trying to help, but it's not your decision, Daddy, is it? Jane's staying here in Minnesota for a while. I don't know. I don't know. Fine! I'll ask her." She covered the phone with her hand and whispered, "Are you coming home for Thanksgiving?"

Tears filled Jane's eyes as she nodded at Spectacular Sara. And then something happened that hadn't happened in a very, very long time…in almost fifteen years. Sara Mays relaxed her shoulders and smiled at Jane Mays like she didn't hate her so much, which made Jane smile back at Sara.

"She said yes, but I imagine she might be bringing a friend with her." There was a long pause, then, and Jane could hear her uncle's muffled voice on the other end of the line. She saw Sara smile as her eyes filled with tears, and her voice was very small when she spoke again. "Just you and me? Yeah. Yeah, of course. I'd love it. I-I love you too, Daddy. Yep. I'll call when I'm home."

Sara pressed the End button and looked up at Jane, her violet eyes bright with surprised tears. "He said he's taking me out to dinner on Wednesday night. Just him and me. I can't remember the last time…"

"He's all yours, Sara. The way it was supposed to be." Tears spilled out of Jane's eyes as she smiled at her cousin. "I think it's going to be okay now."

Sara took a deep breath and pushed Jane's curls off her forehead. "You were always the smart one, Janie."

"And you were always the pretty one." She smiled at her beautiful cousin and added, "Thanks for making that phone call."

"I didn't do that just for you. Look what I got out of it: dinner with my daddy!" She chuckled, then cupped Jane's cheeks and tilted her head to the side, looking at her cousin closely like modeling agents were always looking at her. "You know, I think Minnesota's been good for you, Janie."

I couldn't agree more.

"See you at Thanksgiving, Cousin Sara," said Jane, grinning.

"See you then, Cousin Jane," smiled Sara.

As Jane turned to cross back over to the parking lot and find Mr. Lindstrom, she heard the dulcet tones of the supermodel known as Samara Amaya bellow: "Sebastian! WATER! NOW!"

And all was right with the world.

***

"Key's under the mat, Jane," Mr. Lindstrom grinned at her as Jane unbuckled her seat belt. "Wish I could take you down to Yeller to look for him, but I got a mess of work to do back at the office. Got no idea where he's at anyhow. No telling when he'll be back. He was hurtin' pretty bad this morning."

Jane nodded. "I'm sorry for that."

"I suspect *Midten*'ll be beside himself when he sees you, girl. Go easy on him."

"Will do," she said, hopping down.

"Sunday dinner, Janie," said Mr. Lindstrom, staring straight ahead. "Whole family gets together every week. Expect to see you there."

"*F-family* dinner? Me?" she asked, her voice thready with emotion.

"Like I said," he repeated, smiling at her gently. "See you there."

She waved goodbye as he backed out of the driveway and pulled away.

Jane let herself in Lars's house and closed the door behind her, walking back to the bedroom to drop her bags. She deposited them at the foot of the bed and sighed, thinking about how they'd left things this morning. He was so angry with her, so cool. She was desperate to see him again and set things right between them.

She picked up the picture on the bureau of Lars with his siblings, looking at the faces of the children closely. Nils, towering over his brothers and sister, didn't smile. His eyes were clear and focused, his jaw square, and he had his arm around Lars, resting his hand on Erik's small shoulder. She guessed Erik to be about seven years old, which would make Lars nine and Nils twelve…and Jenny five. Jenny smiled with the fresh-faced exuberance of a happy little girl, her hand clasped in Erik's, her blonde braids falling past her shoulders. Erik smiled too, but his head tilted softly to the side, toward Jenny, and his smile didn't quite reach his eyes, as though he was trying to please someone, but wary. Finally Jane stared at young Lars, so handsome even at nine years old, and realized he was the easiest of the four, the most carefree. He didn't smile, he grinned, and his eyes crinkled. He didn't have his arms around anyone or hold anyone's hand. He was the only one of the four who held ski poles, and looked ready to tear down a mountainside as soon as the photo was taken. Happy to take a picture. Happy to go back to skiing. Happy to be alive.

Uncomplicated.

Jane smiled back at him, placing the photograph gently back on the bureau. She took a deep breath and shucked off the covers, then remade the bed, expertly, accustomed to making her own and, sometimes—but not anymore—Sara's.

She took her phone out of her back pocket and plugged in her charger, placing the phone on the table beside the reading chair in the corner—the chair Jane had sat in the first time she'd been in Lars's room, the first night he'd made love to her, asking if she preferred the chair or the bed. She swallowed a grin, remembering how much she had wanted him.

Leaving the bedroom, Jane headed to the kitchen and turned on the kettle. She found some sort of Swedish tea in Lars's cabinet, and took a mug from the cabinet over the sink. It read "Midsummer isn't just for Shakespeare" surrounded by a garland of yellow and blue flowers, no doubt some Swedish reference that was lost on Jane. She would learn.

While waiting for the water to boil, she wandered around the small living room. There was a beige sofa (*with that heavenly back*) and two brown chairs arranged in a sitting area in front of a fireplace, and several photos framed on the walls. An eagle. A bear and cub. A waterfall. Jane looked at each one, taking her time to admire the light and angles, before jumping at the sound of the kettle whistle, signaling her to return. She poured the water and let it steep, enjoying the light fragrance of flowers and honey rising from the steam.

She threw the tea bag away and repositioned the kettle where she had found it, hoping that it wouldn't be too long before she didn't feel like a guest anymore. She returned to the bedroom where she felt the most comfortable, the most at-home, and opened Lars's closet to find a woolen blanket folded neatly on a top shelf. She pulled it down, burying her face in it with closed eyes, loving that it smelled like Lars.

She kicked off her flip-flops and settled in her favorite chair, curling up with her tea. And for the first time in years, in too many years to count, Jane Mays felt safe and free and wanted. She felt like she belonged somewhere as she never had with the Mayses or working for Sara. She didn't regret the years spent with her guardians, which provided the comfort of her uncle's face, or even the years she'd spent traveling the world as an ungrateful supermodel's assistant. All of that history led to today, so none was wasted, and she had little remorse. But she *would* have regretted leaving Lars.

How strange that she should come to a place as remote

as Gardiner, Montana, only to meet Lars, to click with him so easily, to recognize him so viscerally, to desire him so desperately, to love him so quickly. If someone had told her two weeks ago what would happen to her life, she wouldn't have believed it. Oh, but she would have hoped. My God, she would have hoped.

Jane took a deep breath, deeply comforted by the smell of Lars all around her.

"I'm home," she whispered in the quiet of Lars Lindstrom's bedroom, closing her eyes to rest. "I'm finally home."

***

Yellowstone didn't help. It didn't comfort him. For the first time in Lars's life, it didn't fill the hole, bridge the gap, teach a lesson, offer peace. It was beautiful, and the fresh air felt good and the sun on his skin was soothing, but his heart stayed heavy and troubled.

Lars stepped onto his porch, surprised, at first, that he had left the front door unlocked, but then, he'd been pretty upset leaving with Jane this morning, pretty distracted. And that upset and distraction had stayed with him all day, only assuaged by the beginnings of a plan.

Lars had decided that despite what he said to Jane last night about not going to New York, he was going to go as soon as possible to see her, which meant the weekend after next, as long as she wasn't away on a shoot. And he'd keep going every two or three weeks until she moved to Montana. He wouldn't let her forget him. He would not let her fade as days turned into weeks turned into months. He loved her more than that—more than her selfish bastard of an uncle who used her for his own purposes. Lars had firmly decided that he would do whatever it took to stay in her life and keep her in his.

He glanced at his watch. Six p.m. Eight o'clock there. She wouldn't be home yet, but her plane would be landing soon. She'd be too busy for a phone call until later, or even tomorrow, but his could be the first text she saw when she turned her phone back on.

He headed into the kitchen, throwing his pack on the kitchen table and pouring himself a glass of water. Leaning up against his kitchen counter he fished his cell phone out of his back pocket, then opened a text box.

Jane, I was an idiot not to drive you to the airport. Thought the park would help, but it hurt more not to take my last shot to get you to stay, or at least kiss you one last time and say goodbye. It was a mistake. I'm sorry.

He pressed send then took a deep breath. From somewhere in his house he heard a slight, soft "ding" and absently wondered if he'd left on the TV in the bedroom this morning. Heck, he left the door unlocked. Anything was possible at this point.

I'm buying a ticket to New York. I'll come in two weeks. On the 21st. Just making sure you'll be around and not on an out-of-town shoot. Let me know.

He pressed send again, watching the message load and send, turning from white to light blue to confirm it had gone. He sipped his water and heard that soft "ding" sound again and looked up. Sounded like it was coming from the bedroom or bathroom. Smoke detector probably needed a new battery. He finished his water and put the glass in the sink, heading leisurely to the back hallway to figure out what it was, as he texted one last message.

We'll make it work. I lied when I said I was falling in love with you. I'm IN love with you. I love you, Jane. I wish I'd told you before you left. But you'll get this when your plane lands, and I'll tell you on the phone tomorrow and to your face in two weeks...

He pressed send and this time the "ding" wasn't as faint. He was closer to it now. He pushed open his bedroom door, and as his eyes adjusted to the dim light, he noticed the glow of an LCD light in the corner of the room hovering in mid-air over his reading chair. And there, curled up under a blanket, her face illuminated by the screen on the phone she was holding, was Jane.

He gasped in surprise.

She looked up at him and his eyes adjusted enough to make out her face, though not her expression.

"Heya," she offered, raspy and low and soft. *Jane's voice.*

"*Jane!*" he half-sobbed, half-breathed, crossing the room to kneel on the floor beside her. He reached up to hold her face in his hands. "You're here."

"I'm here."

"I love you."

She glanced at her phone then smiled up at him. "I know. I saw."

Her face was tender as she reached out her hand, which he took, pulling it to his mouth, pressing his lips to her palm.

He was glad it was dark. He was glad she couldn't see the tears filling his eyes.

"How?" he murmured. "What happened? You were leaving."

She pulled the blanket off her lap, and untucked her legs from under her, standing up. He stood up in front of her, snaking an arm around her waist, suddenly aware of how dusty and dirty he must be. Inconvenient, that, because he was going to take off her clothes, take off his, and make love to her. Really, really slowly. They'd just have to shower together after he was done.

She tilted her face up to catch his eyes.

"I couldn't go. I would have regretted leaving you."

"Your uncle?"

"Can't be mad. I got fired."

"Fired?"

"Mmmm. Apparently, I was too mopey to work for Samara Amaya. She fired me this morning."

He felt like he wasn't getting the whole story, but it didn't matter. He'd get it some other time. Nothing mattered but having her restored to him. He searched her eyes, just needing to know...

"Is this temporary or permanent?"

"I love you, Lars. I'm all in, too. I'm staying."

His reaction was instantaneous. He pulled her into his arms and his mouth came down on hers possessively. He swept his tongue into her mouth and Jane responded with a small moan of relief and delight, weaving her hands through his blond hair, then lacing her hands behind his neck. He trailed kisses down her neck to her ear, taking the lobe between his teeth and biting gently, loving the way she tensed up against him and moaned deep in her throat. It made him smile to know her so well. It made him smile that they had so much time ahead of them for him to learn everything.

He laid his head on her shoulder then, and closed his eyes, gratitude coursing through his body, crashing over him in waves of relief.

"Just try and get rid of me now," she whispered.

Oh, man, that warm, honey voice.

"No chance," he breathed. "I will do whatever it takes so that you never regret staying, Jane."

Jane leaned her head back, moving her hands to his face, holding him in place, as her eyes held his.

"No regrets," she whispered. "I'm staying with you."

"You're staying with me," he repeated with wonder, and his heart thundered in his chest, bursting with love for her as he finally believed it was true. He smiled so wide that it turned into laughter, and he held her tightly, knowing this kind of happiness was only possible when you finally receive the one thing you wanted more than anything else in the world.

They held each other for a while in the quiet of the dim bedroom, until Jane leaned back, with teasing eyes, and licked her lips. His eyes sparkled then narrowed, as he watched her, his body responding to her. He sat down on the edge of the bed, pulling her between his legs, spanning her waist with his rough hands, his fingers brushing the satin of bare skin under her t-shirt.

"Heya, Lars."

"Heya, Minx."

"Got anything on the agenda for tonight?" she asked, little fingers unbuttoning his shirt.

"Could be," he answered, pushing her shirt up and over her head.

"Something you want to share with me?"

"Yep. Something special just for you."

He reached for the clasp at her back.

"Is that right?" she asked, shrugging out of her bra.

"That's right," he answered, as he unbuttoned her jeans, his heart racing with anticipation for the sweetness that was to come.

"Tell me what you want, *Just-Lars*," she whispered, low and taut.

He pulled her naked body into his arms, then down on the bed behind them, staring at her beloved face.

"I already got what I wanted," he breathed, pulling her left hand to his lips. He kissed the fourth finger, which he fully intended to decorate with a ring by Thanksgiving. "I got Jane to choose me."

THE END

EPILOGUE

Two months ago

Maggie Campbell couldn't stand it that her best friend, Paul Johansson, who was one of the finest people she'd ever met in her entire life, couldn't catch a break with love. She'd done all she could do to help, but as she had frequently heard Paul and Lars Lindstrom lament, there weren't many eligible young women in Gardiner.

The difference between Paul and Lars, however, was that Lars didn't lack for female companionship, flashing his ice-blue eyes at every pretty park girl who came through town. Paul, on the other hand, seemed to be waiting for something special, some*one* special.

She refilled the coffee mugs sitting in front of them on the copper bar.

"So you're game?" Lars was asking Paul. "Lower Slide? Tomorrow morning?"

Paul looked wary. "Who's coming with us?"

"Just you and me," said Lars.

"Right. Last time you said 'just you and me', we ended up with those girls tagging along."

"Misty and Mandy? Come on! They were fun."

Paul gave his friend a look. "They were barely eighteen. They could have been seniors at my school. It matters what folks around here think of me, Lars."

"Principal Paul," Lars sighed, rolling his eyes. "You've got to loosen up."

"I'm as loose as the next man. Trout fishing with my buddy sounds great. With Misty and Mandy? Not so much."

"I miss Erik."

"I miss him too. When he lived here, you never tried to get me to go horn dogging with you."

"Okay. No Misty and Mandy." Lars took his phone out of his hip pocket and sent a quick text, no doubt canceling on whatever bimbos were supposed to join them tomorrow. When he looked up again, his eyes twinkled with amusement. "Speaking of ladies, I heard you took Mary Phillips out on the town a few nights back."

Paul shook his head, giving Maggie a sideways look and taking a long sip of coffee.

Mary Phillips, the forty-something secretary from Grace Church didn't look a whole decade older than Paul when Maggie had set up the date. Maggie had no idea Mary would spend most of the evening blathering on about her health problems like an old lady.

Maggie shrugged. "How was I supposed to know she has crabs?"

Lars's mouth fell open in shock.

"Shingles!" Paul blurted out, a mouthful of coffee spewing onto the bar. "Shingles! Not crabs, for God's sake, Maggie!"

"Crabs!" exclaimed Lars, his shoulder shaking with laughter. "Maggie said craaaaabs!"

"Och, for heaven's—Shingles, I mean! Shingles!"

Lars howled with laughter as he headed to the door, waving goodnight to both of them as he swiped at the tears in his eyes. They could still hear him laughing as he made his way down the street toward home.

"*Really*, Maggie?"

Maggie shrugged. She hadn't meant to say crabs. She was so distracted lately. And she missed Nils. With him in the park for a whole month with a tour group—

"Mags?"

She looked up to find Paul staring at her.

"Let me give you a refill. Sorry, Paul. I mean, I just…" She shrugged helplessly, turning to grab the coffee pot. She poured the scalding liquid into his cup, pushing it to him, then put the pot back on the warmer and wiped the mixture of coffee and Lars's spit from the copper bar, shining it until it gleamed.

Paul chuckled. "Your heart's in the right place, but promise me something, okay? No more meddling in my love life, okay?"

"What love life?"

"I'm a happy bachelor, Mags."

"I don't buy that for a second."

"Well, it's not your problem."

"But you're like a brother to me and I just want—"

"No more, Maggie. I mean it."

He held her eyes and she made a face, but nodded.

Paul eased off the barstool. "Early day tomorrow."

She grinned at him. "If you swing in at seven, I'll have two hot coffees waitin' for the road."

"Will do. Thanks."

She watched him go, the café door slamming lightly behind him. Besides two old codgers finishing up their tea and dominoes in the corner, the only sound in the café was the soft drone of music.

Maggie wiped down the bar and placed Lars's and Paul's cups in the little sink.

Ding!

She looked to her left where her laptop sat behind the counter. She touched the space bar lightly and her email program came up. One new message.

Maggie clicked on her inbox, and then on the message entitled "Meet the One."

MeetTheOne.com, the Internet's most proven dating website!

Under the header was a picture of a pretty blonde woman. She stood in front of a weeping willow, wearing a simple white sundress and sunglasses, smiling into the camera. She was full of life and innocence, her pretty smile fetching without crossing into come-hither.

Perfect for Paul.

She snapped her laptop shut, remembering her promise, then reopened it, peeking around the café quickly with guilty eyes. What he didn't know wouldn't hurt him, right? And maybe this…

She looked down at the young woman's face. The caption beside the picture read *"Could Holly Morgan be the girl for you?"*

…Holly Morgan was the very person for her friend Paul.

Paul Johansson's story continues in:
VIRTUALLY MINE

ALSO AVAILABLE
from Katy Regnery

a modern fairytale
(A collection)

The Vixen and the Vet
Never Let You Go
Ginger's Heart
Dark Sexy Knight
Don't Speak
Shear Heaven

THE BLUEBERRY LANE SERIES

THE ENGLISH BROTHERS
(Blueberry Lane Books #1–7)

Breaking Up with Barrett
Falling for Fitz
Anyone but Alex
Seduced by Stratton
Wild about Weston
Kiss Me Kate
Marrying Mr. English

THE WINSLOW BROTHERS
(Blueberry Lane Books #8–11)

Bidding on Brooks
Proposing to Preston
Crazy about Cameron
Campaigning for Christopher

THE ROUSSEAUS
(Blueberry Lane Books #12–14)

Jonquils for Jax
Marry Me Mad
J.C. and the Bijoux Jolis

THE STORY SISTERS
(Blueberry Lane Books #15–17)

The Bohemian and the Businessman

CHOOSE ME

The Director and Don Juan
Countdown to Midnight

THE SUMMERHAVEN SERIES

Fighting Irish
Smiling Irish
Loving Irish
Catching Irish

THE ARRANGED DUO

Arrange Me
Arrange Us

ODDS ARE GOOD SERIES

Single in Sitka
Nome-o Seeks Juliet
A Fairbanks Affair
My Valdez Valentine

STAND-ALONE BOOKS:

After We Break
(a stand-alone second-chance romance)

Braveheart
(a stand-alone suspenseful romance)

Frosted
(a stand-alone romance novella for mature readers)

Unloved, a love story
(a stand-alone suspenseful romance)

Under the sweet-romance pen name
Katy Paige

THE LINDSTROMS

Proxy Bride
Missy's Wish
Sweet Hearts
Choose Me
Virtually Mine

KATY PAIGE

Unforgettable You

**Under the paranormal pen name
K. P. Kelley**

It's You, Book 1
It's You, Book 2

**Under the YA pen name
Callie Henry**

A Date for Hannah

ABOUT THE AUTHOR

 *New York Times* and *USA Today* bestselling author **Katy Regnery** started her writing career by enrolling in a short story class in January 2012. One year later, she signed her first contract, and Katy's first novel was published in September 2013.

More than forty-five books and three RITA® nominations later, Katy claims authorship of the multititled Blueberry Lane series, the A Modern Fairytale collection, the Summerhaven series, the Arranged duo, and several other stand-alone romances, including the critically acclaimed mainstream fiction novel *Unloved, a love story*.

Katy's books are available in English, French, German, Hebrew, Italian, Polish, Portuguese, and Turkish.

CHOOSE ME